NO ONE LIVES FOREVER

By Jordan Dane

No One Lives Forever
No One Left to Tell
No One Heard Her Scream

JORDAN DANE

NO ONE LIVES FOREVER

AVON

An Imprint of HarperCollinsPublishers

AVON BOOKS
An Imprint of HarperCollins*Publishers*
10 East 53rd Street
New York, New York 10022-5299

Copyright © 2008 by Cosas Finas, LLC
ISBN 978-0-7394-9539-1

Printed in the U.S.A.

CHAPTER 1

HOTEL PALMA DOURADA
CUIABÁ, BRAZIL

Gripping his nine-millimeter Beretta, Nicholas Charboneau peered through the peephole of the penthouse suite, responding to a soft knock. The red and black uniforms of hotel personnel should not have given him any cause for alarm. And yet, the hair at the nape of his neck reacted to a rush of adrenaline. Two men stood by a rolling cart of white linen, covered with food platters and a bottle of Brazilian merlot with a distinctive label.

Compliments of the house . . . or a Trojan horse? The bottle of wine told the tale.

A lazy smile curved his lips. At his age, he relied more on wit and cunning, leaving the chest thumping to younger men. He had no intention of answering the door, making himself vulnerable.

"No way," he scoffed, muttering under his breath. "Nice try, but never would've happened."

"Who is at the door?" The voice of his young body-guard, Jasmine Lee, drew his attention. Drying her black hair with a towel, she stood near the wet bar dressed only in the white robe of the hotel. "Did you order room service, Nicky?"

He raised his hand and shook his head, silently mouthing the word *No.*

Her body tensed, dark eyes flared in alert.

The sound of shattered glass from across the room broke his concentration. Jasmine darted from his sight, heading toward the noise.

As he rounded the foyer corner, three men dressed in black paramilitary uniforms burst into the room from the balcony, guns raised. Without hesitation, Jasmine tossed her towel toward the nearest man, a distraction. She punched a fist to his solar plexus, doubling him over. To finish her attacker, she elbowed the back of his head, toppling him to the carpet. Now she faced another, chin down and fists raised in defiance.

One down. White queen takes black knight's pawn, threatening the rook.

Nicholas's body reacted on pure instinct as chess maneuvers ran through his head, a practice in discipline and control. Adrenaline fueled his anger. He raced across the room, Beretta leveled. Unarmed, she wouldn't stand a chance if they started to shoot. He chose a spot to her far right, forcing the men to split their attack. A tactical maneuver.

Nicholas squared off with the man he'd coerced into turning his back on Jasmine. His assailant flinched, fear in his eyes as he faced the Beretta. Not wanting to start any gunplay, Nicholas backhanded him across the jaw, knocking him down.

"*Arrgh.*" Wincing in pain, the man writhed on the

floor, holding his jaw. Blood dripped through his fingers.

Two down. White knight to king four, checkmate in two moves.

He smelled victory. With Jasmine at his side, he tilted his head and glared at the final man, his gun aimed dead center between the stranger's eyes. "Who sent you? And you better pray I believe you."

"*Mãos ao alto.*" The stern voice came from behind him.

Clenching his jaw, Nicholas wavered for an instant. He gripped the Beretta, maintaining what little tactical leverage remained. But he had a feeling all that was about to change. Unwilling to lower his weapon until he knew for certain, he shifted his gaze to catch a reflection in the mirror behind the wet bar.

The seductive country of Brazil had beckoned Nicholas to its borders, the fertile ground of corruption awaiting his influence. Now, the reality of that summons had a face. The room service attendant narrowed his eyes in challenge, matching his stare in the mirror.

Despite the night air coming from the open doors to the balcony, he noticed the man had a bead of sweat at his temple. The droplet lingered on the brink of a sun-weathered crease, one of many lines marking his face.

Nicholas did not speak Portuguese, but since the uniformed man held a Kalasnikov assault rifle aimed at his head, understanding the native tongue became a moot point. The universal language of the AK–47 made his meaning perfectly clear. He lowered his weapon, allowing one of the men to take it, then raised his hands in compliance.

He had no option. Given the odds against a semiauto rifle in tight quarters, they were severely outnumbered. And one of the men held a gun on Jasmine. *Check. The black bishop had taken his queen out of play.* As in the game of chess, he would voluntarily topple his king to concede, not wanting to risk Jasmine's life.

Checkmate. Game over. In an instant everything changed.

Glancing toward Jasmine, Nicholas noticed her dark eyes communicating a clear message. He knew from experience she would fight if he gave her the slightest encouragement. The beautiful woman's unspoken connection to him made words unnecessary. With a subtle shake of his head, he gave his order.

You and I shall live to fight another day, my love. He would not challenge the inevitable. Whatever the purpose of these intruders, he would soon find out.

"I'm sure there's been some kind of mistake." He glared at the menacing faces of the five men. The two who entered through the front door via passkey had wheeled in a large portable table. Aroma from the food wafted in the air, making his stomach grind. "The hotel knows never to send me wine made in Brazil."

Insulting the local wine was his calculated attempt to determine whether these men spoke English. The leader's expression remained deadly focused on him. The man held the rifle tight to his shoulder, clenching the weapon in a taut grip. With no reaction to his first offense, he ventured a second for good measure.

"I hope you realize . . ." Nicholas raised an eyebrow. ". . . there will be no gratuity."

The head honcho had no sense of humor, nor did he

apparently speak any English. Nicholas would not be dissuading him with his keen negotiating skills. Without the use of his quick wit, his best weapon would be gone from his arsenal, along with his gun. He churned his brain, considering his limited options.

The intruder spoke again.

"*Você quer tirar sarro de mim, porco americano? Respeite quem aponta a arma na sua cabeça. Você vai saber logo quem esta engarregado ou vai morrer.*"

The comment had been directed at him. With so few visits to this country, he had picked up very little Portuguese, but he did recognize the term *American pig,* and the word *morrer* had something to do with death.

All things considered—this was not a good sign.

The man standing before him clearly had Indian blood coursing through his veins, with his mocha brown skin, pitch-black hair, flat nose, and high, angular cheekbones. The hotel uniform did little to disguise his raw, primitive intensity. An ancient lineage reflected in his dark eyes. The man looked out of place in this urban setting.

So why was he here—and holding a rifle with deadly determination? Desperation forced men to take chances. Unlike the men in this room, Nicholas was not desperate. At least, not yet. Greed was a familiar vice in his area of the world, but Brazil had refined it to an art.

"I'm sure we can come to some . . . arrangement. If you would allow me to get my wallet, I'll reconsider your gratuity." Carefully, he gestured with his hands, making the universal sign of payola.

Encouraged, he watched the head man give a nod,

directing one of his followers to act. Nicholas heard a sound behind his back. Maintaining eye contact with the leader, he resisted turning around until—

He gasped when something pierced his neck, a sharp sting. Pain forced him to wince and shrug a shoulder.

Too late. The damage had been done.

"What have you—"

Within seconds the skin at his neck burned. Muscles in his legs tingled. His equilibrium challenged, he felt weightless and the room swayed. Walls drained their color.

Gravity pulled at him, forcing him to submit to its will. Nicholas dropped to his knees, his arms falling limp by his sides. He no longer had the strength to lift them. From the corner of his eye he caught a motion.

Jasmine fought for her freedom, a blur of white. Sounds of a struggle distorted in his head, as if filtered through mounds of cotton. Noise deadened to a dull throb—an erratic and faint pulse. A dark shadow eclipsed his line of sight, and an arm was flung in retaliation. He sensed Jasmine's loss. It spurred him to stay conscious. His concern for her overwhelmed his body's surrender to the drugs injected into his system—drugs flooding him with an unmerciful indifference.

Falling face first to the carpet, he held one eye open, searching for her. The muffled sound of his breaths came in shallow pants, slowing with each passing second. With his eyesight failing, he sensed Jasmine's dark hair near his face. Her familiar scent penetrated the veil of his stupor. The coppery smell of blood tainted the memory.

Was she . . . ?

The possibility of her lying dead by his side made his heart ache. Dulled outrage compounded his torment. If anything happened to his beloved and loyal bodyguard, the eternal damnation of hell would appear like a day at the spa for the bastard committing the deed.

He vowed this with his last moment of consciousness, before he drifted through a threshold to his own brand of hell.

The foreign woman lay at the feet of Mario Araujo. Blood trailed from her mouth. Drops of deep red marred the luxurious white robe. It had not been necessary.

But time was of the essence if his plan were to work at all. With a quick gesture, he ordered his men to move into action.

"Esta na hora de sair da cidade com a nosso premio, camaradas. Vamos sequir conforme a plano. Rapido."

They hoisted the American's body, jamming him into the hidden compartment of the room service cart. Tomorrow he'd feel the pain of his unceremonious departure from the city. For now, the drugs in his body made him a compliant guest.

As leader of his people, Mario had taken the job of scout. He would not order his men to undertake such a risky job if he wouldn't make the same sacrifice. After all, the idea of kidnapping for profit had been his from the start. So for two years he worked at the menial job of bellhop under the name of Rodrigo Santo. He'd taken the name and identification of a young boy who had died years ago in his village.

The dead rarely took offense to fraud and were good at keeping secrets.

Mario studied his usual prey at the deluxe hotel and suffered the indignities of the *civilized* world. Normally, he resorted to luring his targets from the hotel by way of an official-looking document from the Interior Ministry of Brazil or a memo from the Prosecutor General's Office. And business had been fruitful.

Then, nearly a year ago, a man made contact with him over the phone.

He remembered the conversation as if it were yesterday. Mario had gotten the call at the hotel, during work hours. The voice on the phone specifically asked for him and threatened to expose his little enterprise. The man claimed to have proof of his involvement, even had times and dates and known accomplices. Mario had listened, sure the police would bust in and make an arrest that instant, hauling him from the hotel in handcuffs. But when that didn't happen, he regained his composure and assessed his situation in a different light.

"What do you want in return?" he had asked.

"In return?"

"Yes. You'd have me arrested if that were your purpose," Mario persisted, hoping he'd guessed right. "What do you want?"

After a long silence the man began to laugh, an abrasive sound.

"You see? I knew I picked the right man. You and I are going to get along."

To this day, Mario hadn't told anyone of the secret alliance he had made, not wanting to put any of his people at risk. And with his new partner, he had no complaints. His enterprise thrived more than before. So when the man had called about a rich American, he listened again. The kidnapping had been ordered and planned in haste, without Mario's usual care. His "associate" had told him the foreigner wouldn't stay long and would be far too cagey to be lured from the hotel, as the others had been.

Normally, Mario's instincts would have cautioned him against moving forward with the plan, but two things swayed him.

First, everything had fallen into place without effort, making it too good to pass up. The rich foreigner was delivered into his hands, yet another generous gift from his anonymous benefactor. Second, and more important, his associate had shared vital information on the American and his purpose in this country. For Mario, this carried far more weight than any ransom.

Whether he trusted the man or not, he couldn't ignore the compelling intel. Although it would take time, he'd verify what he could, but shortly it wouldn't matter.

His mysterious comrade made a big show of this being their last venture together, even giving him a special encrypted phone to take with him, for emergency contact only. The phone would work where they were going. And the man had made it worth his while with the American too. Mario would soon return a hero to his beloved home and provide well for his people. Nothing would make him more proud.

Far enough away from the lowland heat, his childhood village had been located at the base of the rocky outcrop known as the Chapada dos Guimarães. Now a distant memory, it had overlooked the flat plain of the Paraguay River and the marshlands of the Pantanal. Still vivid in his dreams, Mario longed for the misty cool of those folding hills. Its pillared rock formations were dotted with the ancient caves of his ancestors. And only the hand of God could have graced such stunning waterfalls.

But too many tourists and the far reach of his own government left him torn apart from his memories. Years ago he relocated his tribe to a spot deeper into the jungle, far from civilization and its corrupt influence. Yet there were days when resentment swelled in his belly like a virulent cancer. He would compromise no more. After today, maybe he wouldn't have to.

"*Até o nosso próximo encontro*," he said in a hushed tone, then watched three of his men escape from the balcony, leaving as they came.

He'd depart with his accomplice, similarly dressed in a hotel uniform. They'd brazenly haul the American to a service elevator. Once in the parking garage, an inconspicuous van awaited for the rendezvous with his men. Soon he would be on his turf, among his own people.

But before Mario left the extravagant hotel suite, he knelt by the side of the Asian-looking woman who had fought so bravely.

"*Para o bem do seu amigo, você tem que obedecer as nossas ordens.*"

He tossed an envelope of hotel stationery on her chest and lightly tapped the side of her cheek. By the time the beautiful woman warrior awoke, they'd be long gone. And she would know what to do.

He only hoped she also knew how to follow orders.

*   *   *

Searing light blinded her. Jasmine squinted and the effort sent electrified shards of glass into her brain. She felt the left side of her face throb, swollen and hot. Yet the night air in the room prickled her skin. The sensation made her aware of a metallic tang in her mouth. With a brush of her tongue, she found the source of the blood.

Unwilling to move, she lay perfectly still, waiting for the pain to subside. It only dulled and spread through her body like venom. Soon her eyes concentrated on the elaborate chandelier overhead. Its iridescent prisms swirled rainbow luster . . . until the shimmer stopped dead center, coming into focus.

Oh, God . . . she had been so careless.

"Nicky? What—"

As she rose up from the carpet, her head nearly exploded. She planted an elbow beneath her weight to keep from collapsing. Nausea churned her stomach. She held back a strand of dark hair and heaved, spitting up pale yellow foam. Her vision dotted with pinpoints of light from the exertion. Signs of a concussion.

Yet Jasmine knew she deserved far worse for her failure.

A dismal ache centered deep within her chest, spreading its heat to her face. She had failed Nicky, allowed him to be taken. For all she knew, he was already dead. She envisioned his handsome face, strangely passive in death. His violet blue eyes glazed in milky white. The image would be forever branded in memory for her sin of failure.

Love blinded her, made her weak and neglectful.

And Nicholas had paid the price. Splaying a hand against the carpet, she lifted her body to a sitting position. Her fingers touched a different texture.

An envelope.

The note inside the hotel stationery provided little information, given the many questions looming in her mind. The instructions were brief and to the point. She had ten days to comply. The ransom to be wired to a Swiss bank account listed in the note—or Nicky would be killed.

Yet with the instructions in English, it left her wondering who was in charge. Did the uniformed man know exactly what Nicky had said in English and only pretended ignorance? Or had someone else pulled the strings? For these men to kidnap Nicholas Charboneau, ignorance would be the least of their problems. They obviously had no idea the extent of their offense.

Once more she stared at the note. No organization laid claim for the abduction. And the ransom was far more money than she had access to. She held no special authority over Nicky's affairs. By outward appearance, he was her employer. End of story. Yet her heart could claim so much more. If only she had disclosed her feelings to him. Now she might never get the chance.

For the first time in her life she felt completely powerless. That was inexcusable.

Her mind began to formulate a strategy. Due to Nicky's reputation, she was not sure how her demand for help would be received. She would direct the attention of the local law enforcement, overseeing the efforts herself. The nearest American consulate would be contacted tonight, the U.S. State Department tomorrow. Time was of the essence.

Surely she could garner support, even in this uncivilized corner of the world. And if money were required, she knew how to get it.

Christian Delacorte owed her a very big favor. Despite Nicky's orders to the contrary, perhaps it was time for Christian to learn about his rightful connection to Nicholas Charboneau.

CHAPTER 2

An odd sensation contributed to Christian Delacorte's fitful sleep, a steady unyielding feeling.

Lying in bed, restless, he stared into the twenty-foot wooden rafters of the old warehouse, an arm wedged between his head and the pillow. Deep shadows edged the pale light of wall sconces he left burning through the night, a necessity since he was ten years old.

Long ago he learned to stay attuned to his feelings, to trust them. Like a sixth sense, his intuition served him well. But this persistent feeling of expectation had been haunting him for days, making sleep almost impossible. He glanced at the red digital clock on his nightstand. Five-twenty in the morning.

Damn! Shake it off, Delacorte.

Maybe it was his new place. Taking a deep breath, he raised up on his elbows to gaze upon his unique accommodations. He had only recently purchased the old three-story building in downtown Chicago off Michigan Avenue, renovating it for his use. He made the top floor into his living quarters. The middle floor was converted to his personal dojo, filled with martial arts weapons and workout gear. And the ground floor held his new business venture. Delacorte Protective Services offered executive protection to wealthy clientele. After quitting Dunhill Corporation as head of security, it was the next logical step—even if logic had little to do with his decision to leave the international conglomerate.

He ran fingers through his dark hair and heaved air from his lungs. A futile attempt to expel the doldrums. Despite the success of his burgeoning enterprise, he felt like a stranger in these surroundings. The old warehouse was not yet home. That would take time. His newfound independence had an empty feel to it, in spite of the fresh start.

Most days, he endured a disconnection from it all. Living near the Chicago Loop with its cultural offerings, exclusive shops, and the yacht club nearby, he watched the energized downtown hurl past him as if he stood still. Adrift under the influence of a strong current, he sensed its pull out to a turbulent sea of an uncertain future. He didn't have the will to stop it. Mindlessly, he took one day at a time to reinvent his life. It was the best he could do.

Barely out of boxes, his personal possessions were close at hand, giving him an anchor of stability. His former home had been a small yet comfortable cottage situated by the pool on the pristine grounds of the Dunhill Estate, a heavily guarded fortress set in the countryside north of Chicago. In his new urban locale, only the red brick walls defined the open living space. A stainless steel kitchen glistened at one end, with a large bed on the other. A seating area separated the two with a leather sofa and chairs sitting on a colorful Persian rug.

Taken from the estate, his unique collection of ornately framed oil paintings and oversized tapestries adorned the massive walls of rough brick, the artwork glorifying ancient battles and death forever frozen in time. As his eyes drifted from one piece to the other, the violence depicted conjured up savage imagery from his past. A dark memorial to mind-numbing loss.

When his somber mood threatened to influence his entire morning, a faint scent kindled his senses with a remembrance.

Her perfume.

He closed his eyes, filling his lungs with the fragrance of Raven Mackenzie. The subtle aroma of her skin, mixed with perfume, created an intoxicating blend. An image of her dark eyes possessed him even when she was not around—eyes capable of great passion, fiery anger, and unforgettable good humor. Feeling like an addict, Christian reached for the pillow next to him, holding it to his face for a fix. He cradled its softness to his bare chest.

God, she's burrowed under my skin!

In his life, serenity was a fleeting commodity. She had been a welcome change, a lush tropical oasis set amidst a fierce, sun-baked desert. Rare and refreshing like a pond of cool water in a thousand miles of hot sand.

Even with the recent upheaval of his past and the misery it launched, Raven's growing influence dominated his well-being. Saying her name aloud had become his mantra to calm his anxiety when he woke up drenched in sweat from another nightmare. And the touch of her cool fingers on his scorching flesh would sweep through his system like a panacea. Somehow, she made all the changes in his life bearable. Using compassion and gentle persuasion, she wielded a power over him unlike anyone else.

"Raven," he whispered as he opened his eyes. Her name was like a morning prayer—or a beckoning.

His phone ringing on the nightstand drew him from his thoughts. Only one person would call him at this hour. He had a smile on his face when he reached for it, and before he had a chance to say hello, her sultry greeting teased his senses.

"What are you wearing, hotshot?"

His smile broadened to a grin. Blood rushed to his cheeks. *And elsewhere.*

"Nothing . . . but a smile." His body reacted to the honeyed sound of her voice. He moved under the sheets, a morning erection inspired by Raven. "I missed you this morning."

"Oh, I like the sound of that. And have I ever told you how much I love your sleepy voice?" Her deep sigh teased his ear, as if she were next to him. He imagined the hot velvet of her skin driving him to the brink of sanity. But the reality of her job, as homicide detective for the Chicago PD, broke the spell.

"Tony and I got called out on a domestic turned bad. Open and shut homicide, but the paperwork still adds up. Not sure when I'll finish here, but I'm heading your way when I'm done, honey. And I'll bring breakfast. Keep the light burning for me?"

"Always. And I'll unlock the elevator, send it down. I'm gonna work out, so look for me in the dojo."

"You should save your strength for my kind of workout," she purred, whispering another suggestion into the receiver. "Maybe we can compromise. When I get there . . . keep the blindfold on. I love a man of mystery."

Christian was a sucker for her blindfold game, Raven's sensual idea of foreplay.

"Can't wait." He laughed softly at her teasing directed at his workout routine.

She had witnessed how he immersed himself in total darkness with a blindfold to hone his hunting skills. His self-contrived method to overcome his fear of the dark had been his redemption and his curse, isolating him from others. But Raven never criticized him for his fixation. She accepted him—demons and all. One of the things he loved most about her. Only one item on a growing list.

After hanging up the phone, he threw the covers back and sat on the edge of his bed, his thoughts lingering on her.

Yet even she couldn't distract him enough to shake the feeling that had plagued him for days. *Anxious* would not begin to describe the hollowness he felt—or the inexplicable anticipation. The combination punch of dread and exhilaration manifested itself in waves of nervous energy and lack of focus. Something had to give. He needed a workout in the worst way. Only complete exhaustion might remedy the unsettling sensation.

Dressed only in his pajama bottoms, he headed for his bathroom. A faint murmur forced him to stop. A premonition tugged at his awareness. Surrendering to the moment, he looked back over his shoulder until his eyes found what he searched for with his heart.

A black and white photograph of Fiona Dunhill hung on a far wall.

Her eyes found his from across the room. The noise he heard earlier held a familiarity. It had sounded like the whisper of a woman, or perhaps merely a distorted recollection. It nudged his consciousness, more of an illusion with words indistinct. Whatever headed his way had something to do with the woman he recently discovered was his mother. As he gazed at her photo, the feeling of dread swelled in his chest and confirmed his suspicion.

He feared the worst. One of his many demons stood at the threshold of his mind. And Christian felt certain it wouldn't wait for an invitation to walk through the door.

A cool morning breeze swept off Lake Michigan and through the city, stirring vitality in its wake. The pale orange dawn prodded the last vestiges of the night sky aside, leaving the wakening sun to spear its brightness across the skyline of downtown Chicago, spreading its warmth. Raven Mackenzie squinted as she stepped out the glass door, the front entrance to Central Station, with Tony Rodriguez at her side. It had been a very long night, but her partner was working off a caffeine high in his usual fashion, sharing his unique view of the world.

"All I'm sayin' is, you should take a vacation together. Now that's a real test. Maybe a little heart-shaped hot tub action in the Poconos or helping each other pick sand out of every nook and cranny on Waikiki beach, slathered in coconut oil. If you survive that, then maybe it's meant to be."

"Surviving a vacation? Sounds like a pitch for a new reality TV show." Raven shrugged into her windbreaker as she stood on the top step. After zipping the lower half of the jacket, she adjusted the waistband over her Glock and the detective's badge fastened to her belt. "It's hard to picture Christian doing the whole vacation thing."

"You mean the camera around the neck, plaid Bermuda shorts, black socks and sandals thing?" Tony reached for the sunglasses in the pocket of his jacket. But before he slipped them over his dark eyes, he grimaced. "God, I just got a mental picture of my uncle Ray in that touristo gear. That's an image I didn't need."

She shook her head and heaved a sigh, infusing her lungs with fresh air. After pulling an all-nighter, she knew that stale coffee and the smoke-tainted air of the bullpen had permeated her clothes. It shaded her disposition with a funk that even Tony's humor couldn't cure.

"It's just that Christian's been so busy setting up his new business, meeting new clients, hiring people, and getting all the renovation done on his new home. Sometimes I think . . ."

Tony squared off in front of her, hands in his slacks. Even through the dark glasses, she saw the concern in her partner's eyes. "What? You can tell me, Mac."

Raven stepped aside, leaning up against the metal railing of the stairs, her eyes on Tony. She had no secrets from a man she considered family. He had proven himself trustworthy on so many fronts.

"I know how he feels about me, Tony. And the way I love him, it scares me sometimes." She stared out toward the lake, its undulating waves glistening in the morning light between the office buildings. A gust of wind caught her next breath, making her shiver. "But he's never shared his grief with me, even after he's grappled with one of his nightmares. It's like a black hole. A bottomless pit that's all bottled up inside him. I can see a memory flash across his eyes, when he thinks I'm not watching, and he looks so lost."

"You ever ask him about that?" He sat next to her, so close she felt the reassuring warmth of his shoulder against hers.

"It's never felt like the right time, so I don't push it. I keep . . . waiting. And you know how much I love the waiting game."

For a moment Tony fell silent. He gazed straight ahead, then dropped his chin to speak, "He's probably still working it out for himself. Guys do that. It gives us an aloof mystique. Women can't resist it. Maybe when the puzzle starts to take shape, he may ask you to help him finish it." He drew her attention when he made eye contact again. "But whatever it is you're feeling, it might be a rift that's permanent. He may never open up. Can you live with that?"

Raven tilted her face toward the sun. She closed her eyes, letting the warmth caress her skin. Her partner was a very perceptive man, latching onto the very question she'd been asking herself for weeks. When she opened her eyes again, she nudged his shoulder with her own.

"I don't know. I want to help him. It's torture to sit back and watch him go through it alone."

"He's not alone. He's got you. And I'm sure he feels your support. Give him time, Mac. Christian loves you. I can see it. But a pain like that takes time." Tony stared down at his boots, nudging the tip of one over a crack in the cement. "It amazes me he's as normal as he is. You talk about having the rug pulled out from under you. A ten-year-old kid having to deal with the massacre of his family overnight, then finding out the ugly reason all those years later. It takes a pretty strong person to pull through it like he has. I admire the guy."

"I don't know if I'm doing him any favors by standing on the sidelines."

"You've got good instincts when it comes to people. Trust yourself. Just be there when he needs to talk." Tony lifted the corner of his mouth into a crooked grin. "You seeing him with what's left of your weekend?"

"Yeah. I've got a stop to make first, but I'm heading over for a little one on one." She returned his smile.

"Just take it a day at a time, Mackenzie."

"I hear ya, partner. And thanks for listening."

"Anytime."

She walked with him down the steps and onto the sidewalk in front of the station house. Heading for her car, she parted company with Tony knowing he was right. She considered every day with Christian a blessing.

Yet why did it feel like those precious days were numbered?

Christian hit the zone where his body reacted on pure instinct, even without the benefit of eyesight. A dark blindfold covered his eyes, yet he sensed absolutely everything from the sweat trailing down the small of his back to the cool air raising the hair on his taut forearms. Holding the sharp *katana* sword in a two-fisted grip, he cut through air, drawing a whisper from the blade. A distinctive sound.

Wearing only the black Samurai pants known as the Hakama, and an *iai obi*—a traditional sword belt cinched at his waist—he moved across the wooden floor of his dojo without effort. As part of the drill, he pictured an imaginary enemy, adapting his *kata* movements to combat his foe. The blindfold made it easier. Only the soft rustle of the wide pant legs accompanied his steady breaths and the lethal murmur of the blade.

When he hunted, he felt true freedom. Fear forged an alliance with discipline, allowing him to focus on his target. With an appreciation for irony, he understood this process infused him with serenity. A balance and symmetry to the art.

He had studied Kenjitsu for years using his favorite *katana,* an elegant, sleek sword. But he also developed his skill with spears and throwing knives. Despite his preparation with weaponry, he preferred the avoidance of conflict—the art of self-defense. Such discipline reflected his own conflict between the violence that fettered his earlier life and his pursuit of tranquility to redirect his future.

The hum of the elevator broke his concentration. Yet he persisted with the blade, cutting at angles to battle his relentless adversary. Vertically down . . . then up in fluid motion. A decisive thrust, forward and back. Rotating his attack, he quickened his cuts.

As the elevator came to rest on the second floor, its wooden freight doors rattled open. He heard her step onto the dojo floor. Almost imperceptibly, the wooden planks echoed her approach.

His blade came to rest in his right hand. In a single motion he resheathed the weapon when she drew closer. And as she instructed, he kept the blindfold in place, awaiting the cool touch of her fingers.

He wasn't disappointed.

"Good timing. I missed you," he said in a hushed tone. His words echoed in the stillness of the large chamber.

Without a word, she placed both hands on his broad chest, splaying her fingers across his muscles. Slowly, she moved down his taut stomach. Minus his eyesight, the move caught him by surprise. He gasped.

"That feels good." His chest heaved in an increasing rhythm. His reaction had more to do with his excitement at having her so near—and the prospect of what would follow. He had lost himself in the moment. Forgetting his discipline, he pleaded, "Don't stop."

He gulped air, almost choking on his hunger.

Still, she did not speak. Her tantalizing game. Instead she moved around to his back, trailing the tips of her fingers up his arm and across his shoulders. Cool satin floated over his inflamed skin. Her nails prickled his body with anticipation. Christian felt a subtle difference in the way she touched him. Raven was usually more direct. The woman's desires matched his need, but this teasing-prolonged foreplay stimulated all his senses. A new level of sensuality. *Amazing!*

Silence fueled his imagination as he conjured up erotic images of Raven, the blindfold enhancing his perception. Vivid mental pictures spawned from his memory. Creamy pale skin and enticing curves of flesh tempted his lips. Dark hair and hypnotic eyes shoved reason from his brain, compelling his body to react. And as her finger traced his left nipple, making it constrict, blood rushed below his waist and hardened him with a familiar sensation.

God, this woman knew how to punch his hot button! His brain raged with pleasure.

"*Awhh* . . . yes," he gasped. Her hands found the clasp to the sword belt. She unclipped it and released the weapon.

"Oh God, Raven. You're driving me insane. How long do I have to—" Before he finished his question, the distant sound of a slamming door distracted him.

"Those stairs are murder. Why didn't you leave the elevator—"

He recognized the voice. Even from under his blindfold he knew something was terribly wrong. And a loud crash confirmed it.

"What the hell!" he bellowed.

"Am I interrupting something?"

The distinctive voice and sarcasm of Raven Mackenzie came from across the room. Christian spun toward her as he yanked the blindfold over his head. He found himself staring at an angry woman wearing a gun and badge. Hands on her hips, she stood over a bag of groceries strewn across the floor. Eyes flared.

"How did you—" He knew by the look of her. For Raven to have been his seductress, she would have to possess skills in teleportation. She had just stepped through the outside entrance off the fire escape using a key he'd given her as backup if the elevator was out of commission.

A woman's voice came from behind him.

"I am sorry for my innocent deception. Seeing you in that blindfold, I could not resist."

He turned his head to gaze upon a familiar face marred with a nasty bruise on her left cheekbone. The beautiful Asian woman slipped a hand conspiratorially through his arm.

"Innocence and you parted company long ago, lady," he said. "I don't appreciate you barging in here." He yanked his arm from her in protest and stepped aside. His reluctance only amused his intruder. And she wasn't doing a very good job of hiding it.

"And I thought you and I were such good friends." Her eyes appraised him. "It's nice to see you in daylight, my love. You are even more handsome than I remembered." The woman smiled like an accomplice, no doubt enjoying her hoax. Dressed in a vivid red silk pantsuit, she looked stunning with her dark features and shoulder-length black hair. "And you are well skilled in the art of Kenjitsu . . . among other things. This pleases me."

Sidestepping a carton of cracked eggs and a melon, Raven narrowed her eyes in disbelief and bounded across the floor in record time.

"I've got skills too, and I'd sure like to demonstrate a few, but by the looks of your face, someone beat me to it. Pun intended." Raven stepped closer to the woman, standing nose-to-nose. "Must be your charm. So who the hell are you?"

Raven's ploy had little effect, despite her attempt at intimidation. Jasmine only returned her glare, not backing down. Having seen the deadly assassin in action, Christian would not have expected otherwise.

"My name is Jasmine Lee. Although I did not share my identity at the time, Christian remembers how we met, don't you?" She shifted her gaze to him, her eyes taking in the length of his body. The gesture added fuel to an already blazing fire.

Not one to back down, Raven inched closer. But before she voiced an opinion, Christian interceded by answering the woman's question.

"Yes, I do," he said, his voice tempered by the gratitude he felt. In reaction to a memory, phantom pain radiated from the scar on his belly, a souvenir from his brush with death nearly a year ago. "I owe her more than I can ever repay."

"I'm glad you remembered, lover . . . and that you are so very grateful." She raised an eyebrow and tilted her head. "I was afraid your memory might be a little . . . vague on some points."

He understood the underlying meaning in her cryptic message—heard it loud and clear.

He could tell by her expression and the innuendo in her voice. Jasmine suspected he hadn't told the complete truth about what happened. Being a cop, Raven wouldn't have understood why he kept his involvement with an assassin to himself. Their pact had been unspoken, for they both had killed that night. He understood *his* motivation, but why Jasmine killed was still a mystery.

In the meantime, ground rules had to be set.

"No matter how grateful I may be . . . that doesn't mean you can barge in here unannounced. I don't appreciate your head games." He pointed a finger at

Jasmine. His raised voice reverberated off the walls.
"So knock it off."

Slowly, she nodded in acknowledgment, making a
graceful gesture with her hand. A sign of her conces-
sion. But the smile lingered, flavoring her truce with
a heaping dose of ridicule.

"I have come to collect on my marker. You owe me,
Christian. And I am afraid *no* is not an option. I do
not have the luxury of time on my side."

Something in the woman's eyes changed, almost
imperceptibly. He heard the urgency of her message.
Yet laced between her words, he found an intriguing
vulnerability. And in that instant the all too familiar
sensation of dread and nervous energy gnawed deep
in his gut. This couldn't be a good sign.

Something was terribly wrong in Jasmine's world—
something frightening and out of control. Whatever
it was, he had a feeling it would turn *his* world upside
down.

CHAPTER 3

Although the woman kept her distance, the room could never be large enough for Raven's preference. While Christian's shower rumbled in the background, Jasmine Lee wandered through his home, leafing through books and handling his personal photos like she belonged. Nothing could be further from the truth. Underneath vivid red silk, the woman's body moved with sensuality, displaying an enviable feminine confidence.

Jealousy reared its ugly head. Raven conjured up a million ways to undermine that confidence with a liberal dosage of *Fear Factor* reality TV. Slithering worms and roaches, steep cliffs, and meaty bull testicles came to mind. She smiled. *Oh, yeah. Now you're talkin'.*

As the coffee maker gurgled fresh aroma in the air, Raven sat at the breakfast bar with an elbow on the armrest of a bar stool, observing Jasmine's every move. The woman would be trouble. Of this she was certain. And the cop in her would not stay silent any longer.

"So how do you know Christian?" Raven asked, raising her voice to make sure the woman heard her across the room.

With her back to the kitchen, Jasmine stopped her pacing, standing near Christian's bed when she turned around. With a deliberate motion she ran her fingers along his bedspread, inch by inch from the pillow to the foot. Red glistening nails set against pale skin tortured Raven. The strange woman's eyes never wavered in their insolence.

"Just lucky, I guess. Lucky for Christian, that is." Defiantly, she sat on the corner of his mattress, crossing her shapely legs with a flaunting smile on her face. "I would have expected you to be more . . . grateful. Christian certainly is. Have you not heard of looking a gift horse in the mouth?"

About the same time, the coffee stopped brewing and the shower ended, leaving Jasmine's not so subtle message hanging in the air. Raven knew she'd been asked to mind her own business. And that had to be the equivalent of waving a red flag in the face of a cranky bull. She hated this woman shared a past with Christian . . . a secret.

"Oh, I've heard of it. I'm just afraid I'm staring at the other end of the horse. The part that produces all the fertilizer."

"You sound like an expert."

The gloves were off, on both sides. Raven preferred it that way. Subtlety took way too much energy. And besides, a full frontal attack felt more honest. Yet Jasmine was anything but honest. Raven suspected the woman would avoid answering any question she had.

Raven trusted Christian with her heart—and her life. And she knew he loved her, enough to risk his life to save her. That kind of love . . . that kind of man, she should have been grateful to have him in her life. But what Christian hadn't shared with her weighed heavy between them, like an impenetrable wall.

And Jasmine only rubbed salt in the wound. Her cop instincts tingled with ferocity as she stared at the unwanted intruder sitting on Christian's bed. She'd have to grease the skids with motor oil to let this one slide.

"It appears we both possess the ability to recognize a heaping pile of horse hockey when we hear it." Raven stepped down from the stool and meandered closer to Jasmine, sitting on the leather sofa in the center of the room. "My horseshit detector is firing on all cylinders."

"The feeling is mutual. And I have no fondness for police."

"I'm a homicide detective with the Chicago PD."

"Yes, I know." Jasmine raised an eyebrow and crooked a wily smile. "My statement stands."

Taking a page from Raven's book, Jasmine rose from the bed and walked toward the living area. Under the guise of complete boredom, she plopped down on the other end of the sofa, across from Raven. Yet her focus told a very different story. The mysterious woman drilled her with a steady gaze, without an ounce of contrition showing in her vague expression.

"In case I have been unclear, you and I have nothing in common. And I do not wish to talk to you. So perhaps it is best you leave Christian and me to discuss our business in private . . . as it should be."

Anger surged under Raven's skin, bringing heat to her face. Just as she prepared to respond to the woman's arrogant audacity, a deep baritone voice filled the space between them.

"Whatever you've come to say, you'll do it in front of Raven. If this is not acceptable, then you should be the one to leave. Hit the bricks . . . now."

Christian Delacorte's appearance was bad timing for Jasmine. Now she risked alienating the one man she needed most. She hoped to be discreet when it came to her open resentment toward the detective's involvement. She would have to be craftier to pry Christian free of this woman's interference. A worthy goal.

Yet when her eyes met his, she nearly forgot to breathe. Every nuance of his face stirred a memory, a bittersweet reminder of why she had sought him out in the first place. Indeed, his face triggered a pang of regret and flooded her with an overwhelming sense of familiarity. So much so that she had to remind herself that this was a very different man. And as he walked toward her with anger in his gaze, a sweeping fragrance of herbal soap and the essence of his skin preceded him, reviving her to the present with all the subtlety of a sharp pinch to tender skin.

He moved with masculine ease, yet his gaze remained guarded and alert. His eyes never wavered from her face. Broad shoulders and narrow hips dominated her imagination. Even with the oversized furniture in the living area, Christian eclipsed the space with his presence, his height well over six feet.

She had nearly forgotten how impressive he was. And once again, she found herself drawn in, completely captivated by the similarity.

His dark wavy hair, still damp from the shower, framed a handsome face. A strong jawline with a day's growth of beard gave him a rugged edge, offset by the sensuality of full lips. Dark lashes accentuated the deep green of his eyes, a complex blending of flecked gold and striations of azure. From this distance, combined with the blue of his chambray shirt, she could not discern the natural color of his most expressive eyes. Although the eye color was vastly different, the resemblance was striking. *Remarkable.*

His masculinity reminded her of—

"Well? What's it gonna be?" he demanded. His gaze drilled her like a weapon.

"It seems I have little choice in the matter." Jolted back to reality, she forced a smile. "May I trouble you for some coffee? It smells delightful."

He raised his chin and narrowed his eyes. After a long moment of silent deliberation, he finally offered, "Yeah. I'll get it."

Christian stepped toward the kitchen, leaving her to face a very perturbed woman at the other end of the sofa. Raven had seen through her subterfuge and her feigned pleasantry. She was too damned smart for her own good and much too inquisitive—annoying qualities in an adversary. Christian would be difficult enough to handle without the added complication of a shrewd police detective.

Yet the emotion the woman wore on her sleeve made her vulnerable. Perhaps it could be used to her advantage, when the time was right.

So much depended upon this meeting with Christian. She could not afford to be distracted again by this woman or thwarted by his stubbornness. Failure was simply not an option. Fear wedged in her throat when she contemplated the consequences. She swallowed hard. Her throat tightened with emotion.

"You are my last hope," Jasmine blurted out as Christian handed her a cup of coffee. She held her cup and saucer in both hands, as he handed Raven her cup, trying to hide the betraying sound of porcelain in trembling hands. "The American Consulate in Brazil and the State Department have refused to intervene. They would prefer to turn a blind eye to the whole distasteful affair. And I have run out of time . . . and resources."

From the kitchen, as Christian served himself coffee, he said, "Hey, you better back it up. Tell me why you're here. I don't understand."

"Yes, of course." She closed her eyes and took a deep breath, letting it out slowly. The side of her face still felt swollen as she moved her head to face him. "My employer, Nicholas Charboneau, was kidnapped three days ago in the city of Cuiabá, Brazil. If I don't wire a million dollars in U.S. currency to a Swiss bank account in seven days, he will be killed."

With a puzzled look, Christian stopped mid-gulp, lowering his coffee mug. But the woman detective interceded. "Wait a minute. I know that name. Charboneau heads up a crime syndicate here in Chicago. He's a tough guy to catch 'cause his assets cover legitimate businesses. As I recall, he makes his money the old-fashioned way, drugs and illegal arms trading mostly. A real specialist. What was he doing in Brazil? Arms trading? Drug dealing? And why do you need help from Christian?"

Jasmine had expected such questions from him, but the intrusion of this woman proved irritating. For now, she had no other option but to tolerate it.

"Mr. Charboneau does not confide his business affairs to me. I am his personal bodyguard. That is all."

With a doubtful expression, Christian chimed in, "I don't know. Someone in your position must see and hear quite a bit. And you look like a smart enough woman to do the math. I think you know *exactly* what he was doing in Brazil."

"And the fact that Charboneau got kidnapped on your watch, that's gotta hurt." Raven cut her to the bone with her perceptive observation. She deserved it. Not a day had gone by that she didn't chastise herself in much the same way. Guilt was a pervasive disease.

"It does," Jasmine replied. "You have no idea." It was the first honest emotion she had shared since her intrusion into their lives. Yet she despised vulnerability. With her eyes downcast, she avoided their stares.

Shifting the focus, she directed her next comment to him. "I am asking for your help. It is not just a matter of collecting on a debt, although that should be a compelling enough reason for an honorable man."

"Don't waste your time with this guilt trip. You're tap dancing around something. What is it?" he demanded.

Clearly, Christian would not make this easy. But there was honesty in his candor. And she respected him for it. Still, going against Nicky's wishes felt like a betrayal.

"My employer would not wish for me to tell you

this. In fact, he expressly asked me not to contact you. But as I have said, I am out of time."

"I don't know the man. Why would he give such an order? You're being painfully cryptic, Jasmine."

Delaying her response, she took a sip of coffee, then slowly set the cup and saucer on a table. It had come to this. Only the truth would satisfy him.

"It is a sensitive matter. Yet I find I have no choice. Your mother, Fiona Dunhill, knew Nicholas quite well. If she knew of his plight, she would help."

"How do you know about Fiona . . . and my relationship to her?"

"The same way I know of your father . . . your biological one." She felt her heart skip a beat, then quicken its pace. It pained her to be the one to break the news, to deny Nicky of his choice in the matter. Her betrayal knew no bounds.

"Nicholas Charboneau is your father, Christian."

"How could you possibly know that? This better not be another one of your mind games," he bellowed, then clenched his jaw in anger. "Besides, I know all I need to know about my *real* father."

Yet his words of denial felt . . . *wrong.*

Christian knew John Delacorte had raised him as a son. And the man had made the ultimate sacrifice, giving his own life to save him from certain death all those years ago. The memory had been buried deep in his mind and only recently unlocked, the dark childhood tragedy that defined him. No one would replace John Delacorte in his role as his real father. Still, Fiona confirmed what he'd already suspected, having kept the identity of his biological father from him for a reason.

Perhaps that reason had a name: Nicholas Charboneau.

"I knew it the moment I set eyes on you, the night we first met. You look just like him. But don't trust me. Talk to your mother. Tell her Nicky is in trouble, or she might continue to keep her secret and deny his . . . contribution. But whatever you do, please . . . make it fast."

Nearly spilling his coffee, Christian collapsed into a nearby chair, unable to take his eyes from Jasmine. The strange sensation he'd been feeling over the past several days bubbled to the surface, churning his stomach with the reality of his life.

Setting down the mug, he shut his eyes. His mind reeled with a flood of old conversations. Fiona's words replayed in his memory. No matter how many times he begged for the true identity of his father, his mother kept her silence. After seeing the pain in her eyes, he knew she would never disclose the truth, as if she were protecting him.

And with what Raven revealed about Charboneau and his connection to organized crime, maybe she had good reason. Yet Fiona's gall boggled his mind. She herself was a matriarch to an enterprise rooted in crime, perhaps a direct rival to Charboneau's. Her disapproval of him as a father made no sense, not if she examined her own life under such scrutiny.

It struck him. He had spent much of his life living in the shadow of her lies. She had kept him apart from "the life," limiting his involvement in the Dunhill family business all those years. Now it appeared he had never fully grasped the depth of her secrets.

Raven's voice yanked him from his dismal thoughts.

"If your employer kept his affairs to himself," she said to Jasmine, "without confiding in you, as you've said, then how do you explain knowing so much about Christian? That seems like pretty sensitive information for a mere bodyguard to have."

"Very perceptive, Detective. I may have misrepresented my relationship with Christian's father. But I will not compromise Nicky by revealing certain aspects of his business affairs. It would be unprofessional . . . and unwise."

Intently, Christian watched the woman speak, as if she communicated in a different language. Perhaps she did. Her world was steeped in shadow and deception. Honesty would be a rare commodity.

"Your instincts are correct, Raven," he said. "This is a woman with secrets. Trusting her would be a mistake." Resentment colored his tone. He glared at Jasmine, searching the subtleties of her face to find a glimmer of the truth.

The woman flashed indignation. "You trusted me once. That night. I could have led you into an ambush."

He stood abruptly and turned his back, crossing his arms over his chest. Looking at her only made him angry. "I was desperate. I had no choice."

"Now you see my predicament. I am out of options as well." Jasmine stepped toward him. Her voice lowered as she pleaded her case. "This is not about me. Nicholas will die in seven days. What would you have me do? How can I prove myself to you? I am only a messenger, speaking for a man who cannot. Please do not condemn him for Fiona's error in judgment."

"What do you mean?" He narrowed his eyes, reading between the lines of her persuasive argument. "And why didn't he want you to contact me?"

"He never really said, but I know him. I believe he resented the fact Fiona kept your birth a secret from him. He didn't find out the truth until only . . . recently."

"And I suppose you want me to take your word for that . . . that he only just found out about me?" Christian turned toward her, searching her eyes for an answer.

"I hope you will, yes." Jasmine touched his arm and spoke in a hushed tone. "She never allowed him the choice—to take his rightful place as your father. Until he examined his heart, I believe he wanted time to consider what such a revelation would do to you."

He wondered how much of this was Jasmine's gift of persuasion. She had all the answers, doling out what he wanted to hear. But his gut jabbed at him, casting doubt on her portrayal of Charboneau as a concerned father with only his best interests at heart.

"So, you think he stayed away, out of concern for me?" He tilted his head and focused his gaze on the woman standing before him. "Don't you think that's a stretch, even by your twisted standards?"

"Please. Do not judge him. Not without Nicky being able to defend himself. And without your help, he won't be alive long enough to do so. Please, I need you."

Despite his cynical nature, he wanted to believe her. But the reality of his situation was simple. He could only discover the truth about Charboneau on his own. He would have to risk his future to uncover his past. Would he regret the decision he was about to make?

"What do you want from me?"

"What the hell do you want, damn it?" Nicholas yelled.

His voice resounded off the walls of the cavern, an inky black and boundless expanse. Some kind of cave. Plunged in total darkness, he wasn't sure anyone heard him. And he hated being ignored.

"You don't know who you're dealing with!"

Anger tempered his voice, but the thick dank air muffled his usual thunder. If he didn't conserve his strength, he'd lose his ability to speak at all. Stale air mixed with an indefinable rotten smell, making it hard to breathe. He fought the urge to take a full breath, afraid the foul air would damage his lungs.

Plop. Tink. Tink. The incessant, mind-numbing noise.

The walls seeped dampness and secreted a pungent mineral odor.

"I can pay for my freedom!" he shouted. Swallowing hard, he found no relief for his parched throat. "You can deal with me!"

No answer. Only a mocking echo. And he didn't like what he heard. At some point desperation tainted his tone, undermining any prospect of influence over the men holding him hostage.

Who was he kidding?

How in the hell could he command respect from his captors? His hands and face felt caked with layers of filth. It clung to his skin, bonded by a scummy sheen of sweat. His body reeked of it . . .and worse.

He couldn't escape the stench from his own urine and other bodily necessities. The foul odor hung heavy in the stagnant air, despite his best efforts. Even though he had been repulsed by the squalor, other creatures scurrying in the darkness rallied to it like greedy vultures. Flies and gnats buzzed, growing in number by the day. So far, he'd kept the rats at bay when he stayed awake, making any real sleep impossible.

This can't be happening. Not to me. Yet with each passing hour, doubt crept into his mind like an affliction.

Nicholas gripped the metal bars of his cell. Set solidly in stone, the barrier appeared escape-proof. He had given up hope of wrenching the blockade free. Yet the feel of the solid object in his hands reinforced his sense of equilibrium in the dark. It gave him something to cling to. His shoulders slack, he leaned his forehead against the bars and allowed defeat to inch closer in the dark. Cool metal next to his skin gave some measure of relief from the suffocating heat that now ebbed and flowed in this hellhole.

But at other times a chilling vapor swept through the emptiness, settling deep within his bones. What remained of his clothing did not provide any relief against such an onslaught. He would brace his hands upon the stony barrier and find a hole to squat, fending off hypothermia as best he could until the sweltering heat returned.

Now, all he could think about was—

"Water. I need . . ." He stared into a sea of black, allowing his voice to fade to a whisper, ". . . water." Nicholas closed his eyes, bone weary.

The bastards kept him guessing, supplying food and water on an irregular basis. A cruel game. Only the distant crunch of footsteps and a faint flicker of a light warned him of their approach. At first he had prepared himself for physical torture, but the isolation proved to be far worse. After a while he found himself eager for any attention at all. Even a one-sided conversation was better than the stone cold silence of his existence.

Without light, the hours melded into nothingness, lacking any sense of morning or night. And worse, he had no idea how long he'd been in this godforsaken place. Drugs initially muddled his perception, but now that his mind had cleared, the reality of his predicament hit hard.

If they never came back, he'd die in this place. He had lost control of everything.

"Defeat comes to no man until he admits it," he muttered, knowing he sounded more like a madman. Even though the old quote sprang into his head, the words implied a defiance he no longer possessed.

Being a prisoner to darkness, only his thoughts kept him company in the endless void—perhaps the greatest cruelty. He had no regrets about his life, so contemplating it would do no good. But what had become of Jasmine? With the power of her spirit, surely he would feel her passing from this life. At least, he'd like to think he would feel it. They shared an undeniable bond.

Surely he would know.

"I still can't believe Nicholas . . ." Jasmine closed her eyes tight and grappled for the words. "Perhaps I should tell you what lead me to your door . . . then we can discuss what I will need . . ."

She shared her story, speaking in a quiet tone as she stood before him.

Christian witnessed her struggle for control over emotion, an uncharacteristic facet of the assassin he'd seen operate up close. As she turned away, he moved closer to Raven, finding a seat next to her on the sofa. Her fingers wrapped in his, making their connection stronger. He felt comforted by her presence, even as Jasmine told her disturbing tale.

". . . After it happened, I planned to stay in Brazil, to lead the search for Nicky. But something felt . . . wrong." She walked toward the kitchen and stopped at the counter. Staring across the room, lost in her memory, she clutched her arms over her chest. "I sensed it was not safe for me to remain, not if I was going to help him."

"What do you mean something felt wrong?" Christian asked, though he fully understood Jasmine heeding her sixth sense. "You were only doing your job. Why was it not safe for you to remain?"

"It seemed like I was the only one who wanted to find Nicky. The American Consulate, the State Department, the local law . . . no one would help soon enough. With politicos and bureaucrats, delay is commonplace, regardless of the urgency of the situation. But I was running out of time."

Normally quite composed, Jasmine gestured with her hands to make her point. Emotion seethed to the surface of her cool facade. It was the most animated he had ever seen her face, even in the instant when she killed. She rejoined them and took a chair. Leaning closer, she held her eyes on him, doing her best to ignore Raven.

"But the real clincher was when I contacted his lawyer in Chicago to arrange for the ransom money. That conversation felt most peculiar . . . like he knew something I did not."

"Come on, Jasmine. You've got to give me something more than that. Having a conversation with a lawyer who acts like he knows more than you do? That's standard procedure, isn't it?" Christian let his annoyance show.

Jasmine's eyes fired with indignation before she regained control.

"It was more than just the inherent arrogance of a man in that profession. I got the distinct impression he suspected me of being involved with the abduction. And if the syndicate believes I am guilty of kidnapping and extortion, then I will soon be a target for a global fox hunt. I do not relish playing the part of a furry creature with a tail, with rabid hounds nipping at my flanks, given the vast resources of the syndicate's holdings. Perhaps Nicky isn't the only one running out of time."

"Did his lawyer come right out and accuse you?" he asked.

"No, not overtly, but the man seemed to know everything that had happened . . . even before I told him." She avoided his eyes.

The thought of Jasmine being involved in her employer's kidnapping had not occurred to him. He chastised himself for not being more alert to her potential deception. The scenario she painted suddenly sounded like a house of cards, ready to collapse at the slightest provocation.

And damn it—he sensed plenty of provocation gusting his way.

Jasmine must have read his mind. She pointed her finger in anger. "And do not insult me by asking if I am involved in Nicky's abduction. I would have to slit your throat."

"I believe you . . . that you might try to slit my throat, that is. But I'll be the judge on whether you're guilty of anything else."

"Then you will help?" Her face brightened with hope.

But the real question remained. "You still haven't answered me. What do you want?"

She took a moment to slow her breathing. Leaning toward him, she reached across Raven to grasp his forearm, pale skin stark against her red nails. "Money."

"Oh yeah, here it comes," Raven muttered. "The big con job."

Jasmine glared at her but overlooked the remark. "I need the funds wired. I cannot trust Nicky's lawyer to follow through with something so vital." She tightened her jaw, then stole a quick glance toward Raven again before focusing on him. "And I would like you to accompany me back to Brazil."

"What? Why do you need Christian?" Raven responded before he had a chance. She leaned forward on the couch, her fingers tightening around his.

He shifted his gaze toward Jasmine and waited for her answer.

"I could use the Dunhill jet . . . for greater flexibility. And I am hesitant to take advantage of my flying privileges with the syndicate's aircraft." Jasmine raised her chin. "The local military police were less than cooperative. It seems corruption is a way of life down there."

"I bet that offended your genteel sensibilities." Mumbling under her breath, Raven made her feelings known, as if there might be some doubt.

Ignoring her, Jasmine continued, "I didn't know whom to trust. A local police captain shadowed my every move. And believe me, that is not an easy feat. Someone is covering up the whole thing and discrediting me in the process. I no longer have resources of my own. And I am afraid Nicky will forfeit his life for my failure."

"Even if I believed you . . ." Christian fell back against the leather couch, frustration tainting his mood. He shook his head. "I don't have access to that kind of money, Jasmine."

"No, but your mother does. I believe Fiona would help if she knew what happened to Nicky." She averted her eyes and spoke softly. "It is my belief they still care deeply for each other . . . even after all these years."

Glaring at Jasmine, he narrowed his eyes in doubt, then found comfort in Raven's loving gaze. Severing ties with Fiona had been painful enough, but to go back to her now was nearly unthinkable. Still, a life hung in the balance. Would he really have a choice?

"Even if I can get the money, you're suggesting we conduct our own search and rescue mission before the funds are wired. Is that it?"

"Yes. And I am certain since the kidnapping took place at the Hotel Palma Dourada in Cuiabá, it must have been an inside job. It was too perfectly executed to think otherwise. We could start there. Between you and I, we would split up, stay one step ahead of the local law. We can trust no one."

"I'll say. Christian, this doesn't add up." Raven turned and placed a hand on the nape of his neck, stroking his hair. "From the way she's talking, this is one big conspiracy—from the local sheriff to the bell-hop and the maid. And let's not forget Charboneau's lawyer too. Hell, I'm sure we can trace this all back to the suspicious creation of the blue M&M and the government cover-up of the alien autopsy at Area 51. Are you really buying all this?"

Raven had a good point, despite her vivid conspiracy analogies. On the surface, Jasmine's story had major holes in logic. It should have been a simple equation. Number one, the kidnappers would want a ransom. Number two, the local law should have been hot after the bad guys. And number three, Charboneau's lawyer should have earned his high-priced retainer by arranging for the funds to be wired. Yet according to Jasmine, only the ransom had been demanded by the kidnappers, nothing more. Something didn't add up.

Or did it?

"Unless someone doesn't want him to make it out of Brazil alive. It might be pretty convenient to get rid of him and blame it on the local cottage indus-try of corporate executive kidnapping." He threw his theory out for consideration, then turned his gaze toward Jasmine. "Why was Charboneau in Brazil?"

A flicker crossed Jasmine's eyes. He knew in an in-stant that whatever response she contemplated would be a fraction of the truth.

"Once or twice a year, he travels there. He gener-ously funds a genetics research facility. He is a be-nevolent man." She'd answered his question, yet he knew she held something back.

He wasn't surprised that Raven didn't buy Jasmine's act.

"Let me take a stab at translating this for you, Christian," Raven offered. "She says Charboneau's involved with a charitable venture in South America. I see an opportunity to launder funds in a foreign country . . . and no doubt tax benefits for his corporation to boot. But I bet that's not all. Hell, I wish I got this much spin out of my washing machine. Ever think about a career in politics?"

"I am only his bodyguard," Jasmine replied, pretending to be insulted. "I cannot respond to such an inference." If the situation were not so grave, he might have seen the humor in her indignation—an assassin who draws the line at associating with known tax evaders. *Strange world!*

"Yeah, right." Raven crossed her arms and tilted her head, her facial expression mocking the woman's reply. "With that song and dance, you should take your act on the road. In fact, I insist."

"Why Brazil?" Christian asked. "Genetics research is conducted in the United States too."

"Maybe Charboneau doesn't like all the pesky laws we have in the good old U.S. of A.," Raven speculated.

Jasmine ignored her insinuation, but not without a steely glare. "The rain forests and marshlands of the nearby Pantanal serve as a virtually untapped resource for new medicines . . . which is an offshoot of the research of Nicky's facility. I have heard him speak of this often."

"Yeah. He sounds like a real humanitarian," Raven interjected. "Maybe the local natives got restless.

They found out what he was doing and are asking for a million dollars in retribution. And who's to say, once the ransom is paid, Charboneau won't be killed anyway, to stop his plundering of their natural resources?"

Christian had to admit Raven's points made sense.

"My only concern is for Nicky," Jasmine said. "I cannot sit back and do nothing. I need to know your answer, Christian." Before he responded, she added, "But know this, if you turn me down, I will find a way to fly back there on my own. I will not leave him to those jackals."

"Very commendable sentiments, but I need time to think. I won't be pressured." He had a lot to consider. And how much would he trust Jasmine's version of the truth? He didn't have many ways to verify it, especially without jeopardizing a rescue attempt.

"Time?" Pulling back, she gripped the armrest of the chair. "If only I had it to give."

"From where I'm sitting, you've got no choice. I have to contact the American consulate and call the State Department."

Jasmine narrowed her eyes and clenched her jaw, knowing he intended to check out her story. She had to know he wouldn't take it at face value. He had a million reasons to make sure this wasn't a scam concocted by her and Daddy dearest. To her credit, Jasmine kept her mouth shut.

"Plus, I have to speak to Fiona about the money . . . and other things," he continued. "Meet me here at seven tomorrow morning. If I decide to help you, I'll be packed and ready to go. If not, you're on your own."

He raised himself off the sofa, letting her know the meeting had ended.

"As you say, I have run out of options. Until tomorrow, then." Jasmine stood and reached for his hand, taking his fingers in hers. "If you decide to join me in this fight, do not take a weapon. With customs and airport security such as it is these days, I've had to make special arrangements." A faint smile quickly faded. "I know you are a man willing to risk a great deal out of loyalty. You have proven this before. Please, I beg of you, don't turn your back on Nicholas."

Christian returned her gesture with a reassuring squeeze of her hand. He watched Jasmine walk toward the elevator and listened as it rumbled to the ground floor. Raven stood silently by his side.

In many ways, he wanted to believe Jasmine. To believe her meant he had all the pieces to the puzzle of his past. His biological father had a name, such as it was. But staring into Jasmine's dark eyes, he'd felt the pull of a dark chasm, filled to the brim with corruption and lies. The woman had grown accustomed to living in such a realm, accepted it. Yet he could not. He felt completely unprepared to enter the world of his so-called father, Nicholas Charboneau.

It was one thing to free a man needing his help, but was it his fight? Even if Fiona confirmed Charboneau to be his father, how much would he risk to uncover the truth about his past?

"It's hard enough to talk to Fiona these days . . . in that place. Now this." He shook his head and pulled Raven to his chest, filling his senses with her warmth.

"Nicholas Charboneau. Just when I thought I'd seen the worst."

Christian's gaze fogged with the image of a face he knew well. Next stop, a long-awaited confrontation with his mother, Fiona. And this time she'd have to tell him the truth.

CHAPTER 4

DAY FOUR

Fiona had no need to fear the never-ending damnation of hell. She lived it, each and every day, cut off from the wealth and privilege—and freedom—she left behind.

Christian could only imagine what it must be like for her to live in a minimum security prison located in downtown Chicago. Beyond the metal bars, the world spun along without her—the charity events, gala openings, and life in general. But her world had stopped dead still, marred forever. For her, nothing would ever be the same again.

As he walked through the door marked for visitors and took a seat, bland gray walls closed in on him. The room smelled of sweat and an indefinable musty odor, masked by industrial pine cleaner. Walls had been stripped bare, functional in their simplicity. Rules of conduct were posted and screwed into painted cinder block, printed in blue, the only real

color in the room. Dull mediocrity and guilt weighed
oppressive in this place.

*God, you deserve better, Fie! If I could switch
places—*

He knew Fiona hated it, her home for the next five
years with good behavior. The judge had been lenient
in exchange for her voluntary confession to the arranged murder of her husband, Charles Dunhill, over
twenty-five years ago. No evidence would have con-
victed her. She came forward, unwilling to deny her
guilt any longer. Perhaps the judge aligned his sym-
pathies on the side of Fiona, given the fact she killed
her husband to save her illegitimate ten-year-old son
from the man's murderous wrath.

All things considered, his life had been built on a
foundation of murder and lies. He had grown weary
of the burden. But he couldn't fathom the depths of
her regret.

He sat in a metal chair, staring through Plexiglas
at the empty seat that would soon hold his mother.
A myriad of fingerprints dotted the dingy surface, a
quiet reminder of the desperation and longing within
these walls. His thoughts turned to Fiona.

He yearned to see her . . . and dreaded it at the
same time.

An annoying buzzer, followed by a slamming door,
preceded footsteps echoing down the hall within the
bowels of the prison. He stood in anticipation, almost
unaware he had moved at all. His gaze shifted to the
door beyond the barrier. Swallowing hard, he had to
remind himself to breathe. Through the small plate
glass in the door, covered with wire mesh, he saw the
grim face of a security guard. The door swung open
with a creak and Fiona walked into the room.

His heart lurched in his chest.

Dressed in an oversized orange jumpsuit, she looked so frail in her misery, so consumed by it. Gray walls drained her skin of color, blanching it to a doughy sheen. Her normally piercing gaze had lost its defiance. Eyes the color of deep jade had faded and now brimmed with tears glistening under fluorescent lighting.

Profound defeat robbed her of dignity. Fiona would never be the same again. This image of his mother would forever stick in his memory. She stared, a tear draining down her cheek. Christian fought the lump building in his throat. He gestured for her to sit, unable to take his eyes off her.

Keep it together, Delacorte—for her sake.

"How are you? You've lost weight." His words sounded trite.

She nodded and wiped fingers across her cheek. "I'm fine. You look . . . Are you getting enough sleep?" Her voice muffled through the speaker in the Plexiglas.

No doubt, the dark circles under his eyes gave him away. Of all people, Fiona knew how he slept, understood his relentless demons. As a child, she comforted him on many nights after one of his recurring nightmares, holding him until he fell asleep again. As a man, the dreams came less frequently, but remained a constant reminder of his past.

So the rift between them left a gaping hole in his heart, stealing the one person he'd known his entire life . . . his confessor. And worse, he could do nothing to ease her suffering.

"Yes. I'm fine," he lied, hating the strain between them. "I miss you. I wish—"

Before he finished, she raised a hand to stop him, pain etched deeply on her face. "Not a day goes by that I don't wish things were different between us . . . that I had made different decisions. But I can't change what happened. I only hope one day you can forgive me."

"I'm trying . . ." He lowered his eyes and took a breath. "So much has happened. I just need . . . time."

Awkward silence. No matter how much he longed to reconnect with her, a part of him knew the link had been severed for good. He would have to get beyond her betrayal, and she would have to survive the guilt. None of it would be easy.

Furrowing her brow, Fiona nodded her head in acknowledgment, yet kept her eyes on him. "You look like you have something on your mind. Please . . . say it."

He could never hide anything from her. Today would be no different.

"On more than one occasion, I've asked you about my father . . . my biological one." He took a deep breath, giving her time to prepare. "This time, I need an answer."

"Please . . . don't ask me again. Believe me, it's for your own good." Her words were engulfed by an underlying fear. He read it in her eyes.

"Why?"

"I made a mistake when I was a very young woman. If I tell you now, then you might convince yourself he is a man worth knowing. I can't let you do that." She diverted her gaze, wringing her thin hands. When she looked up, tears filled her eyes, her lips quivered. "Even if you don't think of me as your mother, I love you more than my own life. Keeping this secret is the last thing I can do for you . . . from in here. Don't make me answer that question. Please."

An uncomfortable stillness filled the space between them. Locked in her gaze, he felt the stalemate, unsure how to proceed. Only one way remained. Her way. *Just say it . . .*

"Nicholas Charboneau has been kidnapped in Brazil." Christian raised his chin, his jaw rigid.

He witnessed her pain, unable to console her. Fiona's eyes widened in shock and the defeat returned, forcing her to stare at her trembling fingers. Without the ability to touch her, he ached with her emptiness.

"His bodyguard, Jasmine Lee, has asked for help to free him. She needs a million dollars wired in seven days and use of the Dunhill jet."

Christian reached into his windbreaker to pull out an envelope containing the wire instructions. He held the unfolded paper against the barrier for her to see, then slid it back into the envelope. A guard would have to approve the exchange before he gave it to her.

"Don't wire the funds until you hear from . . ." Christian hesitated, catching himself. ". . . until you hear from Jasmine Lee. She'll have your contact information."

"You trust this woman?"

"Yes, I do," he lied.

Of course, he'd be the one to make the call on the payout, but he didn't have the heart to tell her he'd be in Brazil to do it. And if the funds got paid early, Charboneau's life would have no more value to the kidnappers. Timing would be everything.

"You still love him, don't you?" Christian knew the answer even before she looked up.

"I would sooner command my heart to stop beating than to deny my love for him."

"Is he my father, Fie?" The question had been unnecessary, but he wanted to hear her say it. Needed to hear it. "He's the one you built that shrine to, the one in the attic at the estate. All those memories locked away."

She chewed her lower lip, no doubt contemplating her options. Time stopped as he waited for her answer. Then resignation stooped her shoulders and she finally replied, "Yes. Nicky is your father."

Finally, the last piece of the puzzle fell into place.

Christian lowered his head and shut his eyes for an instant, letting everything sink in. When he looked up, he spoke softly. "If it means anything, Jasmine is convinced he still loves you."

Haunted laughter echoed in the small room, Fiona's amusement tainted by the agony of her expression. "Yes, I know . . . but he has a most peculiar way of expressing his feelings, my love. I suppose he always did."

With a renewed urgency, she placed her hand on the glass, leaving her print smudges, mingling her desperation with the many coming before. Her voice cracked under the weight of emotion.

"Please, Christian, I beg of you. I'll arrange for the money and the aircraft for his bodyguard's use, but please don't get involved with him. He's a dangerous man."

"So I hear."

Slowly, he raised his hand to meet hers, pressing it to the barrier. There was nothing more to say. Christian stood, giving the metal chair a shove across the floor. He should have told her the truth. His lie by omission shamed him. But if Fiona knew he planned to accompany Jasmine to Brazil, she might pull her support in order to protect him. He couldn't allow that.

"Thank you, Fie. I'll let you know how things turn out."

He headed for the door, avoiding her scrutiny. *Just walk out . . . only four steps.* Before he made his escape, she stopped him with her words.

"You're going with her . . . to free him. Aren't you?" Her voice choked with insight. She knew him well.

Christian couldn't turn around. If he looked in her eyes, he might never do what must be done. Clinching his fists, he stood still for a moment, the muscles in his back rigid with regret. He wanted to comfort her, to hold her in his arms. But that was not possible. And he knew no words would console her. So he chose silence as his only reply. He walked out the door, leaving his mother in a prison far worse than the law would ever impose. He had no choice.

"Strength . . . and quiet endurance, Mother," he whispered, his prayer for her as he walked down the hallway. "One day at a time . . ."

Now, time to face Raven.

Their meal was over . . . maybe even before it had begun. In denial, Raven's eyes focused on a stain smack dab in the middle of her good lace tablecloth, a faded spot of red wine. She'd been so preoccupied, she hadn't noticed it when she set the table earlier. Staring at it now, she couldn't remember when or how it had happened. Her thoughts turned to spot removal, anything but the trouble at hand.

Across from her, Christian sat in stone cold silence—a million miles away. Brazil, to be exact. She looked up and caught her own reflection in an antique mirror on the wall of her formal dining room. And she didn't like what she saw. Avoidance. Totally not like her. Only a damned ostrich would stick its head in the sand this deep.

Meet it head on, woman! Face it . . . deal with it.

She shifted focus to the remnants of their dinner, congealed on her mother's best china. She had hoped for a quiet dinner at her bungalow in the 'burbs, a chance to reason with him. Instead, neither of them had eaten much. Her pasta Alfredo sat cold on the plate, with salads nearly untouched. Ivory candlesticks had melted down, their flicker casting shadows on his handsome face.

Christian had been overly polite, awkward around her. She thought she'd seen the last of that behavior . . . so long ago. Now it returned with gusto. Something lay in ambush within his brain. She saw it coming—like a train wreck.

"You've been quiet. And you haven't said much about the visit you had with Fiona today. Want to talk about it?"

He shook his head, staring into his wineglass, rolling the crystal stem between his fingers. Candlelight speared through swirling chardonnay, its golden haze dancing over lace. "I don't know how you can love somebody so much . . . and hurt them like that."

"Being a member of law enforcement, I can't condone what she did . . . but Fiona acted out of love."

"I'm not talking about what she did to hurt me. I'm the bastard who dished it out today." Darkness shrouded his face. He avoided her eyes. "I used her . . . to get what I wanted."

"To help your father, Christian. There's a big difference."

Struggling for words, he looked at her, his jaw torqued in anger. "It doesn't feel so different, Raven."

"Look. This is not a good situation. None of it. Will you let me inside long enough to help? Can we talk about this?"

She pleaded her case, laying it all out as plain as the red stain on lace.

His gaze drifted to her, a somber, unreadable change. The stillness of the room wedged between them. Only the soft ticking from a wall clock tempered the silence. Time slipping away. Too much time. She knew by his reticence she had lost him.

"Nothing to talk about. I gotta go. Thanks for dinner." He wiped his mouth with a linen napkin and tossed it on the table by his plate. When he stood and started to help her clear off the table, she stopped him.

"Please don't. Leave 'em. I want to talk."

Christian hesitated only for a moment, set his plate down and said, "Sorry. I can't stay. I've got a lot to . . . think about." He headed for her front door, looking eager to be free of her accusing stare.

"Oh, no. I'd say the thinking has been done. You've made up your mind, haven't you?"

Voice raised, she kept pace with him, maneuvering through her small living room. By his actions, he had drawn a line in the sand. A line he didn't want her to cross.

You should know better, Christian!

Framed portraits of her family witnessed their argument. Her father posed in police uniform, the photo taken a month before he was killed in the line of duty. The face of a mother she never knew, smiling. They had been the foundation of her life, but Christian . . . She hoped he'd be her future.

You're my family now, Delacorte . . . like it or not.

In her experience, life never played fair. After her family had been taken from her by tragedy, she developed a pretty tough hide over the years. Yet with Christian, she'd let her guard down, not wanting any barriers to stand between them. *Hell, love made you downright defenseless.* And he was the one man who could hurt her . . . deeply. But in her heart, she trusted him not to.

"You're shutting me out. Why?" she demanded. "If you're so hell-bent on doing this, then I'm going with you."

Her words stopped him dead in his tracks, something logic and common sense couldn't do. Christian turned to face her.

"Yeah? Well, what if I don't want you to go? Do I have any say in the matter of my life?" he argued, gesturing to make his point. "I'd just be worrying about you . . . maybe make mistakes that could cost both of us. I couldn't live with that."

He grimaced as if he were in pain, raked a hand through his dark hair. "Don't make this harder than it needs to be . . . please." His gaze softened for only an instant. "I love you. That hasn't changed."

"But not enough to stay here . . . with me." She blurted out those words, without thinking how needy she sounded. In her brain, the clock ticked louder, harsh and abrasive. The sound mocked her. It reminded her that those precious days with him might have been numbered all along.

"Don't make me choose between the life of my father . . . and you." In the dim light, his green eyes muted to dark gray.

Raven crossed her arms, clutching them to her chest. She paced the floor and blocked his escape.

"I don't trust Jasmine, Christian. She'll have a million dollars and the Dunhill jet at her disposal . . . and you. She could parlay the money, up the ante on her next victim." Raven raised her voice, heaping any argument before him. Desperation hammered her sense of reason. "If Fiona would pay a million bucks for her precious Nicky, what would she pay for you? And what if Jasmine is behind your father's kidnapping? I don't like it."

"And I can't walk away." Christian matched her tone, squaring off in front of her. "I'm not gonna start a new life here and wonder whatever happened to my . . . He's the last piece to this puzzle of my life. I have to do this. Why can't you understand?"

"I do understand, Christian. I just wish you'd let me help. Let me go with you," she pleaded. But when she stepped closer, he raised a hand to stop her.

"Out of the question." He shook his head and stepped around her to grab the door, but stopped when she spoke.

"When it comes to your family . . . and the hurt you've got festering inside, you shut me out, Christian." She let her words hang in the air, waiting for him to face her.

With head down in profile, he sighed as he stood in the open doorway, taking a moment to gather his thoughts. A gust of cool night air drifted by him and soothed her cheek with its caress, making her ache for his touch.

With barely a glance back, he said softly, "I'll call you when we get there. That is, if you're still speaking to me."

He would leave her behind. Gritting her teeth, she responded in kind, letting anger get the better of her. "Try calling collect. If I don't accept the charges, then you'll know."

He narrowed his eyes and raised his chin in defiance, but didn't say another word. He shut the door behind him, leaving her feeling empty.

Damn! Everything had gone to hell, right before her eyes. And she'd been powerless to stop it. She fought the lump in her throat and a blur of tears, listening as he drove away.

"God, Christian. You'd better come back to me." She knew him well enough to believe if he didn't return from Brazil, there would only be one reason. And that reality made her heart ache with regret. "Damn it."

He'd taken a shot to the gut, the wind knocked out of him. Seeing the hurt in her eyes felt every bit as painful.

You, bastard!

Christian gripped the steering wheel, glaring out his windshield with only the drone of his SUV's engine and his self-recriminations to keep him company. Center lane stripes zipped by his wheels, illuminated by his headlights. He set a course for downtown with the anonymity of darkness closing in—the faces of Fiona and Raven haunting his conscience.

Today, he'd hurt the two people he loved most. And Raven's voice replayed in his head, over and over again. Picking a fight with her had been deliberate on his part.

Yeah, you're a real gentleman, Delacorte.

For her sake, he had severed their tightening bond, knowing she would've tried to accompany him to Brazil. The trip would be risky enough, given the scenarios Jasmine presented. He wouldn't give Raven the option. He loved her too much.

For much of his life, he felt alone even in a crowd. Raven tempered the feeling after Fiona had been sentenced to prison, giving him a reason to look forward to each and every day. A miraculous gift. But with the possibility of losing her now, the hollowness of being lonely, once again stretched across his horizon—an endless, familiar chasm.

He couldn't face such a bleak future—not now. Somehow, he'd make it up to her, become the kind of man she deserved. With great effort, he cleared his mind, dismissing the guilt and the emptiness.

He started to compile lists in his head, things he would need. Plans took shape. As it was, he'd be up half the night, packing and making arrangements. Only the mission to rescue Charboneau would take center stage now.

But aligning himself with Jasmine would be tricky. With the holes in her story, he might bring down the wrath of Charboneau's syndicate on his head. And the dangerous tri-border area of Brazil would be no place to outrun a well-funded criminal organization.

With his main operation in Chicago, what the hell was Charboneau doing in Cuiabá, Brazil? Maybe he could pull something off the Internet. One more item to add to his growing list of things to do. Yet the answer to that question might be the key.

His mind conjured up images of a face he'd never seen—his father. *"You look just like him," Jasmine had said.*

If he would ever see Raven again, he'd have to dig deep and rely on his discipline and training to steer clear of trouble. He glanced into the rearview mirror, seeing his face wavering in and out of shadows. Given his distrust of Jasmine and the corrupt world of his notorious father, he found his only ally staring back.

You better trust yourself, Delacorte. 'Cause you're on your own, pal.

CHAPTER 5

He smelled foreboding in the air like impending rain. A steel gray morning cleaved to an ominous night sky. Clouds darkened the horizon, masking the downtown Chicago skyline. He imagined the storm carried its usual rumble, but the incessant drone of airplane engines flying in and out of the private airstrip muffled the distant thunder. The ground crew had worked efficiently as they prepared the Dunhill jet for departure, but now the flurry of activity on the tarmac dwindled. Christian knew it was only a matter of time.

Put up . . . or shut up, Delacorte. No turning back, hero. With their imminent departure, he knew they'd beat the onslaught of rain once they reached cruising altitude. Still, the dismal morning made it tough to shake the blues.

Raven's dark eyes haunted him without mercy.

Slow and deliberate, Christian sipped his black coffee. Holding the steaming mug close to his lips, he stared out the window of the small waiting area, letting the heat linger on his skin. He half expected to see her.

"You looking for someone, boss?" A familiar voice drew him back. As he looked over his shoulder, he heard the Dunhill man say, "We've got the jet loaded. Waiting for anyone else?"

A faint smile crossed his lips. "I'm not your boss anymore, Coop." When the man shrugged and returned a grin, he added, "And no, not expecting anyone else."

Christian turned back toward the window, his eyes on the front gate of the hangar. The cyclone fence gaped open. No sign of Raven. A part of him felt grateful she remained behind and would stay safe, but a nagging selfish side of his nature prayed like hell she'd drive through those gates, ready for round two. No such luck.

"How's Mrs. Dunhill?" Cooper asked.

"Holding up . . . considering. Thanks for having the balls to ask about her. Everyone's been walking on eggshells around the subject."

Fiona being in prison, serving time for an age-old murder for hire scheme, had become the elephant standing in the middle of the room that everyone chose to ignore. Cooper's candor struck him as refreshingly honest by comparison.

Once he'd uncovered the truth about Fiona being his mother, he kept the information to himself. No one needed to know. Most people asked too many questions, more out of morbid curiosity than from any real concern. Only a handful of Dunhill employees knew the real story of why he'd quit. He preferred it that way.

"I've been working for Mrs. Dunhill too long not to ask about her. Doesn't mean she's not in my prayers." Cooper smiled, then added, "Anytime you're ready."

Christian nodded his acknowledgment, gulping more coffee as the man left the room. Alone and rapt in his thoughts, he watched the gate, eyes fixed. Then a scent teased his awareness. He felt a subtle shift. A presence displaced the air in the room. Closing his eyes for an instant, he focused on his senses, waiting for her.

With expectation tugging at his gut, he turned, fighting a smile as his heart lifted. But his mood quickly changed.

"The detective isn't coming?" Jasmine entered the room so quietly he almost hadn't noticed.

"No," he replied.

The woman didn't bother to hide her amusement. It hit him the wrong way.

"Don't read anything into it. Thelma isn't making the road trip, Louise. That's all." With eyes downcast, he looked into his empty mug and muttered. "It's for the best."

Christian got a refill on coffee and stared steadfast at Jasmine. "I did some research last night on the Internet. Got a lot of hits off the name Charboneau."

As expected, the woman flinched, a slight move he might have missed if he hadn't been watching. Feeling encouraged, he went on.

"That genetics research facility Charboneau has been associated with? It was one of the organizations working on the human genome-mapping project, identifying the gene linked to drug and alcohol addiction a few years back."

He stepped closer to her, a hand in his pocket. He nursed his coffee and waited for the right moment to bait her.

"But I find it hard to believe a man who allegedly makes a living off the drug-addicted fringe of society would suddenly have a change in heart. How do you explain that?"

"Ah, the key word is 'allegedly.' But as you well know, I am only a bodyguard. I know nothing about—"

"Just . . . stop." He raised a hand and shook his head. "Save the bullshit for someone who might buy what you're slinging."

The woman stood her ground, not backing down. To the contrary, she smiled and stepped closer. Jasmine placed a hand on his chest. A bold move.

"Despite my preferences toward complete candor, I won't betray him," she said, her voice throaty and sensual.

He clenched his jaw. Whatever she peddled, he wasn't buying. "Oh, yeah, you're a beacon for truth and the American way." Then out of the blue, a thought occurred to him, something he'd read between the lines. He followed his gut instincts and tossed out a zinger from left field.

"Do you love him?"

For an instant, surprise registered across her dark eyes. Recovering, she masked the reaction. Her expression morphed into her usual distant facade. She turned her back and walked to the window, arms clutched to her chest.

"He is my employer."

"Answer the question." He pressed, knowing he had crossed the line.

She spun toward him, eyes flared with indignation. "That is none of your business."

Her strong reaction forced him to replay something she'd told him yesterday about the enduring connection between Fiona and her old flame. Before he could stop himself, he voiced his theory. "You love him, but he still loves my—"

"Don't say it." Cutting the distance between them, Jasmine strut closer with a finger raised in challenge. "Let's get something straight between us. We are here to intervene in Nicky's destiny, to save his life. That is all. If you have another agenda, then you're out . . . now."

Her face suddenly animated, he got a glimpse of what it would be like to suffer the woman's anger. Most probably, he deserved her outrage for intruding on personal turf, but the woman bluffed—big-time.

"Pretty cocky for someone who came begging for my help yesterday. And with the short fuse on this trip, you can't afford a Plan B." He called her bluff, punctuating his gall with a swig of coffee.

Jasmine raised her chin in defiance. She spoke in a quiet rock-steady voice, eyes aimed with deadly accuracy.

"It would not be in Nicky's best interest . . . no. But make no mistake. I will not tolerate mutiny, regardless of your connection to him. I would answer such a threat with my blade."

Now standing within inches of his chest, she toyed with a button on his shirt. Normally, the gesture would be flirtatious and seductive, but he'd seen the woman at work. Her moves had the signature of a coiled rattler, fangs bared, waiting for him to turn his back.

Slowly, her eyes trailed up his chest. Nails in glistening red tugged at his shirt. Her expression softened with her voice. "Besides, you're curious about your . . . new father. Admit it. You have to know just how far you've fallen from the base of that magnificent tree, don't you, little acorn?"

Anyone catching the scene might have assumed he was having an intimate conversation with a lover. But Jasmine worked best up close, her words as cutting as her lethal knife. Especially when her incisions stung with the harsh reality of truth.

Still, he fought to maintain control. *Little acorn, my ass!*

"John Delacorte will *always* be my real father. And from what I found out about Charboneau, I've decided any connection I have to the man is merely a result of adolescent libido." He grabbed her hand and shoved it aside. "No thanks, not interested in making a love connection with daddy dearest."

She raised an eyebrow and curved her lips into a smirk. "Perhaps you should be the one to conserve on the bullshit, Christian. We might find a market for it in Brazil." In jaunty arrogance, she turned toward the door, not looking back. "Can we go?"

Without waiting for his reply, she stepped out of the room, heading for the plane. In her wake, sounds of the airport intruded upon the stillness of the room, then dissipated as the door shut behind her. Dressed in pressed jeans and boots, Jasmine clutched at her blue windbreaker, drawing it to her body. He watched her walk toward the jet, her long dark hair wafting in the breeze.

"If there's a market for bullshit in Brazil, I'd be a wealthy man," he mumbled under his breath. "But you, Jasmine, would be Oprah."

Taking one final look toward the gate, Christian looked off into the distance and sighed before heading for the door.

Next stop—Cuiabá, Brazil.

CUIABÁ, BRAZIL,
MARECHAL RONDON AIRPORT
8:58 P.M.

Christian didn't need this. The airport was a hive of activity . . . and not in a good way. After flying via private jet, he'd hoped for a simpler process to disembark. But the last bank of commercial planes arrived at the gates about the same time the Dunhill jet touched down. The influx of people crowded customs and bottlenecked the process.

Bad luck followed him like a shadow, hard to shake.

Despite the hour, travelers with places to go hauled bags through the bustling corridors . Their faces told a mixed tale. Some were energetic and filled with impatience to begin their Brazilian adventure, while others looked frustrated and tired.

Christian identified with the latter.

Several large groups of tourists arrived in a rush and were now being ushered to buses waiting on the curb outside baggage claim. The terminal echoed with the language of Portuguese, Spanish, and other dialects. Christian heard very little English spoken. The predominance of dark skin and hair, coupled with the bulk of the facial features appearing native, reminded him of his foreigner status.

By the time he got through customs and the baggage claim process, he felt every hour of travel deep in his bones. Even Jasmine, the Queen of Serene, couldn't hide her exhaustion. It showed in her eyes and in her sullen mood.

"I have to make a stop." She led him to a large locker along one of the corridors off the baggage claim area. She fished a key from her pocket, inserted it into the lock, and opened the door. A black duffel bag inside. And another smaller carryon. "This is the special arrangement I spoke to you about. We'll need a porter now."

Weapons and whatever else she carried. The woman always came prepared. She either maintained the locker year-round or had arranged it before she left Brazil a few days ago. She hailed a man in an airport uniform hauling a cart. As the man approached, Christian reached into the locker for the smaller bag on top. Feeling its weight, he shook it and turned his attention to Jasmine.

"What's in here? It's lighter than I expected."

At first he wasn't sure she'd answer. Eventually, she did.

"Nicky's clothes. He'll need something fresh when we rescue him." The words made her sound self-assured, but her eyes betrayed her.

"Good idea," he nodded, unsure what else to say.

Acting as a convenient and well-timed distraction, the smiling porter loaded their bags onto his cart and followed them through the airport, jabbering in broken English. Christian only understood every fifth word, his mind too fatigued to listen.

Outside, the dense air felt like a wall of moisture, the heat sustained even after dark. With evening temps like this, what would tomorrow bring? Diesel fuel and smoke mingled with humidity, making it hard to take a full breath.

Several uniformed men directed traffic with exaggerated hand gestures and the shrill sounds of whistles. The porter took control, stepping in front of Christian and ordering a taxi with a shout and a commanding wave of his hand.

Two cabs surged forward from the mix of vehicles, nearly colliding to gain advantage in driving the foreigners to the city. Neither driver blinked in their game of chicken. After a few well-chosen hand gestures and an exchange of colorful local lingo, one man reaped the spoils. He leapt from his taxi with a smile and a nod, now the picture of hospitality.

"Welcome. Where you go?" The cabbie hustled to open the door.

Jasmine avoided looking at the man. "Hotel Palma Dourada," she answered as she slid into the backseat of the bright yellow cab, fanning herself with a map of the city. The cabbie left the door open for Christian to join her.

Still standing on the curb, Christian watched the porter load up the last of their bags into the cab. With the trunk slammed shut, he slipped U.S. dollars into the porter's hand and started to join Jasmine. But an unmarked police car rolled past the tour buses to block the taxi from taking off, a rotating beacon of red fixed to the dash. A car door opened and one man emerged.

"Welcome to Cuiabá, Mr. Delacorte." Hands against the police car, a lean man in khaki uniform with steely black eyes glared at him. No cordiality on his face. "Please allow me to accompany you to the hotel. You ride with me."

Christian raised his chin and eyed the man with wariness.

"How do you know my name? And my ETA?" He asked the questions, but suspected only one answer. No doubt the man had an informant within customs.

"You will find nothing escapes me in my town. I make it my business to know such things. Please . . . I must insist." The man gestured with a hand, indicating the passenger door.

"He's the police captain who followed me," Jasmine whispered from inside the cab. "Be very careful. I do not trust him."

Seeing the woman's reaction to the cop raised a red flag. On the issue of being trustworthy, Jasmine hoisted stones from her house of glass. By his way of thinking, if she didn't trust the police captain— that alone would be a ringing endorsement—making the cop the lesser of two evils. Yet by the looks of the man's stern expression, Christian couldn't tell if he'd be friend or foe. The guy looked scrappy, a street fighter. Not as tall as Christian, he had a muscular build, looking native, with his dark skin and hair. His piercing stare commanded respect. An age-weathered face framed the severity of his eyes and sent a clear message.

This was not a man to mess with.

According to the research on Brazil Christian read on the jet, corruption had become a major thread woven into the fabric of this country—an accepted practice to supplement low wages. Was the man standing before him getting his fair share, or fighting against others who did?

One thing was certain. Cuiabá was his town.

Christian considered Duarte's invitation and shut the taxi door, with Jasmine grimacing at him from inside. With reluctance, he walked toward the man's car.

"How could I refuse such hospitality?"

Once Christian slid into the passenger seat, the man introduced himself, without offering a hand in greeting. This was not a social occasion. "My name is Captain Luis Duarte. I wanted us to have a moment alone, you and I. Your female companion and I have already had the pleasure."

As the man spoke, he turned off the red cherry and pulled from the curb, heading for town. With the windows rolled down, Christian rested his elbow on the car door. He glared out the front windshield, only his peripheral vision on the man behind the wheel.

Once beyond the airport terminal, a canopy of stars filled the night sky, fading near the horizon with the lights of the city ahead. Headlights drilled the blackness, luring insects from the gloom. And Duarte's face ebbed in and out of shadows, silhouetted by the eerie light from the dashboard.

As it usually did, darkness closed in on Christian, weighing heavy like a vise around his chest. It squeezed tight, a constant pressure. To distract himself, he kept his eyes focused on the road ahead, glancing in the side mirror at the taxi following close behind.

With effort, he tapped into his senses, almost a heightened meditative state. Hot wind whipped through the car, buffeting his hair and shirt as Duarte drove. The hum of the engine and the drone of road noise absorbed the lull in conversation. His thoughts drifted to Raven, his calming mantra ritual. Eventually, the essence of this strange world washed over him like cleansing rain, invigorating his spirit.

"Yes, Jasmine mentioned your interest in her . . . activities." Christian heard his own voice like an out of body experience. "Do you always greet visitors to your country with such a warm reception?"

"No, but I made an exception for you. Then again, you are not just *any* tourist. You are here in Brazil to search for Nicholas Charboneau, are you not?" He didn't wait for an answer. "How do you know him?"

Christian took a gamble that the police captain didn't know everything and skirted the truth about his relationship to Charboneau.

"Actually, I've come because of Jasmine. I've never met the man." He didn't *exactly* lie.

"So you are not connected to his . . . organization? The syndicate in Chicago?"

Duarte had definitely done his homework.

"No, not at all. I have my own company, Delacorte Protective Services, but I'm here because I owe her a favor."

"Such a huge favor. You must owe her quite a debt to repay it in this manner." The man's dark eyes cut through the murky black. "She does not strike me as a woman with many friends."

"I didn't say we were friends." Christian returned the lawman's stare. "Besides . . . she wouldn't exactly take no for an answer."

Duarte found amusement in that. "No, beautiful women seldom do."

"Have the kidnappers provided any proof of life evidence? They can't possibly expect payment if they haven't shown he's still alive."

"It is true most abductions communicate such things, usually a photograph of the victim holding a current newspaper. But I have not seen such proof. Has the bodyguard been contacted?"

"No. She would've told me."

"Are you sure of that? She seems to be a woman of many secrets."

Christian shifted his gaze to Duarte. The man's face drifted in and out of the dark as he kept his eyes on the road. He had asked a simple question, one Christian couldn't answer in good faith. By his silence, he gave the police captain all the confirmation he needed.

Score one for the home team.

Grimacing out the window, Christian distracted himself with the changing terrain. Entering Cuiabá, the capital of the state of Mato Grosso, he found the city held traces of its colonial past mingled with newer development.

Known as the southern gateway to the Amazon, the city served as a beacon of civilization on the edge of Brazil's great wilderness. He had seen photos of the city in his latest research, but nothing like seeing the real thing. Intersected by a river named after the city, the urban setting looked peaceful in the photos, with its flat terrain and skyscrapers nestled between an abundance of trees.

But after what happened to Charboneau, Christian knew a seedy underbelly existed in this picturesque place. Mankind tainted perfection with its very nature.

Still, Cuiabá had an undeniable old-world charm.

Only a sidewalk's width away from the bustling street, multicolored facades of old villas lined the thoroughfares. The artist Van Gogh wouldn't have enough pigment on his palate to do the city justice. Tall, ornate custom window cornices and colonnades were painted in white and set against walls of vivid blue, yellow, green, and burnt orange, giving the city a festive appearance. Under streetlights, the splashes of brilliance assaulted his eyes, a departure from the more conservative use of color in Chicago. Wrought-iron balconies and gateways accented the quaint colonial manor houses. Without much thought to city planning, apartment buildings stood next to more modern office high-rises and ancient cathedrals. The new sprouted amidst the old, a hodge-podge of culture.

On the tepid night air, strange smells overwhelmed his senses, an unfamiliar fusion of a people's culture and the earth. The enticing aroma of exotic foods mixed with the pungent smells of sweet, rich soil, livestock, and the surrounding marshlands, Brazil's lifeblood. Laughter and music served as the backdrop for a lyric language he did not understand, but welcomed. The flood of new sensations bombarded his senses like a hail of bullets, sweet torture. This time, his heightened awareness felt like a gift—a gift he wanted to share with only one woman.

God, I wish you were here. His heart ached for Raven. He closed his eyes and fought to clear his head, wanting to stay in the moment.

When he opened them again, a flash of light drew his attention, a well-timed distraction. Candles burned in votives or glowed within old broken liquor bottles. They were displayed in windows, on sidewalks, and on several of the front stoops to shops. A variety of tributes hung beside them, from religious symbols to cigars, the shapes murky in the flickering light. The unfamiliar practice caught his eye.

"What's with the candles?"

"Macumba ritual. In your country, you might have heard it called voodoo. The people of my country are superstitious. They are drawn to the supernatural, an influence brought to Brazil from the days of slavery. The custom comes from a blending of African spiritual beliefs with that of the Roman Catholic faith."

"Why burning candles? What are they for?"

"I am not an expert, but I have heard the rituals are an attempt to make contact with the Orixás, or spirits. Perhaps they ask for protection from evil or hope to gain good fortune."

Gazing out the passenger window, Christian mumbled under his breath, "Maybe it wouldn't hurt to burn a candle for good luck."

"Never underestimate the necessity to protect yourself against evil. You can never be too careful. The curse of the evil eye has its power."

The police captain's statement struck him as odd. Yet when he glanced toward the man, Duarte kept his eyes on the road, diminishing the significance of his words. Regardless of the man's intention, Christian sensed his implied threat.

"You sound like you believe in Macumba, Captain."

Duarte shrugged. "In my line of work, I find many people like to blame the spirits for their actions. Convenient, I think. But I suppose for me, superstitions are hard to ignore. I grew up with them." His face settled into a frown. "I see the evil eye cast on the street, I take a wide path around it. It is no different than you avoiding a walk under a ladder, is it not?"

Christian smiled. "I suppose so."

He felt content to wait for Duarte to make the first move, knowing the man would eventually get around to business. Biding his time, he fixed upon the local color again, catching a commotion ahead. Duarte slowed down, putting both hands on the wheel. Cars lined the narrow streets of a pedestrian plaza with shoppers strolling by retail store windows in their leisure, without a care for the late hour.

"Does this place ever shut down? I'd expect shops to be closed by now," he asked his self-appointed host.

"You'll find we do things differently in my country, Mr. Delacorte. It is our way. We do things at our own pace." The captain finally began to make his point. Cryptic as it might be, Christian didn't miss the message.

"Sometimes a slow pace doesn't get the job done." He looked Duarte in the eye. "Maybe a busy man of responsibility could use some help."

The police captain gripped the steering wheel, not appreciating Christian's underlying meaning. "Those wishing to help sometimes get in the way, maybe get themselves killed in the process. And that would require countless administrative forms to be completed. I wouldn't appreciate the added work . . . or the extra attention from my government."

Duarte turned down a side street, beyond the central square. The taxi followed.

"I don't suppose we're talking about the street merchants anymore," Christian said. "Unless the competition for sales in this town is that brutal." Christian shifted in the seat and turned toward the man. "Is the economy that bad or are you threatening me?"

"I had hoped to be more subtle." The policeman pulled into the circular drive of a posh hotel. Valets and bellhops jumped to attention, standing along the curb, but Duarte waved them off. He wasn't done delivering his message. "I would advise you to respect our laws. Do not test me. You are a guest in my country. Do not forget that."

Seeing a movement out the side mirror, Christian spotted Jasmine stepping from the cab behind them. She paid the cabbie and gave direction to a hotel valet to unload the luggage onto a cart. Her eyes remained on him as he sat in Duarte's car.

"Subtle or not, message received loud and clear. But let me deliver one of my own." Taking his eyes off the reflection of Jasmine in the mirror, he leaned toward the captain, an elbow propped against the seat back. "I'm here to find Charboneau. I'm sure it would be in my best interest to abide by the law, as you say, but this is a matter of life or death. With or without your help, I'll find the man and bring him back with me."

Captain Duarte curved his lips into a sneer. "Do not make me angry, Mr. Delacorte. You would only disappoint me. And you'll find I'm not a tolerant man. I have been told I make a formidable enemy."

"I have no doubt of that, Captain. So let's agree to cooperate with each other. Then maybe we won't discover how truly ruthless we can be as enemies." He shoved open the car door and stepped out, leaning in for one last exchange. "Thanks for the lift."

"I will be keeping my eye on you. Do not disappoint me, Mr. Delacorte."

"Wouldn't think of it."

Christian shut the car door and watched the man drive away. More than likely, he'd made his first enemy, and he hadn't been in town five minutes. Narrowing his eyes, he stuffed his hands in his jeans.

Jasmine nudged his arm with her shoulder. "See what I mean? Duarte is a snake, lower than a reptile. The man can't be trusted."

Christian stared at the red taillights of Duarte's car as it headed down the street and turned a corner. Without glancing at Jasmine, he filled his lungs with muggy air.

"I'll be the judge of that."

Benign dark eyes stared back at him. "Have you stayed with us before, Mr. Delacorte?"

The uniformed hotel clerk behind the registration desk looked bored as he asked the obligatory question yet another time. The young man didn't care what his answer would be.

"No, I haven't. It's my first time to Cuiabá." Christian watched the clerk work the keyboard to the hotel computer with eyes glazed over. Time to get the man's attention. "Were you working the night Nicholas Charboneau was kidnapped from this hotel?"

Like getting hit with a cattle prod, the man jerked his head, eyes struggling for a discreet look at the hotel guest asking the question. His fingers flattened on the computer keys. The clerk no longer looked bored.

"Yes, sir, I was. But I don't know anything about it." He resumed his work, trying hard to avoid Christian's stare.

Jasmine had stopped her pacing, but he felt the heat

of her glare. She kept her mouth shut, willing to see where he'd take this. On trivial matters, the woman could be a real team player.

Christian lowered his voice. "That's too bad. Because if you did know something, you could be a rich man." He leaned across the front desk, locking eyes with the clerk. "I'm offering a sizable reward in U.S. dollars to anyone with information leading to the return of Charboneau . . . alive. No questions asked."

Jasmine resumed her pacing but kept her silence. She let the sharp staccato of her footsteps on the marble floor do all her talking.

He handed the clerk his business card. "I can be reached on my cell phone. I'd appreciate you passing the word. The sooner the better."

Christian had a tri-band cell phone with international roaming, a necessity of the job.

"Like I said, I know nothing." The man handed him the card key to their accommodations, his jaw knotted with tension. "I hope you enjoy your stay in Cuiabá. And as always, it is a pleasure to see you, Ms. Lee." He nodded to Jasmine, a nervous display of good manners and a gesture she didn't acknowledge.

As Christian turned for the bank of elevators, bellhop and luggage in tow at a respectful distance, Jasmine slipped her arm into his and muttered under her breath. "What the hell was *that* all about? I don't appreciate working under the limelight. Shadows are more to my liking."

"Yeah, but we don't have the luxury of time on our side. We gotta jump-start our search." He punched the button for the elevator, keeping his voice low. "Besides, I thought a surprise game of Russian roulette would appeal to a woman like you."

"Oh, don't get me wrong. I'm an adrenaline junkie, but I've always believed Russian roulette is best played with a rigged game. I prefer someone else's name on the bullet."

"Nice to see you've got a strong sense of fair play. Glad you're on my side."

Even as he said the words, Christian didn't believe Jasmine picked sides. Why complicate the issue when no one else mattered but número uno? He knew the exotic woman played by her own set of rules. No way in hell *fair* would ever muddle her playbook.

Yet Jasmine had sought him out and risked her life to rescue Charboneau. Out of loyalty? Or out of something more? None of it made sense, given what he believed of this woman. Maybe Raven had been right to warn him. Had he stepped into some grand conspiracy concocted by Jasmine . . . or Charboneau? Another retribution scheme against Fiona?

He'd leapt into the fray head first, way too vulnerable to anything associated with his past and the father he never knew. *Fine time for second thoughts, Delacorte.* He caught a glimpse of wariness darkening Jasmine's eyes, but eventually her lips nudged into a smile.

"Few things surprise me anymore," she said, her fingers slithering up his arm like a nest of snakes zeroing in on their next meal. "But I am willing to see what you have up your sleeve, Christian."

Not half as much as I want to see what's up yours, Jasmine.

CHAPTER 6

A red blinking eye drew his attention. Christian walked down the hallway to his hotel suite with Jasmine. She caught his eye movement and nodded acknowledgment with a sideways glance. They were on the same wavelength, checking out the security of the penthouse floor. Two security cameras had a shot of the corridor, one on either end, with another focused on the bank of elevators. A final camera had been positioned toward the doors into the private suites. Adequate, nothing more.

Christian lived most of his life in Fiona's world, an existence defined by the power of money. Still, the Hotel Palma Dourada distinguished itself. Exquisite oil paintings in extravagant frames brought color to tan walls. Plush rugs and carpeting deadened the sound in the hall. The air smelled fresh and crisp. By all appearances, the hotel earned its elite status, making it hard for him to believe any crime had been committed here.

As the bellhop opened the door and pulled in the luggage on wheels, Christian let Jasmine deal with the man's gratuity while he scoped out the room. Charboneau's suite. He pictured his father standing in this very spot only four days ago, contemplating what tomorrow would bring.

Now he found himself doing the same thing.

The impressive front entry had a marble floor covered by an elaborate native print rug. A crystal chandelier hung from the high-pitched ceiling in the foyer, with similar fixtures dazzling the interior. Ornate mirrors, classic Brazilian sculpture and artwork, adorned the suite, bringing richness to ivory and gold walls. Lush, tropical plants grew from huge ceramic pots spaced throughout the penthouse. From the front entry, Christian saw that the suite had two bedrooms with private baths and a massive living room. To the left of the wet bar, imposing French doors led to the private balcony.

Living quarters fit for Nicholas Charboneau. *A damned palace!*

After the bellhop left, he said to Jasmine, "I know we agreed on reserving the same room you and Charboneau shared—in case the kidnappers tried to contact us—but you could've booked another room for me."

"Oh, please. There are two bedrooms in this suite and more than enough space to share. Besides, your detective is not here. She will never know of our cozy accommodations." Jasmine stepped closer, brushing a finger across his waist. Another smile tugged at her lips.

Then her expression grew more solemn. Fatigue might have played a part in her tiring of the long-

standing game between them. For an instant she let
her defenses down and spoke her mind. "Besides,
having you here reminds me of Nicky. I hoped you
wouldn't mind."

"Let's just say I would've preferred my privacy."

From his vantage point, Christian watched her expression reflected in the mirror behind the wet bar.
A veil of concern clouded her eyes. He knew so little
about the woman, but one thing was certain. Jasmine
had a deep connection to Charboneau, a link he
didn't understand. Her flirting with him might only
be a distraction, a way to cover up her true feelings
for his father. At least, he hoped that's all it was.

"It's time to take care of business." With a stern
face, Jasmine fell into her role as bodyguard, checking out the other rooms with efficiency. "You will
take this room." She gave the order, directing him
with a wave of her hand, eyes alert. "If we have
eavesdroppers, I want to know about it."

She rummaged through the black duffel and retrieved scanning gear. State-of-the-art and very
high tech. The best Charboneau's money could buy.
With ear jack in place, she ran the equipment quietly
through each room, over walls, light fixtures, and
phones. As a professional himself, he admired her
thoroughness. When the place had been swept without incident, Jasmine set up her countersurveillance
gear, to jam eavesdroppers from a distance.

Standing by his side, she gave her assessment.
"Looks like the suite's clean, but from outside, par-
abolic mics and laser surveillance are still a threat.
Doesn't hurt to take precautions."

"Good, I agree. But before we get to your agenda,
I need to ask you something." He stepped closer to

her. In typical Jasmine fashion, she gave her acceptance with only a tilt of her head, words unnecessary. "If the kidnappers contacted you for any reason, you would let me know, right?"

She merely stared at him, her dark eyes a blank slate.

God, she'd make a helluva poker player!

"This is not a game, Christian. I know you and I do not trust one another, but we have to get past that, for Nicky's sake." She sighed with drama. "Yes, I would tell you."

Even hearing the words, he wasn't convinced. The woman could sell time-share condos to men on death row. Still, he would play the cards he'd been dealt.

"Now can we get on with this?" She stepped to the French doors located near the balcony. "That is where they came in. They punched the glass and opened the door."

She touched a windowpane. "Right here. It seems they were prompt to make repairs, like Nicky was never here." Annoyance creased her brow.

Christian nodded. "With the cameras along the hall, we should have a record of what happened outside the suite that night. We'll ask hotel security tomorrow, see if they'll cooperate if given enough monetary incentive. Let's hope Captain Duarte hasn't taken custody of everything."

"Not likely." She crossed her arms over her chest and leaned a shoulder against a wall. "The man does not strike me as inept. Did you see the eyes on that snake?"

One reptile to another, Jasmine had an inside track, but Christian only shrugged and opened the doors to the balcony to step outside. Sounds of the city swelled below as he peered over the balustrade. Colorful lights of Cuiabá churned beneath him like a witch's caldron, casting its spell. Eventually, he broke free of its seductive pull to search the darkness, looking for a means of escape for the men who had kidnapped his father.

"No easy way out. Rappeling to the street from here would've drawn too much attention. And security cameras would've nailed 'em if they left by the front door. If they dropped from the roof, maybe they left the same way. What's on the back side of this building?"

"The hotel parking garage." She nodded. "So you figure they escaped to the garage rooftop, probably to a waiting vehicle?"

"It makes the most sense." He narrowed his eyes and raised his chin. "And if the garage has surveillance, maybe . . ."

She grinned. "Perhaps Captain Duarte missed the security cameras in the garage. Now that's a notion with possibility. Good thinking, little acorn."

She caught him by surprise with the familiarity. In her mind, he was the acorn that hadn't fallen far from the imposing Charboneau tree, the spitting image of his father.

"You know I hate that name, don't you?" He fixed a stern expression to his face and folded his arms across his chest.

"Most assuredly. There are many ways to get a rise out of a man." She pursed her lips and raised an eyebrow, matching his stance. "Please don't deny me my fun."

He shook his head. "Lady, we haven't gotten to the fun part yet. Not by a long shot."

* * *

Dr. Tyson Phillips had gone to bed with his wife over an hour ago, knowing sleep would be a lost cause. His demons weren't that humane.

When Elizabeth's breathing settled to a steady pace, he rolled out of bed, shrugged into his robe, and nudged his feet into slippers in the dark. Guided by the dim nightlights along the upstairs hallway, he walked toward the bedrooms of his boy and girl. He touched a hand to each door, his way of grounding himself in reality. They were his world. His kids and his wife of sixteen years meant everything.

Too bad he hadn't realized it sooner. Guilt tugged at his heart.

He made his way to the study. After flipping on a desk lamp, he poured himself a glass of brandy from a crystal carafe on a console table, gulping down the first of many. With the decanter in one hand and a glass in the other, he wandered farther into the room filled with scholarly books and his credentials framed on the wall.

Raising a glass, he saluted the sham of his life.

"A man isn't a failure until he starts blaming someone else." He paraphrased an old quote that held more significance for him now. "Well, if you're looking for someone to blame, look in the mirror."

He slouched into the leather chair behind his desk and set the carafe in front of him.

When he was a younger man, he believed providing for his family meant material things. Money was power. But all that changed after he'd been downsized at the prestigious Biotech Industries back in the States. He felt like such a failure on all fronts—a stigma he couldn't outrun.

"You used to be bulletproof, Phillips." He downed another glass. "And oh, so gullible, you egotistical loser."

When presented with an escape to Brazil, it seemed like such a fresh start at first. Charboneau enticed him with the position of director at a notable genetics research facility in Cuiabá—Genotech Labs. It made him feel whole again. In the end, the man's flattery seduced him completely. Why didn't he question such a gift horse? Like being offered an apple in the Garden of Eden, he got suckered by bogus promises.

Soon after he'd moved, the cold reality hit. His feelings of impotence had been a beacon to Charboneau. Now he wished he'd never met the man.

"God, you fucked up everything." He torqued his jaw in frustration.

Every damned day, he lived like a king in this country, thriving in complete denial of his fraud. He perpetuated the lie in front of his wife and kids, knowing he was little more than a common criminal. In time, guilt softened his backbone and sapped his strength.

Now, he sat at his imported cherrywood desk in his extensive library, all the trappings of his life surrounding him. He stared at his reflection in the empty crystal snifter of brandy. His face warped with the thin coating of liquor on the glass. Failure had aged him, infused his blond hair with streaks of gray. Creases along his forehead and around his pale gray eyes had deepened with his inadequacies. Like *The Picture of Dorian Gray*, the sins of his life had taken their toll, producing a distorted vision of the truth.

And time had run out.

Along the far wall, a grandfather clock stroked the top of the hour. Slowly, his eyes searched for the cell phone sitting on his desktop. He waited for the call he knew would come. It had been prearranged.

Even still, when it chirped, the harsh sound made him nearly jump out of his skin, yanking him from his self-indulgence. He grappled for the phone and flipped it open in a rush, his hands trembling with the heat of too much alcohol. Before he uttered a word, a man's voice commanded his attention.

"She's back. And this time, the foreign woman has someone named Delacorte with her. He says that the woman is the reason he's here. He claims not to even know Charboneau . . . and that he has no link to the Chicago syndicate." The man's voice was low and furtive, his accent more pronounced than usual.

Gritting his teeth, Phillips condemned the man on the other end of the line. Yet he despised himself even more. He'd been tethered to the bastard for what felt like an eternity. No matter what happened now, he would deserve whatever fate held in store.

"Oh, and because he says so, you believe him? How nice." The doctor stood and paced the floor behind his desk. He found it more and more difficult to hide his disdain. One day his arrogance would get him killed. "You assured me that when she left she'd be arranging for the ransom. The money was supposed to be a distraction to get her out of town, but now she's back. And she's got company. Why is this man with her?"

"He says he's here to free Charboneau. And he's demanding proof of life or no payday. The arrogant bastard." A wicked chuckle told him the man found Delacorte's purpose to be a ridiculous endeavor. Yet no matter how hard he tried, he couldn't hide the alarm filtering through his voice.

"What? How can we do that now? You said—"

Phillips stopped, trying to regain his composure. His head throbbed with a mounting pain. "We're in way over our heads. I didn't sign on for this. Charboneau is one thing, but now—"

"Don't panic. Believe me, Delacorte will find out how dangerous a path he walks. I have a grand welcome planned."

"Oh, just great." He spat his reply before he could stop himself. Closing his eyes, he waited for the response he knew would come.

"You know what's at stake, you pompous ass. And you're not going to fuck this up . . . not when we're so close to pulling this thing off." Uncharacteristic humor tinged his voice. "Besides, one little Polaroid and we might even get them to wire the ransom to the Swiss account. Pure gravy."

"I thought you weren't interested in the money."

"I'm not. A million dollars is nothing by comparison. Yet for a man who grew up with so little, I find money hard to ignore. In the end, if they don't pay, it won't matter. I've got bigger plans." His tone grew adamant with a familiar resentment. "Charboneau's an outsider. He had no right to rape my country. If anyone has the privilege of doing that, it is me."

Rape was rape, no matter who performed the despicable act. The subtlety of this concept in exploitation missed the mark with his partner in crime. Phillips felt the blood rushing through his system. The heat of it flushed his face. Slowing his breathing, he collapsed into the leather chair once again, defeat in his voice.

"I just wanna stop the killing."

Again a vulgar cackle erupted from the phone.

The man's sinister laugh mocked his plea. The sound made his skin crawl. "Don't tell me you've suddenly developed a conscience, not after what you and Charboneau tried to do. There's only been one change since this whole thing began. You've got a new benefactor, that is all."

This time his voice hushed to a macabre whisper. "And your old backer is not going home, except in a box . . . if they even find the body."

The room closed in on him, the eerie gloom suffocating him. Would the killing ever stop? How had he gotten sucked into this quagmire of corruption?

"Oh, God, please don't remind me." He pressed his fingers to the side of his head, trying to squelch the migraine he knew would be inevitable. "I just can't—"

"You can . . . and you will." Cruelty shaded the man's voice. He knew the sound well. Then a repeated threat churned beneath the surface, like the many caimans and piranhas in the Paraguay River of the Pantanal, ready to strike with razor sharp teeth. "How is your lovely family, by the way? I hope they are in good health . . . and will remain so."

He wouldn't have to wait for the torment of hell. Hell's fire was on the other end of the line. "Please . . . you've got nothing to worry about. We still have a deal. Just leave my family out of this." He closed his eyes, drawing in a shaky breath. Sweat trickled down his temple, even in the cool stillness of his home.

"Nothing would please me more. Stick to the plan. These Americans have nothing, but it will not stop them from visiting the clinic . . . from wanting to speak to you."

"What if something goes wrong?"

"Look, if they become a nuisance, I'll take care of everything. I've got surveillance on them now. Remember, this is my turf. Are we clear?"

"Yes, I—" The dial tone interrupted him. The man had already hung up, not waiting for his answer—so cocksure he knew what it would be.

"Time for phase two." Christian stood at Jasmine's bedroom door and gestured with a wave of his hand. At the small of his back, under his shirt, he carried a Glock 19 that Jasmine had held for him in her black duffel. "You're coming with me."

He interrupted her as she hung a blouse in the closet, emptying her suitcase. By the looks of things, the woman donated her fair share of dollars to the bottomless coffers of designers everywhere. And Lord only knew what she stashed in her bags to appease the more lethal side of her nature. Killer couture at its best.

"Where are we going?" she asked.

"I'll know it when I see it. How do you feel about fishing?" He knew she'd hate his cryptic response. The woman liked being in charge. Christian smiled as he ushered her to the door of the suite, under protest.

"I'd sooner go bowling."

The image of Jasmine in rented shoes, hoisting a Brunswick in one hand and a cold brew in the other, almost made him laugh out loud.

"You know, I might pay good money to see you wage war on tenpins. But no, I've gotta see what fifty thousand in green might buy us. Stir things up."

To make sure no one bugged the rooms undetected,

the woman had set up surveillance with hidden cameras rigged for motion before unpacking her clothes. Given all the high-tech equipment inside the room, he felt sure they'd know if the suite had been tampered with once they returned. But just in case, he stopped outside the hallway door for one last measure.

"*Ow.*" Jasmine turned around, looking appalled. Rubbing her scalp, she turned to face him. "What the hell are you doing?"

He held a strand of her hair and dangled it in front of her face, fighting a smirk. *Some tough assassin.*

She grimaced. "With all the surveillance gear I've got set up in the room, what good will *that* do?"

Curiosity replaced annoyance as she watched him hang the DO NOT DISTURB sign on the doorknob and make use of her personal donation to their added security. He wedged the single strand of hair into the crack of the door, above their heads. A small piece hung barely visible.

"An early warning system . . . of sorts."

"I would've expected something a little more high-tech from a guy with your background."

"Nothing wrong with a low-tech advance warning to give us an edge. After all, if it's good enough for MacGyver, it's good enough for me. What I could've done if I had a gum wrapper and a toothpick."

"Really?" She raised an eyebrow.

"No." Christian headed down the corridor.

The woman had no sense of humor.

As they left the main lobby, heading for the street, Christian made a point to catch the eye of the clerk who'd checked them into the hotel earlier. A seed had definitely been planted with the man whose eyes burned Christian's back as he left the hotel.

They grabbed a quick bite at a local street café, then killed an hour walking the dark streets of Cuiabá, getting familiar with the city.

At first Christian chose well-lit avenues and crowded thoroughfares. Not hard to find. Even with the late hour, many of the downtown boulevards thrived with action. Along streets lined with palm trees, scooters dodged small sedans and engines revved to a high whine as they blew exhaust into the muggy air. High heels clacked fast on cement sidewalks, accompanied by the low steady rhythm of their male companions, lounge lizards making the rounds bar to bar. Jazz music wafted sultry in the night air, competing with the seductive beat of the samba.

The city had its own tempo. And although traffic fumes and smells hung heavy, an underlying primitive scent refused to be denied. On the edge of civilization, the great rain forest endured, a piece of its heart carved out by man. Christian sensed the wilderness on the outskirts of Cuiabá, and the restless sensation he wanted to forget returned.

"You've grown quiet." Jasmine broke the silence. "I understand the demons that haunt you. In that way, we have much in common. More than you know."

Death was nothing to have in common. Not with her. He had no need to make a connection with Jasmine. He didn't want to like her . . . or need to. And he had no faith in the glimpse of humanity she shared with him now, even if there was more to her story.

"There's only one thing we have in common. Let's stay focused on that, shall we?"

If she'd been hurt by his remark, she never let it show. Her face remained a blank slate as she said, "Yes, for Nicky."

The damned heat had finally gotten to him, and his manners were the first to go. At least, that's what he told himself, but he didn't feel the need to apologize.

Instead, with great deliberation, he strolled through landscaped parks and stuck to the shadows. Not a wise move for the average tourist, but if anyone followed them, he wanted to draw them out. They walked for another thirty minutes. Still nothing.

Strike one. Self-doubt flashed through his brain as slick as a fastball over home plate.

After stopping to admire far too many monuments and statues, he finally broke the silence. "Damn it. Thought the reward would pay off, get us a lead, but no one's tailing us."

"Or perhaps you and I have met our match. Skilled pursuers could still be out there, besting us." She narrowed her eyes.

"There you go, looking on the bright side again." He kept his eyes vigilant. "Quit tryin' to cheer me up."

"Ah, I forget. The male ego is easily bruised. Forgive my rudeness." With his glare, she winked without humor. "Don't worry. Your plan still might work, and your instincts were solid."

"You're just pissed 'cause the reward wasn't your idea." He smirked as she slipped her arm in his.

"You might have a point," Jasmine conceded without a fight. "Let's head back to the hotel. Something might turn up there. Besides, is it not wise for the fisherman to remain patient?"

"I thought you didn't know much about the sport?"

"Yes, but when luring men, I am an expert."

He arched an eyebrow at his companion. "Good point."

* * *

Jasmine's single strand of hair still dangled from the suite door undisturbed. A good news, bad news scenario. Good news, his low-tech advance warning system worked. But when it came to bad news, his heart sank. No one had broken into their hotel suite using the front door.

A strange thing to wish for. *Strike two. Damn it.*

Christian pulled the Glock 19 from the waistband of his jeans, hiding it from the hotel security cameras in the hallway as he entered the suite, Jasmine at his back. In silence, they split up and searched the rooms, weapons in hand. His heart pumped with adrenaline, the muscles in his arms tense. When they found nothing out of place, Jasmine checked her surveillance equipment. The only motion recorded had been them.

Strike three.

But as he exchanged a look of disappointment with his companion, something caught his eye. Over her shoulder, a light flickered behind drawn sheers.

"What the hell?"

He recognized the danger. It hit the pit of his stomach in a rush, forced him to move.

"Fire . . . on the balcony." He jerked his head, calling to Jasmine as he rushed by her.

Christian ran to the French doors and threw them open, but stopped dead when his eyes found the source of the flame. Even in the stifling heat, a chill raced across his skin. The hair on his neck stood on end. *What the hell had his father been into?*

CHAPTER 7

For the first time since Christian met her, Jasmine looked baffled, but she covered it up with a heaping dose of sarcasm.

"I never knew the devil made house calls."

"Apparently so." Christian glared down at the unsettling sight. He'd never been confronted by something like this.

The entire balcony had been converted into a bizarre religious rite. Flickering black candles melted into broken liquor bottles circling an altar made of old bones, sticks, and frayed hemp. A dead chicken, throat slit, bled into a sticky pool that seeped through the crevices of the tile. Blood spatter marred the pristine white balustrade, but most of it had been doused onto what looked like a human skull. Its jawbone gaped open and black eye sockets stared in accusation.

The smell of old death.

"How quaint. Perhaps we should tell housekeeping we prefer a simple mint on our pillows."

Jasmine had an edge to her voice, but her attempt at humor didn't dispel her uneasiness.

"This doesn't look like any goodwill gesture, more like . . . foul play." His chicken pun didn't fare any better. Christian leaned closer, careful not to disturb the scene. "What's this? Do you recognize where this was taken?"

A newspaper clipping of Charboneau had his head cut and pinned to a doll made from straw and burlap. Blood from the chicken covered the likeness. And three small wooden skewers impaled the effigy. Although he wasn't an expert, it didn't take a genius to recognize black magic.

"No. The image is too small." Jasmine crossed her arms as if a chill ran along her skin.

"This makes no sense." Christian straightened up, glaring at the hideous array.

Charboneau had been cursed, but why now? Being hijacked from his hotel room should have been enough of a bad omen. What had his father been into?

If this elaborate atrocity had been intended to ward off their interference into the kidnapping, why use a photo of his father on the voodoo doll? And why risk scaring off their ransom meal ticket? It looked like two factions were involved in Charboneau's abduction—one interested in the money and another setting roadblocks in their path, every step of the way.

More questions roiled in his head like an approaching thunderstorm, but one pushed ahead of the rest. "If the bastards didn't come through the front door, then how'd they set this up?"

Suddenly, Jasmine reached for him. "Did you see that?"

Eyes wide, she tightened her grip on his arm. With her other hand, she went for a knife she had stashed in her bra. *One of Victoria's secrets.*

"What?" He turned and looked down, following her gaze.

"I think the skull moved."

Christian watched the skull for a moment. Nothing. "You're seeing things."

To prove his point, he kicked the bones with the toe of his boot, only enough to nudge it. The skull rolled to one side, tipping over.

"Holy shit!" He leapt back when he saw it.

An angular head lashed out, barely missing his leg. Fangs bared. Hissing spit. A slithering snake raced across the tile, straight for him.

He backed up and fumbled for his gun, knowing he'd never make it. The damned thing moved too fast. But from nowhere, a flash of silver flew by him.

Whap! Ssssss . . . thump . . . thump . . . ssssssss.

Jasmine's knife sliced through the head of the snake, almost severing it. Blood spilled onto the floor. The slick body coiled, writhing in death, out of control. As it thrust from side to side, the body pulled itself apart from the head . . . and continued its vile dance. Smears of blood trailed under it like a macabre finger painting. Christian and Jasmine backed away, each with a look of disgust.

"Let's tear this place apart, inside and out. I don't want any more surprises." Christian swallowed hard. "And by the way . . . thanks."

Thanks didn't cover it. He didn't know much about snakes, poisonous or otherwise. But he had a feeling

Jasmine had saved his life a second time. A regular habit for her, one he had no problem encouraging.

"Don't worry. You'll have plenty of opportunity to repay my generosity. I assure you." She stepped closer to the French doors, pushing her back against the door frame, not taking her eyes off the thrashing snake. "Think I'll collect my knife tomorrow. If that thing's still moving in the morning, I'll consider it a lost cause."

"Come on. We'll search the rooms . . . together."

Jasmine nodded, a quick shake of her head. "I don't have a problem with that."

Neither did he. Together worked for him too.

HOURS LATER

Christian left a lamp on. Its pale light washed over his bedroom, casting shadows into the corners. White bed linens spread across his bare chest as he lay on his king-sized bed, several pillows propped against the headboard. Since Jasmine came back into his life, he'd been plagued by thoughts of a father he'd never met and an indefinable influence that kept him on edge. Now he had a new nightmare.

God, I hate snakes!

In this country, where not even a man like Charboneau was safe, something primitive tapped into his senses and lurked in the dark corners of his mind. A threatening malevolence. And tonight a coward almost took him out, using a cheap shot with fangs. The candles were intended to draw them in, and the snake would do its damage. If Jasmine hadn't been on her game, the bastard might have succeeded.

He felt like an interloper into Charboneau's world, an amateur to the danger. For all he knew, his father was already dead. He hated this limbo of not knowing.

And heaped on top, the fight he'd picked with Raven kept replaying in his head. The hurt in her eyes flashed over and over. He had called her, but only left a message about where he was staying with her phone voice mail, though he wanted to say so much more. She should have been home, but Raven hadn't picked up the line. He hoped she'd cooled off enough to recognize the white flag of surrender in his voice, but nothing doing. No amount of good intention would overcome the regret in his heart. He should have trusted her, been willing to share his darkest nightmare. Why hadn't he?

Raven had earned the right to know everything about him, but shame held him back. He'd never be *normal*. Death defined his past and had a stranglehold on his future. It carried a crippling stigma, one he couldn't shake. He had never felt entitled to happiness. And yet, having Raven in his life was the closest he'd come to touching it. Did he have the right to make his burden hers?

Damn it, forget about sleep. To hell with it.

He'd had enough. Throwing back the covers, he hoisted himself out of bed, unwilling to waste any more time. His mind wouldn't allow it. Dragging fingers through his hair, he wandered out his bedroom door dressed in his pajama bottoms.

In the stillness of the hotel suite, Christian closed his eyes for a few seconds, acquiring his night vision. He listened and quieted his heart to focus on his hearing. He knew he was alone in the room. He felt it.

No lights. Darkness gave him the gift of anonymity. Yet the lights from the city shone through the doors leading to the balcony. A bluish haze cast into the room. On instinct, he stepped toward the French doors, cell phone in hand. He wanted another look at the Macumba housewarming present outside, snake and all. He intended to take digital photos of the setup with his cell phone, then break it apart and stuff the contents into a pillowcase borrowed from the hotel.

But something cautioned him against opening the doors right away. *Good thing.*

As he stood steeped in shadows, he saw a red ember flare and die away on the rooftop across the street. *What the hell?* With his eyes locked, he waited. *A cigarette.* Another faint reflection captured light from the streets below, then melded into the shadows once more. *Eyeglasses or binoculars?* He couldn't tell from where he stood. He tilted his head and furrowed his brow, watching in the dark.

It happened again. No, it hadn't been his imagination. Someone stood on the roof across the way, an office building or warehouse. An odd place to catch a smoke in the middle of the night. Folding his arms over his bare chest, he watched awhile longer, to make sure.

"Haven't you heard?" he whispered, heading for his bedroom to change. "Smoking is bad for your health."

For only a second, he thought about waking Jasmine to tell her where he was going. But he felt certain she would want to come along . . . and bring her knife as a companion.

No way, José Cuervo! He'd fly solo on this mission.

CHAPTER 8

DAY SIX

Nearly four in the morning and the hotel lobby was quiet as Christian slipped out a side entrance. Very little activity. Outside, muggy air seized his skin like a warm washcloth. And without a breeze, the air felt thick and oppressive. Motionless, it deadened sound, muffling noise in its vacuum.

Given the temperature, he already regretted his choice in clothing, but his gear had been picked more for stealth than comfort. Dressed in dark clothes and boots, he would meld into the night. As he crept along an alley, he stuck close to a brick wall, mingling with its shadows. He felt the Glock pressed against the small of his back, tucked into the waistband of his pants with a black T-shirt worn loose over the weapon.

On cue, the darkness closed in as it usually did. To regain control, he shut his eyes and focused, allowing his senses to take hold. He steadied his breathing and tapped into his abilities. The act had become second nature. In no time the hunter emerged and exhilaration infused his blood. Eyes vigilant, he now searched for the best spot to cross the street—unseen from above.

Already his skin felt damp, a layer of sheen glistened on his forearms. The extreme humidity sucked the moisture from his pores. Christian glanced down the street. Parked cars along the thoroughfare held his attention as he looked for movement.

Nothing. Before he darted across, he glanced to the rooftop. No sign of his prey.

But as he made his move, he heard a sound. In the distance, a high-pitched splinter of broken glass followed by the shriek of a cat. The eerie cry resonated along the buildings of the side street, prickling his skin. Despite his reaction, he smiled. Another creature of the night . . . a kindred spirit.

Finding a likely spot to cross the deserted street, he zeroed in on the building. The doors to the street were locked, but he located a fire escape to the roof. With little effort, he leapt to grab the ladder and pulled it to the asphalt. The metal groaned in complaint, rust on its hinges. He winced at the sound.

Why don't you send up a flare? Make a real announcement, Delacorte!

Whoever watched the penthouse surely knew he was coming now. Still, he had to see for himself. He pulled the Glock, pointing it toward the night sky. He climbed step by step, focusing on the parapet wall of the building. His muscles tensed, ready to dive for cover if necessary. He waited for a shadow to peer over the edge. No sign of the man.

As he drew closer, reaching the landing on the

final flight of stairs, Christian dropped to a knee. He pressed a shoulder to the wall and listened. Nothing.

He craned his neck and peered over the top of the wall, grip taut on his weapon. On the far side of the roof, a brick structure housed a door, presumably a stairwell shaft into the building. The easiest place for someone to hide.

Relying on gut instincts, he switched his hunting mode into high gear. In one fluid motion he leapt over the edge and crept toward the door, ducking near the mechanical room housing a commercial grade air-conditioning unit. As he did, the equipment kicked on, an abrupt whirring sound. He cursed under his breath until he realized he could use it to his advantage, moving closer without being heard. But the noise would interfere with his hearing too.

Hell! He was going into this blind.

With his element of surprise questionable, he knew he had one other distinct edge. Following a marginal plan, he navigated the exhaust vents to circle the brick structure, keeping to the pockets of murky dark. It put the light from his hotel across the street to his back, keeping his face in shadow. The man would be forced to deal with the glare. Repositioned on the far side, his back pressed against the wall, he hoisted his gun, inching his way to the corner.

As he drew near, the damned AC unit droned on, deadening his senses. He swallowed hard, knowing he'd have to move or risk the tables being turned on him.

Now or never, hot shot!

He sprang from his hiding spot, gun drawn. In that same instant, the AC unit stopped and the stillness of the night closed in. In a voice way too loud, he shouted, *"Freeze!"* hoping to sound like a cop. Pretty lame since he only spoke English.

No one. *Damn it!* His eyes searched the shadows. He found nothing out of the ordinary, except—

The lingering stench confirmed his suspicions. A cigarette had been tossed aside, as if the smoker had just lit up. Smoke wafted into the air, lazy swirls made heavy by the humidity. He hadn't imagined it. Someone had been there, but left in a hurry.

After he inspected every dark corner of the rooftop and found no one, Christian slipped his gun into his waistband. He walked back to the discarded cigarette butt and shifted his gaze across the street to the balcony of his suite. From this distance, with the hotel room dark, he couldn't see much. But if someone had the right surveillance gear, the range wouldn't be a factor. Jasmine's precautions to thwart surveillance had been prudent after all.

With the release of tension, Christian raked a hand through his hair and headed for the parapet wall. The Glock pressed against his belly, he climbed back over the building ledge and tromped down the fire escape stairs. *Stealth, be damned!*

Once on ground level, he meandered down the short alleyway, heading for the street and his hotel. Fatigue eased into the muscles of his shoulders. As he approached the quiet intersection and stepped into the street, a harsh sound pierced the night air.

Tires screeched. He caught motion to his right.

Faint light glinted off a windshield as gloved hands braced the steering wheel. A face veiled in shadow. A dark sedan with no lights barreled down. It crossed the center lane, swerving straight for him.

Shit! Without thinking, he lunged left.

The car fishtailed. Grinding metal, it crashed into another vehicle, forcing the shrill cry of a car alarm. The sedan careened by. Its mirror grazed his hip as he turned. With the impact, he spun out of control, falling against a parked car. The momentum hurled his body to the ground like a rag doll. He slammed to the asphalt—hard.

"*Arrghh.*" He gasped, air rushing from his lungs.

To break his fall, he braced his forearms in front of his face as he skidded to a stop, scraping his hands and elbows. He struggled for air, chest heaving. And the sting of road rash burned his skin. Bits of gravel stuck to raw flesh.

Car alarms blared without compassion, head and taillights flashing in cadence to the siren—two-toned, high-pitched. The noise served as cruel torment for his aching head.

"Ahh . . . hell," he groaned, leveling his eyes to catch a glimpse of the car speeding away. But a flashing headlight blinded him. He squinted in pain, trying to recall the make or model of the getaway car. Other than the description of a dark sedan, nothing registered in his mind. It happened too fast.

He strained to get a look at the license plate, but his vision was blurred. His own hand, held inches from his face, would have been a challenge. Now the vehicle weaved in and out of shadows, racing from his sight with tires squealing as it turned a corner. *Gone.* Only the smell of its exhaust fumes lingered.

Christian struggled to catch his breath, assessing the damage. Nothing broken, but his chest felt like a mule had kicked it—twice. The Glock wedged in his pants had bruised his ribs. For a long moment he lay on the ground, unable to budge, trying to shake loose the cobwebs. Lights whirled and vanished to an inky black as he faded in and out.

With effort, he braced his hands and rose to his knees, forcing himself to move. Otherwise, it might have been too easy to lose consciousness. Sweat trickled down his forearms . . . or maybe it was blood.

Curious onlookers peered from the hotel, their bodies eclipsing the lobby lights. Soon they would come with their questions—questions he'd have no answers for. He had to clear out soon or else attract Captain Duarte's attention. A part of him suspected the man already knew about the incident, or maybe ordered it.

Christian moved to stand, but reconsidered.

"Being vertical is highly overrated," he muttered under his breath.

Too dazed, he decided to stay put, slumped against the nearest car. Leaning his head back, he closed his eyes. He'd wait for the city of Cuiabá to stop spinning. But one thought cut through the fog swirling in his brain. He'd let his guard down—never saw it coming.

He couldn't afford to do that again.

Several hours later, under stark overhead lights, he stared at his reflection in the bathroom mirror, grimacing.

He looked exactly how he felt—*like the by-product of a meat grinder.*

He only had a few hours sleep or maybe he'd passed out. The scrapes on his hands and forearms had stiffened and his body looked mottled with bruises. He'd taken a hot shower to loosen up. His muscles felt better, but the hot water only aggravated his wounds, making them red and swollen. Now, with a towel wrapped around his waist, he contemplated a shave, but couldn't muster the energy. Stubble would have to do.

Running a comb through his damp hair, he mentally psyched himself up for the long day ahead until—

"What the hell happened to you?"

Under the heading *What Else Could Go Wrong*, he heard Jasmine's voice behind him. Barging into his personal bathroom, she hadn't bothered to announce herself.

"Remind me to complain to hotel management. The bed sheets had too much starch." His muscles ached. Answering her questions came dead last on his list of priorities. "Ever heard of knocking?"

"Yes, a boring American ritual."

Dressed in khakis and a crisp white blouse, Jasmine sauntered by him and hopped onto his bathroom counter.

"Feel free to barge into my room any time . . . day or night." She smiled and winked. "I assure you, you'd find a much warmer reception."

"I'll bet. Guess if this assassin gig doesn't work out, Wal-Mart could use a greeter." He finished combing through his damp hair and tossed the comb onto the countertop. The dull ache in his head throbbed, fueling a mega dose of cynicism. "And be sure to include your knife skills on your résumé. It'd come in handy when they slash prices. I've seen you in action."

"Action? You haven't seen anything, my sweet."

He ignored her usual brand of sexual innuendo. Something in her tone suggested she persisted simply because it got a rise out of him. After last night, he didn't have the frame of mind to put up with it. And to completely make his day, one of the gashes on his elbow started to drip blood down his forearm. He reached around her to grab a white washcloth.

Jasmine only shook her head. "Next time you feel the urge for a little one on one, try me. You might still be black and blue in the morning, but at least you'll have a smile on your face."

With her back propped against the mirror, she scowled as she touched a bruise on his ribs, pretending to care. He hadn't expected it. The cold touch of her fingers on his sore spot made the muscles of his belly flinch.

"Hey, Florence Nightingale. Back off."

But even his foul mood didn't dissuade her.

"So, what's with all the cuts and bruises, tough guy?" She crossed her arms over her chest. "I'd really like to know."

"And I'd really like to be left alone. What are the odds of you disappearing?" He soaked the washcloth in cold water and dabbed at his left elbow, getting a bead on the cut from the reflection in the bathroom mirror.

"Not good odds, I'm afraid. Only because I know my presence truly annoys you." She raised her chin and grinned. "But I've got something you need."

"Can't wait," he muttered as Jasmine slid off the counter and left the room.

She returned a minute later with a white zippered bag.

"You always travel with a first aid kit?" he asked.

"I've been in a few scrapes before, when going to a hospital was out of the question. Now hold still."

Without a smart remark, she swabbed down his wounds with an antiseptic and applied antibiotic ointment with a cotton ball. Covering the worst abrasions with bandages, she worked with enviable efficiency. And to her credit, she avoided making her usual sexual inferences, even when her hands took liberties with his body out of necessity. Like a comrade in arms, she patched him up with the competence of a medical doctor.

"Now, I want the real truth about last night. I overheard a couple of tourists talking about it this morning. Rumor has it that a close-mouthed American almost got himself killed in the street out front . . . before dawn. Do you know anything about that?"

"Unfortunately, yes. Firsthand knowledge." He filled her in on the details, which got sketchier when he explained what drew him to the roof and what he'd found once he got there.

She nodded when he was through. "So it would appear the vultures are circling. That didn't take long."

"I don't appreciate the analogy. Call me sensitive on the subject of becoming pavement paste before my time. That attempted hit and run was no accident." He grimaced. "Whatever happened, it doesn't make sense the kidnappers would kill the ransom wrangler. You and I are in charge of the payoff. Why would someone want to take me out *before* the money had been wired?"

"Unless your original theory applies. Perhaps Nicky's abduction is a cover-up for something more. Maybe he's not supposed to make it out alive." Concern edged her voice.

"He could already be dead, for all we know."

"No. I would feel it, I think. I have to believe he's alive. You and I must believe." Desperate hope filtered through her expression.

She let a strained moment pass between them. Uncharacteristic emotion etched her face. Christian witnessed the woman shoving aside her worst fears, closing her eyes. But soon the old Jasmine reemerged, brimming with her usual cynicism.

"While you were sleeping in like a self-indulgent prima donna, I've been busy. It seems Captain Duarte *did* confiscate the hotel security recordings. A pity." She pouted, then grinned. "But I managed to make a digital copy of something very interesting from the garage surveillance system. I've got a disk downloaded to my laptop. You were right—the hotel staff is very cooperative with the right motivation in American dollars."

"Capitalism at its best. Good job." He nodded. "If we find enough on the garage camera, we won't need the hotel surveillance. Testing Duarte's spirit of cooperation would've been interesting, though."

"Optimist." Jasmine hopped off the counter and smacked him on the butt with the back of her hand as she strolled to turn off the shower. "Come on. Get dressed. We haven't got all day."

Christian shot an irritated glance in the mirror. With another long day ahead, he wasn't in the mood for *Moo Goo Gal Pal*.

Dressed in lightweight Moschino beige jeans, boots, and a short-sleeve khaki shirt worn loose over a white polo, Christian walked out of his bedroom and found Jasmine preoccupied with her laptop. The glow of the monitor cast shadows on her face as images flashed across it. As intrigued as he was to see the digital surveillance, the smell of fresh brewed coffee captured his interest in a hurry. The caffeine would jolt his brain into first gear.

Jasmine had a coffeepot placed on a service tray at the wet bar. Christian poured himself a cup and joined her on the sofa, taking his first sip. He heard the keystrokes of her laptop once she lowered the sound of the stereo system with the remote. But even with the music low, he drew the line at hearing the classic lounge lizard rendition of "Feelings" sung in Portuguese.

"Even without understanding the lyrics, this song sucks. If there's a hell, Muzak would play it for eternity." He narrowed his eyes, pleading his case. "At the risk of sounding like a high maintenance guy, can you change to another station?"

"Finally, we agree on something." She scanned the local radio stations until she found an instrumental jazz piece, then she directed his attention to her computer. "Check this out."

Jasmine hit a few keys and replayed what she had already seen. Coming into view from the lower left-hand side of the camera frame, two waiters in hotel uniforms pushed a food cart through the deserted level eight of the parking garage.

"Heavy load. Takes two to push." After setting his coffee down on a table, Christian rested his elbows on his knees and leaned forward, his eyes glued to the computer monitor. "I'm impressed. Full service hotel, catering food to the garage."

She pointed again. "See the dark blue van at the end of the row? Those men standing around it? Just as I remembered. Five of them took my Nicky."

Hearing the crack in her voice, Christian turned to catch Jasmine's eyes welling in tears. She coughed and cleared her throat, wiping a quick finger across her cheek. To give her time to compose herself, he shifted his attention back to the digital recording. The kidnappers loaded his father into the back of the van and shoved a much lighter food cart against a wall of the parking garage. The men piled inside. The vehicle pulled out and headed toward the camera.

"The man driving looks like he's in charge."

"Yes, he was." She nodded. "You tend to remember the man who held an AK-47 aimed at your head."

"Did your informant know him?"

"Yes. He told me the guy used to work for the hotel, until four days ago. He went by the name of Rodrigo Santo. The other one dressed in uniform didn't work here, according to my guy. Santo must have given him the monkey suit."

"Hell, the bastard isn't likely to use his real name. Kidnapping an American while on the clock? Not a smart move."

"Kidnapping Nicky is not the work of an intelligent man. Who would do such a thing if they knew who he was?"

"Maybe he didn't. Maybe all he saw was opportunity. But it makes sense this was an inside job, someone working at the hotel." He raised his hand and nudged his chin toward the TV. "Freeze that, right there."

Christian stared at the face of the native man who kidnapped his father, memorizing every detail. He searched for compassion in the dark eyes but found none.

"Can you get a print of his face?"

"Already done. My contact was most obliging."
She pulled out a handful of hard copies printed of
the digital frame. Fuzzy but workable.

"Good. Did anyone find it odd that Santo quit like
that?"

Shifting her weight on the sofa, Jasmine crossed
her legs and leaned closer.

"Well, technically, he never gave notice. When he
didn't show up for work, the hotel sent someone to
check his local address. He had a dingy little motel
room he rented by the week. He'd cleared out, walked
away from his life here in Cuiabá. Everything gone,
no forwarding."

"He didn't collect his paycheck? That's unusual in
this economy."

"Apparently, he's got a bigger payoff in mind."
Christian glared at the face frozen on the screen.
"So no trail to follow."

"Not exactly." She smiled and winked. "My source
told me the man kept to himself. But he was very
traditional in his beliefs, very old school. He talked
about his people like he belonged to a tribe."

"Not much to go on. I hoped the reward would
jump-start things."

But the gleam in Jasmine's eye told him she had
more. She reminded him of a slick black jaguar on
the prowl. The woman sure enjoyed her vocation.

"Perhaps it has. Ever since our slithering care
package on the balcony, I racked my brain trying to
remember someone Nicky and I met at a local fund-
raiser a while back. Then the name came to me. A
shop owner, Bianca Salvador. She owns Guia Do Espírito, catering to the lunatic fringe of Cuiabá. The
place sells herbs, charms, and other ritualistic items."

Jasmine smiled. "She performs rituals for many of the indigenous people in the area. Perhaps she can help us take the next step to finding Nicky."

He shrugged and nodded. "She's a local and knows the area. Plus, she might shed light on our voodoo welcome wagon. Sounds solid."

"I could talk to her while you—"

"Oh, no. We're doing this together," he insisted.

"That makes no sense. We can cover more ground if we split up . . ."

Christian finished his coffee while he listened to the logic of her argument, but eventually he interrupted her.

"Look, someone waited for me to let my guard down last night. And I almost got strained through the grillwork of a sedan, a human lube job. We're stickin' together."

She narrowed her eyes, not used to taking orders. "I'm touched by your concern, but as you know, I can take care of myself."

"No way. Hallmark doesn't make a card for 'Sorry I got you killed.' Ain't happenin' on my watch. We're doing this together. No arguments."

"I'll remind you of that the next time you play a solo game of dodge ball with four thousand pounds of steel."

The woman had a point.

To change the subject, he asked, "Did last night's surveillance show how the damned snake got to the penthouse balcony? Some bastard gained access outside the hotel."

"No, I found that quite strange." She shook her head, a troubled look on her face.

"With what we're paying for this damned room, you'd think it'd buy us a snake-free zone. Something like that wouldn't materialize out of thin air, complete with flamin' candles and a dead chicken. We just didn't catch it on surveillance, that's all."

"Yes, I suppose so."

The doubt in her voice caused him to turn and face her. "Don't tell me you believe in this voodoo stuff."

"No, don't be silly." She shrugged and waved him off with her hand, not very convincingly. "I like to think we make our own fortune, good and bad."

"Not sure what that says about Charboneau. Let's hope his luck turns for the better real soon."

Jasmine nodded, avoiding his eyes. After a long moment of silence, she finally said, "So what's your plan?"

Christian looked at his watch. "It might be a little early to make a call on the shop owner. The place won't be open at this hour. Let's hit the genetics facility first."

"Why? We have a better lead chasing down this shop owner. The genetics angle is a complete waste of time, something Nicky doesn't have."

Christian knew by her reaction that the genetics lab was a taboo subject. That only made him want to know more about it.

"You're coverin' up his involvement with the facility, aren't you?" By her glare, he knew he'd hit a nerve. "Well, guess what? If we don't find your precious Nicky in time, his connection to that so-called genetics front will be a moot point. I think you need to get your priorities straight."

"Look, we have to work together, but I'm beginning to think you don't trust me." From righteous indignation to a coy smile, Jasmine ran hot and cold like a water spigot.

"Oh, yeah? Can't imagine where you got *that* idea. Maybe I'm just an equal opportunity cynic."

"Point taken." With a raised eyebrow, she crossed her arms over her chest. "So what's your angle on this genetics thing?"

"Just feeling the need for a little education on genetics research, that's all. Let's check out your employer's little charity, to rule out any connection." He stood and stared down at her. "Then we can follow the lead on Santo and your local jinx monger. Come on. We're burnin' daylight."

Christian walked into his bedroom, leaving Jasmine alone with her thoughts. Before leaving the suite, he'd get his digital photos of the care package on the balcony and pack it up in a small carryon bag. With what Jasmine had discovered, the voodoo vendor might shed some light on the materials and its slithering messenger.

He sat on the edge of the bed, his muscles stiff and the fresh wounds on his body aching. After rummaging through the weapons and gear Jasmine had provided, he slipped a knife into his right boot, double-checked the Glock 19, and tucked it into a holster he wore under his khaki shirt. The rest he locked away in a bag in his closet.

Today had to bear fruit. Like Jasmine said, they couldn't afford to waste time. Minutes ticked into hours and he felt the pressure. Soon, his father would run out of time. And he had far too many skeletons in his closet to be cavalier about adding one more.

CHAPTER 9

From the day Jasmine rocked his world with news of his biological father, a clock ticked in Christian's head—nagging and persistent—in perfect rhythm with Nicholas Charboneau's beating heart. The fact that he'd never met the man didn't diminish the blood link they shared.

He felt the pressure of that connection. Today, something had to happen.

On the ground floor of the hotel, the man at the concierge desk gave him a map of the city and the location of police headquarters for future reference, only a few blocks from Hotel Palma Dourada. How convenient for Duarte.

As he walked outside, to catch a taxicab for the genetics lab, the sunlight reflected off the sidewalk. The glare made him squint, which started a throbbing headache. Already the heat had become a factor. He slipped on sunglasses and stepped into the brightness of morning as a valet blew a shrill whistle to hail a cab. The sound triggered a domino of pain from his neck down. This day had gone from bad to worse in the span of five minutes. He couldn't wait for their adventure to begin.

Slung over his shoulder, Christian held a small carryon bag containing the dead snake and the Macumba ritual offerings. His creepy cargo messed with his head. He wanted to ditch it, forget it ever happened. But like Jasmine, he had high hopes for a lead with the local voodoo peddler—their next stop.

"Remind me to leave a large tip for housekeeping. Today, they're gonna earn it," he muttered under his breath to his companion. His headache had shifted to behind his eyes.

A sly smile nudged the corner of Jasmine's lips. "I'd love to be a fly on the wall when they find the dead chicken."

"Let's not talk about flies . . . or deceased poultry. Show some respect for animal rights."

Admonishing an assassin on animal rights struck him as ludicrous. In all probability, the life of a chicken ranked higher than people she considered to be a "waste of skin." But he didn't want to begin a philosophical debate with her. He had a hard enough time sleeping.

As Christian waited for the cab, he watched the bustling streets of Cuiabá. Even under the expansive portico of the elite hotel, the mass of humanity closed in on him. Traffic in the city hummed in the background, the smell of diesel fuel in the air. The blare of a horn down the street muffled the engine and brakes of a bus coming to a stop. It soured his stomach. Across the boulevard, a café worker hosed water onto the sidewalk, dampening the lingering smells of the night before—a strange blend of muggy odors coupled with the refreshing start of a new day. A city awakening.

Jasmine had no appreciation for this place. He caught a glimpse of the woman. Her expression had changed to a mix of disdain and suppressed emotion. He knew why he felt like crap and he had the bruises to prove it, but she had no excuse.

"What? You not a morning person?" he asked.

"Not particularly. Except for the language, this place reminds me of . . . Chinatown in Chicago." She offered nothing more. Cagey as ever, she answered his question, only conjuring a greater curiosity in his mind.

"Did you grow up there?"

A cab pulled to the curb. Christian took care of the valet's tip and opened the back door, letting Jasmine slide in. She gave the driver their destination as he joined her. He shifted his gaze to Jasmine, waiting for an answer he knew would have little substance. Her typical mode of communication.

"Let's say I spent time there . . ." Her eyes grew darker, if that were possible. ". . . like a prison sentence." Her voice faded, muffled by a dispatcher's voice crackling in the background and the idle humming of the driver.

More of a gut reaction, Christian suspected one thing. Jasmine had shared her past with his father. He had no idea how he knew this. The woman trusted no one. She'd become a tightly woven tapestry of dark memories. Still, Jasmine shared a bond with Charboneau, his enigmatic father, who had plenty of his own well-kept secrets.

Her loyalty to Charboneau intrigued Christian. It shed a strange light on his father's character. Charboneau traversed the line between the underbelly criminal element and the lofty influences of high society—and was equally at home with either. And he had taken the time to harness and cultivate this woman's devotion without rival. No doubt, she would die for him.

Even his own mother, Fiona, shared a lifelong commitment to the man. A tribute to Charboneau's charisma, or his ability to manipulate? How had his father earned such allegiance? Christian wanted to believe the man deserved it, but didn't want to jump to any unfounded conclusions.

"Did you meet my . . . did you meet Charboneau there? How long have you worked for him?"

"I met him when I was quite young . . . in Chicago. Perhaps you can say he recognized my talents long before I did." She smiled, her gaze locked in memory. "He showed me the world. And with Nicky, you can live a lifetime in a day. Your father is the most amazing man. He knows what he wants, and he would take it like a thief if it pleased him. A dangerous combination, some might say."

"But not for you. You like danger." No question. Only his observation from the limited time he'd known the woman.

She shrugged, fighting a faint smile. The word *smug* came to his mind.

"Well then, you should really be lovin' this little adventure. A real adrenaline rush for a danger junkie like you. But here's what I believe." Christian went with his gut, taking a stab at the truth. "I think you and Charboneau got yourselves into a mess you hadn't anticipated. Got caught with your pants down."

"How dare you! I resent your . . ." She raised her voice, punctuating her sentiments with an angry glare. The cabbie stopped humming. His eyes darted to the rearview mirror.

Before she built up a good head of steam, Christian countered, "Save the bogus indignation, J. I think you and your employer are accustomed to being the big fish in a very small pond. Maybe you're used to getting your way. Only this time you picked the wrong swimmin' hole . . . one a little far from home and chocked full of piranha."

She held his gaze for a long moment, only a hint of emotion lingering. Then her face eased into a blank slate. The picture of composure. Her voice low and menacing, she leaned closer to him.

"Piranha is a delicacy here in Brazil, an aphrodisiac. I plan to eat my fill." Chin held high, she turned away, dismissing his insinuation.

"Yeah," he muttered. "Guess I figured that."

A sex kitten like Jasmine needed an aphrodisiac like Paris Hilton could use more media attention. He settled back in his seat and stared out the window, letting the drone of the taxi engine settle between them.

Eventually, the bustling city tapered to residential neighborhoods, then ultimately to a dirt road that cut a swath through the dense jungle—civilization only a faded image in the rearview mirror. Red dust kicked up behind them. But through the lush greenery, Christian caught a glimpse of an impressive complex in a valley below. Genotech Labs.

A wall of security and armed guards surrounded the place. Good thing he called ahead for an appointment. Their passports would serve as ID. The facility director agreed to meet him only after he claimed to be investigating Charboneau's abduction, and that he would be accompanied by the man's bodyguard. Dropping Jasmine's name got him in.

But Christian knew she would be nothing more than an albatross around his neck at the genetics facility. A double agent. Getting at the truth ranked low on her list of priorities if it meant betraying Charboneau in any way. Whatever her reasons, she'd be of no use to him. The mysterious woman might even toss a few obstacles in his path.

Yet with that thought, he gazed out the window and focused on the imposing facility ahead, resisting the urge to smile. Because of Jasmine's strong reaction, he knew he was on the right track.

He only hoped it wouldn't be too late for his father.

Lying on his back, Nicholas opened his eyes after hearing the sound again. At first he thought he'd been dreaming. A damned nightmare. But something *had* rushed by his ear, kicking up dirt. Awake now, he held his breath. Listening. His eyes searched the darkness, but nothing took shape.

An endless void. Pitch-black.

A musty mineral smell swept over him, coupled with the recurring chill and the stench from his own body. He rose from the cold ground. His muscles ached with the torture of how he'd slept. When he moved, tiny feet scurried away, deeper into the inky black.

"Foul beggars. You had better keep your distance or I'll—"

"Or you'll what, Nicholas?" A man's voice resonated from the dank tunnel. A sinister whisper. "Perhaps you're not capable of intimidating even a rodent . . . in your present circumstance, that is."

The voice sounded familiar. His mind raced with possibilities. He hadn't seen anyone approach. How had this man gotten so close without detection . . . or a light to guide him? More than likely, in his exhaustion he'd allowed it to happen.

"Yet you haven't shown your face. Now why is that?" He kept his voice stern.

A crunch of dirt underfoot to his left. The man crawled out from his hiding spot, flipping a switch to a large flashlight. A blinding glare. Nicholas held a hand up, blocking the intense light. His eyes watered with the strain.

"And still, you won't let me see you," he said, provoking the man. "Are you a coward?"

A low menacing laugh echoed in the cavern. Eerie shadows gyrated along the wall as the stranger moved.

"Even now you taunt me. I do not think that is wise, do you? Given your predicament . . . You have the attitude of a man in control of his own destiny. And that is far from the truth."

With the light lingering in all the dark crevices, Nicholas used his limited eyesight to scope out his surroundings, hoping to find a means of escape. He'd been right about the cave and the locked jail cell. Metal bars caught the reflection. Beyond his cell, a yawning chasm held most of its secrets. Massive boulders glistened with their own sweat and the incessant droplets from jagged formations overhead. Decades of time passing drop by drop.

His perverse host spoke again.

"Besides, my face is unimportant. I've only come to learn more about my enemy . . . to look into the eyes of a man without reverence for life."

"That's simply not true." He raised his chin and squinted into the beam of light, mustering his audacity. "I value my own."

"Ah, yes, you do. For once, you speak the truth. And the lives of others be damned, is that it?" The man's profile, outlined in the pale light, triggered a memory for Nicholas. His voice teased that recollection, but still, the man's face remained in the dark recesses of his mind.

"What happened—" Nicholas stopped, not sure he wanted to know the answer to a question that had plagued him since he first opened his eyes in this place. "Where is Jasmine . . . my bodyguard? If she's dead, I'll—"

"Threats? Always with the threats. Even now." The man laughed. The sound rumbled through the cave—cruel and haunting. Superior. "She is no longer your concern."

Jasmine dead? The pain of the man's insinuation gripped him hard. His gut twisted with the image of her beautiful face mired in death. A sickness rose hot in his belly.

"You'd better pray I don't make it out of here, friend." He spat contempt with each word.

Finally, the last piece of the puzzle fell into place. The dark-skinned, sun-creased face pulled from his memory, the one who pretended not to speak English. The man with the AK-47, his kidnapper. The jailer now had a face.

"So your heart is not made of granite, I see. Too little, too late, I'm afraid."

What the hell does that mean? he wondered.

The man tossed a section of the newspaper to the dirt floor of his cell. "Seeing you think of me as . . . a friend." Sarcasm punctuated the man's use of the word *friend*. "You shouldn't mind doing me a favor. Hold the front page across your chest and smile. A man like you must enjoy a good photo op."

With reluctance, Nicholas played along, minus the smile. He leaned over and picked up the paper. The sooner he got on with this, the sooner he'd be free. His abductor took a couple of quick photos. The flash caused Nicholas to wince, not his most flattering shot.

"Don't worry about your appearance, my friend. You won't be leaving this place."

"What?" *Had he heard right?* "What do you mean?"

"My people have suffered far too much because of men like you. Users. And until recently, I saw no end in sight. But now, I can make a stand . . . for my people."

"I don't get it. Why kidnap me and bring me here? What's the point? You could have killed me at the hotel."

"I have to admit. At first you were just another rich American to be . . . harvested. But I have learned why you come to my country, and it sickens me. I know all I need to about you." The man shone the light in his face. Nicholas raised his hand to shield his eyes.

"For crimes against the people of Brazil, you will die here. I think that is more fitting."

"What crimes? Who's been talking to you about me?" He raised his voice in objection, filling it with indignation. "I demand a lawyer . . . or someone from the American consulate. There's been a mistake."

"Justice has been dealt, sir. Demand all you want. No one will hear you. Then maybe you will understand what it feels like to be without power." The man turned to leave, taking the light with him. Shadows surged in his wake. His voice echoed. "And these rats you despise so much? They will become your only companions . . . until they pick your bones clean."

"No! I tell you, someone has lied to you. I'm a businessman from America. I have done nothing wrong. You can't do this," he demanded as he gripped the bars, his lungs burning. "Damn it, don't go. Come back here!"

But with each step the man took, the flashlight flickered into shadows. And as the light faded, Nicholas felt hope drain from his body.

"Don't . . . do this."

He always imagined going out in a blaze of gunfire, a fitting send-off for the life he'd chosen. *Hell, no one lives forever.* But dying in this rat infested squalor? No, he couldn't die here. *Not here!*

Mahogany and black leather. Tasteful decor. The office for the facility director of Genotech Labs had been well-appointed. Family photos told Christian what was important to Dr. Tyson Phillips. Smiling happy faces framed in gold were strategically placed at every angle of the impressive suite. Only now, the man's somber expression contradicted his attempt at idle chatter.

"Thanks for meeting with us." Christian sat in a guest chair across from the man.

"It's always nice to speak to another American. Don't get me wrong. My family and I love it here, it's just that . . ." Dr. Phillips held a pen in his fingers, tapping an end of it onto his desk. He cleared his throat and narrowed his eyes. "What did you say your name was again?"

"Christian Delacorte . . . from Chicago." Christian handed him a business card.

Jasmine wandered the room, keeping her eyes trained on the man. She hadn't said a word since coming into Dr. Phillips's office, even when she'd been introduced. Christian learned long ago silence could be a useful tool. Most people felt the need to fill the void in conversation—especially when they had something to hide. Apparently, Jasmine understood the concept.

"Ah, Chicago," the man repeated. A forced smile. "Yes, you said you were here about Mr. Charboneau. I recognized the name of Ms. Lee as his bodyguard." He turned his head and kept an eye on Jasmine, who stepped behind his chair. She enjoyed her little game of intimidation.

The facility director continued, "His kidnapping came as a real shock."

"Yes, I would imagine." Christian nodded.

The doctor seemed to expect his visit and acted like they'd met before. He should've been more curious, like any outsider to a case. Phillips should have wondered whether he'd been hired to investigate the kidnapping, or if his protective services firm was responsible for Charboneau's security from the start. Did Jasmine work for him? Was he working with the local police? Did he have any inside information to share? But none of those questions occurred to Phillips. Instead, the man looked like he'd bitten into a habanero pepper and couldn't spit it out.

Christian pulled the photo of Rodrigo Santo from his pocket and handed it to Phillips. "Tell me, Doctor. You ever see this man?"

The doctor pursed his lips and shook his head. "No, can't say that I have."

Again, the natural question would be for Phillips to ask if the man in the photo was connected to the kidnapping, but he didn't ask it. Very strange.

"Tell me, Doc. The kidnapping. Does this kind of thing happen often in Cuiabá?"

"Unfortunately, more times than I care to admit. It's become a means of support for a struggling economy, I'm afraid." He swallowed, avoiding Christian's eyes.

"Looks like you have a nice family. You say they like it here?"

"Oh, yes, very much."

Another strained smile. More silence.

"Boy, they gotta hate all the added protection. Do you keep your family under lock and key, like the way you do at this place?"

"What do you mean? They come and go—" The man stopped himself and backpedaled. "It's not that bad, really."

"If abductions are so commonplace, why haven't you added any protection for your wife and kids? Especially right after the incident with Charboneau."

He had baited the doctor, and the man knew it.

"I do hope they find Mr. Charboneau soon." Phillips shifted his eyes to the pen in his hand. *Tap tap tap.* "He's been a staunch supporter of our work here. Without his backing, our funding will be severely limited."

"Who are the other supporters of this facility?"

"We're privately financed. I'm afraid that's confidential." *Another roadblock.*

Until he spoke the words, Christian hadn't thought about other potential backers for such research. All this time, he'd convinced himself his father had ulterior motives, for his own personal gain. And the man may still be up to his nose hairs in illegal motives, but what about others who might capitalize on this endeavor? Would Jasmine know the players involved? *Keep an open mind, Delacorte.* His old man thrived in a world of smoke and mirrors, a labyrinth of illusion to obscure the truth. Nothing would be simple.

Phillips cleared his throat and changed the subject. "Why are you here, Mr. Delacorte? I'm not sure I can help."

Alarms blared in Christian's head. The doctor's body language told him the man was a bundle of nerves, wrapped way too tight.

"I'd like to understand why Nicholas Charboneau was in Brazil . . . and his connection to genetics research. Can you help me with that?"

Before the facility director answered, another voice interrupted.

"Dr. Phillips has already said he can't help, but perhaps I can."

Jasmine's eyes flashed anger as she recognized Captain Luis Duarte. He leaned against the doorway, dressed in his khaki uniform, eyeing Christian with suspicion.

"If you have questions regarding the investigation, it would be best to direct them to me." The captain crooked his lips into a half smile.

"I'll take you up on that, Captain." Christian returned the man's grin. On the outside, he kept a confident facade, but on the inside was another story. How did Duarte have the inside track on everything? "But first, I was hoping to get a tour of this impressive facility. Can that be arranged, Dr. Phillips?"

All eyes went back to Phillips. The facility director looked for a reprieve from the police captain, but none came.

"I suppose . . . maybe a quick tour." The man stood and buttoned his suit coat.

Duarte let Jasmine and the doctor pass, but held an arm across the door when Christian approached. He leaned in, his voice low.

"When you are done wasting your time here, stop by my office. I am curious why you failed to report your hit and run outside the hotel last night."

"I figured you already knew about it, Captain."

"What's that supposed to mean?"

Christian didn't hesitate. "You said it yourself, this is your town. Nothing gets by you."

"And still, you believe you can hide things from me. A blood sacrifice in your penthouse suite?"

"Hey, when in Rome . . ." Christian shrugged, then reconsidered. "I can explain . . ."

"Yes, you will."

Duarte didn't look impressed by his sense of humor. And now the captain eyed the bag he had slung over his shoulder, the Macumba paraphernalia and the dead snake. *Please . . . don't ask.* The man narrowed his eyes. Hoping for the best, Christian raised his chin and waited to see what the cop would do. *When steeped in hot water up to your pie hole, what's ten more degrees?*

Duarte furrowed his brow and heaved a sigh. "My office, after your tour. And you'd better have answers to my questions, Mr. Delacorte."

The man dropped his arm to let him pass. With his footsteps echoing down the hall, Christian replayed the cop's words in his head from the night they'd met. *Never underestimate the necessity to protect yourself against evil. The curse of the evil eye has its power.*

Pure insight or subtle threat? With every face-to-face, the answer to that question took shape.

Plus, the man knew his next moves even before he did. How had the captain found out about their visit to Genotech Labs . . . and so soon? He'd barely sat down before Duarte made his appearance. Had Dr. Phillips told him, or did Duarte have another informant inside the lab?

Clearly, there were reasons for his growing paranoia. Even now, he didn't have to look over his shoulder to know Duarte stared a hole in his back. He felt the searing heat of it.

"What we've gained from human genome-mapping is a better understanding of how certain diseases act on a molecular and cellular level, the brain's pathways associated with the affliction." In his element, Dr. Phillips grinned as he ushered Christian and Jasmine through another massive lab.

Pointing to a microscope, the doctor added, "And with advances in atomic force microscopy, we have

improved our DNA mapping and sequencing tech-
niques. Cell tissue yields its secrets when explored
under high-resolution imaging. It may not be long
before we can predict, with pinpoint accuracy, what
risk a person may have for certain ailments. Then we
can tailor a remedy specific to them, one without the
usual side effects."

The man beamed with pride, hands on his hips.
"And there are so many other gains to be made. It's
an exciting field, I can assure you."

Lab technicians in white coats barely looked up
from their work. A sea of white and stainless steel
blended with high-tech equipment Christian had
never seen before. A medicinal smell remained a constant in the air. And despite the hot temperature outside, the indoor rooms were maintained at a chilly
level, probably for the benefit of all the pricey computers utilized across the expansive facility.

"Quite impressive, Doctor." Christian returned his
smile, sneaking a glance toward Jasmine, who had
not changed her expression. "Would this research
help with natural addictions, such as overeating, ad-
dition to gambling, or . . ." He winked at Jasmine.
". . . compulsive shopping?" That finally got a rise
out of her, her usual poise replaced by a threatening
glare.

"Yes, yes, you're right, Mr. Delacorte." Phillips
seemed pleased. "We have scientific evidence that
supports this theory. I'm delighted you understand."

"Tell me how it works." His sole objective was to keep
the man talking, especially as he maneuvered the doctor
toward the subject he really wanted to chat about.

"The cerebral cortex of the brain stores and pro-
cesses such things as language, math, and strate-

gies. It's the 'thinking' part of you. And buried deep within the cerebral cortex is the limbic system, which is responsible for survival and human emotion. It remembers and creates an appetite for the things that keep you alive, such as good food and the company of other human beings."

Phillips used his hands to point to the areas of the brain he spoke about.

"I've heard the limbic system controls the four F's— fleeing, fighting, feeding, and fu—" Christian stopped himself, catching a look at Jasmine. "—hooking up."

Jasmine rolled her eyes but didn't say a word.

"Yes, I suppose that describes it." The doctor raised an eyebrow and paused for effect. "Since natural pleasures are necessary for survival, the limbic system creates an appetite that drives human beings to seek them out. And when someone experiences unnaturally intense feelings of pleasure, the limbic system is flooded with dopamine. So the behavior is reinforced."

The doctor walked slowly down the aisle as he explained the complex topic.

"So we believe the brain circuits regulate a person's responses to food, sex, or certain risky behaviors, and acts like a natural reinforcement for survival. Well, what if this natural order is somehow commandeered from its usual path? If this happens, it's conceivable a person might become addicted to overeating, for example."

"And I suppose this also explains how drug addiction works, right?" Christian asked. "The drug high signals the brain to release the dopamine and the behavior is reinforced, time and time again, at greater and greater levels."

The facility director stopped walking, losing his enthusiasm for the subject. The eye contact he'd been exchanging vanished, replaced by a glare tinged with caution. The man stuffed his hands in his slacks.

"Yes, the principle works for all types of addictions," he said, picking up his pace through the laboratory. "A person's genetic makeup probably plays a role, but after enough doses, an addict's limbic system craves the drug. And dependency is made worse over time. Without a dose of the drug, dopamine levels in the abuser's brain are low. They feel flat, lifeless, and depressed. So the addict needs drugs to overcome these feelings. Larger amounts are needed to create a dopamine flood or high, an effect known as tolerance. And so the cycle goes."

A flurry of familiar questions bombarded Christian, but one stood out. Why would a man associated with drug trafficking in the States be involved with a genetics lab committed to curing the disease in South America? His gut wrenched as he followed Dr. Phillips. He had a feeling he wouldn't like the answer.

When they exited the lab and turned toward the offices, he knew the tour was almost over. Even though his body felt stiff, his mind churned with questions, perhaps stemming from his need to procrastinate.

"With the rain forest nearby, does your research include a broader scope? A search for new medicines, for example?"

The doctor brightened, thankful for the change in topic. "It is one of the very reasons this facility has achieved what it has. Our close proximity to Mother Nature's own pantry has afforded us great opportunities."

Phillips directed them into another room. A climate-controlled structure stood in the center of the floor. Technicians in white coats blurred behind opaque walls. The usual high-tech gear and computers lined the walls of the room, but the main focus was the arboretum.

"Can we see inside?" Christian asked.

Phillips was getting tired of accommodating him, but the man complied after a quick glance at his watch, "Certainly. I suppose I can spare a little more time."

Stifling heat stemmed his next breath as Christian walked inside the conservatory. The temperature shift from chilly to hot made him want to sneeze. He fought the sensation, but Jasmine wasn't so lucky. She suppressed a set of three sneezes.

"Bless you." He responded on pure reflex, but had second thoughts about blessing an assassin. Somehow, it went against the grain.

The interior of the greenhouse was set up like a mini-rain forest, complete with artificial light. Butterflies fluttered amidst the flowers, and small colorful birds chirped in the trees. Man-made streams and fountains provided a soothing white noise. And water misters purged their contents onto the picturesque setting at timed intervals. In a perfect world, nothing was left to chance. Someone had an eye for style over function. Even Jasmine appreciated it. She walked next to him, brushing his arm as she lost her balance looking into the lush trees, her eyes wide with wonder.

"Did you have a hand in this, Dr. Phillips? It's beautiful." Christian meant it.

"Yes, I did. Rather proud of it, actually." The man smiled. "I sometimes eat my lunch here. It's quiet. Peaceful."

Christian appreciated the need for a quiet mind. His own demons rarely cooperated.

A female technician hunched over a small shrub ahead, digging at the yellow-tinted root bark. The vivid color combination of the exotic plant caught his attention. He hadn't seen anything like it. Small green leaves set off delicate white flowers with bright pink spots. And elongated oval-shaped fruit, the color of an orange, hung from its stems. The lab tech extracted clippings from the root system.

"What is she doing, Doctor?"

"Ah, Tabernanthe Iboga, also known as black bugbane, or simply the Iboga. It's a perennial, more plentiful in western Africa. Although it's found in our rain forests, it is not as common, so we cultivate a crop of it here." Phillips's eyes wandered around the room and he kept looking at his watch, making sure Christian got the message that he wanted this tour to be over. "But we've also discovered a similar plant that's showing great promise. It grows near the base of the Chapada dos Guimarães foothills that overlook the Pantanal near the Paraguay River. The local tribes have been . . . generous to the efforts of this research facility. We have a great deal more research to do, but our initial studies show amazing similarities without the same downside in side effects."

Phillips turned around, directing them away, but Christian had another question.

"With all the exotic vegetation in this country, why the fascination with this plant and the one in the foothills?"

The man stopped short and sighed. He let a long moment pass before he replied, "The Iboga and its distant cousin stimulate the central nervous system.

Under scientific testing conditions, Ibogaine has been found to be effective in stopping addiction to hard drugs such as heroin or cocaine. It may also help interrupt chemical dependency to alcohol and nicotine. We are simply studying this aspect to see if there is a genetic correlation. Standard procedure, really."

The facility director dismissed his curiosity once again. Even Jasmine gave him the stink eye. But Christian was having none of it.

"This doesn't sound like something the FDA would approve."

"No, unfortunately not." Dr. Phillips let out a loud sigh, making a show of his impatience. "Even though the pharmaceutical aspects have been extolled in countless peer reviews and position papers, no formal clinical studies have been completed."

With a grin, the man added, "But there is growing support in the U.S. for legislation making it permissible for Ibogaine—and perhaps other derivative plants not yet on their legal radar—to be used for medicinal purposes, similar to marijuana."

"No harm, no foul, just as long as no one inhales?"

"Excuse me?"

"Ah, nothing." Christian shook his head. "So Charboneau and the backers of this facility would be ahead of the game if a worldwide Ibogaine market opened up . . . or some derivation of that by-product that might be uncovered through your studies. Operating in a country that allows such research would give them an edge."

For what purpose, he still had no idea. His speculation sounded like a legitimate business enterprise, but curing addiction wasn't much of a game plan for a drug lord bent on world domination.

"Yes, I suppose. And you are right. We have discovered other plants similar to the Iboga that are not banned in the U.S." The doctor shrugged. "We're making strides."

Strides? Strides in their agenda. Maybe that was the point. Interesting that Phillips was more concerned by a U.S. ban than the therapeutic aspects. Finding a way around U.S. laws and international borders handed them a get-out-of-jail card in case they needed it. Making strides around the law on a global scale could be quite lucrative until they were deterred by legal measures. And with enough distribution infrastructures, they could operate for a long time before they were shut down, country by country. The arm of the law moved slowly across jurisdictions. But he realized he had to know more about the plant itself.

"You said the Iboga stimulates the nervous system. How does it work exactly?"

Phillips appeared uneasy by his interrogation.

"When taken in small doses, it reduces sleep, makes it possible to resist hunger and fatigue, and activates circulation and respiration. The root material has an astringent bitter taste when chewed, causing an anesthetic sensation in the mouth and numbness to the skin," the doctor explained. "Local natives use it in rituals and tribal dances to stimulate spiritual hallucinations, particularly at night. Apparently, darkness accentuates the haunting experience. And because it's not addictive, they consider it quite harmless. Now I really must be going."

"Yeah, but human nature being what it is . . ." Christian touched the man's arm to grab his attention. ". . . someone always pushes the limit. What happens when the dose is upped to overload, Doc?"

He knew he pushed the guy's buttons, but his mind was filled with questions. Jasmine, impatient as well, stood behind Phillips and glared at him, arms crossed and foot tapping. Some forms of communication needed no translation.

A concerned look shadowed the doctor's face, an uneasy fear. "In massive doses, it can cause death by paralysis of the respiratory muscles. Not a pleasant way to go, I'm afraid. The victim suffers extensive hallucinations in a frenzied state. And they endure profound paranoia before they simply suffocate, strangled by the failure of their crippled lungs. Agonizing."

That sounded way too personal.

"You've witnessed an overdose before?"

The doctor stared off into the distance, his mind in another time and place.

"Once." The peaceful setting of the arboretum mocked the memory he relived. "And once is quite enough."

The man cleared his throat and ushered them out of the hothouse and back into the main corridor.

"I'm afraid that's all the time I have today." The director turned for the offices up front, expecting them to follow.

"Wait a minute. What's down here?" Christian pointed to a corridor the man had avoided.

"Oh, that's nothing. A medical clinic we set up to serve the local community." Phillips turned to go, but neither Jasmine nor Christian followed. When the man looked back over his shoulder, he added, "I assure you it's nothing. Minor injuries, immunizations, really basic health care for the locals. It was negotiated . . . recently."

"Such a humanitarian gesture. I would think you'd want to show it off." Christian shrugged and stood his ground.

Jasmine joined him, crossing her arms. "The last time my employer came for a visit, this clinic was not in service. I would also like to see it for myself."

Dr. Phillips sighed. "Very well. Follow me," he conceded, and headed toward the health facility. His jaw was knotted with tension, nudging a nasty cluster of purple veins jutting from his temple.

With a pained grimace, Christian hoisted the tote carrying the dead snake and voodoo artifacts onto his sore shoulder and waved an arm for Jasmine to pass.

"After you, Ms. Lee."

The beautiful woman said nothing. Her sly wink gave him the only *Atta boy* he'd get.

CHAPTER 10

Like a Russian nesting doll, the clinic was burrowed neatly within the much larger genetics facility, only a fraction of the puzzle Charboneau's money had funded. If Christian hadn't paid attention on the tour, he might never have noticed the breezeway link to this section of the compound. The medical clinic had been cordoned off from the rest of the secured research laboratory, with a circular drive and a small parking lot outside. On the taxi ride in, he hadn't noticed any signs directing traffic to a health-care clinic. Yet it looked like an entrance allowed the public through an open gate without security during the day, giving the community better access.

Being the cordial guide, Dr. Phillips now led them through the main ward. Contrary to what the doctor had led them to believe, the facility mainly catered to expectant mothers, not just general health concerns. Christian might not have given this a second thought since everything appeared in order—except for Jasmine's behavior. Her classic stoic face morphed into edgy apprehension. When the doctor's back was turned, she stepped toward the bed of a pregnant teenage girl, grabbed her chart and scanned the girl's medical history.

"What's wrong?" Christian whispered, turning his back on their host. She kept reading, a troubled look on her face.

Eventually, Dr. Phillips stepped between them and yanked the chart from Jasmine. "In this facility, we respect a patient's right to privacy."

"Yes, of course." Jasmine nodded her apology, a courteous bow of her head. "I was merely curious."

She walked up to the young girl, who couldn't have been more than fifteen years old. Shoulder length black hair, skin the color of caramel, and large hazel eyes brimming with uncertainty. Even with her swollen belly, she looked small and frail in the hospital bed. But the young girl managed a smile. Jasmine reached for her, ran fingers through her bangs and touched her cheek.

Christian had no idea she could muster such affection. *Well, I'll be damned!* When the doctor headed back to see what Jasmine was up to, he waved the man off.

"The girl reminded her of someone. Let it go." He knew Jasmine had something on her mind. To deflect attention away from her, he went on the offensive. "Is this place linked to the research conducted at the lab?"

"No, this clinic is purely humanitarian in nature. What are you implying?"

Christian stepped in, closing the gap with Dr. Phillips, while Jasmine made the rounds.

"Come on, Doc. You mean you're not even tempted to further your research with discarded tissue samples? You do fertility work here?"

From the corner of his eye, Christian saw Jasmine steal a peek at other med charts. No doubt, she had something on her mind. And for his part in the diversion—making a belligerent ass of himself—he expected Jasmine's cooperation when it came time to share her suspicions.

The doctor's skin grew flush, almost purple, to match the veins on his face.

"Mr. Delacorte. Are you suggesting this clinic is involved in stem cell research with unsuspecting donors?"

Christian had no idea where he would go with this line of questioning. He only wanted to stall. From the corner of his eye he caught Jasmine motioning with her hand, a signal for him to keep going. *Well, damn it! Read faster.* As she flipped through another chart, he dug through his memory for something more to say.

"I've heard a lot of embryos are tossed in the fertility process. I bet that seems like a waste for a researcher like you. Too much temptation?"

Before the man blew a gasket, Christian saved the best for last.

"And what about genetic engineering?" He waggled a finger. "A controversial subject. But with the genome for drug addiction identified, wouldn't it be possible to reengineer a junkie, steer him away from his addiction?"

From fertility and pregnant mothers to a point counterpoint on crazed meth heads, Dr. Phillips grappled with the change in topic. But the way Christian figured it, when grasping at straws, sound reasoning only got in the way.

The man took a deep breath and nodded. "Yes, that's our hope."

"Is it, Dr. Phillips? Is that what Nicholas Charboneau had in mind with this privately funded research?" When the director didn't answer, Christian pressed. "Isn't it also possible to engineer a normal person into *becoming* an addict? Or make the dependency that much stronger on someone already addicted?"

Indignation replaced the sudden panic on Phillips's face, but not before Christian got a good look at his initial reaction. *Score one for the visiting team.*

"That's . . . preposterous. I see you've been reading all the propaganda from people who don't understand the benefits mankind can derive from stem cell research. For your information, adult stem cells have been extracted from bone marrow since the sixties, for crying out loud. Besides, why would someone knowingly subject themselves to be rewired into an addict?"

"Key word being 'knowingly,'" Christian countered.

"I resent the implication, sir."

"Implication? Maybe I haven't made myself clear. How are you getting your test samples, Doc? Before I came here, I did a little light reading on genetics, something about legislation on human tissue."

"I'm well aware of the Human Tissues Act." Phillips crossed his arms over his chest.

"Yeah, well . . ." Christian nodded. "International law puts a tight lid on testing human genetic material without informed consent from the patient. Tell me, are you and this facility in compliance, Dr. Phillips?"

"I assure you, none of the people you've seen here today have had their rights violated."

"Very clever semantics, Doc. What about all the people we haven't seen?"

"That's enough." Jasmine weighed in. She'd made her rounds. Now, in a low voice, she intervened. Christian had crossed a line she would defend. Charboneau's line.

"You feel the conflict, Jasmine? Maybe your beloved employer put himself in the line of fire without knowing it. Maybe the people behind this so-called research got greedy and took him out. You gotta pick sides. What's it gonna be?"

She looked surprised. He'd caught her off guard, not an easy feat.

Christian knew what the doctor said made sense. Even if someone's genes were manipulated without their knowledge, how would the subterfuge be implemented on a grand scale? With Charboneau out of the picture, he knew he might never know the answer. He had to find his father to uncover the truth behind such a conspiracy. Now there was more at stake than a rescue mission for one man. And Jasmine would have to choose sides.

"I think this tour is ended." Phillips seethed with anger.

"I agree," Jasmine chimed in, with less conviction.

Seeing his chance to evade Christian's questions, the doctor took advantage of his rift with Jasmine and waved over a security guard. "Call a taxi for our guests and see that they are escorted off the property. Don't let them get lost." To Christian, he added, "I hope you understand when I say our meeting is concluded and you're not welcome back."

Bile rose in Christian's belly. He didn't want to think about Charboneau's role in all this. Research of this magnitude took time and money. What was his father's blueprint for implementation? How did he plan to take advantage of genetic engineering? Most of all, he wondered how he could so easily believe Charboneau was guilty.

As they were escorted out, Christian whispered to his questionable comrade, "Thanks for the teamwork back there. You're a real gem."

"And the fragile male ego rears its head once more." Jasmine flashed her best Mona Lisa smile and another wink. "We got what we came for."

Christian did a double take, catching her subtle gesture. "We? Lady, you put a whole new emphasis on the 'me' in the word team. I'm not exactly feeling the love here."

"Oh, but you will."

Jasmine had something to share, but would she? And if she did, how much could he trust? The start of a festering headache took hold, along with a growing soreness to his shoulders. With Duarte waiting, and no likely moment for a private conversation with Jasmine, he'd have to put off getting his answers.

He hated being in the dark, in more ways than one.

MILITARY POLICE HEADQUARTERS,
STATE OF MATO GRASSO
DOWNTOWN CUIABÁ

From his taxi window at a busy intersection, Christian spied police headquarters up ahead, a glass and stone building. Given all the history in this town, the structure was modern and relatively uninspired. Not much to look at, except for the impressive palm trees and fountains in the median of a bustling boulevard.

At the curb, he paid off the cabbie. Getting out of the vehicle took effort. His body ached from head to toe. Jasmine made a beeline for the entrance, but Christian's mind was elsewhere when he caught up to her. Soon he'd be staring into a set of dark eyes—eyes that bristled with a capacity for danger. Captain Duarte would require special handling. Christian believed when negotiating with a hungry, unpredictable beast, it was best not to look like a side of beef.

He'd consider it a moral victory if he walked away with all his original body parts.

"Let me do all the talking," he said to Jasmine, like that was an issue. The Asian beauty made the Terminator look neighborly and downright chatty.

"By all means. I'd rather not be blamed for tightening the noose around your neck." She smiled. Sometimes Jasmine had all the charm of a croc swallowing a baby antelope whole.

At the first floor security kiosk, they showed ID and signed into the building. Directed to the second floor, they wore visitor badges clipped to their collars. Captain Duarte had a corner office to the far right of the detectives' bullpen, off the bank of elevators. Even crossing international borders, some things went without saying—the universal language of police work never changed.

Christian knocked on the man's open door.

"Glad to see you are prompt, Mr. Delacorte." The captain did not extend his hand, only waved them to take a seat.

As usual, Jasmine did not respond well to cordiality. She donned her cloak of invisibility and melded into her surroundings like a slithering chameleon in self-preservation mode. She chose to stay mobile.

"Do I get points for cutting our lab tour short?" He broke the ice with a lame attempt at humor as he sat down, trying to hide his wince of pain. Duarte barely sneered, so he went for round two. "I love what you've done to the place. Real cozy."

Bare bones and no frills, Duarte's office gave no hint of the man he was. No family photos. Nothing personal. The unpretentious room held a fatigue green metal desk with oak veneer, a matching bookshelf and credenza, and a few chairs. The sparse decor made the furniture showroom at Ikea look ostentatious and overdone.

"I prefer things . . . simple," Duarte said. "I don't often get my way."

Christian raised an eyebrow. "I find that hard to believe."

"Just as I find it hard to believe a visitor to my country does not register a formal complaint after he is very nearly killed on the streets of my town. Why did you not report the incident, Mr. Delacorte?"

Playing hard ball already; the man had no patience for idle chitchat.

"It wasn't a big deal." He shrugged.

"All evidence to the contrary. The bruises on your body say otherwise."

Christian considered the man seated behind the desk. Did Duarte exert control to force his cooperation, or did the man have an affinity for interference? What was his agenda?

"I didn't get a good look at the license plate or the car. Filing a report would've been a waste of time. And we don't have much of that."

Duarte stared at him. His black eyes looked like bottomless pits.

"And I suppose you hoped the blood sacrifice of a chicken would bring good fortune in your search?"

How many times would he hear *that* question in a lifetime? *Count 'em, one.*

He knew he had to give Duarte something. He broke down and shared what he could about the Macumba house warming on their balcony last night, but he held back a choice tidbit or two. Their next stop, to the voodoo peddler, to see Bianca Salvador, was his lead to keep. And he wouldn't mention the contents of the carryon bag at his feet or the digital photos captured on his cell phone. Until he figured out whose side the man was on, Duarte didn't need to know everything.

"So, Captain, you have any ideas on who might think a poisonous snake makes a good key to the city?"

"Placing a curse on Mr. Charboneau after the fact seems a waste of time, don't you think? Perhaps the scare tactic was directed at you and your delightful companion. A message to mind your own business."

Jasmine stopped her pacing. She drilled her eyes

on Duarte. Clearly, the man brought out the best in her. If looks dealt a mortal blow, Duarte would have been sporting a garrote necktie, his throat severed by a lethal wire.

"That's what I thought too, but I find it hard to believe kidnappers would tamper with their meal ticket." Christian offered his theory. "Usually ransom money is the main driver for an abduction, but whoever is behind this thing is sending mixed messages, like they don't care about the payoff."

"I've witnessed families of victims take different approaches to recovering their loved ones, to pay or not to pay. I am not offering advice, but I've seen a severed ear or finger put things in perspective."

"I appreciate your . . . sensitivity." Christian scowled, leaning forward in his chair. "Forgive me if I don't wait for body parts to show up on my doorstep."

"I'm not suggesting—" Duarte stopped and slouched back in his seat, making the brown vinyl crinkle. He pulled something from his desk drawer. "You asked if any proof of life evidence had been received. Well, this arrived an hour ago."

The captain dropped a plastic bag onto his desk. It contained a Polaroid photo and a white envelope, the photo of a man holding a newspaper. When it landed in front of Christian, he recognized the face. His father, Nicholas Charboneau. He looked gaunt, his clothes rumpled and his skin smeared with grime and sweat. Before Christian picked up the bagged photo, Jasmine beat him to it. She held it close, in both hands, as if it were fragile.

"Did you see who left it?" she whispered, not taking her eyes off the Polaroid. "I can't see the date clearly. Did you recognize the headline?"

"The paper was yesterday's. And unfortunately, a small boy dropped it off before anyone questioned him. It came inside a sealed envelope. It's unlikely we will find the child, but even if we did, he probably couldn't tell us much."

How convenient. He had asked about proof of life when he first met the captain on the ride from the airport. Now this photo arrived, materializing out of thin air. His skepticism tainted anything Duarte had to say.

"He's in some kind of jail cell, but with the shadows and the poor quality of the photo, we can't determine much else. And we found no fingerprints on the photo or the envelope." Duarte leaned forward in his chair. "If it's any consolation, it does confirm he's alive. More news than what we had before."

"I'd like to know what you've been doing to find him." Christian gritted his teeth, holding back his anger.

Second thoughts and instinct stopped him from showing the photos of Rodrigo Santo. Why didn't he trust the captain? If Duarte was covering for Santo, Christian would be stepping into the middle of the conspiracy without knowing the players. And having the photo would only bring up questions on how they'd acquired it. No, at this point he had no faith in Captain Duarte. And with his abrupt change in attitude, Christian's true colors showed.

"What leads do you have, Captain?"

Before Duarte replied, a booming voice came from behind him. Jasmine turned her attention to the newcomer, her expression unreadable.

"And if I were in your shoes, I would want to know the answer to that question myself."

Duarte glared at the intruder standing at his door. Tall and well groomed, a man in an expensive suit extended his hand, walking toward Christian. He stood, grimacing with pain as he knocked out all the kinks.

"Mr. Delacorte, my name is Chief Ricardo Zharan. I'm sorry for what has happened to Mr. Charboneau."

The man already knew his name. Did everyone in this town get the memo on his arrival?

"Pleased to meet you, Chief," he replied. Zharan had a firm grip.

"And it is a pleasure to see you again, Ms. Lee." The police chief nodded in her direction. Without a word, Jasmine leaned an elbow against a bookshelf and nodded. She raised a finger in greeting, going all out. The woman knew how to conserve energy.

Dressed in a dark navy suit, crisp white shirt, and a red power tie, Chief Zharan carried himself like a man of privilege, head held high and rock-solid eye contact. Seeing him on the street, Christian might have mistaken him for a politician or a successful movie actor. Charismatic. Confident. A head of thick dark hair grayed at his temples. And his strong jaw and white teeth projected a polished image.

"Understand this, Mr. Delacorte. I will not tolerate such a travesty in my city."

Apparently, Duarte had competition for control of Cuiabá. And by the looks of him, the good captain didn't appreciate the opposition from his boss.

Zharan continued, "It is despicable. I have formed a special task force to work with your American consulate, coordinating the rescue efforts. Captain Duarte has agreed to turn over his files to me, along with the evidence he's gathered thus far."

The chief's sideways glance toward his police captain sent a clear message to Christian. Zharan was taking charge and Duarte resented it. Nothing like getting your manhood whacked in front of an audience.

"And furthermore, I plan to match your reward offer for any information leading to the arrest of all those involved."

"I'm more interested in getting Mr. Charboneau back alive."

"Yes, of course. That goes without saying." The chief grinned, white teeth setting off dark olive skin. "Do you have a card? I will be in touch, of course."

After Christian handed the man his business card, the chief gave one of his own.

"Call me anytime . . . for any reason." Zharan gave a quick dismissive look toward Duarte and left the room. The silence in his wake was deafening.

Although Jasmine kept quiet, her smug attitude spoke for her. She enjoyed the degrading show of disrespect Duarte just got from his superior, but Christian had never developed a fondness for gloating.

"I hope you know I had nothing to do with that." He didn't know what to make of this sudden turn of events. No point alienating Duarte.

"I have survived many chiefs, Mr. Delacorte. And I am still here. This one has ambition for politics . . . and other things. One way or another, he will not stay long."

"And what ambitions do you have, Captain?" Christian couldn't resist asking the question.

The man narrowed his eyes and flexed his jaw. "As I have said, I am a simple man. What I want does not concern you."

"I hope not, Captain Duarte. For both our sakes, I hope that's true."

With Jasmine on his heels, Christian left Duarte's office, feeling the weight of tension in his chest. His shoulders and neck felt like crap. Charboneau's case had escalated into the hands of the military police chief, with a hefty bump in reward money. He should have been satisfied for the added attention to his father's case. Instead, he felt adrift in a strong current, being pulled out to sea. A familiar sensation these days.

Had the police chief taken over too late? Or worse, was Zharan only an image-conscious figurehead without clout—more buff than stuff? And if Duarte had a secret agenda, would he sabotage Zharan's investigation?

All things considered, his short-fused mission to save his father's life had grown hair. And he didn't need the added complication.

"Come on. I could use some caffeine," he declared as he headed for the elevators with Jasmine. In his best Ricky Ricardo impersonation, he added, "And you have some 'splainin' to do, Lucy."

Christian picked a sidewalk café down the street from Guia Do Espírito, their next stop. With the carryon bag at his feet under the shade of the table, he indulged in a jolt of espresso and a sweet roll as he watched the comings and goings of the voodoo store and listened to Jasmine.

"That clinic was not in operation the last time Nicky and I came." She sipped her tea. Her eyes hid behind dark glasses. "I'm guessing, but I don't think Nicky knew of its existence."

"But you're only his bodyguard. How would you know that?" He smiled.

He had no proof, but he suspected she glared at him from under her sunglasses. No way she'd answer his sarcastic attempt to get a rise out of her.

"You saw something in those med charts. Talk to me."

She kept her silence for a long time. Finally, she said, "You raised a good point at the lab. Maybe we haven't seen everything going on there, only what they allowed us to see. With the focus of that clinic on pregnant mothers, especially the young ones or women unable to afford good health care, it makes me wonder. They could be conducting illegal embryonic and fetal stem cell research without the consent of these women, not to mention what they might be doing with the discarded umbilical cords. How would that poor young girl know any better?"

"I'm taking a wild guess here, but you're not a doctor, are you?"

Nothing about Jasmine would have surprised him at this point.

"I know enough. Hear me out." She leaned closer, elbows on the table, and glanced over her shoulder to make sure no one overheard. "When you said other backers of this facility may be behind Nicky's abduction, it made me think. Someone is operating in the shadows, escalating the research with this clinic and its so-called humanitarian efforts. With all the advanced technology at the lab and an abundance of human tissue to harvest, the opportunity may be too tempting to pass up. And like your Raven, I do not believe in coincidence."

Hearing Raven's name sent a sharp pang of guilt through Christian. He missed her. He took a deep breath to purge his system of her memory, for now.

"Don't try and convince me your precious Nicky is an innocent pawn in all this. You may be right about someone operating on the side and dealing him out, but Charboneau is just as guilty of raping and pillaging this country and its people. Don't whitewash his involvement." He had a growing headache and Jasmine wasn't making things easier.

"I knew you wouldn't understand." For an instant anger swept her face—biting like a winter chill over Lake Michigan—then it was gone. "If Nicky knew they were conducting research on women and babies, he wouldn't condone it. Some lines should never be crossed."

This coming from an assassin?

"What kind of research, Jasmine?"

She sat back in her chair and crossed her arms, unwilling to betray him. Christian shook his head and stared across the street. His father lived in a strange world, one with double standards. He made his money off peddling addiction, a vile soul-robbing commodity. And yet, according to Jasmine, he would defend a pregnant teen?

As if she read his mind, Jasmine said, "Please, do not judge him. You know nothing. I am here to save Nicky's life. If you've changed your mind about helping, I can and will do this alone." In a distant voice, she added, "I have to."

Christian searched for her eyes beneath the dark shades, looking for some semblance of humanity.

He only saw his own reflection. Being on the wrong side of this fight could get him killed. And yet, he wouldn't turn his back on his father. If they were lucky enough to find Charboneau and free him, he would worry about the morality of his decision later. Right now he had a job to do.

"I'm still in, but you better be telling me the truth. You hold back now and both of us could get killed. Whoever is behind this thing has invested big bucks. And they won't stop at killing to protect their investment."

She nodded and whispered, "Thank you."

"Let's go." Christian left money on the table for a tip and started to stand, unraveling his aching muscles. Jasmine reached for his arm. She had his attention.

"You asked me before—" She stopped. "I *do* love Nicky, but he doesn't know. You have to understand I'm walking a fine line to protect his interests. Now, I'm asking you to trust me."

Ay, there's the rub. His very action of following her to Brazil demonstrated some level of faith, but she had to earn his trust. And so far she'd shown no aptitude for the task.

"I could ask the same of you, but we both know how that would turn out." He hit home with a double barrel shot, dead center.

Jasmine heaved a sigh and looked toward Guia Do Espírito, resigned to losing her small verbal skirmish with him. "Let's go. We are burning daytime."

He grabbed his carryon bag and followed her to the voodoo store, walking off a fresh limp. From weird science to black magic, his day kept getting better.

He didn't have the heart to correct Jasmine's bastardized version of the old saying "burning daylight." Sometimes a guy had to know when to quit. He only hoped that when it came time to let go of his obsession with the tragedies of his past, he'd be able to do it.

CHAPTER 11

"So what's it mean . . . the name on the store?" Christian asked. He winced as he flexed his aching shoulders. And Brazil's heat had inflamed his abrasions and bruises.

"Spirit Guide, I think." Jasmine's dark hair wafted in the marginal breeze as she walked across the street toward Bianca Salvador's Macumba shop. "And before you ask, I've never been inside. I'm not exactly the religious type."

"Oh, don't sell yourself short, J. I bet you've put the fear of God into plenty of men."

When Christian looked down at Jasmine, he caught her sly smile as he opened the door to let her pass. A bell tinkled overhead.

Looking over her sunglasses, she stopped in front of him, blocking his way into the store.

"I prefer to think of it as improving the gene pool."

She winked, the smile gone. He shook his head and followed her in.

When Christian closed the door behind him, the darkness took over. He fought an unexpected panic, his usual reaction to the dark. Removing his sunglasses, he let his eyes adjust and slowed his breathing. Veiled in murky shadows, the room closed in. In this place, time stopped dead. Off the beaten path of the tourist trade, the store was a throwback to another century, an ancient dwelling operating the same way for a very long time.

If he had any preconceived notions what Guia Do Espírito looked like inside, those images disappeared faster than loose cash on a subway. The words *controlled chaos* came to mind. Every square inch of the store accommodated its inventory, no space unutilized. And although the shelves looked cluttered to his way of thinking, they were clean and dusted. Someone had laid out the store in a grand scheme and maintained it.

The heavy aroma of incense and herbs made the air thick and smell stagnant. But on the side of good news, the incense masked an underlying odor probably best left to the imagination. Closer to the front door, rows of candles in every color were mixed in with tall glass jars and an amazing array of religious statues. Pretty tame stuff, which he'd seen before. But as his eyes wandered into the deeper shadows toward the back, the creep factor kicked into high gear. Jars and glass containers were filled with unnamed roots, herbs, feathers, and animal parts. Rows of them. Small vials contained a dark oozy substance bearing an uncanny resemblance to blood. No labels.

Some things you're better off not knowing.

Flickering candles called attention to altars that commemorated graphic and bloody crucifixions. Martyred faces of Catholic saints twisted in agony and stood alongside fierce pagan monsters and spirits he didn't recognize. A religious alternative universe, *Guia Do Espírito* peddled fear and redemption at retail prices.

Jasmine seemed oblivious to the macabre spectacle as she took off her shades and tucked them into a pocket. She had targeted the young man behind the register like a deer hunter dressed in blaze orange on opening day. Christian only hoped she had a limit of one.

"Let me do all the talking." She grabbed the bag from his shoulder and put it on the floor. With her back to the clerk, she undid the top two buttons of her white blouse. After a second look, she unbuttoned a third. "How do I look?"

Christian raised an eyebrow, his expression flat and his tone mechanical. "Hold me back."

With a practiced glare, Jasmine jutted her chin. "Watch . . . and learn, grasshoppa." Working her hips, she headed for the register, not taking her eyes off the unsuspecting rutting buck in her sights behind the counter.

"Can I help you?" A heavy Portuguese accent, but so far the guy's English was understandable.

The young man had no interest in Christian. He smiled at Jasmine with eager eyes and brilliant white teeth against dark skin. A handsome kid in a land of good-looking people. By the looks of him, Jasmine had bagged her buck without even trying. The clerk being a flagrant horn dog made it far too easy for a woman like Jasmine. Christian cocked his head and narrowed his eyes. He had the urge to confiscate the kid's man card, send him back to the factory for re-tooling.

The guy's badge carried his first name.

"Hector," she began, placing the bag on the counter, "you look like a smart guy. Help me out, will ya?"

Heaping on the sex appeal, Jasmine leaned on the counter, making sure good old Hector got an eyeful. Christian veered left and down the nearest aisle, staying within earshot. He pretended to shop—as if he'd suddenly run out of yak fetus and chicken feet—but he kept an eye on the clerk. The guy's body language might give a clue if he lied or hid something.

Ironically, Jasmine had a real flair for bullshit and stacked it high without breaking a sweat. He found it increasingly difficult to chalk her skill up to a good thing.

"My ex-husband cheated on me. And now, when I'm trying to move on with someone new . . ." She smiled at Christian and gave a perky shrug, practically blowing him a kiss. ". . . the lying bastard is trying to ruin everything. He wants me back."

Hector gave him a skeptical sideways glance, probably wondering why the beautiful woman hadn't traded up in the process. Unable to hide all his bruises, Christian knew what he must look like. Jasmine milked the sympathy factor, twirling a strand of hair with her finger. The guy ate it up, watching every move she made.

"Some men have no idea the best way to treat a woman." Hector tweaked an eyebrow, making a move of his own.

Christian rolled his eyes and let out an exasperated sigh. *Yep, a real horn dog.*

"I thought by leaving the U.S. for a while, my ex would cool off, but he's hired a local thug to scare me," she went on, embellishing her story. "I don't want to report this to the police. It's a private matter. I just want it to stop."

Hector leaned closer, more engaged by the treasures underneath the white blouse than her sob story. "But what I can do for you . . . Miss . . . ?" The kid fished for a name, his English challenged.

"Jasmine. Please . . . call me Jasmine." She smiled and held out her hand. He took it, holding on too long. "First, that bastard left a calling card at my hotel room. What can you tell me about this?"

She dumped the contents of the carryon bag in front of the clerk. The black magic paraphernalia caught the guy's attention, but not half as much as the headless snake. It thumped onto the countertop. Hector gasped and jumped back. Christian knew the feeling.

Try this sucker with fangs, bro. Talk about changin' your shorts.

"This is . . . jararaca. Is deadly. Bad, very bad." Hector pushed his back against a wall, not taking his eyes off the snake. "You got the head? Where's the head?"

"Last night this thing came as a matched set, head and all. My ex-husband's idea of a prank." Jasmine cocked her hip and fought back her amusement as Hector regained control of himself. "See what I mean? The sick bastard's out of control."

"And the rest of this?" The guy peeled himself off

the wall and stepped back to the counter . . . slowly.
"What is it?"

"You tell me."

Hector kept one eye on the dead snake like it was
playing possum . . . without a head. With the other
eye, he searched through the remains of the make-
shift black magic altar and noticed Charboneau's
voodoo pincushion.

"This you?" the guy asked with another sideways
glance, noticing the family resemblance.

Guess all tourists looked alike to Hector.

"Yeah. Creepy, huh?" Christian spied a glimmer
over the clerk's shoulder.

A small pinpoint of light broke through the murky
shadows, coming from a peephole in a door behind
the counter. Movement. Someone eclipsed a light.
Given the location of the doorway and the frame-
work of the walls, Christian assumed the really nasty
stuff was under lock and key, reserved for special pa-
trons. But someone behind the door wanted a closer
look at the tourists. Most probably, the peephole had
been installed for that reason.

Hector shook his head. "I only sell this. Can't help
you, but someone set the evil eye on you, man. Nasty
curse."

"The doll and the altar materials look home-
grown," Christian said, "like someone built it from
scratch. It looks different than the merchandise in
your store. Can you tell me anything more about it?"
Christian asked.

The clerk shrugged. "Sorry. Maybe if you leave
your number. I can reach you, have someone call.
Leave this with me."

At this point, Christian knew he had few alternatives . . . and no need for a dead snake or a voodoo doll with a used up curse on it. He nodded and handed the kid his business card, saying, "We're staying at the Hotel Palma Dourada."

"Nice." Hector grinned and wrote the hotel on the back of the card. "Anything else I do for you?"

Since Christian was on a roll, he reached into his pocket for a copy of the photo of Rodrigo Santo. "Yeah, you ever see this guy?"

The kid took the photo and glanced down. A muscle under his eye ticked and his jaw flinched, a subtle move.

"That's the guy my ex hired to harass us." Jasmine pointed at the photo but shot a heated glare at Christian. She looked surprised by his direct approach, especially since she was supposed to do all the talking. Maybe she hadn't seen the light flicker through the peephole behind Hector.

More under control now, the clerk pursed his lips and shook his head. "No, man. I never see him." He handed the photo back.

It all happened so fast. Had he imagined the kid's reaction? He pressed. "Someone told us Bianca Salvador might know the man in this photo. Is she in?"

"No. Me, I only one here." He smiled, cool under fire now. Apparently, lying in a second language came naturally. "Bianca Salvador is old. She no come here . . . much. Her health no good, you know?"

"So you know all about this hinky inventory? I thought you only sold the stuff." Christian caught a moment of hesitation in Hector. "I mean, none of these jars are labeled. If Bianca Salvador isn't here, she must have the utmost confidence in your ability to serve her customers."

Hector narrowed his eyes, knowing he'd been set up, but without skipping a beat, conjured up a steaming pile of horse dung. *Fresh.* He must have learned a thing or two from Jasmine.

"Not me." Hector shook his head. "Mrs. Salvador works with customers by appointment only. She has different peoples who help, they have specialties. Each different. She match customer to these peoples. You see? That's how it works." He shrugged. "Besides, most peoples come here? They know what they want."

Was it his imagination or was this guy's English getting worse by the lie? If Christian had any hopes of getting insight from Hector on the local tribes, he quickly changed his mind. He wouldn't find an ally here. Christian forced a smile.

He'd just hit a roadblock named Hector.

Jasmine diverted the kid's attention. "Please . . . call me. I won't be able to sleep until I know what all this means." She pointed to the Macumba ritual gear on the counter.

"Yeah, I see." But Hector had his eye on Christian this time.

Guess he'd made an impression.

Bianca Salvador heard every word from the shadows of the storeroom in back. With aged hands, she touched the single strand of pearls at her neck, a gift from her deceased husband. It had become a nervous habit. Her fingers trembled. Through the peephole, she watched her nephew deal with the Americans. Now, she sat at the small wooden chair at her desk in the back. Her legs weren't what they used to be, especially after what she had seen in the stranger.

The tall man with emerald green eyes held her fascination. He had sensed her presence but did nothing to confront her. That intrigued her and may have drawn her out, but something else kept her hidden.

The stranger had the strongest aura she had ever seen—a complex combination of evil and goodness at constant struggle for control. He knew death all too well. The young man had survived it more than once. And somehow, he came to battle it again. Would he be strong enough to stand alone in this remote place on the edge of the world?

Bianca did not question how she knew this. She had been taught in the old ways, rituals passed from one ancestor to another. She had witnessed the power of the spirits, the Orixás in all forms, and trusted in her faith. She would not doubt her instincts now.

Her nephew opened the storeroom door and called to her. Hector had a bag in his hand. "I have to go out. Can you manage the store? It's getting late anyway. I can put the Closed sign out."

Hector's English had suddenly improved. A miracle. She shook her head. Her nephew liked to play games with foreigners, to watch them try and cheat him when they thought he didn't understand. But this time his game came in handy. He'd handled himself well.

But she knew of the reward money offered by the Americans. Word of it spread like a plague. A young man like Hector would be tempted to walk the line between easy money and the betrayal of his own people. And she had no faith in his judgment to do the right thing when a small fortune was involved. Before she answered him, Bianca waved him over, not hiding the concern on her face.

"Let me see the card that man gave you . . . and show me what's in the bag," she demanded, her voice stern. Like a stubborn child, Hector trudged closer and did as she asked.

The contents of the bag confused her. Some elements looked authentic, but most were products of someone's vivid imagination. A nonbeliever. Why would someone go to so much trouble to break into a foreigner's hotel room to plant a curse with no substance? Even worse, using a deadly snake meant whoever did this wasn't above killing to get what they wanted. Who would do such a thing . . . and why?

Since she had met the Asian woman before, she knew her story about an ex-husband wasn't true. Definitely inventive, but true? No. Bianca understood why they had come to her store for answers. She was considered a local authority on religious beliefs and rituals. Yet after seeing the contents of the bag, she feared for the safety of her people, especially the man in the photo. None of this bode well for him or his tribe. It would be far too easy to plant evidence against the local natives, especially if they had a face to blame. Her people would serve as a scapegoat yet again.

After setting the tote aside, Bianca read the name on the business card and softened her tone. "Please don't do this, Hector."

"Do what?" He shrugged and leaned against a corner of her desk, looking nonchalant. He forced a smile, but she knew better.

"The Asian woman deals in death. I have felt this more than once, nephew. I've met her before." Bianca touched Hector's arm when he rolled his eyes. "And her employer, Nicholas Charboneau, is much more dangerous. But that one with the green eyes, he scares me most. The Orixás have marked him. I hear their whispers. The evil may be too strong for him to overcome. Please don't get involved."

"You are a superstitious old woman." He leaned over to kiss her forehead, more eager to do what he intended. He pointed a finger at her. "Stay out of this."

"The spirits have spoken. Their whispers warn of evil and should not be ignored. Hector?" She cried out to her nephew, but the high-pitched tinkle of bells told her he had already left the store. He had no faith in the old ways. One day it might get him killed.

But Bianca had the power to intervene. With one hand, she clutched at her pearls. With the other, she grabbed a pen to make a list of what she would need. To summon the spirit, Ayza the Protector, she would need her most powerful magic.

The sun had dropped below the skyline, blazing liquid fire across the horizon. Neon lights competed with nature's show, a city getting its second wind. As beautiful as it was, he missed Chicago . . . and Raven. And to make matters worse, the stiffness in his body couldn't be ignored. He felt like crap. Lack of sleep and his narrow escape from the hit and run had taken their toll. Only thoughts of Raven made the pain tolerable. She had that effect on him, even across the world.

But when his thoughts drifted to Charboneau, Christian knew he was running out of options as he walked back to the hotel with Jasmine. Without the heft of the bag on his shoulder, the absence of it served to remind him how abysmal the day had gone.

Hoofing it gave him time to think, and he hoped the exercise would do him good. Since Jasmine hadn't said a word since the voodoo store, he assumed she felt the same until . . .

"You didn't let me do all the talking." Eyes forward, she kept the anger from her voice.

"Someone in the back storeroom was looking through the peephole."

"Yeah, I know."

Christian did a double take. Jasmine was full of surprises.

"Don't worry, little acorn. You played it right." She smiled, still not glancing his way.

Meandering like a shopper, she kept her eyes alert, even using the reflection in store windows to check behind them. She looked uneasy, a subtle nuance to her demeanor.

"What's up?" he asked.

"Don't know yet. I've had the feeling all day. Someone is tailing us, but they're too good to spot."

"You want to ditch 'em?" He kept his eyes straight ahead. "Out of principle?"

"No. We're heading back to the hotel. Let them feel in control . . . for now. When we need to shake them, we will." She smirked. "So what did you make of Hector?"

Christian gave her his point of view. The guy behind the register at Guia Do Espírito got a little testy after Jasmine dumped the dead snake and the Macumba gear on the counter. Who could blame him? Working retail brought out the worst in folks. And whoever kept their distance in the back stockroom certainly got his attention, but did the place warrant a return visit or a nighttime surveillance gig? He wasn't sure they had the time to spend on an operation that might not pan out. Hector didn't seem to know much.

Genotech Labs and Dr. Tyson Phillips were more likely candidates for pulling an all-nighter. Getting onto the grounds of the lab would be a major undertaking, with all the security, but maybe they didn't need to get inside the walls. Besides, if they got thrown in jail for trespassing, Charboneau would pay the price. Jasmine agreed with his assessment.

Yet he still needed a heads-up from a local, someone familiar with the tribes. By now Chief Zharan might have Duarte's surveillance recordings from the hotel. Maybe he would know Rodrigo Santo, the guy with the AK-47.

"So . . . you think we can trust Chief Zharan?" he asked Jasmine.

She stared at him, considering the question. To her credit, she didn't cut his throat for even thinking it. Sometimes, it was the little things that could perk a guy up.

"I am not a good one to ask about the trustworthy nature of anyone in law enforcement. Why?"

"We need a next step, and he may know Rodrigo Santo or whatever his real name is. Maybe Zharan can recommend someone who knows the local tribes." He shrugged. "And if Duarte had a line on Mr. AK-47, he would've already taken steps to bring him in for questioning or covered the guy's tracks. If we ask him right, Zharan might tell us which."

She pursed her lips and nodded. Neon lights and a dying sun reflected off the sunglasses she still wore. "It's worth a shot."

Christian pulled out Chief Zharan's business card from his wallet and placed the call. With a hand stuffed into his pocket and the other holding the phone, he leaned against a brick storefront on the street. Jasmine paced in front of him, eyes alert.

Zharan answered on the second ring. "Chief Zharan."

"This is Christian Delacorte."

"Yes, Mr. Delacorte. Please, what can I do for you?"

"I was wondering if you'd seen the hotel surveillance on the Charboneau kidnapping yet."

"Yes, I've reviewed it. How can I help?" Strong and self-assured, the chief's voice gave him comfort.

Jasmine crossed her arms and narrowed her eyes, trying to read Christian's reaction to what the chief had to say.

"It's my understanding that a man named Rodrigo Santo worked at the hotel and may have been one of the men who kidnapped Charboneau. Do you know this man?"

"No, I'm sorry. I don't."

"I doubt that Santo is his real name, but was Captain Duarte searching for him?"

Silence. Christian heard Zharan sigh on the phone. Jasmine started to pace again.

"Unfortunately, Captain Duarte had not pursued the matter. I'm sure he would have eventually, but rest assured, I have issued a bulletin for Santo. I will get to the bottom of this very soon."

The chief covered for Duarte like any good supervisor would, but he did not lie. Instead, he focused on the positive of the investigation moving forward. Christian respected him for that.

"Santo may have connections to a local tribe. Can you suggest someone who might know the area natives? I'd like to speak to them."

Jasmine turned and raised an eyebrow, waiting for Christian's reaction.

"Are you sure you want to do that, Mr. Delacorte? These tribes can live in remote areas, and generally would not tolerate being accused of kidnapping. I'm concerned for your safety."

"I appreciate that, Chief, but I have to do something. If you don't want to get involved, I understand. I can pursue this on my own."

It took a while for the man to answer. Christian didn't want to alienate him, but he'd follow this lead whether he got Zharan's endorsement or not.

"Actually, Mr. Delacorte, I do commend your perseverance. But my task force has already made several inquiries. I don't want to get your hopes up, but we've narrowed down some possibilities. Please don't do anything until you hear what I have to say."

Zharan shared what he had so far. The details were sketchy, but the new lead gave him hope. Finally.

"I'll call you tomorrow at your hotel when my men have something. We're working through the night." Zharan cleared his throat. "And Mr. Delacorte? Please know that I intend to oversee this investigation myself. Nothing will happen without me knowing about it."

"I appreciate that, Chief Zharan. Thank you." Christian ended the call.

Despite the good news of a fresh lead, he felt his belly twist into a tight knot. If Zharan hadn't taken Captain Duarte off the case, they would have been back to square one. Precious time had slipped through their fingers—all because of Duarte's clever stall tactics. Christian wondered if the captain had been paid to look the other way or was involved up to his eyeballs with a much larger pay out.

With a long waiting game ahead, he needed something to fill the void or he'd go stir crazy. He glared through Jasmine, not really seeing her.

"Zharan's working through the night. I think we oughta do the same. I've got an idea."

MILITARY POLICE HEADQUARTERS
DUARTE'S OFFICE

With his door locked and only minimal lighting, Captain Duarte sat at his desk. Only a skeleton crew worked the night shift in the detective's bullpen outside his office. He didn't want anyone else to know he stayed behind, with other things on his mind.

His jaw tight, Duarte pulled off the headset and stopped the recording. The telephone conversation between the American and his chief still played in his head.

The chief was building a case against him. No surprise. He had seen it coming long before today. But with Christian Delacorte knowing about Rodrigo Santo's role in the kidnapping, Chief Zharan would be forced to act. The American had tipped the first domino, leaving him no way out. *Damn it!* From here on things would get . . . complicated. With all the stealth and patience of a snake in tall grass, he would bide his time before he struck.

Timing would be everything.

"You were warned, Christian Delacorte," he whispered as he picked up the phone to make a call. "You can't say I never warned you."

CHAPTER 12

Dr. Phillips slipped away from dinner with his family to take the call in his study, pretending it pertained to a situation at the lab. He knew he might need the excuse later, something to tell his wife when he would leave in the middle of the night. Phillips hoped it wouldn't come to that, but his luck had been flushed down the toilet long ago.

He reported what happened on the tour with the Americans.

"I'm telling you, Delacorte's going to be trouble. He asked way too many questions. Good questions. And Jasmine gave me the creeps. She stared at me like I was food." Dr. Phillips gripped the phone, trying to mask his unsteady nerves. "I think they know what's going on."

"They know nothing." The man didn't hide his perverse amusement. "Don't ever play poker, my friend. You wouldn't be good at it."

"This isn't a game. I don't want—"

"I don't care what you want or don't want." *Venom. Pure venom.* "I have everything under control. It would be in your best interest if you remembered I'm the one in charge now."

Phillips shut his eyes. He was afraid to ask the question on his mind, but he had to know. "Are we still on for tonight? I think we ought to lay low for a while. At least until this is all over."

Even as he said the words, he knew what *all over* meant. Charboneau would be dead and his living torment would be worse. His new partner lived in Cuiabá, way too close for comfort.

Phillips had no doubt Charboneau was deadly, but at least the man had a certain civility. He knew the game of manipulation and how to play it, a much more tolerable bullet to the head. But the man on the phone wasn't encumbered by courtesy of any kind. Phillips had traded his seat in the frying pan for one in the fires of hell.

The silence on the phone made him swallow, hard. He waited for the man's answer.

"I have no interest in what you think, Doctor." A sickening throaty chuckle sent chills along the doctor's skin. "I've got Delacorte and his friend under surveillance. Focus on your end and you'll have nothing to worry about. Give my regards to your lovely wife."

The line went dead, but the man's threat came across loud and clear. Fear gripped the doctor's throat, the strain amassing to overload. If he made a mistake now, his family would pay the price. He knew he was in a no-win scenario.

But if presented with an opportunity to be free of all this, would he be man enough to take that chance?

Hard to tell how many tailed them. After comparing notes from earlier in the day, Christian and Jasmine knew it had to be more than one or two guys. Whenever they got a fix on a face, the target would blend into the crowd and they assumed someone new took his place. They had to start all over again, searching the crowds for familiar faces from place to place. No doubt about it, whoever pulled surveillance over the last few days knew what they were doing.

But would their surveillance setup handle what Christian had planned?

Leaving the hotel once again, he walked with Jasmine, a repeat of their first night in Cuiabá, out for dinner. They strolled down the main drag in front of the hotel as if they had the whole evening and weren't in a rush. Nearing a busy intersection, the light changed. Dressed in dark attire to blend in, they stood on the street corner amidst other pedestrians. Christian stared straight ahead but directed his comment to Jasmine on the sly.

"You know what to do?"

"Yeah, I'll meet you as agreed, but keep in mind . . ." She glanced toward him, issuing a personal challenge he knew would come. ". . . if one of us doesn't make it, I'm going it alone."

One of us? Christian smirked at the implication. Obviously, Jasmine planned not to fail.

"Don't you worry about me." He grinned. "We'll see who gets there first."

As the light changed, Christian took off left against

traffic and Jasmine went straight, hiding within the crowd. Being shorter and with dark hair, she would blend in. He dodged traffic and picked up his pace after crossing the street, then immediately ducked into a crowded restaurant with dim lighting. He had seen the café earlier on his walk from the Macumba store. With only furtive glances over his shoulder, he quickened his steps as he pushed through the dinner crowd, careful not to make a scene.

Catching the eye of a waitress, he asked as he kept moving, "You got a back way out?"

Christian followed where the young woman pointed and skipped through a hallway by the kitchen and out the back. Now he faced an alley, dark and murky. To his right, it led to traffic. To the left, it looked like a dead end, branching off in another direction. He didn't want to make a mistake and get boxed in. He jogged toward traffic and hailed a cab. No hesitation.

"Just drive," he ordered after slipping inside the taxi.

Crouching low in the backseat, he turned to catch a glimpse of a man running out of the alley, dressed like a local in nondescript casual clothes. The guy looked both ways, unsure which way to go. His frustration showed. Christian smiled and turned to face forward, staying low so he wouldn't make a good target.

He hoped Jasmine had the same kind of luck . . . only not as quick.

After riding in the cab for nearly twenty minutes, he gave the cabbie directions to drop him six blocks from the sidewalk café they had coffee earlier in the day. They were to meet on the southeast corner. He kept to the shadows, avoiding storefronts and street lamps. He walked the block and ducked into alleyways and side streets to make sure he hadn't been followed. Now he sat on a concrete step leading to a subterranean basement of an older hotel. His head barely visible, he craned his neck to keep an eye out for Jasmine.

Just when he thought he'd won the challenge, and began to worry that she'd gotten into trouble, a red Fiat Grande Punto pulled to the curb near him. The windows were tinted. He couldn't see the driver. Christian tensed. His hand reached for the Glock 19 and pulled it from the holster when the passenger side window rolled down.

"What took you so long? I got bored waiting, so I grabbed us some wheels. You like?" Not waiting for an answer, Jasmine demanded, "Hurry up. Get in. We ride in style."

The woman was certifiably nuts. She would get them arrested yet. Holstering his weapon, Christian shook his head and darted for the car. *Hell, he had carryon luggage bigger than this damned Fiat.*

At six-four, Christian had trouble getting into many vehicles. He yanked open the passenger door and shoved into the tight seat. Not wanting to call attention to the stolen Fiat, he didn't have a choice but to make it quick. He crammed into the front, his knees practically to his chin. Once inside, his head bumped the ceiling as he fidgeted to adjust the seat.

Jasmine couldn't hide her amusement.

"You see? Big is not always better." The words were out of her mouth before she had time to think. "On second thought, forget I said that."

"You did this on purpose," he complained, folded

into the future piece of scrap metal like a glassy-eyed sardine.

Jasmine didn't say a word. Her grin said it all.

Using only running lights for the last few miles, Jasmine drove the red Fiat with both hands on the wheel, using the curves in the road and the dense treeline to mask their approach to Genotech Labs. Without a full moon, the night closed in on Christian, pitch-black. The pale lights cast eerie shadows onto the road and the thick vegetation along it, playing tricks on the eyes. An animal darting into their path would cause serious damage. His companion leaned forward, peering through the windshield, searching the darkness for man and beast.

"We won't get much closer. I don't want to risk being heard. Sound carries out here," she reminded him. "I'm pulling over if I can find a good spot. We can walk the rest of the way."

"Works for me." Out of reflex, Christian reached for the gun in his holster. His elbow hit the door panel. "There's a dirt road to the right up here, just before the last bend. I remember it from our taxi ride."

He pointed, and Jasmine pulled onto the shoulder. The change in terrain caused the vehicle to lurch right and take a hard bump. Christian rammed his head into the ceiling.

"Hey, watch it." He ducked and shoved a hand onto the dash. "I'd like to make it out of this tin can in one piece . . . and without a brain tumor."

"Sorry." She pretended to care, but the smirk on her face told him otherwise. "You know, technically, you can't get a brain tumor from a little bump on the head," she mumbled loud enough for him to hear. "A concussion perhaps. Or maybe a little head-trauma-induced brain bleed."

Christian gritted his teeth and stared straight ahead, cursing himself for the lack of foresight to bring earplugs.

Jasmine followed a narrow dirt trail until she was satisfied the vehicle wouldn't be seen from the main road. She doused the lights, drove into the brush, and killed the engine. Christian flipped the switch for the interior lights so they wouldn't go on when the doors opened and jack with their adapting night vision. While he did, Jasmine reached into the backseat and pulled out her backpack. She unzipped a pocket and retrieved a small plastic bottle. When she opened the cap, the smell of it hit his nose in the tight quarters of the Fiat. Bug juice. The woman thought of everything.

"Put this on. You'll need it." She slathered it onto her face and exposed skin.

"I love the smell of DEET in the morning," he teased, doing his best Robert Duvall impersonation from *Apocalypse Now*. Jasmine gave him a sideways glance, clearly not a fan of movie trivia.

Once outside the car, they shut the doors, careful not to make a sound. Mosquitoes bombarded him in a thick swarm, but the bug juice kept most of them away.

"Stick to the treeline. Follow me." Jasmine gestured and led the way, shrugging into her backpack.

She traversed a gully, digging in her heels and leaning into the hill to keep her balance. Jasmine cut a path diagonally, then back down, heading for the valley floor. Christian followed, keeping the security floodlights of the lab in his sights through the dense trees, an orientation point. In the dark, tree limbs and shrubs slapped his pant legs and arms. He couldn't avoid them. But as they crept closer, the sounds of the night muffled to deathlike stillness. Any noise they made drew attention from the nocturnal wildlife. He sensed their eyes on him, quietly watching.

Eventually the terrain leveled and Christian became aware of water nearby, a convergence of several tributaries. The swirling water captured the moonlight on its surface, giving shape and size to the streams. Jasmine headed for the water and veered left to follow its confluence. Heavy brush grabbed at his boots.

Suddenly, a shrill cry ripped through the night. Pitiful and agonizing. Then it stopped . . . dead. Thrashing of water followed. In a swell, other animals screeched and yowled, rippling through the hillside.

What the hell was that?

The sound sent adrenaline coursing through Christian's blood as he dropped to a knee. A primal reaction. He peered through murky shadows toward the noise. Caught in the bluish haze of night, a large caiman surged down the creek. A distant relation to the crocodile, the creature undulated beneath the surface of the water, dragging its prey from the bank. In seconds it was over.

In this place, death came silent and in the blink of an eye.

Jasmine knelt by his side and waited for the quiet to return. "Let's go," she whispered.

Being in a valley west of the lab gave them cover from the security lights that strafed the night sky, but the refuge wouldn't last long. They angled toward the side entrance to the lab's med clinic and clamored up a small hill on all fours, staying low. Halfway up, he and Jasmine stopped to listen.

Dense humidity and the close vegetation intensified the heat. Every scratch and cut on his body ached, inflamed. And to exacerbate the condition, his clothes clung to his skin, damp from perspiration. Sweat trailed from his forehead down the side of his face. More trickled down the small of his back. When he wiped the back of his hand across his face and mouth, he got a serious taste of bug repellent. Nasty stuff.

Satisfied they were alone, Jasmine pressed ahead. "Last push, slow and easy."

At the crest of a hill, she scrambled into a thicket and slipped out of her pack. Christian knew the woman came prepared for a small skirmish, but mostly he wanted the water she carried in her pouch.

After she tossed him a bottle, he downed a large swig, cooling his throat. Jasmine quenched her thirst with another one, then retrieved night vision binoculars and shifted her focus to the west entrance of the heavily guarded facility. She assessed the situation.

"Two men at the gate. Armed," Jasmine muttered. She passed the binoculars to him for a look. "More walking the grounds inside. Hard to tell how many."

Christian rolled onto his belly and checked out the layout for himself.

"We could be in for a long night." He knew this would be a long shot. But after today's tour, something didn't feel right about this place. He trusted his instincts.

An hour stretched into two. And Christian's headache had returned with a vengeance. After sweating away the bug repellent, they applied more. Just when

Christian thought their efforts would be a lost cause, Jasmine punched him in the arm.

"We got company."

Headlights along the ridge flickered between the trees. The sound of a car approaching carried through the night. It turned into the main entrance to Genotech and made the switchbacks, heading into the valley. Dust kicked up in its red taillights.

On cue, the guards looked like they expected company. They raised their weapons and stood aside as the gate slowly opened. Obviously, they waited for someone they knew. Dressed in a white lab coat, Dr. Phillips joined them and paced, looking at his watch. A familiar gesture.

"He's working late," Christian whispered, binoculars up. "No rest for the wicked."

A dark sedan pulled into the light and stopped at the guard station. From the shadows in the vehicle, Christian saw more than one man, but not much else. Phillips leaned down to speak to the driver. The doctor gestured for him to pull ahead. After the car parked, two men in suits got out of the front seat. Christian caught a glimmer off the belt of one of the men when his suit coat opened. A badge reflected the light. The men were . . .

"Cops," Jasmine said as if she invented a new curse word. "I can smell them from here." She didn't have his clear-cut view, but there was nothing wrong with her senses.

Christian couldn't imagine why they were at the lab, yet something unfathomable gripped his throat. He held his breath, waiting.

Two men in handcuffs and disheveled clothes were hauled from the backseat. They stumbled and had trouble walking a straight line. Homeless vagrants. They were either inebriated or stoned on something far worse than alcohol. Christian took in the scene, peering through the night vision gear, his jaw tight.

"What's this all about?" Jasmine whispered as she reached for the binoculars again. "Are they doing what I think they're doing?"

"Yeah, I'd say Doc Phillips just got two more volunteers for his genetics research." He furrowed his brow. "Those two don't look like amateur drinkers either. Addicts fresh off the street."

But a bigger question lurked in the back of his mind. With cops handing over the unsuspecting men to Genotech as lab rats, who had given the order—Captain Duarte or Chief Zharan? All the hope Christian had for progress in his father's case suddenly got sucked away in a cruel twist.

Who would he trust now?

There was cruelty in silence, and isolation made it worse. Jasmine knew this firsthand.

Once they walked back to the hotel after ditching the "borrowed" Fiat, Christian withdrew into himself and ignored her attempts at conversation, which were few and far between on a good day. He tried to call his lover, but had no luck. His woman had cut him off from what little comfort she could bring long distance. On top of what they witnessed at Genotech Labs, he didn't need this personal blow. His frame of mind changed. He'd grown sullen and moody, not entirely his style.

Jasmine suspected that Christian's detective was not happy about the way he left the States, with another woman. And she had chosen to punish him in the worst way possible. Watching his pain only reminded her of words unsaid between her and Nicky.

A Kevlar vest gave protection from a bullet, but no such invention existed to safeguard the heart. Pity.

"Takin' a shower." Christian headed for his room. "G'night."

To him, she might as well have been a ghost. Jasmine wasn't sure she liked the new experience of being invisible to a man. He even tried to shut the door behind him—like mere wood could keep her out—but it remained open a crack.

She knew she should have followed his lead and washed off the disappointment, but her mind wouldn't stop. Anxiety mixed with adrenaline and kept her moving. She paced the living room and downed a shot of vodka. Nothing helped. When the shower rumbled in the next room, her eyes shifted to his door, more out of reflex. Yet once she caught a glimpse of Christian in the mirror of his dresser, she couldn't take her eyes away. The mirror angled toward the bathroom, giving her a spectacle she had no right to see.

Had she been hindered by a conscience, she might have exercised restraint. Instead, she stepped closer, figuring if she got caught, she'd slam the door and act offended by his display. But with his back turned, her voyeurism held no such consequence, so she indulged herself.

She narrowed her eyes and peered in.

Christian removed his holster and put away his gun. Heading for the bathroom, he stripped off his dark shirt and tossed it to the floor. The steam in the shower billowed, but the sound of it faded away. The stillness of the moment closed in. With his black undershirt stuck to his skin, he tugged it over his head—tanned skin and lean muscles with the hint of pale skin below the waistband of his pants.

Jasmine swallowed. Her cheeks flushed with heat. And the air-conditioning made the salt from her dried sweat prickle her skin.

When Christian unzipped, she should have turned away. Instead, she nibbled her lower lip and held her breath. Piece by piece the rest of his clothes hit the floor until he was down to his natural assets. His thick, dark hair curled at the nape of his neck. Broad shoulders tapered to narrow hips. A striking man.

Like father . . . like son.

Christian stepped into the billowing steam, his body moving behind the opaque shower door. She pictured hot streams of water rolling down his skin. But when her fingertips touched the doorknob, all she thought about was Nicholas . . . how it felt to lie with him. She shut her eyes, fighting back the lump in her throat.

Jasmine took a deep trembling breath and shut Christian's door. Left alone with her thoughts, she walked across the room and sat at the wet bar. Still smelling of insect repellent and sweat, she downed more vodka as images of Nicholas ran through her mind. As pathetic as she felt, she couldn't shake the blues.

So when Christian joined her again twenty minutes later, she welcomed the company.

"Thought you were going to bed," she said.

"Too wound up."

Barefoot and dressed in khakis and a navy tank, he brushed by her smelling of herbal soap. He looked exhausted. Dark circles had formed under his eyes. They made the bruising on his body look worse.

After taking a glass and a bottle of vintage Macallan single malt whiskey from the bar, he sprawled on the sofa and indulged. Jasmine recognized the pricey label. One of Nicky's favorites. It made her all the more sad. Without a word, Christian drank in the dark, not bothering to put on the lights, except for the one she had lit by the suite door.

Once again she'd been relegated to ghost status. To distract him, she asked the one question they had both avoided.

"At Genotech. Do you think Zharan is involved?" The thought punched her in the gut when she said it aloud. She had hopes Zharan might have a solution to finding Nicky. She needed to believe it. Now, she had no idea. "Or is Duarte acting alone?"

Jasmine knew Christian had been disappointed with the day, and she couldn't blame him. She felt the same. It took everything she had to keep herself together, the facade of self-reliance and strength.

"I don't know what to think. Not anymore," Christian mumbled, and took another gulp. She barely heard him.

"Are you in pain?"

He didn't answer, only waved a dismissive hand. Typical tough guy. She knew if he drank himself into oblivion, he'd be no good to her tomorrow. She went to her room and came back with something from her well-equipped first aid kit. She could take care of his physical pain—and maybe with a little bit of luck, he'd get a night's reprieve from his emotional scars. The best she could do.

"Here. Take these." She held out two pain pills. With the alcohol he'd consumed, he'd be dead to the world. He turned to ask what they were, but she anticipated his question.

"Pain meds. They'll dull the aches and you'll get some sleep. With no lingering hangover the next day."

She lied about the hangover. In his current condition, she gave no guarantees. Christian swallowed them both and washed them down with the last of his drink. Neither of them could afford the luxury of self-pity. She had to keep him focused and his mind open to possibilities. Jasmine joined him on the couch. Her eyes fixed on him, even though he didn't return the gesture. Christian was too absorbed in his thoughts. She had to get her point across before the drugs and alcohol took over.

"Duarte's a lone wolf. Can't see him being one in a crowd. And I can't imagine they staged Zharan taking over Nicky's case just for our benefit. It would serve no purpose."

Christian raised his head, his brow knitted as he considered her assessment.

She continued, "If Zharan continues to make progress, what harm would it do to follow his lead?" Jasmine found it hard to believe she had proposed working with the police, under any circumstance.

"You've got a point. Maybe we can see what tomorrow brings." He wiped his face with both hands, an attempt to clear the fog. "If he comes through with his promises, we may get an opportunity to fill him in. Otherwise, we keep our mouths shut."

She nodded. "Agreed."

Even though Christian continued to speculate about Genotech and the role of the men in handcuffs,

Jasmine only listened and offered little. She had to protect Nicky's interests the only way she knew how. When Christian's words started to slur and his beautiful green eyes grew droopy, she noticed the change.

"The pills have kicked in. Don't bother to argue the point." She stood and tugged at his elbow, pulling him to his feet. Not an easy feat. "Let's get you to bed, little acorn."

"I told you . . ." He garbled his words. "Don't c-call me that."

Christian nearly toppled to one side as he took his first steps.

"Whoa." He braced himself onto the back of the sofa, but when Jasmine stepped in to help, he grimaced. "Hey . . . do I smell DEET?"

"Give it a rest, Delacorte."

She rolled her eyes and forced his arm over her shoulder, gripping his wrist. With her other arm wrapped around his waist, she led him to his bedroom and flipped a light switch. Recessed lighting across one wall cast a pale glow onto the room. Surprisingly, Christian let her help as he rehashed his theories on Genotech. Perhaps in his condition, he had forgotten she was practically the enemy.

"They g-gotta be looking . . . for a new . . . addiction . . ." He yawned and moaned with the effort. Jasmine pulled back his bed linens with one hand, not trusting Christian to stand on his own. He kept talking. ". . . something to rewire a person's brain . . . without them knowing it. They'll wrap it up in a n-nice bow . . . s-saying it's . . . medicinal. A miracle cure for something . . . maybe depression. Hell . . . who knows . . . what the lasting effects w-would be . . . when you're talking ge-genetics. And . . . and they're using the natives of Brazil . . . as lab rats. What do you th-think?"

Even doped up, Christian and his sharp mind explored a trail that made logical sense. Jasmine had a feeling Nicky would be proud of his son, in a peculiar sort of way.

"I think you need to let it go. Let the pain meds do their job." She sat him on the bed, toppling onto him when he shifted his weight. When Christian collapsed onto the mattress, clothes and all, she covered him with the blanket.

After he shut his eyes, she resisted the urge to touch his cheek and brush back a strand of hair that had fallen across his forehead. In this light, he reminded her of Nicky when he was younger. She took a deep breath and blocked the image from her mind as she walked toward the door to his room.

"Good night, Christian." She glanced over her shoulder and saw him fast asleep. But when she turned off the light switch, he called out to her.

"Please d-don't," he pleaded. "Leave them on."

Of all people, Jasmine understood whatever demons plagued his sleep. She had more than a few of her own. She left the recessed lights on and shut the door.

Out of habit, Jasmine performed her duty and checked all the surveillance gear throughout the suite. No one had entered the room besides housekeeping staff. She closed the drapes and shut the place down for the night. Standing by the French doors, she touched the windowpane where the glass had been broken, the sting of her mistake fresh in her mind.

Her nightly ritual of self-torment.

If only Nicky had let her fight. That night, he shook

his head, a gentle no, probably trying to protect her. Didn't he know her job was to defend him? She would have died for him. If she had it to do over, she would have. Anything was better than living with regret. Nicky always said regret was a waste of time, but at this moment she indulged in it. Wallowed in it. Let it swallow her whole.

"Stay alive, my love," she whispered. After a long moment, she headed for her room by way of the bar, grabbing a bottle of vodka and a glass. All she wanted was a hot bath and enough mind-numbing liquor to mask the steady barrage of guilt she felt coming back to Brazil.

She had no choice, really. Her destiny, one way or another, was here . . . with Nicky.

Her thoughts never strayed from him. She saw him everywhere, felt her connection to him, especially here in this suite. The last place she saw him alive. She fought back a tear as his handsome face came to her again. His luscious, wicked smile. The violet blue of his eyes. His absolute masculinity. She smelled his warm skin on her pillow, even after the linens were changed. The man could stop her heart . . . and often did. She knew Nicky had branded her soul and left his mark. No one else would ever take his place.

In her room, she filled the tub with steamy water and sank into the suds, glass of vodka in hand. She stared across the bathroom, her mind lost in the past. Without much in her stomach, the alcohol worked through her muscles, leaving her legs and arms sluggish and heavy. And the hot water only intensified the sensation, making her feel weak.

Tonight, the ghosts of her past would visit. And without Nicky, she would be alone to face them.

* * *

Nicholas stared into blackness, his lungs heaving for air. Fear gripped him like a fist crushing his heart. He couldn't catch his breath.

"H-Help me."

Without warning, a flashbulb burst light across his cell, blinding him. *Pop . . . pop . . . flash.* Cowering, he shoved his back against the wall and held up a hand to shield his watering eyes. As he moved, a sick wheeze got worse, deep in his throat. A death rattle. Muscles in his chest burned, the heat blossoming from the pit of his stomach. It radiated through his arms and legs, making them feel sluggish and heavy.

"Can't b-breathe," he cried. "I c-can't . . ."

Flashes of light strafed the murky black as he clutched his shirt, tugging at the collar. Buttons popped off. His shirt tore. A bitter taste in his mouth forced him to spit, but the growing numbness of his tongue swelled his throat, constricting his windpipe.

"W-What h-have you . . . d-done?" A raspy whisper, his voice sounded more like a garbled gag. He heaved, but fought the urge to throw up. In his condition, he might drown in his own vomit.

Amidst flickering shadows and the throbbing light, he watched with strange fascination as the bars to his jail cell began to melt. Liquid silver drained to the ground and pooled near his feet. Even with the bars down, he was too weak to free himself. Then the silver took on life and slithered toward him like a nest of venomous snakes. With his lungs on fire and his gasping worse, he scrambled to get away with nowhere to go. The molten pool touched his heel and a massive numbing sensation invaded his body, crawling up his legs inch by inch.

"No . . . Nooo."

The realization hit him, hard. His hallucinations were drug induced. Wide-eyed, he found what was left of his evening meal and kicked the tin plate with his foot. Too late.

"P-Poi . . . son," he choked.

Somewhere in the dark, a man laughed. It grew louder and louder. His cruel cackle echoed off walls, magnifying his captor's degrading brutality. Nicholas slumped against the wall, his chest barely moving now. His violet blue eyes glazed over, milky white. Spittle ran down his chin as he thrashed, his body fighting for every breath.

Unmerciful laughter filled the room again, muffling his dying gasps, until there was nothing but eerie silence. Nicky no longer struggled for air. He had no need for it now.

Heavy footsteps on wooden stairs intruded upon the quiet, with no reverence for his death. A dark memory emerged, compounding the atrocity.

This couldn't be happening. Not again.

"Nooo!" The high-pitched scream, muffled at first, then grew louder. *"Nooooo!"*

Jasmine sat bolt upright in bed. Her heart pounded, jarring her rib cage and pulsing against her eardrums. She had never known such fear, not since she was a little girl. Her eyes searched the darkness to anchor her in the present, hoping to escape Nicky's dead eyes and the horror of her childhood terror revisited.

Hotel Palma Dourada. Haze from the moon filtered through the sheers of her hotel window, a feeble match against the neon city lights below. Still panting, she peered around the bedroom, orienting herself to time and place. Yet the vivid nightmare of Nicky dying meshed with the sound of her drunk uncle climbing the stairs, coming to her room in the middle of the night. Her childhood tormentor.

An icy chill raced across her skin, made worse by the cool sheen of sweat covering her body. Jasmine clutched at her blankets, pulling them close, but nothing warmed her.

In the dark, the graphic memory permeated every fiber of her being as if it were happening again.

Even fully awake, she couldn't shake it. A familiar whimper teased her senses. On countless nights, her screams muffled with her small face shoved into a pillow. Powerful hands took over and her uncle's brutish grunting and explosive release never summoned help. Abusive threats followed each violation, a whispered taunt meant only for her, even as she writhed in pain. And if she dared to resist, he inflicted greater punishment, invading her small body . . . and her very soul.

Paralyzed by her past, Jasmine recalled the greatest betrayal of all—the face of her hypocritical mother. The woman refused to help and left Jasmine to her fate—time and time again—with dull, beat-down eyes mixed with a hardened apathy. Her mother denied the transgression by dutifully washing Jasmine's bloody sheets without question, avoiding her child's accusing eyes.

"Fuck you, Mother!" Jasmine cursed the image of the woman's face. The hurt stung like a fresh wound.

After her bad dreams, Nicky had always heard her cries and held her until she fell back to sleep. Sometimes she tried to entice him with sex, but Nicky knew what she needed. He would pull her to his chest and stroke her hair with a tenderness she had never known. The beat of his heart gave her comfort, her ear nuzzled against his warm skin. And his deep baritone reassured her, the words less important than the safety of his arms.

Now, overwhelming grief filled her heart, as if the ordeal of his death had come true, an overdose of the Iboga root. Guilt mixed with profound regret and tears filled her eyes. Without thinking, Jasmine yanked back the bed covers and headed for Christian's room in the dark.

If she couldn't have Nicky, she would have the next best thing.

She crept to his bedroom, her eyes on the pale light spilling onto the carpet beneath his door. In her mind, she devised a story to tell him if he would wake, why she needed to talk. She turned his doorknob, careful not to make a sound.

After she slipped inside, she watched Christian, dead asleep. The combination of his exhaustion and the warm effects of alcohol and the pain meds had done their job. She doused the lights. Without a window in the room, everything went pitch-black. She listened for a change in his breathing. None came. He still slept.

Jasmine tugged at the black silk lingerie against her skin. The flimsy material was damp from perspiration, giving her chills. And to make matters worse, her body tensed with a rush of adrenaline. Slowly, she stepped toward his bed, her body shaking. When a tear rolled down her cheek, she knew she had to steady her nerves. She closed her eyes and imagined the beat of Nicky's heart, hearing the gentle pulse of it close to her ear.

In the dark, she pictured Nicky under the sheets.

In the dark, Jasmine would be with him . . . even if it were for the last time.

CHAPTER 13

Christian felt a soft hand touch his forehead, cool velvet across his skin. He smiled at the sensation as his mind filled with . . .

Raven.

In the twilight of sleep, before he opened his eyes, she stirred his body with little effort. Dream or not, heat rushed through him, churning his blood until his mind filled with nothing but her. Pale skin and enticing curves of flesh came to life in his memory.

"Oh, Raven . . . yes," he whispered, loving the sound of her name in the stillness.

Playing her favorite game of seduction in the early hours of the morning, he kept his eyes shut tight and moved under the sheets, surrendering to her. In the most vivid dream he'd had of her, Raven slipped under the sheets next to him. Cool air kissed the heat of his raging skin. She nuzzled her head into his shoulder, an arm over his chest. Her caress gave him comfort, but with the alcohol in his system, he wasn't in the mood for sleep.

"Come here, baby," he whispered. "I love you."

"Hold me." So faint, he barely heard her. "Just hold me."

With his eyes still shut, Christian rolled to one elbow and stroked the side of her face, pressing his lips to hers. She returned his urgency at first, her tongue entwined with his.

Slowly, he pulled down her lingerie and held her breast, licking her nipple. Slow circles turned into arousing flicks of his tongue. When she moaned, he heard the sound of it ripple through her body.

"No . . . please," she murmured. In a show of domination, Raven pushed him onto his back and nestled against his chest once more. "Hold me."

"I'm trying, baby." He rolled on top of her again, cradling her head with a hand, his fingers entwined in her hair. "You feel so good."

He wanted her . . . needed her.

Unable to play the game any longer, Christian opened his eyes, his mind reeling with the vividness of the dream. No lights. Raven had turned them off. That struck him as odd. Something was off. But in the darkness, even with the room spinning, when he caught sight of her faint silhouette under him, he had no interest in anything other than toe-curling sex.

Once more he pressed his lips to hers. And Raven cried out, "Christian . . . please. Stop. I only want you to hold me," she sobbed. "Please stop."

He fought to regain control, but his body still re-acted to her. His erection hammered against his pants, straining for release. He stared into the black-ness, replaying everything in his head. Why was he still wearing his clothes? *Damn it! What the hell?* In the dark, he couldn't see much, but a flash memory of the hotel room came to mind. And reality hit hard.

This wasn't Chicago. He wasn't home . . . with Raven. *Then who . . . ?*

He shoved the woman aside, his erection on a downhill slide, and reached for the lamp on his nightstand. Before he hit the switch, he knew what he would find. The light flooded the room and he discovered Jasmine lying beside him.

"Wha . . . ? Why are you . . . ?" Confusion muddled his mind. He suddenly felt nauseous. "I think I'm gonna be sick."

"Oh, God." Jasmine pulled away from him, avoiding his eyes. She wiped her cheeks and tugged at a lingerie strap, placing it back on her shoulder.

She'd been crying. Male ego aside, a woman crying in bed was never a good thing. And this wasn't a sudden outburst, faked to get out of her predicament. Seeing her like this brought Christian to his knees. Point a gun to his head and he'd still try to outmaneuver his assailant, despite the odds. But a woman in tears left him downright defenseless.

For the first time, she looked as vulnerable as a small child.

He opened his mouth to speak but nothing came out. On his back and propped on his elbows, Christian stared at Jasmine, his brain completely wasted. He didn't even know what to ask. Had he gone to her room, thinking she was Raven? What kind of lowlife asshole would do that? He looked around the room. When he saw his things, a whole new set of questions crowded his mind.

Jasmine stopped him cold by reaching out a hand.

The move caught him by surprise. Although Christian held his face stern, the rest of him melted like a double scoop of Ben & Jerry's Chunky Monkey on a hot Chicago sidewalk in August.

"Please don't . . . let me explain." Jasmine fought to catch her breath with her fresh onslaught of tears. "P-Please . . . this is not what you think."

"Lady, I'm not exactly doing a lot of thinking right now. You better help me out."

She told him about her nightmare, with each detail more shocking than the last. In her dream, she had witnessed her lover's death in all its cruelty. Dr. Phillips and his tale of the Iboga overdose had no doubt instigated her worst fears. She held nothing back, her face twisted in grief. Christian pictured the same happening to Raven and knew exactly how Jasmine felt.

"I needed to be held, like Nicky used to . . ." She stopped, her eyes avoiding his. "That is all. I didn't think you'd wake up." And with a fresh batch of tears, she admitted, "I've lost him, Christian. I think he might be dead. And it's my fault."

She looked so broken . . . and lost. Feeling alone for most of his life, he understood the need for emotional closeness, the touch of another human being. Her need to be held resonated with him. He rolled toward her and wiped a tear away with his thumb.

"This isn't your fault. I'm sure my father brought a lot of this on himself, with the life he chose." Christian lifted her chin and pulled back a strand of her hair. "Look, all you had was a bad dream. We're gonna find him."

Tears in fragile balance teetered on the edge. But her dark eyes brimmed with something else—hope.

"You really think so?" After he nodded, she let a faint smile influence her lips. "You realize this is the first time you have called him your father in front of me?"

Well, I'll be damned. Apparently, she'd been keeping track. Before he could stop himself, the words were out of his mouth.

"Tell me about him."

One in a million odds she would do it, but he had to take a shot. After a long moment of silence, Jasmine started to tell him about his father, the man she loved.

"Nicholas and I met for the first time in a jazz club in downtown Chicago. Believe me, I was not there to enjoy the music. I'd come to kill a man."

"You came to kill someone? Why?"

"The bastard had raped my younger sister." She looked away, fighting the tears welling in her eyes, but gravity won. "She was only nine years old . . . and I could not stop it from happening to her too." Anger flared, a distant hurt revisited. "My uncle had a gambling debt and she became part of the deal when he could not pay."

"You said you couldn't keep it from happening to her too. Did you . . . ?" Hearing the words aloud sickened him. He couldn't finish his question.

"You are a good listener . . . like your father." A sad smile came and went. "Yes. I endured my uncle for too many years. It was too late for me, but when I saw it happening again, I lost it. I tracked down the man who violated her. And I unleashed all the rage I had in me for all those years. To this day I don't remember much of the details, except for one thing. I remember your father."

She wiped her face with her fingers. It took her a moment to start again.

"He forced the blade from my hands and kept whispering in my ear. I don't remember what he said, but my heart slowed and I collapsed into his arms. He took me to his home, made me feel safe for the first time in my life. He bathed me, washed my hair, and put me into bed. A guest room. Never once did he take advantage of me. I became his lover much later . . . when I wanted and needed him far more than my next breath."

"And the police never came for you?"

"No. Nicky took care of that too. I had come for one thing and didn't care what happened to me afterward, but he became my witness for self-defense. He was so convincing, others came forward too. I don't know how he pulled it off, but he did."

"And you never saw your uncle again?"

"We crossed paths once more. On the day of his funeral. It seems my uncle met with an unexplained and most peculiar accident. Closed casket." This time Jasmine's smile stayed. "I've been with Nicky ever since."

Jasmine went on, telling him more about his father. He laid back against his pillows, trying to catch up on a lifetime missed. Although his father was nothing like him in the things that really mattered, like the ethics of right and wrong, he saw bits and pieces of himself reflected in her many stories and felt an eerie connection to a man he'd never met. And with her guard down, Jasmine took on a whole new level of beauty. She had a delicate shyness to her, an extraordinary innocence he found captivating. And with her as a portal, he saw his father in a different light.

How long they talked, he would never remember. Christian didn't exactly hold up his end of the conversation. He faded in and out to the sounds of her voice, his eyelids heavy. He found it hard to stay alert.

Jasmine touched his arm and smiled as he jerked awake.

"Huh? What happened?"

She shook her head. "You know, we are more alike than you know, Christian."

He fought the drugs in his system. It took him a moment to focus.

"I sense you have a place in your heart no one sees, perhaps not even you. I hide such a place from Nicky . . . and he from me. But lovers should not have such secrets from each other."

Jasmine had summed up his relationship with Raven. He had yet to open his heart completely to her, to trust Raven with his dark places.

"What if I never get my second chance with Nicky?"

"You'll get it, Jasmine. Hell, we both need a second chance." He sounded more confident than he felt. "Sometimes I think we get one defining moment to say what's in our hearts. And if we don't grab it, that moment rolls by on a one-way trip."

He could tell by the look on her face, she wondered the same as he did. Had that opportunity come and gone? They both had too much unsaid and too much undone with the ones they loved. After a long silence, Jasmine rolled off his bed and headed for his door. She turned for one last look. He had no idea what she was thinking.

"You okay?" he asked.

Jasmine had a pitiful expression on her face, a depth of sadness uniquely her own. Without a word, she slipped through the door and shut it behind her. Christian stared at the closed door for a long time, until the pain meds washed over him in a second wave. He slumped back onto the pillows and shut his eyes, pulling the sheets to his chest.

"No . . . guess I'm not either."

THE NEXT MORNING
DAY SEVEN

Barefoot and dressed in faded jeans with a white T-shirt, Christian stumbled from his room with the worst hangover in the history of the known world. Why had he been so worthy? He could have done without the experience. Not even a quick shower did any good to rake the cobwebs from his brain. He leaned against the doorjamb to his room to steady himself and dragged fingers through his damp hair bleary eyed. Every hair follicle ached to the touch. Even his teeth hurt.

And to compound his misery, the sun glared through the windows to the suite, nearly blinding him. He squinted and opened his mouth to speak, but stopped short when he saw Jasmine. Images of her in his bed catapulted through his mind, most of them a blur.

He felt the rush of heat to his cheeks and neck.

"Did anything happen? I remember . . ." He almost clarified his point, but stopped shy of full disclosure. "Well, not sure what I remember. Maybe it was a dream."

"Admit it, you fantasized about me. Plenty of men do, my love." On the sofa, she sipped her coffee with feet up, winking over the brim of her cup. Her usual attitude doled out in heaping doses, except for a hint of uncertainty in her eyes. Jasmine looked as if she were holding her breath, waiting for his reply.

A strained moment passed. Christian chose the path of least resistance.

"Sorry to burst your bubble, but there's only one woman who occupies my three pounds of gray matter these days." His thoughts turned to Raven. "And at the moment, she's not taking my calls."

Jasmine set her coffee down and gave him her full attention. "Funny. I never thought a man used his brain with a woman." She smiled, but the gesture quickly faded. "Your detective could use a lesson in forgiveness. Love should not be discarded so lightly."

An awkward silence.

"I know you mean well," he said, "but stay out of my personal life . . . please."

A throbbing pain pulsed over his left eyebrow, but damned if he'd let her know how much he hurt. Catching a whiff of coffee, he walked over to the wet bar and poured himself a cup. Black.

"Thank God some things are no-brainers," he muttered, and took a gulp.

When the hotel phone rang, he winced at the shrill sound, but Jasmine got up to answer it.

"Hello?" She raised her chin and turned her eyes on him. "I see." After a long moment she added, "No, that'll be fine."

When she hung up the phone, Christian asked, "Who was that? You look like we got trouble."

Jasmine took a deep breath. "Yeah, the worst kind."

Without explanation, she hurried to her bedroom. He heard her rummaging through her things, but she rushed out, heading for the door.

"Hey, where are you going?" He narrowed his eyes. "Who was that on the phone?"

"I know we've had our issues with trust . . ." She smiled as she stood in the open doorway. A strange, sad smile. ". . . but this time, you're gonna have to trust me. Some things you just have to do alone." Jasmine left, shutting the door behind her.

What the hell did that mean? *Do what alone?*

After she left, Christian downed his coffee and set the cup on the bar. He rushed to his room, grabbing the Glock and his wallet, his mind racing. Jasmine wasn't going anywhere without him. Too risky to fly solo. He thought she understood that. But when he got to the suite door and swung it open, he stopped cold.

His jaw dropped. Standing in the hall, with her arm raised, ready to knock, was. . .

"Raven," he whispered.

This time she wasn't a dream.

CHAPTER 14

In the quiet of the morning, speaking Raven's name gave Christian the feeling of . . . home. Wide dark eyes held him in place and the smell of her perfume mingled with the warmth of her skin. *Intoxicating.* His eyes, his senses, took everything in. A lump wedged in his throat.

"Christian." Raven took a guarded step toward him, unsure how she'd be received. She held her breath, then spoke, "I had to come."

Her voice shot tingles over his skin.

Before she said another word, Christian wrapped her in his arms and lowered his lips to hers. Nothing felt so right. He forgot all the reasons for her not to come to Brazil.

Now, none of them mattered.

Dr. Phillips stared at himself in his bathroom mirror, having trouble with the Windsor knot in his tie. He'd done it a million times, but today his nerves were shot. Anxiety raced through him like an electrical charge. He had a bad feeling about today.

"Damn it." He yanked the knot apart again and undid the top button of his white dress shirt to get some air.

His predicament had come to a head. He couldn't go back to change things, and moving forward left him wondering: Move forward to where?

Head down, Phillips shut his eyes and flattened his palms on the bathroom counter. Taking deep breaths, he let the sounds of his family downstairs wash over him, hoping their normalcy over the breakfast table would calm his raw nerves. When he looked up, he caught the movement of a dark shadow behind him . . . in the mirror.

"What the hell?" He turned around, eyes wide. Abject fear gripped his throat. "What are you doing here?"

Jasmine Lee inched closer. Her eyes never strayed from his. In a low seductive voice she whispered, "Bet you wished you had added security now, don't you, Doctor?"

His next breath wedged deep in his throat. He swallowed hard. When she reached for his tie, Phillips tensed, grounded where he stood. Like staring into the hypnotic eyes of a cobra about to strike, he couldn't turn away . . . or move. His feet were rooted.

"I suppose you are wondering how I knew where you lived." Charboneau's so-called bodyguard tugged at his tie, drawing it tight around his neck. A slow, deliberate move. "You'd be surprised what I know about you, Doc. Mr. Charboneau makes it a habit to know his associates."

"Please . . . my family is downstairs. Don't hurt them," he begged, despising the tremble in his voice.

"That is entirely up to you, as it's always been." Her voice was low and throaty.

Jasmine released the tension from the tie and initiated the knot, not looking at her handiwork. She kept her gaze drilled on him like a weapon. Even though he outweighed her, something in her eyes told him that he wouldn't stand a chance if he resisted.

"Tell me where they have Nicholas Charboneau." She wrapped the wide end of his tie over the narrow part, tugging at his neck. When he didn't answer fast enough, she added, "Surely your family means more to you than keeping their secret."

"Please . . . don't do this," he begged. "I don't know who is pulling the strings or where they're keeping Mr. Charboneau. They threatened to kill my family if I didn't cooperate. If I knew more, I'd tell you. I'm not a brave man. Please believe me."

"Oh, that, I do believe, Dr. Phillips. Go on." She pulled one end of the tie under and over, tucking it through a loop. Her eyes never drifted from his.

"Some time back I started getting phone calls. The kind that made my skin crawl. He threatened my family and sent messages home with my kids. It made me sick." Phillips grimaced. The veins at his temple pulsed. "I've never met the guy. All I know is he's local and has a Brazilian accent. He calls me. Communication is a one-way street. I don't have a number for him."

"How is this man connected to Santo . . . the one who took Nicholas?"

"I told you the truth when I said I didn't recognize Santo. I have no idea who he is."

She tensed her jaw, not happy. "And the clinic? How did he get you to add the medical facility if you never met? Mr. Charboneau didn't know about it . . . or approve the capital expenditure." Jasmine finished the knot and tightened it, yanking him forward to make her point. She cut off his air with a twist of her fist around the tie. "You better start making sense, Doc."

"Before I got the first call, someone contacted me asking to verify my passport. They said they were from the government and the inspection was just a formality, standard protocol. They wanted to see not only my passport, but for every member of my family." His eyes glazed over, bitterness reflected in them. "Several men in suits came to my office at Geno-tech, part of the arrangement. When I presented our documents, they confiscated them without giving me a reason. After that, the calls began. Now, even if I arranged for my wife to visit her parents back in the States, I couldn't get them to safety."

A voice muffled outside the bedroom door.

"Honey, your breakfast is getting cold," his wife called from downstairs. "You better get moving."

"Oh, God." His heart thrashed in his chest.

In reflex, Phillips pulled away from Jasmine's grip. His back hit a wall, giving him no place to go. Anticipating his move, she swept a foot under him and toppled him to the floor, using the tie for leverage. His hip hit the tile and sent a jolt of pain down his leg.

"Arrghh."

Before he knew where it came from, Jasmine held a knife to his throat and used his dress tie to pin him down. She shoved a knee to his chest. Her long hair hung over him, shadowing her menacing face.

His lungs burned and his face rushed with heat. She cut off his air, choking him.

"You make a move like that again . . ." She glared with fierce eyes. ". . . you're gonna mess up my tie. And that is no way to repay my . . . good deed."

The tip of the blade stung his neck. A warm trickle rolled along his jaw and the coppery smell of blood filled his senses. *Oh God, she's cut my throat.*

"Don't . . . p-please." He forced his arms to the floor, raising them above his head. A complete show of submission. "Just don't . . . hurt my . . . family."

He barely got the words out. No air.

"This silent partner of yours. He must be linked to the police." She loosened her grip on his tie so he could breathe. "We saw you take two homeless men into your lab last night, with the help of local cops. Guess that little point slipped your mind. What else are you leaving out, Doctor?"

Damn it! The man had told him Delacorte and Lee were under surveillance and everything was under control. He should have been warned when they lost them. Phillips saw where he ranked in priority. Rock bottom. All of it was coming undone. And he'd be caught in the middle . . . if he survived.

"Look, I told you. He threatened to kill my family. I couldn't—"

"And what do you think I'm going to do? You think this is a social call? You think I came to shop with your sweet little wife? Attend a PTA meeting?" She pressed on the blade and drew more blood. The necktie tightened, worse than before.

"Okay . . . okay." He gagged. "The guy is connected all over town. He knows everything. And yes, I think he's with the police, even though I can't confirm it. The bastard has you and Delacorte under surveillance."

"Had us under surveillance," she corrected with a wicked smirk. "We ditched his watchful eye last night to do the reconnaissance at Genotech. And as you can see, I avoided his scrutiny this morning to pay a call on you and your lovely family. In case you hadn't noticed, no one is safe."

Jasmine moved the edge of her blade down his cheek. His raspy breath filled the inside of his head, along with the throttling punch of his heart. When she traced the knife under his eye, a tear rolled across his skin and into his hair.

Oh, God . . . No!

"Now you're gonna tell me what's really happening at the lab . . . and at that clinic. And believe me, I'll know if you leave anything out." She pressed her knee into his chest. "Start talking."

To Jasmine, the setting was as foreign as Brazil, another place for her to feel like an outsider. Dense trees surrounded the split-level home. Suburbia, Brazil-style. Sunlight danced through branches and along pale yellow stucco walls and a red terra cotta roof. A stone terraced walkway led to the front door, a massive portico bordered by flowers.

The picture of domesticity.

She watched the Phillips villa for a long while after his wife took the kids to school with a stop for groceries after. Jasmine overheard the woman's plans when she told Phillips on the front driveway. She had a pretty good idea of the family routine.

All looked normal, whatever that meant.

Jasmine had stuck around to see if the good doctor

would stir things up, call for reinforcements. Phillips had plenty of time to make contact and report the incident with her, but no cops showed. Unfortunately, his connected partner remained a mystery.

Her gut instinct? Phillips had been a scared little man, more fearful for his family than himself. Commendable but pathetic. He would have told her anything he knew, and made up the rest, if he thought she'd buy it. No doubt the man behind Nicky's abduction knew this about Phillips and kept him in the dark.

But the meeting with the doctor hadn't been a total waste of time. At least now she knew more about Genotech, the plans beyond Nicky's original purpose.

Jasmine watched Phillips leave his home. He'd changed shirts, favoring a pale blue one without bloodstains. The man could have taken a lesson from her on how to tie a Windsor knot. After he took off in his car, presumably for work, she eventually came out of hiding in the park across the street. She stuck to the treeline and headed through the greenbelt, away from the quiet residential neighborhood.

She glanced at her watch and wondered about Christian. A lazy smile softened her face as images of last night in the dark stirred her mind.

"Raven Mackenzie," she whispered. "You are a lucky woman."

Such memories only reminded her of Nicky. And the heartache of regret returned with a vengeance. She had to remain focused—and strong—for him. She'd catch a cab soon and head back toward town to the Guia Do Espírito.

Hector hadn't been truthful and held something

back. She sensed it. And without Christian's interference, or his damnable ethics, she'd get her answers using her own methods. As she told Delacorte, some things had to be done alone. This time the gloves would be off.

Nicky's life depended on it, and nothing else mattered to her. *Nothing.*

The first time they made love, Raven couldn't get enough of Christian. Nothing was too hard or too fast for her. His urgency only matched her driving need. As much as she gave herself to him, she let her body demand from him in return.

Christian filled her now, thrusting into her, slow and deep. His skin glistened with a sheen of perspiration. The weight of his muscular body intensified his surges.

"I love you, Raven," he whispered in her ear. ". . . missed you."

His warm breath on her neck sent a ripple of chills over her body. He had that effect on her. Christian touched her in every way.

As he took her earlobe between his lips, she cried, "I love you too."

The words came out too intense, more a cry of surrender. But when his tongue penetrated her ear, mimicking the steady pounding motion he made inside her, she lost it completely.

Oh, God!

Raven wrapped her legs tight around his hips, using him as leverage to move. The rush of an orgasm gripped deep in her belly and jolted through her body, wave after wave. She flexed the muscles of her legs, toes curled in pure ecstasy.

"Oh . . . Christian," she moaned. Raven held onto him, not letting go. *"Ahhh."*

She felt his body react. An urgent release. Christian arched his back and spilled into her, shuddering in violent swells.

"Aarrgghhh." He jerked in a torrent of spasms, every shove another gift to prolong her pleasure. "Oh . . . Raven."

After his body quieted, he collapsed onto her. Cradling her in his arms, Christian pulled her to his chest and rolled onto his back. He covered her with bed linens and kissed the top of her head, stroking her hair with his fingers.

In this place, Raven had lost all track of time. The flight to Brazil had been a grueling overnighter, especially not knowing how Christian would react to her surprise visit. Now, the rhythm of their panting filled the room, coupled with the musk of sex. And she had her answer. She lay in the crook of his arm, rapt in his love.

"I feel so lucky to love you." His deep voice rumbled through his rib cage, teasing the ear she had pressed to him.

"It's more than luck, Christian. We're . . . blessed." Raven smiled and nestled her cheek to his chest. "It's like I've spent my whole life waiting for you to come into my life. I've never felt so loved."

After a long moment she closed her eyes and listened to the gentle pulse of his heart. A sweet steady rhythm. When she felt certain Christian had drifted off to sleep, she joined him, forgetting the horrible reason that had brought her to Brazil.

Every moment with Christian was a precious gift,

like they were living on borrowed time. No matter what tomorrow would bring, she would have this moment alone with him. It might have to be enough to last a lifetime.

In broad daylight, any move Jasmine made held the risk of being spotted by a surveillance team. She had taken great pains to make sure she wasn't followed from the Phillips villa. A half block from Guia Do Espírito, she would soon have what she wanted. Private time with Hector.

Hiding in an alleyway down the street from the Macumba store, she searched the street, her eyes vigilant. No one stood out. No one watched her. Moments earlier she'd tried the back of the shop, hoping an alley might give her anonymity from the street, but the door was locked.

Jasmine didn't want to break in and find the store had customers or other witnesses. And she couldn't afford to be arrested, not now. With her eyes searching the street and every car, she made her final move and meandered onto the sidewalk, heading for the store. Posing as a shopper, she kept an even pace, not wanting to draw attention.

When she got within a few feet of the storefront, she heard a screech of tires behind her and turned in time to see two unmarked cars pull to the curb. Two sedans. One gray, one dark blue. Dressed in similar colors, stern-faced men in suits emerged from the cars and moved toward her.

"Hands up. Now!" one man yelled. He held her at gunpoint while another man raced closer, his weapon drawn. "Do as I say, Ms. Lee."

They knew her name. Slowly, she raised her hands. Her eyes searched the vehicles, knowing she'd soon find a familiar face. She recognized the last man to get out of his car. A slow smile emerged, having nothing to do with humor or a warm greeting.

"Captain Duarte. I wish I could say it's a pleasure to see you again."

The captain returned her gesture, his dark eyes relishing the moment.

"The feeling's mutual, Ms. Lee." Duarte's lip twitched into a faint sneer. "Check her for weapons and be thorough."

As one man patted her down, another retrieved her weapons—a gun and a knife. With her hands behind her back, Jasmine felt one of Duarte's men slap handcuffs to her wrists. She could have fought and made a run for it, but a part of her wanted to discover the truth only Duarte would know. Jasmine tensed her jaw and gave in to their demands.

But before she got shoved into one of the unmarked cars, Jasmine caught a motion from the corner of her eye. Hector's face peeked out from the shop window. He cowered in the shadows, barely letting her see him. Yet his move looked deliberate.

Jasmine smiled at the young man, appreciating the irony.

Only a moment ago, she wouldn't have shown Hector any mercy in demanding what he knew. Now she prayed he'd take pity on her and call Christian, to let him know what had happened to her.

It might be her only hope.

CHAPTER 15

By the looks of the pretty Asian woman, being hauled off in handcuffs by a stone-faced cop was commonplace in her world. She smiled at Hector, as if she flirted without a care. The same could not be said for him.

He ducked back into the shadows of the store window, careful to avoid being seen. Of late, Hector had heard stories about the military police—stories of the missing and unaccounted for—men arrested and never seen again.

"What's happening?" Aunt Bianca called from the back storeroom. The door stood open. The old woman had been restocking her inventory and dusting the shelves, a daily ritual.

"Nothing. A driver was careless," he lied, barely looking over his shoulder. She had probably heard the screech of tires out front. "He almost hit a car when he pulled from the curb. There's nothing to see now."

Hector walked back to the counter, his thoughts in a jumble. After a long moment, he knew what he had to do. He sorted through his wallet for the business card, searching for the man's name. Christian Delacorte. He claimed to stay at the Hotel Palma Dourada. Hector remembered writing that on the back of his card.

"If you can afford such accommodations, you can surely toss some coin my way," Hector muttered under his breath. And the American had no idea he knew about the reward for information on the rich man recently kidnapped from the hotel. Word about money traveled fast in his town.

Hector slid behind the counter and found his aunt working in the storeroom at her desk in the back. He kicked away the wooden block that held the door open. It shut with a hiss. He didn't want to take the chance of her overhearing his plans. She wouldn't like what he had in mind, but he had to do what he thought best. She'd done so much for him, this might be his way to repay her.

Hector looked up the phone number for the hotel and dialed it, glancing over his shoulder again to watch for Aunt Bianca. She had a habit of turning up when he least expected it. He grinned as he dialed, smelling the opportunity practically dumped on his doorstep. Times like this, he almost believed in the spirits his aunt revered. Fate had indeed played a hand.

He would be a fool to ignore the Orixás now.

Sitting at her desk, Bianca looked up from her inventory work, hearing the low murmur of a familiar voice. It puzzled her. She hadn't heard the customary ring of the bell over the front door, warning her a client had entered the premises.

Who was Hector speaking with?

When she turned, she noticed the storeroom door had been shut. The boy thought he fooled her with his maneuverings. Many times Hector claimed her age had something to do with her forgetful memory, but she knew better. When she chose to act her age, she did so, but always to her advantage. They played this game, each by their own rules, only she was much better at it than Hector.

Bianca crept toward the door and peered through the peephole, on tiptoe. Instead of clutching the pearls at her neck, she held a charm at the end of a chain—a recently conjured talisman. She had prayed for Ayza the Protector to keep Hector and her people safe. And guide the stranger Delacorte.

With the talisman in her grasp, Bianca pressed an ear to the door, listening. She knew Hector would not approve, but at her age she had earned the right not to give a damn.

No woman had ever worn him out, through and through, like Raven Mackenzie. In the dim light of his bedroom, he opened his eyes and embraced the moment of complete exhaustion. Wrapped up in Raven, he felt her arm over his chest and a leg entwined in his. The faint scent of her perfume played second fiddle to the sweet fragrance of her skin.

Although he felt the stirrings of another erection and wondered if he'd be up to the challenge, mostly he wanted to hold her. And listen to her breathe as she slept.

For many years he felt alone in his grief. Death had invaded his life and taken hold of it. Raven made him see how much he had given in to the loneliness. She made him want to reclaim his life and so much more. She hadn't been wrong.

He kissed the top of her head and laced his fingers through her hair.

"Oh please . . ." she muttered. "Don't move. Anyone ever tell you? You make an excellent pillow."

"Always happy to be of service." Christian smiled, breathing in the scent of her hair.

"Oh, now that you've brought it up. Have I ever told you? You've really got that whole servicing thing down. Even better than the pillow thang."

He heard the grin in her voice as she drew a finger over his nipple, making it hard. His bare skin erupted in goose bumps. The really good kind.

"Speaking of bringing it up . . ." Christian pulled Raven to his chest, her naked body pressed against him. "You keep up the foreplay and you're gonna get a rise out of me."

"And this is a threat . . . how?" she teased, nestling her chin on his chest. Her dark eyes stared into his. "You think I can't handle another go? I've got the ovaries to tackle anything you can dish out, bucko. Watch me."

With a glimmer of the devil in her eye, Raven rolled on top and stared down at him, her legs between his. His body responded to her move. No doubt about it, he was up for the challenge.

"Love to." Christian cupped her face in his hands, aroused by the warmth of her skin next to his. He kissed her long and hard, his tongue finding familiar territory. With her breasts pressed to him and her hips writhing between his legs, he wasn't sure he could hold back. His hands grasped her body, never getting enough of her.

But like a quick douse of ice cold water, the phone on his nightstand rang, loud and shrill. His heart leapt at the abrasive noise.

"What the hell?" For a split second he thought about not answering, but Chief Zharan had promised to get in touch. He kissed Raven again, saying, "I gotta take this."

"Sure." She nodded and rolled off him, drawing a hand through her hair.

"Hello?"

"Is this Christian Delacorte?" A low quiet voice.

Christian didn't recognize it. Whoever it was sounded nervous and about ready to hang up.

"Yes. Who's this?"

"Hector Salvador. You remember me . . . from the Guia Do Espírito?"

Christian sat up in bed, a sudden jerking motion. The kid had the same last name as Bianca Salvador. A relative? Interesting.

"Of course I remember. What's going on, Hector?" He tried to keep his voice calm and steady. Raven sat up beside him. Her eyes were fixed on his, reading into the importance of the call.

"I have information you might find useful. Very timely, in fact." Hector let the silence build between them. The kid knew how to milk the moment. "Your pretty Asian lady friend might consider my call to be . . . beyond price."

Hector was fishing for money and making no

bones about it. And his English had improved . . . immensely. A regular scholar.

"But I bet you have a price in mind. What do you want, Hector?"

"I am a struggling student, working part-time at my aunt's store. In this economy, we could use the money. Perhaps what information I have would be worth your charity, to support my . . . education."

"Call it what you want, Hector. Extortion is no way to fund your college tuition," he said, knowing he had to play this right. "Innovative, yes. Smart? Not so much."

"This isn't only for me. I am motivated for a number of reasons."

"Who are you kidding? Your motive is measured in U.S. dollars, nothing more." Christian found it hard to hide his skepticism.

He knew when he was being played. The kid spoke so low, he barely heard him. Bianca probably stood within earshot, behind a nearby peephole. Or maybe Hector made the call with her complete blessing. Christian shook his head.

"I'm not paying anything until I hear what you have."

"That means I have to trust you."

"Smart kid. See? You're learning already. The Hector Salvador college fund is working wonders." He switched the phone to his other ear and glanced at Raven. She leaned closer and touched a hand to his shoulder, a show of support. "If you have something good, we'll negotiate your college fund. You need a translator for that?"

"No . . . no, I don't."

"Didn't think so. What's up, Hector? Spill it."

Silence. Christian pictured him pondering his situation. He all but heard the slick wheels of Hector's brain working, greased by the promise of U.S. dollars. Or maybe he was conferring with his aunt. After a long moment he got back on the line.

"Your lady friend . . . she was arrested outside the store . . . on the street. Not ten minutes ago."

Christian bolted upright, his eyes narrowed.

"Jasmine arrested? By whom? Did you recognize the cop?"

"Cops, but they were led by one man. She called him Captain Duarte. Your friend seemed to know him, and she didn't look pleased to see him. He took her away in handcuffs. Two unmarked sedans full of his men. One gray. One dark blue."

Now he took a deep breath and shut his eyes. Jasmine had warned him some things were best accomplished alone. After he saw Raven at the suite door, he assumed she had meant accomplished by him. Now, he understood what she really had in mind. Jasmine saw this as her opportunity to go it alone, knowing he'd be . . . occupied.

Damn it!

Now he had no way of knowing where Duarte had taken her. The bastard had no grounds for an arrest, at least none that Christian knew of. If she weren't being held at police headquarters, he'd have no clue where to look. He might need someone on the inside.

"Hector, I appreciate your help. If all this works out, I promise you I'll be plenty generous. You hear anything else, call me."

Before the kid answered, Christian hung up the phone.

"Bad news." Raven didn't phrase it as a question.

Christian tossed aside the bed sheets and headed for the bathroom, his brain working on some semblance of a strategy. Without looking back over his shoulder, he answered, "Yeah. Get dressed. Jasmine's in trouble."

Dressed in khaki shorts and a camo green tank and hiking boots, Raven crossed the living room to listen to Christian on the phone in the bedroom. He tried to get Captain Duarte on the line, but no one at police headquarters claimed to know his whereabouts. She knew a cover-up when she heard it. Cops across the globe protected each other's backsides, the universal code of her brothers in blue. And by the sounds of it, Christian had his bullshit detector on high gear. With voice raised, he didn't appear to be making much progress. She gritted her teeth, catching glimpses of him through the crack in the door.

And what was up with this grand palace of a penthouse suite? Christian was used to this lifestyle, but the pretentiousness made her uneasy. The whole thing was bigger than her bungalow in Chi-town. And with the second bedroom door closed, she didn't have to guess about Jasmine taking up residence there. That made her downright mad. She trusted Christian beyond a doubt, but Charboneau's version of a female Kato was another story. The Asian beauty grated on her nerves.

No, she didn't think much of Jasmine Lee, but Christian had obviously formed a bond with the woman while searching for his father, or else he would never have lived in such close quarters. Whether she agreed with it or not, she had to respect his feelings. Besides,

Duarte sounded like a loose cannon. And a rogue cop made a deadly enemy.

A soft knock at the suite door caught her attention. *What now?* After a peek through the peephole, she narrowed her eyes, unsure whether she should be grateful for the distraction.

A handsome man in a sharp suit stood in the hallway, with another man at his side.

"Yes?" she called out, not opening the door.

"Police Chief Zharan to see Mr. Christian Delacorte."

"Hold on a sec." Raven glanced over her shoulder to Christian, who was still on the phone, but she had his attention. "The chief of police is here to see you."

He nodded and gave her a thumbs-up sign, talking fast and making excuses to end the call. Raven opened the door.

"Come in . . . please." She forced a smile. "Christian is on the phone. He'll be off shortly."

"I am Police Chief Ricardo Zharan, at your service, miss. This is one of my investigators, Detective Arturo Fuentes."

Both men nodded a greeting and entered the foyer. Very gallant. Very formal.

"I'm Raven Mackenzie, a homicide detective out of Chicago, back in the States. Pleased to meet fellow officers in Brazil."

She kept a watchful eye on the half-open bedroom door, waiting for Christian to come out.

"I had no idea Mr. Delacorte traveled with another woman . . . and one so beautiful. I have only met Ms. Lee. He is a lucky man to travel in such company." Zharan steadied his gaze on her.

Raven ignored the chauvinistic flattery. Even wrapped in a seductive Brazilian accent, she knew the bullshit of a flagrant come on.

"Actually, I only just arrived today." She kept the banter light, not wanting to broach the subject of Jasmine's disappearance or Duarte's alleged involvement until Christian joined them. As far as she was concerned, this was his turf. With her being a latecomer to the game, Christian knew far more about the situation than she did.

The police chief meandered to the French doors for a look outside, showing only marginal interest in her explanation.

"Sorry to keep you waiting, Chief Zharan. Can I get you or your man some coffee?" Christian offered, entering the room.

"No, Detective Fuentes and I can't stay long," the chief said, declining for both of them.

"You have anything new on Charboneau's abduction?" Christian caught her eye, giving Raven a vague sign to follow his lead.

She knew him well enough to pick up on it. A rogue cop and a police chief he didn't trust entirely. Raven didn't need a wake-up call to know Christian should handle this. She went for the wet bar, poured a cup of coffee, and moved to the sofa.

"Well, as I told you, we worked through the night following leads and backtracking Captain Duarte's investigation."

When Christian heard Duarte's name, he jumped on the opportunity to ask about the man.

"Excuse me for saying this, but if you had to backtrack Duarte, that must mean you questioned his work. Do you suspect him of something?"

Zharan glanced to his man Fuentes with a pained expression. Clearly he did not feel comfortable speculating about one of his own men.

"We don't have evidence to support that . . . yet. But it is not above our consideration." He looked away and cleared his throat. "I hope you know if there is any proof of his misconduct, steps will be taken. I assure you. I have made my career on stamping out corruption wherever I find it. No one is above scrutiny."

"I appreciate your candor, Chief."

Fuentes nodded in support of his superior officer. The detective held his hands behind his back, looking like ex-military, with a lean physique, thick neck, and buzz cut, his face stern and unreadable. Duarte had insinuated that Zharan might be more of a political figurehead, in name only. Yet from what Christian saw, the chief commanded respect from the men under his command, and got it. Another Duarte lie?

"You said you worked through the night. Did you find anything new on Mr. Charboneau's case?"

Chief Zharan laid out his exhaustive measures to stir up new leads, including an update on his communications with the American consulate and his plans for a raid on a tribal village in a remote area. Taking action held great appeal for Christian. Finally, someone with authority had taken control of the case.

"So how good is your reconnaissance on this village? Any proof Charboneau is being held there?"

"I'm waiting for confirmation now, but I've gotten pretty reliable statements from individuals who would have reason to know such things. Still, I want to be sure." The man shrugged, but maintained eye contact. "Mobilizing men in an area so remote is not an endeavor to be taken lightly."

"Yes, I agree." Christian gave a quick glance to Raven. "In the spirit of our newfound cooperation on this case, I have something to share, Chief Zharan."

"Oh? Please." The man nodded, gesturing for him to continue.

"It's come to my attention . . ." Christian didn't know how to phrase it. No matter how he did it, the chief would know he'd held back until now. "Someone called me to say Duarte arrested Jasmine on the street earlier today. I've been trying to locate her, to get a lawyer if need be, but no one at police headquarters has been able to give me information on where Duarte booked her. Frankly, I'm worried. Can you help locate her? I could sure use someone on the inside."

"Captain Duarte arrested her? On what grounds?"

"The caller didn't say."

"Who reported this?"

Christian hesitated, unsure about giving up Hector's name.

"Please, I know you have no reason to do so, but you must trust me." Chief Zharan snapped his fingers, and Fuentes turned his eyes toward his boss. "Detective Fuentes, call headquarters and see what you can find out. If Duarte cannot be located, advise me. We will not hesitate to put out a bulletin for his whereabouts."

Fuentes pulled out his cell phone and punched in numbers.

"Hector Salvador works at a Macumba store called Guia Do Espírito. He witnessed the arrest firsthand and called me."

"How did he know to call you, Mr. Delacorte?"

Fuentes interrupted, a convenient distraction. "Sir, I can't get a good signal for my cell phone here in the hotel."

"Try the balcony, or downstairs if necessary," the chief suggested.

The detective headed for the French doors, rattling in Portuguese once he got outside.

"You've been very generous with your communication, and I appreciate all you've done," Christian offered, his eyes shifting from the chief to Fuentes on the balcony.

"I can imagine your frustration at having to sit and wait. I see it is not in your nature." The man smiled. "You have a stubborn streak, I would imagine."

"Guess that's true enough."

When Fuentes came in from the balcony, all eyes were on him. The man shook his head and explained, in English this time.

"Captain Duarte is nowhere to be found. And Ms. Lee has not been booked."

Chief Zharan tensed his jaw. His anger could not be contained. Trying to regain his composure, he turned to Christian.

"I will get to the bottom of this. When I return to headquarters, I'll put out a bulletin on the captain. In the meantime, we will confirm our plans for the raid on the village. I'll be in touch."

Zharan and Fuentes headed for the door, but the chief turned when he got there.

"I hope for the sake of Hector Salvador that Captain Duarte does not know of his involvement. He may be tempted to make another . . . arrest."

"Well, he's not gonna hear it from me." Christian

shook hands with both men and shut the door behind them.

He pulled Raven to his chest and held her in silence. What the chief said shocked him, the honesty of it. The man showed more of his cards and didn't cover up his obvious disdain for Captain Duarte. That made Christian worry all the more for Jasmine. Normally, the woman could take care of herself, but with Duarte, she'd be severely outnumbered.

This time, Jasmine may have met her match.

Perhaps Hector was right, age had caught up to her. Bianca hadn't heard much through the door. Either that or Hector had gotten better at keeping his secrets. With dust rag in hand, she emerged from the storeroom, keeping an eye on her nephew. In time he would tell her all she wanted to know. It was his way. And she was a patient aunt.

"You look happy." She smiled at the handsome young man, her dead sister's son. "Like a cat with a belly full of canary."

Even in the pale light of the store, his dark eyes gleamed and he fought back a grin. His smile always reminded Bianca of his mother, her beloved younger sister Pilar.

Hector had been the product of an out-of-wedlock union with her sister never naming the father. So when a virulent cancer claimed Pilar's life ten years ago, Bianca took her son in and adopted him, giving him a name. She shamed the rest of her family into accepting Hector. Eventually, it worked. An uphill battle she hid from him.

When Hector came to work for her, he put in hours that would not hinder his schooling. Her offer had become more than an opportunity for employment and a means of support. The boy needed a woman's hand. Although Hector bore his grief like a man, at times he let his guard down enough to reveal the hurt eyes of a child. She had become a surrogate mother to him and had learned to read his moods.

Now, without being asked, Hector joined her and took up a cloth.

"Do my eyes deceive me? Hector Salvador stooping to do woman's work?" She shook her head and raised an eyebrow. "To what do I owe this honor?"

One of her decanters of cemetery dirt was only half full. She'd grabbed the depleted jar and headed for the back room to fill it when her nephew opened his mouth.

"My luck is about to turn. I can feel it." He teased. "Maybe that talisman around your neck will bring us good fortune."

Ah, the exuberance and bottomless optimism of youth.

Bianca fingered her talisman and rolled her eyes, but before she left, Hector grabbed her arm and kissed her cheek. The boy was devoted, but the sudden display of affection caught her off guard. Her cheeks bloomed with heat and she laughed out loud, stroking her fingers across her pearl necklace.

"Sometimes . . . you make me feel like a young woman, Hector." She beamed, then furrowed her brow and waggled a finger at his mischievous face. "But most days, you remind me that youth is wasted on the very young."

Before she turned away, he called after her. "Aunt Bianca?" His face turned serious. "One day, I hope I can repay all you've done for me."

For an instant they had a moment. He held her gaze without a wisecrack. And Bianca returned it with a mother's pride. Eventually she shrugged and smiled.

"You don't owe me anything, sweet boy."

She fought a knot in the back of her throat. Before Bianca ducked into the stockroom, she glanced at Hector and caught his shy crooked grin, no doubt an asset when courting young ladies.

Yes, baby sister had done well.

At the counter, Bianca poured herself a half cup of coffee, careful not to let Hector see. The boy worried she wasn't sleeping, and the caffeine wouldn't help. At her age, sleep was only a distant acquaintance, but a rich cup of coffee was an old familiar friend.

With the glass jar wedged in an arm, she enjoyed a few sips of coffee, her guilty pleasure. The storage door hissed closed behind her. She wandered to her desk and set down her cup, saving her indulgence for after her chore.

Bianca busied herself, scooping cemetery dirt into the decanter, careful not to lose any. To be careless would be disrespectful. Worse, she believed it would bring bad luck. She barely heard the bell tinkle overhead. Someone had entered the front door to the shop.

Voices muffled. Angry voices.

She turned her head and listened, sure she had misunderstood. When the noise continued, she pulled the light string over her desk and the storeroom turned pitch-black. Bianca couldn't wait for her eyes to acclimate to the dark. She held her hands out in front of her, trying to find the door. A small pinpoint of light from the peephole guided her. At the door, she stood on tiptoe and squinted, clutching her Ayza talisman and holding her breath as if someone might hear her.

Before she got a good look, something heavy hit the storeroom door. *Thud!*

In a panic, she almost fell backward.

"Oh, my God."

Cowering, Bianca covered her mouth to stifle a scream. Her heart hammered her ribs and chills ravaged her skin. She worked up the courage to take another peek—for Hector's sake. What she saw stole her breath.

"Hector," she sobbed, her voice a raspy whisper.

Chapter 16

A bald-headed thug had cold-cocked Hector. A savage blow. Now he yanked him off the floor by the collar. Seeing stars, Hector was too weak to fight. He felt a warm stream roll down his chin and smelled blood. Tears of pain flooded his eyes.

"Anyone ever tell you to mind your own business, *cabrão*?" The guy balled his fist again and slugged Hector.

He fell against the storeroom door, jamming an elbow. A jolt of pain shot through his arm and he slid to the floor. This time, the bastard nearly dislocated his jaw, loosened a tooth. His face felt on fire.

"*Aargh.*" Hector held up his good arm and waved a hand. He searched for mercy in the faces of the three men standing over him, his eye swollen. "Please . . . st-stop. Why are you doing this? If it's money you want—"

Cold dead eyes stared back. He would find no mercy. Fear gripped him. Aunt Bianca hid behind the door he'd fallen against. He felt her presence and prayed these men would not search the store. If they found her, she would not survive such treatment.

"Not so simple, asshole. You should've followed your own advice and stopped before you got involved."

"Involved in what?" he pleaded, spitting blood. "What are you talking about?"

The man rolled Hector on his belly and rammed a knee into the back of his neck. Yanking his arm back, the jerk almost separated his shoulder. When he felt the handcuffs slammed to his wrists, Hector's eyes grew wide.

"You guys are cops?" He raised his voice, a warning for his aunt. "But I didn't do anything wrong. Why am I being arrested?"

The three men were dressed like a street gang. He thought they would rob him. None of them looked like military police. Now all the rumors of men disappearing off the streets flooded his mind. Cops had been rumored to be behind the conspiracy. His stomach lurched. He fought back the urge to throw up. He'd brought this on himself, with his grand scheme for money and taking care of his aunt as the man of the house. *Big ego, Hector, you idiot.*

He had only wanted to help. Now his foolishness might cost his life . . . and Aunt Bianca's. Hector started to cry. Tears mixed with blood.

But damned if he'd take his aunt down with him.

"Okay . . . okay. I'll go with you. Just let me close the shop and lock up."

"*Vai a merda!* We'll take care of that." The guy sneered. "See what you get when you resist arrest?" The men laughed. A perverted and cruel joke.

The mean son of a bitch hauled Hector to his feet

and shoved him into the next man. Hitting a wall of muscle, Hector stumbled, his legs not working. Two men grabbed his arms and dragged him to the front door, not waiting for him to stand.

"I'll search the place. Take him to the car."

Oh, God . . . no! Hector craned his neck, catching a glimpse of the man who'd beat him. The guy headed behind the counter . . . toward the storeroom. As they hustled him out the door, dragging him across the threshold, the bell tingled overhead and made a mockery of his predicament. The noise barely registered.

Between the steady thud of his heart, Hector listened to a faint whisper. And as the men shoved him into the backseat of a dark sedan and locked the door, the sound grew louder in his head. More urgent.

It took him a while to recognize . . . the sound of his prayer.

Cramming his pockets with cash from the register, Eduardo Silva opened the door to the supply room, looking for anything else to steal. Side benefits to the job. In the back, it looked like only more of what stocked the shelves in front. Roots, dried herbs, preserved animal parts floating in murky liquid, and macabre religious figures with faces twisted in agony. He'd grown up with superstition. This shithole reminded him of everything he hated from his childhood.

And to think, some people paid good money for a shot at redemption. *What a waste!*

He had almost made up his mind to forget about the back, but in the quiet, he thought he heard a faint rustle of fabric. It reminded him of the rats skittering through the walls of the bedroom he had to share with his three brothers when he was a kid.

What the hell? Fuckin' place gives me the creeps.

"Tem alguém aqui? I could use some help up front . . . anyone back there?" he cried out. "Hello?"

He didn't need any complications.

Silence. Nothing moved. Eduardo peered into the dark corners of the room. From what little he saw, wooden shelves lined the main aisle and a ladder leaned against them. A small desk in the back. It smelled of herbs and an underlying foul odor, like something musty or dead. He wedged the door open with a wooden block to let in the meager light of the storefront. Not much to speak of, but every little bit helped. When he found a chain dangling from the ceiling, he pulled the cord and the small desk was washed in a harsh light.

"Jesus." He squinted, letting his eyes adjust.

Someone had been working. A pen atop a pad of paper, scribbled with a list. An inventory. The handwriting looked too neat to belong to the kid. A woman's touch, he guessed. Eduardo spied a coffee mug on the desktop and ran his fingers along the liquid line outside the cup. Still warm. His senses went on full alert.

Did the kid drink coffee or was someone else here?

He pulled open every drawer in the desk, tossing files and shoving aside paperwork until he found a purse in the bottom drawer. A grin spread across his face. The kid wouldn't have one of these. Dumping the contents on the desktop, he tossed the purse aside and nabbed the wallet, scrounging for a photo ID.

After he pocketed the money in the wallet, he gazed

at the face on the driver's license and read the name:
BIANCA SALVADOR.

She had to be here somewhere. His eyes searched
the gloom. Slowly, he walked down the aisle, peering
through the massive shelves. Then he bent over and
hustled down the row, shifting his moves in hopes of
catching anyone lurking in the shadows. The inventory of the supply room looked eerie in the gloom.

Eduardo didn't consider himself a superstitious
man, only a cautious one.

After a long while, he gritted his teeth and scratched
his bald head. Did he have a witness to the kid's so-
called arrest or had the bitch stepped out before they
got there? He hated loose ends.

"Hey, you done?" one of his men called from up
front. "We gotta roll."

Fed up, Eduardo turned and headed for the front
door, but his eye caught something out of place, a job
left undone. Set atop a workbench was a tall jar with
dirt in it. A scoop lay on the soil, propped against the
inside lip of the container. *Superstitious crap!* With
a sneer, he dumped the contents onto the floor and
smashed the decanter. Dirt and shards of glass spilled
everywhere, making a mess.

That's when he heard the creak of a door. A soft
muffled sound.

Eduardo jerked his head and searched the darkness. His hand went instinctively for his Taurus
1911 pistol, tucked under his T-shirt at the small of
his back. He pulled out the .45 caliber weapon and
flexed his grip, his palms slick with sweat.

Against inky black, the bright light overhead played
tricks on his eyes. Images drifted in the shadows, but

why hadn't he seen any lights when the door opened? Maybe he'd missed it. That pissed him off. If the old lady hid in a closet, he'd make her pay for putting him through the extra effort. Teeth gritted and gun in hand, he headed toward the noise.

And the darkness swallowed him.

Chapter 17

It broke Bianca's heart to leave Hector behind. She slipped out the back door and into the light of a fading sun. Squinting, she held up a hand to block the glare and get her bearings. Soon it would be dark, but not soon enough to help her escape. She thought she heard heavy footsteps behind her, or perhaps it had been her imagination.

But wishful thinking could get her in plenty of trouble.

Absentmindedly, she clutched at the talisman around her neck as she ran down the alley. She gasped for breath with the effort, her heart pounding. Deep inside she knew there wasn't much time, no doubt the voice of Ayza the Protector.

As she ran toward the nearest door, the sound of her feet hitting the pavement was soon replaced by the horror of Hector's beating. It replayed in her head, over and over. Even now she flinched at the brutality of the shocking blows. Her precious boy.

His pleas to warn her gripped her throat, making it hard to breathe. And her eyes filled with tears.

She grabbed the doorknob of a shop down the alley. Locked. With her hand clenched in a fist ready to pound on the door, Bianca looked over her shoulder, back the way she'd come. When the back door to Guia Do Espírito opened with a faint yet familiar creak, she changed her mind about calling attention to herself.

Time had run out.

She ducked behind a Dumpster near a corner to the alley that branched off. She crouched behind the metal refuse bin, the stench of it stifling her breath. In the distance, she heard the crunch of gravel underfoot. Too late to move.

Was he coming? Had he seen where she hid?

She didn't dare look. Bianca pressed her back against the brick wall behind her and prayed. She shut her eyes and held the talisman to her lips. Her throat dry, her breathing labored. She had to calm her heart or the man would hear her for sure. She cowered behind the Dumpster, too scared to budge.

Most of all, she prayed for strength. Bianca turned herself over to Ayza, trusting in his benevolence and power. In the end, it was all she had.

Taking a risk, Eduardo Silva shoved the door open and leveled his weapon, but the sun's glare blinded him, watering his eyes. He held up a hand to see, looking up the alley and down. In the distance he spotted foot traffic near a busy street, but it was too far away to matter. Sounds of the city closed in.

"Foda!" he swore under his breath.

Had he been wrong about hearing the creak of the

door? Old buildings played tricks with your head. Anger had gotten the better of him. Lowering the gun to his side, he picked a direction and walked. His eyes searched for movement.

How far could an old woman get?

Heading for the nearest door, he tried to anticipate where a scared old lady would go. If he was right, this one had nerves of steel to stay quiet so long. Reaching out a hand, he gripped the doorknob and turned. It didn't budge.

Eduardo caught a shadow near the Dumpster. He clenched the grip of his weapon and crept closer, careful not to make a sound. The metal refuse bin lined up near a brick wall, square with it. But it had a noticeable gap from the wall, big enough for someone to hide behind. He held his breath—listening—filtering out the sounds that didn't matter.

A slow sneer slid across his face.

In a sudden burst he lowered his shoulder and shoved against the huge metal container. The groan of steel echoed down the alley, resonating off the walls. It slammed against the brick in a loud thud. He didn't wait for a scream.

Gun drawn, Eduardo raced around the bin and found . . .

Nothing. *Damn it!* Absolutely nothing.

After a long moment, he quit gnashing his teeth and lowered his gun, tucking it in the waistband of his pants. His men were waiting out front and they had to get the kid off the street. Before he left, Eduardo reached into his pocket and pulled out the ID he'd found in the purse, memorizing Bianca Salvador's face. This wasn't over. He'd meet the old woman on his turf.

He hated complications.

*   *   *

Bianca had trusted the spirits. And Ayza told her to run, even when everything in her gut yelled, *No, stay put!* Hesitation would have gotten her killed. She knew it as surely as she understood the Orixás were with her.

Using the Dumpster as a shield, she had stayed low and crept along the wall, heading for the corner ahead. It felt like forever, but she eventually made the turn. The talisman swung from her neck. She felt its burden. Bianca grabbed the hem of her skirt and watched every footstep, avoiding broken glass or the scuff of a shoe that might give her away. After she'd gotten far enough from that place, she picked up the pace and never looked back.

Bianca ran.

She felt the steady thump of the talisman against her chest, in perfect rhythm with her frantic heart. Every breath pained her. And tears made it hard to see.

Still, she ran.

If the police had taken Hector, she would be on her own. As she saw it, she had only one place to go. And she would not doubt the spirit Ayza now. Her only hope to save her nephew lay in the hands of a man with striking green eyes, the one laden with a heavy aura of death. Her rational mind told her it was foolhardy to trust a stranger, but blind faith had gotten her this far. In truth, she had no other choice.

She had made the talisman for a reason. Now she understood its purpose.

CHAPTER 18

"I can't stand waiting. I'm no good at it." Christian stalked the suite, dragging a hand through his hair.

"Good to know we have something else in common." Raven's oddball humor didn't defuse the stress of the situation. Christian may not have heard her at all.

The late-afternoon sun hung low in the sky, casting shadows into the room. Raven watched him from the couch, understanding the frustration he must be feeling. She felt it too.

"What can we do?" She leaned forward. "If you have a plan, I'm with you."

He stopped and stared, his mind working.

"Maybe they have Jasmine at Genotech." Christian narrowed his eyes and chewed a corner of his lip, hands on his hips. "That place is a damned fortress. Plenty of security. And Duarte probably has a holding cell there. Those addicts I told you about wouldn't last long in a hospital ward. They'd find a way to escape if they weren't confined."

"Makes sense." She nodded. "You trust Chief Zharan?"

A simple question without an easy answer.

"I've got no choice. I need someone on the inside. Someone with resources." He shook his head. "Duarte's not a guy to mess with, not without a game plan. And this is his home turf. He's well connected . . . been ahead of us all the way. Can't believe I let Jasmine out of here on her own. Damn it! I should've known she was up to something."

He clenched his jaw and pinched the bridge of his nose. A tension headache brewing.

"Don't blame yourself." Raven stood and walked toward him. She put an arm around his waist and caressed the side of his face with her hand. "I got a feeling that woman rarely hears the word no. She must've played a hunch. You and I might've done the same."

Christian closed his eyes and nudged her hand with his cheek, a tender gesture she'd grown to love. But the moment didn't last.

"This waiting is killing me." He lowered his head, glancing at his watch. "Can't imagine the chief launching an operation this time of day. It's gonna be dark soon."

"Jasmine being taken by Duarte has been a real distraction from Charboneau's case." Raven shrugged. "Maybe that's the whole point."

After a long moment she asked, "How about the ransom? You have it arranged?"

"I told Fiona not to pay until she heard from me. If the kidnappers got the money early, my father's life wouldn't be worth a dime. I had hoped to know more by now."

The reality of his deadline hit Christian hard. He would have to contact Fiona soon if he thought paying the money would help Charboneau's chances. If not, there would be a point of no return that he'd take upon himself. Could he live with the guilt if he guessed wrong? The muscles of his shoulders knotted with tension. He wrapped his arms around her, but comfort wouldn't come so easy.

Suddenly, the phone rang, making Raven jump. His anxiety was contagious. Christian kissed her forehead and rushed across the room to answer it, expecting it would be Chief Zharan.

"Yes?"

"Is this Christian Delacorte?" The timid voice of a woman.

"Yes. Who is this?" He shook his head and shrugged to Raven. What now? he wondered.

"We've never met, but I need to speak to you. Please." The woman cleared her throat, the sound more of a sob held in check. "My name is Bianca Salvador. Something has happened—"

Christian heard sounds in the background, but the woman never finished.

"Where are you?" He listened and looked up, locking eyes with Raven. "Stay put. I'll be right there."

Raven stepped closer, standing by his side. Her dark eyes narrowed. When Christian hung up the phone, he grabbed her hand and kissed it, her skin warm to the touch.

"When I come back, I'll introduce you to someone I've been dying for you to meet."

* * *

It wasn't easy to spot her. Dressed in a dark floral skirt and a white blouse, a woman cowered near the guest phones across from registration. The huge lobby with its activity dwarfed her tiny frame, obscuring her presence. Her gray hair was mussed, her dark eyes wary. She looked as though the devil would swoop to claim her soul if she didn't stay vigilant. As he stepped closer, Christian saw something else. Draped off her neck, the woman wore a chain with a peculiar leather pouch dangling from it. Strange, but what could be expected from an owner of a Macumba shop? Even though they'd never met, Christian knew he'd found Bianca Salvador.

The older woman spotted him, confirming his suspicions that she'd been the one behind the peephole the other day.

"Mrs. Salvador?" Christian waited for her to extend a hand. She didn't. The woman only nodded, not looking him in the eye.

"Yes. I'm sorry to intrude, but I didn't know who else might help." Bianca lowered her voice.

"Please believe me, this is no imposition; quite the contrary. Follow me. We'll have more privacy in my room."

She followed him, keeping a step behind. And she never said a word during the elevator ride. The silence felt awkward, yet unavoidable. Something he read in her body language made it clear she preferred the quiet. Once they got to the suite, the woman looked shocked to see Raven. She stopped and almost turned away. Christian interceded.

"It's okay. Please, I'd like to introduce you to Raven Mackenzie from Chicago, Illinois."

Bianca stared at the man with the green eyes as he touched the shoulder of the beautiful woman, clearly a sign of affection. In Bianca's mind, these two fit. They had a connection, unlike the Asian woman he'd brought to her store.

"Raven? This is Mrs. Bianca Salvador. She owns the Guia Do Espírito, a local store specializing in spirit ritual and religious artifacts."

"Pleased to meet you." The young woman smiled.

"Can I get you anything to drink?" He extended his hand and directed Bianca to take a seat on the sofa.

She nodded. "Please. A glass of water."

While he stepped behind the wet bar, Bianca caught her reflection in a mirror and wondered what these Americans had thought of her frazzled appearance. She pressed flyaway hairs with her fingers, her mind racing. After he handed her the water, the American sat and waited for her to speak. Since she had no time for pleasantries, it didn't take long.

"The military police, they took my Hector, my nephew." With a voice low, she choked back a sob and pressed a hand to her lips. "They beat and dragged him from the store. Maybe he couldn't walk on his own. I don't know how bad—" She grimaced; reliving the horror brought pain.

"When did this happen?"

"Earlier this afternoon. I ran straight here. I didn't know where else to go."

"Did you see any of the men who took him?" he asked. "Do you know Captain Luis Duarte?"

"No, I saw no one. And I do not know the captain you mentioned."

"Did you see their vehicle? Get a license tag?" the young woman asked.

"I'm afraid I won't be any help. I only heard the attack from the stockroom, from behind a closed door." Fresh tears rolled down her cheeks. " I was too afraid to stop it. I would have called the police, but Hector made sure I knew those men *were* the police. He sacrificed himself to protect me." A strained moment passed as Bianca wept. In a quiet voice, the man named Delacorte broke the stillness.

"For reasons I can't get into right now, I believe Captain Duarte took Hector. He's on the police payroll, but I think he's found a way to subsidize his income."

"So much corruption in my country. I wish it were not so."

"And we believe this captain took a friend of mine, the one who visited your store the other day. He called it an arrest, but we have proof he never booked her. We don't know where she is."

"Do you think this woman is dead?" The reality of her question hit too close to home, reminding Bianca of Hector.

"I have nothing to back up my claims, only a hunch. But maybe the chief of police can do something about it. I can tell Chief Ricardo Zharan what happened to your nephew. He might be able to find Hector. He's looking for Duarte and Jasmine now."

"You would do this thing for me?"

"Yes, I don't know what good it'll do, but it may help. Being a foreigner here, I don't have much choice in the matter."

The American stared at her. Finally, Delacorte reached for her hand. She drew from his strength before she pulled away.

"Hector is a good boy. Sure, he has grand schemes.

What young man doesn't? He has the body of a virile man, but the tender innocence of a child. He has so much to learn." Bianca fought back the fear that her nephew wouldn't get the chance to learn life's lessons. "Hector only wants to take care of me. And he's not patient. He probably thought that money was his big opportunity."

"That money? What do you mean?"

"He knew of the reward money you offered for information on the kidnapped man." She forced the words from her mouth, hating how they sounded aloud. "I think the wrong people heard of his interest. Maybe they were afraid he'd learn something to hurt them and say too much."

"Actually, I have another theory. Hector contacted me here earlier today."

Bianca wasn't surprised. She'd heard her nephew on the phone, but never knew where he placed the call.

"I do not mean to pry, but can you tell me why he called you, Mr. Delacorte?"

"He called to tell me about my friend Jasmine. He witnessed her arrest outside your store today. He heard her mention Captain Duarte by name." His green eyes fixed on her. "Hector wanted money for the heads-up. I thought he wanted it for himself, but after listening to you, I think he wanted it for your sake. Guess I was wrong about him."

Delacorte exchanged a glance with the young woman sitting next to him. In turn, she reached a hand to him in consolation. These two were definitely in love. Love was always a gift meant for sharing. And it brought back memories.

"Hector's mother died of cancer years ago. My

baby sister. Her boy is like a son to me." She fought the lump in her throat.

"How can I help you? You came here for a reason."

Even with all his troubles, Delacorte offered his help. Bianca knew she'd come to the right man. The spirits had been right about him.

"This may sound strange." Bianca didn't know how to explain to a non-believer. "I cannot go to the police. To do so might get Hector killed, if he is not already—"

The thought of Hector dead tore a hole in her heart. Bianca fought for composure. She sipped water until she could continue.

"The day you came into my shop, I saw you from the storeroom in the back. For security, we installed a . . . how you say?" She gestured with her finger, pointing to her eye.

"A peephole," Christian offered.

"Yes, a peephole. We put one in the door." She nodded. "When I saw you, you intrigued me, but something about you scared me. I didn't understand at first, but now I think I do."

"Understand what? why would I scare you?" he asked.

"You are the vessel for Ayza, the Protector, one of the Orixás. I don't know how you'll help Hector, but I trust in the spirits. They've spoken to me."

By the skeptical expression on Delacorte's face, she knew she'd lost him. Bianca reached across and squeezed his hand.

"I have made a strong talisman for Ayza and you must wear it, Mr. Delacorte. I know you aren't a believer, but I'm asking for your trust. Please take my gift and wear it, even if you don't understand. What harm can it do? My talisman is yours. Once you put it on, don't take it off. Please, I beg of you."

Bianca reached for the charm she wore. Pulling the chain over her head, she held the leather pouch, a sacred fetish. Her fingers trembled with her burden.

"Will you allow me?" She held out the chain.

Eventually, Delacorte nodded. Bianca stood and placed the chain around his neck with all the reverence she had in her. She bestowed him with Ayza's talisman and tucked it inside his shirt next to his skin. After it was done, she sat. Delacorte was a broad-shouldered, masculine man, with fierce intelligent eyes. He could intimidate men or soften a woman's heart. Now the compassion in his eyes warmed her heart and made her believe Ayza had been right about him.

"You have a place to stay for a while?" he asked. "You can stay here if you like. I don't think you should go home."

Bianca shook her head. "Oh, no. I could not impose. I have friends in the city and won't go home. I'll be fine."

"Then here, take this. You'll need money." Christian stood and pulled out his wallet. Bianca raised her hand.

"No, please. You've been more than generous. My friends will take care of me. They're like family." She wiped her eyes and took a breath. "I'll call this hotel and leave a message where I can be reached. Please call me if you have news."

"I will," he promised.

His woman friend smiled. A kind face with trustworthy eyes. A woman in love. Bianca returned her gesture. One last time, she touched Delacorte's chest with trembling fingers, feeling the talisman under his shirt. He gave her that moment without embarrassment. She relied on her faith, but more depended upon the strength of Christian Delacorte.

"Thank you. I pray we will see each other soon. Good fortune in your journey," she said as she stood.

He cocked his head and looked at her with questions in his eyes, but he didn't ask them. Both Americans walked her to the door and allowed her to leave on her own. Bianca rode the elevator to the ground floor, avoiding eye contact. Once she got to the lobby, she pushed through the revolving door and onto the crowded street, in step with a group of businessmen. She had done what she came to do.

Now Hector's life was in the hands of Ayza—and a stranger.

Sitting in a silver Fiat Siena sedan, Eduardo sucked on a cigarette, taking his last drag. He flicked the butt out the window and blew smoke out his nose, his eyes fixed on the plump ass of a young woman strutting down the street. A real handful. No, make that two. In his mind, the urban landscape faded to black and the noise of traffic died.

He pictured himself humping her—hard and fast. The sound of flesh slapping flesh filled his brain. His skin beaded with sweat, the veins of his neck distending. She clawed his back, wanting more, crying out his name. In his fantasy, he was always a wanted man.

Eduardo shut his eyes and leaned back against the headrest. A hard-on throbbed in his pants, making demands.

"Hey, check it out."

When the guy sitting next to him punched his arm, Eduardo blinked rapid fire, resenting the intrusion. Without complaint, he shifted his gaze to where the man pointed, back to his left. His cock thwarted by the interruption.

"Is that her?"

"Where?" It took Eduardo a moment to find her. He shifted in his seat behind the wheel.

At first she blended into a crowd of businessmen leaving the hotel. Being short gave her an advantage she didn't keep for long. The suits headed across the street and she broke away on her own. When he caught a glimpse of Bianca Salvador, Eduardo grabbed her driver's license and compared the image to the old lady heading down the sidewalk, looking over her shoulder. Now he kept an eye on her through his rearview mirror. Dark skirt with flowers and a white blouse. Salt and pepper hair, cut short. Bone thin.

"Yeah." He smirked. "Keep an eye on her."

Eduardo turned the key in his ignition, waited for a break in the traffic, and made a U-turn to follow her. With his cell, he hit the speed dial of a familiar number and held the phone to his ear. When the call was answered, he said, "Your hunch paid off. We found her."

Eduardo listened for further instructions, then smiled again.

"Count on it." He ended the call, shoving the cell into his shirt pocket. "Let's pick our spot, somewhere nice and quiet. That bitch is going for a ride. Before it gets dark, we'll know what she told Delacorte."

CHAPTER 19

DAY SEVEN
NIGHTFALL

"What did you make of that?" Raven touched Christian's arm, the meeting with Bianca Salvador on her mind.

The same thoughts plagued him. The older woman had definitely been on edge and had a lot to lose. She loved her nephew. That much was plain to see, but the strangest part was Bianca's true purpose. She conveyed what happened to Hector, yet seemed more bent on making sure he carried her talisman—as if life or death depended on it. Strange world, he thought.

"Not sure. Hector getting picked up by Duarte so soon after Jasmine? Maybe someone saw him or knew we'd been to the Macumba store before." Christian took her in his arms, his mind working double-time. "But why? What would Hector know about all this?"

"Maybe it's not what he knows, but what he witnessed. People disappearing on the streets of Cuiabá can stir up an investigation. And it sounds like your chief of police is already curious enough to make that happen." Raven speculated. "If that lab has something to hide, they'd do just about anything to keep their secrets. My guess."

"But why abduct my father?"

"In a case like this, I'd say follow the money. And I'd bet serious coin that this is linked to Genotech Labs. Someone has invested in the genetics of drug addiction, and not for the good of mankind. Whoever is behind this wanted Charboneau out, maybe to take his place. Greed is a powerful motivator." She narrowed her eyes. Her cop instincts had taken over.

He heard it from across the room and pulled from her arms to answer it.

"Delacorte." He listened, his face taking on a sense of urgency when he recognized the voice. "Chief Zharan. You have anything new?"

"I have no news on your friend, Jasmine Lee. My men have canvassed the neighborhood where she was taken and we found no other witnesses, a common outcome in these times. No one wants to get involved." He sighed heavily on the phone. "I still have men working this, but if Captain Duarte is involved, we may never know what happened. He would know how to dispose of a body that would never be found. I'm sorry to be so blunt, but if this were my acquaintance, I would want to be mentally prepared for the worst. By nature, perhaps I am a fatalist, a consequence of the work I have chosen."

Christian shut his eyes, letting the world fade to black. He pictured Jasmine's face and felt the loss of a comrade in arms, but he didn't want to believe it. The woman had saved his life and Raven's—a lifetime ago.

A part of him wanted to rage at the injustice, but another part understood the consequence of the "work" Jasmine had chosen. What goes around, comes around—and kicks you hard in the butt—but who's to say what was deserved or what was truly unfair?

In hindsight, he had no business judging Jasmine Lee—and yet, he had.

Raven sensed his worry and laid a hand on his chest, her fingers touching the talisman under his shirt. Her beautiful dark eyes gave him comfort, beyond any words he could ever express. Christian brushed back a strand of her hair and forced a smile, but she saw through his facade, a sad expression on her face.

And he loved her all the more for it.

Most of his life, people didn't have a clue what he was about. They considered him a mystery and never bothered to learn more. Maybe he scared people. His emotional scars kept others away. His mother was the exception, but Fiona had secrets of her own, and plenty of them.

Raven had no such agenda. She accepted him faults and all, reading him like an old familiar book. Christian liked the feeling.

He didn't feel alone anymore.

"On the side of good news, we have reason to believe we know where Mr. Charboneau is being held." The chief had optimism resonating in his voice. "At this point, however, I can't say anything more. You understand?"

"Yes, certainly."

"We can't mobilize tonight, but we're leaving at dawn."

Christian read between the lines, in what the chief didn't say. Working logistics for a tactical maneuver in the jungle involved coordination and planning for all contingencies.

"I don't suppose you can share any of the details."

"No, sorry. I can't, but we're preparing tonight at an undisclosed location. I've hand-selected my men, not even headquarters knows the location of this op. The fewer who know, the better. If all goes as planned, we can attempt a rescue, perhaps one without bloodshed. That is my hope." Zharan cleared his throat. "I apologize for being so mysterious. I hope you understand."

"Yeah, I do, believe me. But I've got a favor to ask."

"Yes, Mr. Delacorte?"

"Take me with you," he pleaded, knowing he'd pay the price. Raven's eyes flashed with shock that evolved into anger. She punched him lightly in the chest, then pointed a finger to herself. She wanted to go too.

Silence. Chief Zharan didn't jump on his offer. Finally, he said, "Taking a civilian is not exactly standard operating procedure."

Raven punched him harder this time, looking more determined. She wasn't going to quit.

"Please . . . can you hold a minute, Chief." Christian covered the phone. Narrowing his eyes at Raven, he whispered, "Sorry, I gotta do this."

"Think about it, Christian. You left Chicago and I came after you. What do you think will happen if you try to leave me behind this time?" She crossed her arms and stared him down.

He'd seen that look—stubborn determination. He cocked his head, knowing he couldn't hide the disbelief on his face.

Still holding the phone to his ear, covering it with a hand, he shook his head. "No. Can't risk it."

Raven softened her expression, a show of love on her beautiful face. Going for his jugular, she pulled out the heavy artillery from her playbook on feminine wiles. He prepared himself for both barrels between the eyes.

"Look, my job is dangerous, Christian. It's what I do." She raised her chin, fixing her gaze on him. "You can't protect me every minute . . . even though I love you for trying." She smiled, a gesture that quickly faded. "Put yourself in my shoes. Think how I'd feel if I let you go and something happened to you. I'd never—" She couldn't finish and looked away.

He knew what she meant. Jasmine had felt the same when Charboneau was kidnapped on her watch. And no way he'd let Raven go without him if their situations were reversed.

He nodded and took his hand away from the phone.

"Sorry, Chief Zharan, I'm back. I just wanted to say that I'm not exactly an inexperienced civilian."

Raven looked upset again, misinterpreting his intentions. He raised a hand, quietly asking for her trust before he continued, "I'm well-trained in weapons, tactics, and I can follow orders. Please . . . with all that's happened. I have to go."

The man sighed again. "To tell you the truth, I'm

concerned for your safety if I leave you in Cuiabá . . . and your lady friend. With a certain captain lost and unaccounted for, I fear he may not hesitate to arrange another 'arrest.'" The man's voice was laden with sarcasm and full of disappointment regarding his own man. "With the rescue operation, I will be preoccupied. And I don't have enough men to protect you while I'm gone. Hard to know who to trust, if you know what I mean."

"Then bring us both along. Raven and I can handle a weapon, if you allow it. Either way, we'd be part of your team."

Nodding, Raven grinned and crossed her fingers. Christian raised an eyebrow and shook his head. You had to love a woman who got jazzed over the prospect of an armed assault, but it sure made dating hard to top.

"Very well." Zharan still didn't sound convinced, but to his credit, he understood Christian's need to go.

"The detective you met previously? I'll have him pick you up at five-thirty A.M. He will meet you in front of the hotel." Referring to Detective Fuentes, Zharan played it cagey to the bitter end. "It will be dark, but sunrise will come soon enough. Bring whatever weapons you choose, purely for self-defense. But make no mistake, Mr. Delacorte. Both of you will follow my orders to the letter. My men will handle any tactical maneuvers. Is that clear?"

"Understood. And thanks, Chief Zharan. You won't regret it." He ended the call and fixed his eyes on Raven. "We're on. I'll fill you in on the details. But tonight I want you all to myself. Deal?"

He held out his hand.

"Deal." She nodded and shook it.

Staring into Raven's deep, soul-branding eyes, Christian thought of only one thing. *You must be abso-frickin'-lutely out of your mind, Delacorte!*

After dinner from room service, Christian and Raven spent a quiet evening, preparing for tomorrow morning. They had showered together, taking time for every caress and holding each other in the hot stream—a loving intimacy he had never experienced. Neither had spoken, during or since.

The grueling trip to Brazil and his complete surrender to Raven had left him drained . . . and more than a little worried.

Dressed in a white hotel bathrobe, Christian forced himself to go through Jasmine's stuff, a necessity that hit him hard. He couldn't get his head wrapped around Jasmine being gone. Here today, gone the next, he wanted to believe life and the human spirit meant more than that. The thought that it might not lurked in his mind and twisted his gut. He felt an obligation to find out what happened to Jasmine. He owed her that much.

Strange too. Somehow, he felt certain she'd do the same for him.

Christian had left Raven in his room, packing a rucksack they'd share tomorrow. The chore wouldn't take long, but he wanted to give her space. Quiet prep time allowed each of them to grapple with the reality of what tomorrow might bring. Death was the silent partner they dealt with each and every day. For Raven, murder was part of her job as a homicide detective. But for him, death had entrenched itself into the emotional baggage he would carry the rest of his life.

Still, as he saw it, a guy comes into this world alone and he goes out the same way. No sugarcoating required. He could deal with his own death, but the thought of something happening to Raven ripped him apart. A wave of serious second thoughts hit him until he put things in perspective.

Raven had followed him to Brazil out of love. How could he argue with that? He would've done the same. She was a headstrong woman with a mind of her own, one of her more endearing qualities—and one of the reasons she put up with him.

As a cop, she faced dangerous situations all the time. Her badge put her in the line of fire. When he started this relationship with her, he knew he'd have to deal with that fact or leave. He chose to stick it out and treat each day with Raven as a gift. The alternative would be living in a vacuum, without risking his heart. He'd been there . . . done that.

Until now, when dealing with Raven's line of work, that reasoning had done the trick. But Zharan's words still resonated with him. If he left Raven behind and Duarte took her into "custody," he would never forgive himself. He couldn't take the chance.

In the end, he didn't want Raven out of his sight.

"Okay . . . that's it," he muttered under his breath.

Every weapon in Jasmine's gear bag had been tossed onto the mattress for his closer inspection. The woman sure knew how to pack. And with what he brought, Raven should have plenty to choose from. Christian stuffed the essentials into a small day pack and locked away the rest. He left Jasmine's room, carrying the bag with him.

But when he got to his bedroom door, he stopped cold. Slowly, he laid the pack on the floor near his bare feet. Raven had been busy all right, but it was not what he expected to see.

The bank of recessed lights in his room had been turned to a soft glow and she'd moved every candle in the suite to the bedroom. They flickered and cast soft shadows on the walls. And no one looked better in candlelight than Raven. Her dark hair shone auburn strands, reflecting the warmth of the flames and the blush of her cheeks.

"Dear Lord," he whispered his thanks, finding it hard to catch his breath. Very hard.

She smiled, a tender yet seductive lure. The pale light accentuated her perfect skin, velvet soft like a rose petal at dawn. And she lay naked under his blankets with nothing but a crisp white bed sheet over her breasts and down the length of her body. He had never conjured up a wet dream as flawless as Raven Mackenzie . . . and never would.

Still spellbound and unable to move, he licked his lips, taking everything in.

"Hey you, those lips are mine and I need my fix." She pulled back the bed covers on his side and patted the mattress, gesturing for him to join her. A lusty smile on her face.

Christian hooked a thumb under the belt to his robe and tugged. He shrugged out of one shoulder, then the other, and let the robe drop to the floor. Every move, every action, was foreplay. He didn't want to rush it. Using every ounce of willpower, he took his time making his way toward the bed, not taking his gaze off her. He loved the way her eyes traveled the length of his body, and he savored the moment. When she saw his erection, her smile faded, replaced by hungry need.

"You've been busy." Christian conjured an inspired grin. "Now I've got all night to return the favor."

DAWN
OUTSIDE CUIABÁ
DAY EIGHT

A molten sun cast its fire across clouds that streaked the parting night sky. Soft billows absorbed the color, borrowing from the marvel of sunrise—an inverted and undulating sea of red. Truly breathtaking. The vivid hue washed over the interior of the vehicle, bathing Christian in its fire. In awe, he watched the rising sun and drank in the beauty of this land as he felt the shape of the talisman Bianca had given him, the soft pouch under his shirt. Ever since he first put the trinket on, the weight of it never let him forget he wore it over his heart. Strange as it was, he couldn't bring himself to leave it behind. Not today.

Along the horizon, the backdrop of the skyscraper city, Cuiaba, stood in dark silhouette. A reminder of man's intrusion. Even at dawn with cloud cover, the temperatures were sweltering.

"Bad weather, I'm afraid." Detective Fuentes drove his unmarked vehicle onto the tarmac of the heliport. Christian sat in the front seat, Raven in the back. "What is it they say about a red sky?"

"Red sky at morn, sailors be warned." Even as Christian smiled at the old adage, he smelled humidity thick in the air. Real muggy. "Good thing we're not navigating by boat."

The detective shrugged. "Yes, but we may need one before the day is done."

"I see your point."

Up ahead, over a dozen men were hard at work, prepping for the mission. Dressed in camo BDUs with tactical-level body armor, Zharan's men looked like a team on maneuvers, a formidable army. They were equipped with Kevlar helmets and protective goggles, binoculars, extra mag pouches, radios with two-way headsets and ear pieces for stealth. For weapons, he saw everything from short-barreled shotguns and sniper-scoped M-14 rifles to shoulder-fired grenade launchers and H&K MP5SD submachine guns with suppressors.

Christian had read about Brazil's military police force being armed with military-grade weapons, trained in counterinsurgency tactics, and armed with machine guns and armored cars—a necessity in a war zone filled with drug smugglers and arms dealers who were better equipped.

Between the drug traffickers, gangs, and the well-armed police, he wondered about the civilian population caught in the middle, but shoved the thought from his mind. The men here today would risk their lives to rescue his father and right an injustice. Enforcing the law brought order to chaos. That had to be enough.

Two Bell 412EP helicopters were the focus of the activity up ahead, metal gray with green and white stripes down the fuselage and on the rear rotor, colors of the Brazilian flag. Each looked to hold up to fifteen men.

"Helicopters?" Christian asked. "How far are we going?"

Detective Fuentes pulled up to a group of vehicles and parked. "It's not how far exactly. Our target is accessible by road, for the most part, but we would lose our element of surprise and run the risk of ambush. I will let my chief explain the details. You understand this, no?"

"Yes, of course." Christian opened the door and got out of the car, Raven sliding out on his side of the vehicle. Nervous tension colored her eyes, no matter how much she tried to brush it off. She carried the rucksack, but Christian took it from her and hoisted it on his shoulder before heading toward the man in charge.

"Be sure to get medical supplies in each aircraft. And extra water bottles and batteries," Chief Zharan said, raising his voice, pointing to one of his men loading the far helicopter. When he saw Christian and Raven, accompanied by Detective Fuentes, he joined them halfway, shaking hands with them.

"Good morning. We are just about loaded." The man narrowed his eyes and shifted his focus between them. "I have rain ponchos and tactical body armor for your protection. I take it you have your own weapons as we discussed?"

"Yes. And extra mags." Christian nodded. "We're set."

"Fuentes, please see they get ponchos and body armor." Zharan gave the order and Fuentes took off. "I've got an aerial map. Let me explain what will happen today."

Grim-faced men hustled by them with a sense of urgency. No idle conversations, only work with a focus on the mission.

The chief escorted them to the open cargo door of the first aircraft and unfolded a topographical map with satellite aerial images. Zharan explained where the village was located and its layout. His men would land miles away, using it as a staging area for the operation, to minimize the sound of their approach. They'd trek from the north over a ridge, circle the village, and find the location where Charboneau was being held before they launched the raid.

After their briefing, Fuentes returned and handed Christian two dark green pouches containing rain gear and the body armor. Although he offered the rain gear to Raven, she declined. Christian noticed none of the other men wore it. Going into a potential skirmish, the rain protection would not only be awkward for hand-to-hand combat, but it might also interfere with any maneuvers involving stealth. The enemy would hear them coming.

Yeah, rain gear would keep them dry and deter the leeches. But the way he figured it, if the enemy hears you and shoots you dead, who the hell cares if you're dry and leech free? The ponchos got stuffed into his backpack. But without a second thought, Christian did shrug into his body armor, then helped Raven into hers by tightening the Velcro. The military-grade body armor would be bulky and hot to wear, but where they were going, they'd need it.

As they got organized, Zharan continued.

"This man, Rodrigo Santo? He's actually Mario Araujo, the leader of these people. We do not know how many in his village are involved with the kidnapping of Mr. Charboneau. There are probably women and children at this location, so we must be very careful. You will stay with me and follow my orders. Agreed?"

"Yes, certainly." Christian nodded.

"Agreed, yes," Raven chimed in.

"Then we are ready." Zharan turned and waved an arm, giving the order. "Green light. We have a go. Load up."

Rain began to fall, spotting the asphalt. It made a gentle patter on Christian's vest as he helped Raven into the first helicopter, holding her hand a little longer than necessary. She turned toward him and smiled, putting on a sturdy front. He climbed in and sat near her. A man on the ground shut the cargo bay door and gave a thumbs-up to the pilot as he backed away, heading for a small building near the helipad.

Two crewmen were in the cockpit, going through their checklist. Zharan sat next to Christian and Raven, with ten other men sitting shoulder-to-shoulder. Rapt in their own thoughts, Zharan's men stared straight ahead, not acknowledging their presence.

Rotor blades cranked overhead for both aircraft. The pilot in the other craft signaled with a nod and waited for his turn to take off. The fuselage rumbled and the skids lifted off the tarmac, the ground drifting out from under. They were airborne. As much as Christian wanted to speak to Raven, he kept his silence. The engine was loud and they had no privacy.

As the craft climbed, then pitched forward, the rain doused the outer hull. Beads of water streaked the windows, but through the rain Christian caught glimpses of the terrain below. Spotty areas of civilization and commercial outbuildings soon gave way to dense jungle. Rivers he didn't know the names of converged into larger tributaries, a maze of wetlands carved through lush foliage and trees. Miles and miles in every direction. The vast expanse made him feel small and insignificant.

The helicopter flew parallel to the other craft, the engine and rotor noise drowning out everything, even hampering his private thoughts. When the aircraft veered left, his stomach lurched. The queasy feeling reminded him of the gravity of what they were about to do. He found Raven staring back, as if she knew what he was thinking, but she wouldn't be completely right.

Yes, he thought about Charboneau and the fact this ordeal would soon be over. Soon he would know what had happened to his father. And soon he would know the price he'd pay for that knowledge.

But with that thought, flashes of Jasmine leapt into his memory, images from their time in Brazil. Raven might misinterpret his gut twisted in guilt, yet now he had a small appreciation for what Jasmine felt about failing to protect his father. He had taken over the rescue. *Her rescue.* She should've been allowed to finish and clear her conscience.

Christian crossed his arms and stared out the window. Although he shoved Jasmine Lee out of his mind, he knew she wouldn't stay put.

Chapter 20

Outskirts of Cuiabá

Dressed in worn jeans and a faded black T-shirt, Luis Duarte stared out the filthy cracked window of a clapboard shack wedged into a terraced shantytown. It was his home away from home since he'd gone underground, staying beyond Chief Zharan's reach. After the chief issued a bulletin on him, Duarte made a difficult choice to walk away from his life. Resentment churned hot in his belly, but he could not afford to confront the bastard. Not until he was stone cold ready.

Today he would be.

His dwelling for the last two days, no bigger than a matchbox, was crammed into the side of a slope with countless others above and below, between narrow dirt streets only wide enough for foot traffic. It had been abandoned long ago, but drug users and hookers still made use of it, at least until he moved in. It smelled of urine, body odor, and the tang of sex.

Trash and clumps of weeds had been shoved into cracks in the walls and ceiling to block bad weather. The recycling effort had not worked. Today, the steady downpour of rain leaked in and puddles of mud were gaining ground. The foul weather only made things worse, forging doubts in his mind about what lay ahead. A bad omen, if he believed such things. And with the feral cat population running rampant throughout the *favela*, feeding on rats and roaches, he could make a point they belonged here more than he did, but he wasn't so sure anymore.

The irony of his choice to retreat to such a place wasn't wasted on Duarte. Long before he became a police officer, he lived in a similar dwelling growing up as a child. It had defined him, irreparably. At the time, he did not realize the desperate poverty his family had endured. It had been his life, but now he didn't think he could return to it. He had seen too much, experienced too much. No, he couldn't go back to that life. And, insult to injury, the slum overlooked the modern silhouette of downtown Cuiabá. He glared at it now.

His personal reminder of the intolerance of this world . . . and what had been taken from him.

"No more," he muttered under his breath. "Not after today."

Reclaiming his life wouldn't be easy, but he had a plan. A duffel bag of personal belongings lay at his feet. Duarte dropped to a knee and stuffed one of his uniform shirts into it, zipping the bag shut before standing. He glanced at his watch, hating to be apart from the action, pinned up like a caged animal.

When his cell phone rang, he answered it, eager for news.

"Yes?"

"Sorry to disturb you, Luis, but our target is on the move." Duarte held the phone to his ear, recognizing the man's voice and the sound of road noise in the background. "As you said, he used a heliport north of the city to launch two helicopters. We counted over twenty men, heavily armed."

The man he had questioned most of last night had spoken the truth about Zharan's operation. Torture had a way of making life simple. A man either wants to live or he does not. Quite simple. He hoped everything the man said had been the truth. Life and death would depend upon it.

"Good work, Manolo." Duarte smirked. "You have a tracking beacon on both aircraft?"

"Yes, sir, we're on it. Time to go . . . but there's something else."

"Oh?" Duarte hated surprises.

"Sir, as you figured, the American went with him. But there is another woman with Delacorte. And we have not yet identified her. Another American."

The complications kept mounting. Duarte was not pleased. "Stick with the plan. We've got no choice now." He heaved the bag onto a shoulder and hustled for the door, phone to his ear. "I'll meet you at the rendezvous point in five."

"Already on my way. What do you want to do with the woman?"

Manolo had not asked about the American woman with his question. Images of Jasmine Lee flooded Duarte's head. Having her along might prove useful.

"Tell them to bring her, but don't let anyone see. She's not a woman easily forgotten . . . or trusted."

Duarte ended the call, wondering if Jasmine Lee or Nicholas Charboneau would have any appreciation for poetic justice. He hoped after today he'd be alive to appreciate the irony himself.

They had outrun the rain—for now—a short reprieve from what would come. The sun stabbed through an accumulation of darker clouds, fighting a losing battle. And as far as Raven's eye could see, the Amazon rain forest spread its dense blanket, covering this corner of the world.

She had no sense of which way they'd flown out of Cuiabá. Not that it mattered. Raven flew over a world so foreign and primitive, none of it felt familiar. With the added tension, the flight seemed to last an eternity, but now the pilot skirted treetops, heading for a small clearing, but big enough for both helicopters to land. Soon she'd leave the safety of the aircraft in search of a native tribe that had kidnapped an American for money.

For all she knew, Christian's father was already dead.

Harsh reality sent a chill over her skin. Raven kept her eyes focused on the ground below, searching the treeline for signs of trouble. She felt the weight of a holstered nine-millimeter Beretta 92FS, a weapon courtesy of Jasmine Lee.

The craft hovered as the pilot scanned the ground for a sturdy place to set the landing skids. When the aircraft touched down, the prop action kicked up dirt and whipped tall grasses and tree branches into a frenzy. Zharan's men shifted in their seats, ready to disembark. Oddly enough, a couple of them had to be nudged in the ribs. They'd fallen asleep. She'd seen it many times and it never ceased to surprise her. Everyone dealt with stress differently.

Raven sought peace of mind, but in her own way. She found herself staring into Christian's eyes. Gazing into their lush green with flecks of gold and sea blue, she indulged herself. This close, the color of his eyes always stole her breath.

Love reflected in their depths and it calmed her heart. With him by her side, she wasn't alone. And more important, neither was he. His fight had become hers.

"I've got your backside, big guy." She smiled.

"Good. Can't think of anyone I'd rather assign that duty." He winked, but the humor in his eyes faded. "Stick close, huh? And no heroics."

"Same goes double for you."

The cargo bay door opened and a rush of wind swept past her, the rotor kicking it up. Zharan and his men rushed through the door, hunched low and weapons drawn, setting up a perimeter.

Once on the ground, Zharan spoke with one of his men in rapid-fire Portuguese, consulting a map. The man must have been a native guide. He wore civilian clothes and a floppy jungle hat in camouflage green, and had a machete in a scabbard on his belt. An old guy with bulgy dark eyes, a scraggly graying beard, and brown skin the texture of rough-hewn leather.

Raven wondered how she had missed him before, but it made sense for Zharan to have an experienced guide as part of the operation.

The native headed toward the trees at a steady pace. Zharan's men followed single file as if they did it everyday. No one spoke. All eyes were on the surrounding jungle. To remain in the clearing meant exposure. In Portuguese, Zharan ordered two men to stay behind with the pilots to protect the aircraft, their only means of escape. The men nodded and ran for cover in the jungle, to defend their position from a distance with rifles. When it came time for reinforcements and the trip home, the chief would contact them via radio and order them to the village. A solid extraction plan.

Zharan pocketed the map in his shirt and joined them.

"You two will stick with me. We have some miles to go yet, so let's get started."

"We're right behind you." Christian nodded and extended his arm, letting her walk in front of him.

In no time Raven's skin felt damp and sticky, her hair and clothing wet with sweat after walking the short distance out of the clearing.

As she drew near the trees, they towered over her, much more impressive than from a distance. She stayed on Zharan's heels, Christian behind her. Walking single file, only those closest remained in sight. Most of the men ahead disappeared, camouflaged by overhanging branches and vines as massive as anacondas dangling from the treetops to the jungle floor. The thick green and brown canopy felt like an ancient house of worship, a sacred place. Heavy-duty root systems dug deep into the earth, dwarfing her presence with their age-old lineage. From centuries of dropped foliage, the jungle floor felt spongy and pliable underfoot and the ground smelled of decay, wet wood, and damp rich earth.

Like an entourage accompanying them, woolly monkeys hooted overhead and leapt from branch to branch. And colorful parrots screeched their passage, while smaller birds with bright plumage flitted between the tree limbs, more curious than fearful.

A cloud of insects swarmed over them, following fresh meat. At first Raven squinted through the hurling bugs, swatting them with a hand. But eventually she gave up and tried her best to ignore them. In no time she'd sweat off the bug repellent she had put on earlier, and she wasn't sure when or if she'd get a chance to put more on.

Then it started to rain again. Tree branches filtered the downpour, but soon she'd be drenched. The air felt muggy and thick. Everything around her grew dark and slick with rain. And the sound of it pummeling the earth filled her senses. A steady incessant drone.

Through it all, the men kept absolutely quiet, with eyes vigilant. Dark-skinned faces, each with a story she would probably never know. Off in the distance, the occasional zing of a machete splitting wood echoed through the jungle as the native guide cleared a path for them up ahead.

The elevation changed and they began to climb, scrambling up a steep and narrow trail. Below and to the right the ground dropped away. She had to watch her step, with the soil turning to slick mud under her boots. Lactic acid churned in the muscles of her legs, her thighs burning. Still, she pressed on without complaint. Her throat felt parched, even with the rain. She wanted a cool drink in the worst way, but none of the others drank, so she held off and satisfied herself with the raindrops that quenched her lips.

She refused to give them any reason to regret bringing a woman.

After a while the rain began to dissipate to a gentle patter. Yet off in the distance, Raven heard a muffled rumble like faraway thunder, only more persistent. Another storm? She had no idea what it was, but her gut knotted all the same. Somewhere in the back of her mind she knew what the sound was, but her brain hadn't registered it yet.

Still, she climbed on, leaning into the steep hill to keep her balance, grateful for any time she had spent on a Stairmaster. But it hadn't been near enough. The trek uphill finally leveled off, providing a welcome break from the torturous climb.

The rain had stopped, but now the rumble grew louder and masked the chime of the machete up ahead and the chatter of animals. The trees thinned and the sun's rays filtered through the leaves and vines and pierced the thick canopy. On this side of the ridge, blue sky penetrated the shadows.

As she crested a small mound and the men ahead of her started downhill, Raven knew what she would find. A massive and raging waterfall surged from the jagged cliffs beneath them. Breathtaking. From her vantage point, she didn't have a clear view of the pool of water below. A thick and constant mist churned, making it disappear. And the coolness of the water-fall billowed and touched her, giving an instant chill against the blistering heat of her skin, still damp with rain.

She turned to find Christian standing at her side. She felt his hand on her neck as he took a moment to enjoy the view. He let a couple of Zharan's men pass.

"Come on. They won't want us to pull up the rear. Time to go. You okay?" he asked.

"Sure." Raven took a swig of water and nodded, wiping her mouth and face with a sleeve. "Let's go."

It took them the better part of an hour to clear the waterfall and start their descent into a valley. But as they did, Raven spied a small patch of grassland below, a break in the surrounding trees. A section had been cleared. She saw the rooftops of a small village, a circle of huts with thatched roofs clustered around a larger communal structure. Although small children played, most of the inhabitants looked busy, preparing for some kind of celebration. Too much was going on for an average day of survival.

A central fire pit burned high, natives milling around it, occasionally flailing into a dance. And a large blackened carcass spun on a spit nearby, smoke spiraling into the air. They were still too far away to see what was happening, but Raven knew Christian had spotted the villagers too. She only took a moment to assess the situation, then turned down the trail with him close behind. No doubt he grasped her sense of urgency.

These people would not be expecting a fight. On the surface, the element of surprise would be in their favor, but she didn't want to take that fact for granted. An offensive could turn deadly in a hurry with men protecting their families. Raven picked up her pace, ignoring her aches, pains, and mounting bug bites.

With women and children involved, Zharan knew this assault operation would be more difficult. He expected it and said so. This would be his show, and she wouldn't second-guess the man. Her experience in tactical operations was limited, but she had a working knowledge of what would happen. Out of reflex, her mind ran through a checklist of preparations after she'd seen the village.

First, the crisis scene, targets, and innocents would have to be identified with solid intel from two-man observation teams. Entry routes and rally points with backup strategies would be nailed down. Each assault team would be comprised of four to five men. They'd be assigned specific responsibilities, position locations, and fields of fire. Some men would be designated as perimeter security, and an officer or two would be tapped for sniper duty.

Given the layout of the village, mission briefings would be conducted on the fly by radio with no practice runs. After the initial round of diversionary tactics, a series of launched flash bang grenades, the teams would sync their assault using the explosives. They'd insert at multiple points to overload Araujo's ability to react. And Chief Zharan would coordinate the command from a central location through radio communications. With heavy firepower, they'd get in and out as quickly as possible.

Despite the expectation of a smooth maneuver, she couldn't help but worry. Her cop instinct kicked in with an underlying restlessness, a familiar sensation before an armed siege. She wanted this day to be over.

But most of all, she prayed no one had to die.

Sitting cross-legged on the ground, hands resting on his elbows, Mario Araujo stared straight ahead. Dressed in a fine colorful tunic, he held his back erect and his head perfectly still, his eyes fixed on the festivities outside the communal hut. The people of his village wore clothes of bright cloth and strings of beads, their cheeks painted with simple shapes. They displayed their finest baskets and pottery, filled to the brim with various food offerings—all in celebration of his return.

They had no idea of his plans to make their feast more memorable, but he had no choice now. The time had come.

He shut his eyes and let the man who knelt before him work.

The village medicine man took great pains in detailing the paint across the skin of Mario's face. With fingertips dipped in black and rich ochre, the man made elaborate geometric shapes, a sign of nobility for his tribe. The face paint smelled of clay and glided on smooth and cool.

It reminded him of his childhood days in the shadow of the great Chapada dos Guimarães. He could hunt alone for days and not see another human being, then return to camp, a person to be admired for his kills. A simpler time.

When he opened his eyes again, he noticed the rain had stopped. Soon the celebration would begin in earnest. The hog had been butchered and was nearly done. His people waited. In anticipation, their eyes shifted toward him as he sat in the shadows of the communal hut.

The medicine man had done his work. He bowed his head, gathered up his materials, and retreated, leaving him alone with his thoughts. Under his tunic, Mario felt the weight of his gun, a weapon he had used countless times in the city. And he also carried the encrypted phone, his only link to the man who had arranged this whole thing.

Soon, he would not need the incriminating connection.

Mario would pay his final visit to Nicholas Charboneau in the cave behind the waterfall. Accompanied by two of his men, he'd pretend to bring the American water and sustenance, food prepared with an overdose of the Iboga. When Charboneau's mind was no longer his own, he would haul him from the cave to the center of his village for all to bear witness.

When they learned what he wanted to do, his people would be shocked at first, but he would make them understand. To return to the old ways, big medicine would be required. And to clean the slate of injustice, they would have to make difficult choices. But it must start here and now, with him as their new leader.

Nicholas Charboneau would be their first human sacrifice. His death would be merciful and quick, before the Iboga did its worst damage. By that time, perhaps a knife through his beating heart would be considered a mercy.

In his village, he would deal justice as he saw fit, with no one to answer to—a truly liberating feeling after years of denying his heritage. There would be no need to ask the opinion of an outsider, using the special phone to reach his mysterious benefactor. Mario had made up his mind, yet he didn't think of himself as a killer. Instead, he considered himself a man who did not shirk his duties. He had a responsibility to protect his people. *Damn the reward money!*

Between what his associate had told him before and what he had verified since, he drew only one conclusion. Someone had ordered the recent changes at

Genotech Labs and must have found a way to profit from the pain of his people's addictions. Although Mario couldn't directly tie Charboneau to this, his accomplice had made the link clear enough, not holding back. As a fellow countryman, the man resented the intrusion of the wealthy American too.

Surely his partner would understand what must be done. Some beliefs transcended the significance of money.

Knowing the truth behind Charboneau changed everything. A simple kidnapping would not suffice now. Charboneau represented much more than just a threat to his people's way of life. He embodied the total disregard for them as human beings. This would not be tolerated.

Mario stood and pulled his tunic around him, his head held high. With the jail cell key in hand, he gathered a jug of water and a tin plate of food he had prepared earlier. Outside the hut, he nodded and gestured for two men to help him carry the special last meal for his American "guest."

Soon it would be over for Nicholas Charboneau. Mario sincerely hoped the man's god would have mercy on his soul—for he would find no forgiveness here.

CHAPTER 21

Chief Zharan lay on his belly, propped on his elbows with binoculars focused on the huts in the clearing below. As Raven had expected, he made his assignments and ordered his men in teams to surround the village. They awaited the final go ahead. The chief spoke Portuguese softly into his headset, gathering intel and communicating his orders. She didn't have to speak the language to understand.

A few things had gone in their favor. The dense foliage and the treeline provided adequate cover for the operation. And the village looked preoccupied with a celebration. The chanting and activity proved quite a distraction. Another good cover for Zharan's maneuverings.

Yet something bothered her.

She didn't want to make an assumption, but these people appeared to be amateurs compared to other South American abductions she had read about.

Hard to believe they had any connection to the city of Cuiabá at all, much less staged a kidnapping there. Could they have pulled it off without help? It made her wonder about the accuracy of Zharan's intel. She watched the village using Jasmine's binoculars. The huts were made of rudimentary materials indigenous to the area—pliable tree limbs, layers of grasses, sod walls—but some were made from bits of corrugated metal and plywood. She estimated forty adult inhabitants, with twenty or more varying under the age of fifteen years. Younger dark-skinned children with swollen bellies and bare bottoms were harder to count. They ran among the adults, playing games in bare feet around the communal fire blazing in the center of the village. And in a separate pit, the villagers cooked a hog carcass.

Raven counted thirty huts with three other structures of unknown purpose. The openings to the dwellings faced inward, making it easy for the tribe to defend the core of the community, yet the arrangement made them vulnerable to more sophisticated surveillance, as the police were doing now.

So far, everything had gone better than expected, except for one thing. They had not found Nicholas Charboneau. Raven hugged the ground next to Christian and handed him the binoculars.

"Don't think they're expecting company," she whispered.

"Good for us." Christian stared through the field glasses, muttering under his breath. "Any signs of Charboneau?"

"No. None so far." She nudged her chin. "He might be in one of those smaller huts, there and the two over to the left." She pointed to the three small huts that didn't look to be inhabited. "But if he were held in one of those, you'd think there'd be a guard out front."

"Yeah, I agree."

"And I haven't seen a weapon either." She grimaced. "But that doesn't mean they don't have them."

"Yeah." Despite his reply, Christian didn't sound convinced. He looked through the binoculars with renewed interest.

Villagers circled the big fire pit, strolling and dancing in one direction. And they chanted, a rhythmic repetitive sound of mostly male voices building to a crescendo. Painted faces, bright colors, and festive robes; Christian felt an air of anticipation running through the village like an electrical charge.

"Something's going down . . . up ahead there." He shifted his focus. "What are they up to?"

The large communal hut was comprised of a woven mat of grasses pitched over the top of a wooden frame. The covering had the texture of dense hemp. One side, facing them, was completely open. They saw hammocks stretched along the back wall inside, hung between heavy wooden stakes pounded into the ground. A man standing in front of the opening waved for a couple of men to follow him. Dressed in an elaborate tunic, with his face almost completely painted, he had the look of a medicine man or native chief.

The three men left the encampment and headed for a well-worn trail—straight toward them. Within minutes the natives would be right on top of their position.

Christian got to his feet and hunched down, turning toward Zharan. "They're bringing food and water to Charboneau. We gotta follow 'em."

"You don't know that for sure."

"It doesn't matter. We can't let them go without someone on 'em," Christian said, pleading his case. "You have your men assigned, you can't afford to send more than one or two men to tail these guys. Let Raven and me do it."

A stern look spread over the chief's face and he narrowed his eyes at the native men on the trail below. Christian knew what he was thinking. The path crossed near enough to their position to matter. And if the natives deviated from it, there would be greater risk. Either way, the men would be upon them soon. Zharan had no time to waste.

"Your woman will stay here," he said in a hushed tone. "Take Fuentes."

Christian caught the move. Raven raised her chin to protest, no doubt upset over getting shot down for the assignment by an overdose of testosterone and chauvinism. To her credit, she kept her silence and only glared at the chief. But the man ignored her and gave an order to Fuentes over the headset without hesitation. They exchanged words in Portuguese. Clearly, Zharan welcomed authority and wielded it with an iron hand, no questions asked.

Within seconds, Fuentes crept up behind Christian, stone quiet and with a grim face.

"Fuentes will stay in touch on the com set." Then Zharan glared at Christian and pointed a finger. "And you'll follow my man's orders without question. Do you understand?"

All business, Christian nodded to the chief. Before

he left, he shot a sympathetic gaze at Raven, followed by a subtle wink. She raised an eyebrow and the corner of her mouth twitched, her version of a smile under duress. Time to go.

If the man wearing the war paint and fancy duds was someone in a position of authority, or even Mario Araujo himself, Christian and Fuentes had a shot at ending this battle before it had even begun. Without a head honcho, the tribe may not resist. And if he and Fuentes found his father alive and unharmed, perhaps this operation might end without bloodshed. They could slip away without the natives knowing they'd been there until it was too late.

Even with the good thoughts, Christian couldn't shake the anxiety welling in his chest. He had no idea what triggered the feeling. And to complicate matters, it began to rain. Dark clouds cast shadows along the ground and deepened the reach of its steamy fingers into the jungle. From experience, he knew drizzle could turn into a deluge in short order. Dirt would dissolve into a slick stream of mud.

One last time, he glanced over his shoulder at Raven, and found her staring back. Although he wasn't a mind reader, he'd double down on his bet that she felt the same way.

Something felt off, but he had no tangible reason to turn back now.

"Caves can be sacred to these people," Fuentes whispered, binoculars up. Raindrops pelted his helmet and shoulders. "The path to the waterfall is well worn. And now they climb. They've got a cave up there." The loud drone of the tumbling water almost made it impossible to hear him.

Christian hunkered down behind thick under-
growth next to the Brazilian detective. His drenched
clothes clung to his body like a second layer of skin
he didn't need. He watched as the three native men
traversed a rock ledge near the base of the waterfall.
The boulders were slick with rain, and the men tread
with slow deliberate moves. A cave made sense. He
couldn't think of any other reason for these men to
make such a treacherous climb.

Eventually, the men disappeared behind the thick
sheet of water and did not emerge again. If a cave did
exist, they had found it.

"Come on. Let's go," Christian prompted. "That
cave. We might lose 'em in there."

"I've got night vision gear. You don't." Fuentes
turned to face him, rain beaded on his cheeks and
drizzled off his chin. "Perhaps you should stay near
the base of the waterfall and wait for me to return."

Fuentes pulled out his tactical night vision head-
gear and fixed it to his helmet. Once inside the cave,
the special goggle would slip over the detective's eyes,
giving him the ability to see in the dark. He had to
stay far enough behind the men they were tracking
to avoid their flashlights, which made his gear inef-
fective.

Christian shook his head. "No worries. Me and
the dark are old friends." He took the lead, slogging
through the mud. He didn't wait for Fuentes to catch
up. The darkness had once been the catalyst for his
greatest fear, only reminding him of the tragic loss of
the Delacorte family who'd raised him all those years
ago. The abject feeling of being powerless had been
at the root of his worst nightmare.

Now, the inky black would be his ally.

* * *

Nicholas thought he saw a play of light on boulders to his left. Sitting alone in the dark had wrought havoc on his senses. Made his brain mush and messed with his equilibrium. Perhaps he had only imagined the dim flicker of light, needed to see it for his own sanity. He pushed his back against the rock wall and used his hands and arms to shove off the ground. He'd grown weak, his throat parched.

He stood and waited. Chin high, he mustered the last bit of dignity he had left. If he had a shot at escaping, he'd have to take it soon—no matter the odds. Eventually, he'd be too weak to make a convincing go of it. The light got brighter, more distinct. Someone was definitely coming. He heard their approach echoing in the cavern. His heart kicked up its usual pace.

Desperation was distasteful. He wanted no part of it.

"Ah, he stands on his own two feet. Good. Room service has brought food and water. This may not be Hotel Palma Dourada fare, but let it not be said I am an inhospitable host."

The native man's face was painted and he wore elaborate ceremonial garb. Nicholas almost didn't recognize his abductor.

"What is this? Trick or treat? Sorry, but I'm fresh out of candy." He couldn't help it. Sarcasm came naturally.

One of the men laid the water jug down and scooted a tin plate through the metal bars. The image shot a moment of déjà vu through Nicholas. The peculiar sensation had something to do with Jasmine, but he couldn't explain how or why. Although he wanted nothing more than to drink and eat, he resisted the urges of his body and heeded his instincts.

"No thanks. I'm quite full, actually. Couldn't eat another bite." He rubbed his lean belly and slouched against the back wall.

His captor walked toward the bars and sat on a nearby boulder, a smug look on his face.

"You are a stubborn man." He shook his head. "In my country, we learn not to squander such opportunities. You never know when or if your next meal will come at all. It makes no difference to me whether you eat or not. Your destiny is sealed."

"Then perhaps we should talk instead. Food for the soul." Nicholas remained standing and crossed his arms, trying to look nonchalant and in control. Hardly the way he felt. "You mentioned that you know why I came to your country. And that I have committed crimes against your people. In the United States, the accused has a right to face his accuser. Surely you would grant me that simple right. Tell me what you think you know."

Even in the dark, Christian took the lead with eyes shut, using his senses more than his eyesight to feel his way. He fought to suppress his trauma-induced fear of the dark, forcing himself to move and remain focused on the hunt. Like a bat with sonar, he maneuvered through pitch-black, second nature from the training he had obsessed over most of his adult life. His hand was never far from his Marine Corps Ka-Bar knife.

The native men had a lead. Their flashlights weren't visible, but he followed their trail all the same. Their rough-hewn damp clothing, the distinctive smell of their skin, and the face paint left a marker in the air for him to follow. Different from the natural smells of the cave.

Fuentes thought he had an advantage wearing his night vision gear and tried to slip ahead, taking a turn down a tunnel that veered right. But Christian stopped him from stepping into a hole, placing an arm across the man's chest. He shook his head after he knew he had the cop's attention.

Christian gestured without speaking, knowing the detective would understand he needed to step around the ditch and stick with him. He didn't have time to explain how he trailed the natives, but he kept Fuentes on track, back to the main cavern. The air in the cave smelled thick with minerals and an earthy dampness. His wet clothes brought a chill to his skin, but he kept moving, Fuentes close at his heels.

When he heard voices in the distance, Christian risked opening his eyes. Beyond the bend, a distant glow shone against a rock wall ahead. The light flickered. He couldn't make out the words that garbled in echo, but Fuentes removed his night vision gear and moved ahead with his Taurus .45 caliber ACP in a two-fisted grip, silent as death.

Christian knew it was out of his hands now. Fuentes would take over.

His captor insisted, "You came to Brazil to conduct genetic experiments on my people that aren't condoned in the U.S. Something to do with drug addiction. Do not deny it. And that so-called new medical clinic you have added to Genotech Labs is a front for all of it."

Nicholas grimaced and shrugged. "What are you

talking about? What clinic? Genotech is a lab for genetics research, yes. And yes, I've funded some of its efforts, but you're mistaken if you think there's some new medical facility there. I would know of such a thing."

The man laughed aloud. His voice carried through the cavernous space.

"Do you think me a fool? I have seen this clinic with my own eyes. I can assure you that I know what I'm talking about, sir." His captor stood, indignant. He paced the front of the cell. "You have the local military police working with you. They take addicted men off the streets and use them to conduct their experiments. And these men are never seen again. This is reprehensible."

Nicholas shook his head and stepped closer to the metal bars. "I admit to purchasing the services of key personnel within the police force and the local government. Such an investment tends to work in my favor, but I prefer to be more discreet. What is this about taking drug addicts off the streets for experiments? I know nothing of this."

"Why do you bother to dispute it? I have spoken to a witness. He confided everything."

"Look, you and I are men who bend the rules when it suits us, but what you're suggesting seems foolhardy and risky. Who is this witness you speak of? Let me confront my accuser. Isn't a man's life worth the extra effort?" He pleaded his case, voice raised.

"That won't be necessary." Another man's voice came from the shadows. Low and threatening.

On instinct, Nicholas rushed to the back wall of his prison cell. His captor reached under his tunic, no doubt in search of a weapon.

The other two native men turned with a start. One raised a flashlight and the other reached for a knife. A shot rang out. Then two more. The one with the knife took a round to the face. His head snapped back and twisted. His body followed the momentum and convulsed when it hit the ground. His brain was dead but the rest of him hadn't gotten the message.

The second man collapsed backward with shock forged in his eyes. The sound of bullets hitting his chest center mass echoed through the cave long after his heart stopped beating. Two meaty thuds. Once a man hears a sound like that, he never forgets it.

The pungent smell of gunpowder hung heavy in the air. It infused with the coppery sweetness of blood and the foul stench of human waste, the familiar mélange of violent death.

"Hold it. Drop your weapon. State of Mato Grosso police." A guy in fatigues materialized out of the dark like a ghost. He held his weapon on the tribal leader, his eyes hard-edged and unflinching.

The man with the painted face and ceremonial robes laid his gun down. His eyes were fixed on the dead men at his feet. His men. In shock, he didn't appear to care what happened next.

"What are you doing? You didn't have to shoot 'em." Another voice came from the dark, but Nicholas couldn't see the man.

He barely heard the words of their exchange. His ears still rang. The sudden brutality left him stunned, yet Nicholas knew what it took to execute men this way.

"Don't worry. No one will hear the gun fire this deep in the cave, especially with the waterfall outside," the guy with the gun and the upper hand insisted. A soul incapable of guilt.

"That's not the point," the other man argued.

When he emerged from the shadows, the second man came into focus. Those eyes. That face. Like standing in front of a mirror that shed twenty years from his age.

It took Nicholas some time to recognize the face of the son he'd never met.

Chapter 22

Christian stared into the eyes of his father for the first time. Until now, he'd been preoccupied with the rescue and hadn't thought about how this would feel. The reality of the moment hit him hard. He stepped closer to the metal bars, unable to take his eyes off Nicholas Charboneau. He searched for the young man that had stolen his mother Fiona's heart all those many years ago. Most of all, he wanted to find his connection to the man. His father.

"You okay?"

With disheveled clothes and hair and a gaunt face, Charboneau looked like hell. And in the dim light, Christian thought he saw a glimmer of tears welling in the man's eyes. Or maybe it was only his imagination, stirred by his own feelings.

"I am now." He nodded. "How did you . . . ? Can't believe you came."

"How could I not?" Christian smiled, but the quiet moment between them faded.

"My name is Detective Arturo Fuentes. I'm with the military police for the state of Mato Grosso. Can you walk, Mr. Charboneau?" Fuentes asked, still holding his gun on the native man.

"Yes. Please . . . get me out of here," Nicholas answered, but hadn't taken his gaze off Christian. Those penetrating eyes took in every detail, as if he wanted to capture the moment. But then again, maybe he was reading into it.

"With all that face paint, I barely recognized you. You must be Mario Araujo," the detective said with amusement in his voice. "Keep your hands up and kick that gun to me. No fast moves."

Araujo did as he was told. The gun skittered across stone to the feet of the detective, but he didn't pick it up. He stayed focused on the tribal leader.

"I know you have the keys. Open the cell." When the man hesitated, Fuentes added, "I can search your body for them. It makes no difference to me."

Araujo slowly moved his hands toward his tunic.

"Be careful, old man," Fuentes threatened, shifting his aim to the man's head. "Real slow."

The native man pulled out the key and opened the lock. Nicholas stepped through the cell door, but stopped in front of Araujo.

"I meant what I said about that clinic. And I don't know anything about people taken off the streets for experiments."

The native man looked up in surprise with eyes narrowed, but didn't say anything.

"Mr. Delacorte. Please assist me by handcuffing this man." The detective held out a set of cuffs, but kept his gun on Araujo. "I will take care of the rest."

After Christian secured the man's hands behind his back, Fuentes picked up the loose gun and searched his prisoner to make sure he didn't have any other surprises. When he found a cell phone, the detective pulled it out and looked at it with interest.

"Nice phone. Who would you need to call from out here?"

Araujo kept his face unreadable. "I use it for emergencies only. For my people."

Fuentes glared at him with skepticism. "We'll see about that."

Once he was satisfied with his search, the cop stuffed the cell phone in one of his vest pockets and tried his com set, but got no reception. The cave caused interference.

"I'll try again when we get out of here. If you would see to Mr. Charboneau, I will take care of Araujo." Fuentes picked up a flashlight from the ground. He stepped over the dead man who had once held it, without giving him a second look. "Grab the other light. You may not need it, but Mr. Charboneau might appreciate it."

Fuentes smirked and holstered his weapon. He yanked Araujo by the arm and hauled him back the way they'd come, taking half the light with him. The cavern grew dark. Shadows stretched across stone. For the sake of his father, Christian reached down and picked up the other flashlight with reluctance. Flecks of blood and tissue covered the still burning light. He couldn't help but look into the accusing eyes of the second dead man. The smell of death hung heavy in the air. Fuentes could have avoided taking the shot. He didn't have to kill. The cop never even gave a warning.

"What did he mean by that? About not needing the light?" his father asked.

"Nothing. Let's get out of here." Christian wiped his hands on his pants and walked beside Charboneau, careful to shine the light on the path in front of him.

"Please tell me something." His father reached for his arm and pulled him to a stop, letting the detective and Araujo stretch their lead. "If you're here, that must mean Jasmine told you what happened, right?"

"Jasmine did ask me to help, yes. And Fiona was willing to put up the ransom."

"So Jasmine must be okay. He let me believe she'd been killed, but somehow I knew. Where is she? Why isn't she here?"

Christian saw the urgency in his eyes. He felt it in his grip. The man had more concern for Jasmine than for his own safety. And that told him a lot.

"I wish I knew." Christian shook his head. "We've got a lot to talk about."

The downpour had come in waves, from a gentle patter to a gully washer. It kept the mosquitoes to a minimum, but had no other redeeming qualities as far as Raven was concerned. Now the rain came steady and unrelenting. She'd have mixed feelings about taking a hot shower when this day ended. The skin of her fingertips had begun to prune.

Drenched head to toe, she kept watch over the villagers with binoculars, yet Chief Zharan drew her attention whenever he moved or spoke into his com set. She hadn't known the man long, but felt his agitation even from a distance. Christian and Fuentes had been gone for what seemed like an eternity. Soon, the villagers would notice the missing men and might go looking for them. They were sitting on a time bomb of their own creation.

And Zharan knew it.

Forcing a confrontation with these people would be hard to explain if Zharan's intel wasn't complete and Charboneau wasn't being held here. So much was riding on word from Detective Fuentes. When it finally came, she felt a fraction of the chief's relief. No one took it quite as hard as the guy in charge.

"Fuentes reports he and your Mr. Delacorte have freed Nicholas Charboneau and he is able to walk. And Mario Araujo is in custody." He smiled.

"That means we can pull out, right?" she asked. "These people have no need to know we were ever here."

"Yes. I've ordered my men to fall back. We will meet Fuentes at the base of the waterfall and continue from there, back the way we came. It's been a good day." He tapped her lightly on the shoulder.

She returned his smile. "Yes, it has."

After the police chief left, Raven took one last look at the natives below while the tactical team maneuvered by her in silent retreat. The simplicity of the villagers' lives intrigued her, but their leader fascinated her even more. Given the choice of so-called civilization and this simpler existence, Mario Araujo had chosen to live here with his people. Not the mind-set of your typical kidnapper. The pieces to this puzzle didn't add up.

But another thought shoved aside her questions about Araujo and his people.

She found her heart racing with the prospect of resuming her life with Christian. *Her future.* He had rescued his father and now would have time to get to know the man. She understood the importance of family. And with Christian, she had a shot at starting one of her own. In that instant, Raven felt the pain and the joy of every moment she had shared with him and came to one conclusion. Finding Christian had been worth it all.

"Yeah, I'd say it's been a very good day," she whispered, then moved out with the rest of the men.

Fighting the lump in her throat, Raven forgot about the rain and the miserable conditions. None of it mattered. She couldn't wait to see Christian. He had anchored her world with his love. Now they would have a lifetime to figure out the rest.

"This Captain Duarte, is he the kind of man who would kill Jasmine?"

It took a long moment for Christian to answer his father's question. Charboneau had been through so much and didn't need this extra burden of guilt, yet his very lifestyle had exposed his bodyguard to this type of danger. What did he expect?

"I really don't know." In the end, he couldn't lie to the man.

"I have to get back. Find her," his father vowed.

Christian nodded. "I'll help." But he doubted Charboneau heard his offer.

His father clenched his jaw. Raindrops beaded on his face, then drained down to drip off his chin. He didn't bother to wipe them away. Kneeling at the water's edge, Nicholas stared across the undulating pool at the base of the falls, his mind as unsettled and turbulent as the water's surface.

Clearly, the man didn't like what he'd heard about Captain Luis Duarte and the new situation with Jasmine. Christian got the distinct feeling it would not be a good move to trade places with the Brazilian cop. He had no idea what drove the enigmatic police captain, but Charboneau was another story. His loyalty to Jasmine, and whatever else he felt for her, would far outweigh his sense of right or wrong, assuming he had a conscience at all. Christian trusted his gut instinct. And it told him his father was a far more dangerous man than Duarte. How he knew this, he couldn't quite put a finger on it. Yet he knew it with certainty.

Nicholas continued cleaning up, his emotions contained once again. "You haven't told the police I'm your father, have you?"

Nicholas didn't wait for his answer. He scooped water into his hands and splashed it onto his face, scrubbing his skin. The rain had turned to drizzle, not enough to do the job. A layer of sweat and grime came off, and he doused his wavy hair, leaving it wringing wet.

When he didn't reply, his father looked over his shoulder, prompting him with an expectant stare.

"No. I thought it would . . . complicate things." Christian straddled a fallen tree and flicked a flat rock along the surface of the water. It skipped four times.

"Or maybe you'd rather distance yourself from someone like me."

"I don't want to pass judgment." The lack of conviction in his voice was hard to miss.

"You may not want to, but it's hard not to have an opinion, isn't it?" his father pressed. The unusual violet color to his eyes turned to midnight blue under the overcast sky. "I'd rather we clear the air. It's more my style, and I hope yours too."

Christian didn't answer at first. He took a quick glance to his right. Fuentes had taken Araujo and given them a wide berth. And with the rumbling waterfall, they would have their privacy. But they'd have little time alone. According to Fuentes, Zharan and his men were only minutes away.

If his father wanted the truth, he'd lay it out for him—his way.

"Why did you come here . . . to Brazil?" he asked. "You've got a connection to Genotech Labs. You admitted that to Araujo. I heard you in the cave." Everything came out in a rush. Indignation mixed with hostility. "Hell, it doesn't take a genius to figure out you're manipulating genetics for the drug addicted, like they aren't already living in a hell on earth."

Christian tossed another stone but didn't watch where it landed. He wasn't done.

"And that so-called clinic? I caught some of the late-night action with Jasmine. Araujo was right. The cops were taking drug addicts off the streets and turning them over to Phillips. I got the distinct feeling it was a one-way trip."

"Whoa." With a grimace, Nicholas raised both hands. "Good thing you aren't here to pass judgment. I'd hate to think what your opinion of the old man might be if you thought I was a lying conniving bastard who took advantage of poor helpless meth heads."

"Don't try taking me on a guilt trip. I'm not buying a ticket." He piled on a heaping dose of sarcasm. "And do us both a favor. Don't deny you have a connection to drug trafficking. My father, the pusher."

Christian hadn't realized the depth of his anger. Everything he'd learned about his father after coming to Brazil had welled to the surface. He tossed another rock across the water. This one sank.

"Makes me wonder what Fiona ever saw in you. Correct that. Still sees in you." There it was. He'd said it.

They sat in silence until Charboneau said, "Believe me, I wonder that myself. I never deserved her love, but oh, how I wanted it."

Nicholas sat back on his haunches and stared at Christian, straightforward and unflinching.

"Perhaps the best way to answer your question is to say I have many regrets in my life." Nicholas stared off into the distance, past Christian, his mind rooted in the past. "But the way I treated your mother is at the top of that long list. She was the road not taken. My dear sweet Fiona will haunt the rest of my days. It's the one constant in my life."

He shut his eyes and sighed, but he wasn't finished.

"And you? She never told me about you, for good reason. She was always the more pragmatic and rational one." Nicholas shook his head, then fixed his eyes on Christian. "It took a lot of guts to risk your neck for someone you don't know or respect. For whatever it's worth, I want to thank you for what you did."

Christian hadn't expected to hear Charboneau talk about regrets with such openness. Sad, but he had no idea if he could trust the words coming from his father's mouth. No matter how much he wanted to.

"Thanks for sharing that . . ." Christian had no idea what to think. "But your involvement with this med clinic at Genotech is so damning."

Indignation flashed across Charboneau's eyes. "Look, I already told Araujo I had nothing to do with any clinic at the lab. What's it going to take to—"

He didn't get a chance to finish. Zharan and his men came up the trail and overtook the small clearing.

When Nicholas saw a smiling Chief Zharan, he slowly stood with hands on his hips, a look of disbelief set in his eyes. "Well, I'll be damned. What the hell are you doing here?"

CHAPTER 23

"You two know each other?" Christian asked, standing between the two men. He raised his voice to be heard over the waterfall. But Fuentes and the rest of Zharan's team drifted into a circle around them, insulating them from the white noise of tumbling water.

"All too well, I'm afraid," his father replied with a subtle shake of his head.

"Does my presence here truly surprise you, Nicholas?" The smug expression on Zharan's face added to the tension already mounting between them. "Did you really think I would back off and let an outsider take from my country?"

"What's he talking about?" Christian asked, shifting his gaze to Charboneau.

His father ignored his question, the corner of his lip curled into a sneer. He drilled Zharan with violet eyes teeming with contempt.

"It wasn't about an outsider taking anything that bothered you, Ricardo. You're not the kind of guy who likes being number two. You wanted it all. With you, it's all about greed and power."

"You looked down your nose at what I could bring to the table. And you never would have thought I had the stroke to pull this off, but here we are. You underestimated me."

"All you brought to the table was poor taste and unwarranted risk. You're the one behind this so-called med clinic with its illicit experiments."

Zharan grimaced. "You weren't moving fast enough to suit me. And I was beginning to question your real motives."

"And my kidnapping? That was you too."

Zharan looked at Fuentes with a sideways glance. His number one man grimaced in question. But no one looked more confused than Mario Araujo himself. His father had struck a chord, but Christian didn't know how to read it. *What the hell was going on?*

"Let's just say I knew what might have happened," Zharan said. "I had only recently become aware of Araujo's activities in my role as chief of police."

"Oh, bullshit. You got Mario involved so you could blame the local natives. But why not just kill me from the start?"

Zharan tensed, then seemed relieved to be off the topic of the kidnapping and eager to change the subject.

"I'd face too many questions and the interest of your crime syndicate. I had to come up with a plausible reason that didn't land on my doorstep. Jasmine

Lee was supposed to bear witness to it all and be the messenger when the time came for your Chicago business associates to hear the bad news of your demise. But she had to bring back help. And Christian Delacorte couldn't leave well enough alone. He had to spotlight the genetics lab and uncover the connection to Araujo. And as you can imagine, I had no interest in finding you alive. Unfortunately, it was only a matter of time before I had to step in and take care of things myself. I fed Delacorte just enough information to get him to trust me."

"So why the rescue? A pretty big operation," his father asked.

Zharan shrugged. "Who am I to deprive Mr. Delacorte and his cop lady friend of hope? I might have spared Ms. Mackenzie, but with her link to law enforcement back in the states, I couldn't risk it." The man shook his head and chuckled under his breath. "I'm not partial to loose ends, as you can see. Your man Delacorte was far too stubborn and determined. I was afraid of his connection to your business back in Chicago, so why not lead the lambs to slaughter by dangling a carrot? They came willingly. Captain Duarte, on the other hand, is a sly fox. He will be a challenge."

The chief cocked his head and waggled a finger at Charboneau. "You know, for someone so perceptive of human nature, it amazes me you never saw this coming, Nicholas." Zharan didn't hide his amusement. He had the upper hand and he knew it. "That ego of yours made you vulnerable. You thought you'd come to this sleepy little Brazilian town on the edge of the great Amazon rain forest and take charge with all your financial resources. Well, down here, you're on my turf. My country. Using my people. I only claimed what was rightfully mine to take."

Nicholas smiled without any real humor, a look of disdain forged in his eyes, and said, "You're right about one thing. I should've known better. Never trust a man you can bribe."

"What's going on?" Raven asked, coming off the trail and slipping next to him.

Zharan had played him. He even coyly listened while Christian pleaded his case to be taken on this raid. *Damn! What an idiot!* The bastard wanted that from the start, and Christian had made it way too easy. He'd gambled with his future to uncover the last piece to the puzzle of his past—and he just threw the dice and came up snake eyes—crapped out.

And now Raven would pay the price for his mistake.

"Glad you could join us, my dear. Now that we are all present and accounted for . . ." Zharan waved a hand to Fuentes. "Would you do the honors, Arturo?"

Fuentes grinned and pulled his gun, barking an order to his men. "Take off the body armor and search for weapons, then cuff them. Remove all forms of identification." When he fixed his gaze on Christian, he added, "You can see in the dark, my friend. But I bet you never saw this coming."

The detective laughed, a haunting abrasive sound. Christian wasn't likely to forget it.

"Base Camp, this is Rally One. Do you read?"

"Copy that, Rally One. Go ahead."

"Rally One requesting clearance for landing. We're about five klicks from your position. You copy?"

Rally One was the call sign for Detective Eduardo Silva's special ops team. Oscar Vasquez grimaced to his fellow officers and shook his head. Only seconds before, the com set had crackled to life. In the background of the transmission, Oscar heard the distinct sound of a helicopter rotor. The unexpected noise and the radio chatter jolted his brain like an electrical shock. He'd almost dozed off in the steamy heat of the jungle. Boring duty. The communication came on the radio frequency designated for the operation. And the call sign was legitimate.

Oscar had met the undercover cop Silva before and didn't care for him much. The *cabrão* was nothing but a bully, both on and off the force. But Oscar had a job to do.

"Stand by Rally One. Hold your position and wait for further orders. I repeat, hold your position. Do not advance until I give the order."

"Copy that, Base Camp."

Protocol was protocol. If Silva disregarded his authority, he might have to send a clear message. A kiss off the hull by a sniper round. The thought made him smile. This time, Oscar would be in charge, at least until he heard back from the chief.

Before he made the call, one of the helicopter pilots sitting nearest him asked, "Are we expecting another chopper?"

Oscar shrugged. "Not up to me to decide. I'm contacting the chief. Let him make the call."

In unison, they all nodded. They weren't paid enough to think.

"Base Camp to Team One. Come in, Team One." He waited for a moment, then repeated. "I say again, Base Camp to Team One. Do you read?"

Over the ridge to the east, Chief Zharan heard the call in his earpiece.

"Base Camp, this is Team One. Read you loud and clear. Go ahead."

His man at the extraction point informed him of the arrival of Detective Eduardo Silva via a third helicopter. He had expected the call. His plan was coming together.

"Affirmative, Base Camp. Rally One is approved to land. Do you read?"

"Will comply, Team One."

"Team One heading back to Base Camp." Looking at his watch, Zharan gave his best estimate for their arrival, then signed off. "Team One clear."

Christian sensed a change in the man's demeanor. "You have an uninvited guest at the clearing?"

"Not at all. Quite the contrary." Chief Zharan grinned at Christian and Charboneau. "A trusted ally and two very reluctant guests. You have not met my special ops man Eduardo Silva, but Bianca and Hector Salvador have. An unfortunate circumstance for them. And they have you to thank for that, Mr. Delacorte. The Macumba curse on your balcony was meant to point a finger at the native population, specifically Mario and his people. And it worked too. But you had to take it a step further. Involving a local Macumba vendor only meant another loose end for me. And today it will cost them dearly."

Mario Araujo jerked his head toward Zharan with a scowl. Christian noticed the man's reaction to the news. The native man opened his mouth to speak for the first time since his so-called arrest.

"I know Bianca Salvador and her nephew. What are you planning to do with them?"

"I believe in equal opportunity. An idealist like you, Mario, should appreciate the concept. What will happen to them will also befall each of you. I wouldn't want them to feel left out, so Silva has brought them here." The chief and Fuentes laughed, starting a chain reaction with the rest of the men.

Zharan walked in front of his prisoners, hands locked behind his back, glaring each one in the eye as he passed.

"Once we arrive at the extraction point, you will be forced to kneel before my men with your backs turned, hands bound behind you. No resistance. No escape. No hope left."

Nicholas rolled his eyes and cocked his head, a look of boredom on his face. Christian had no idea what was going through his father's head except a heavy dose of insolence. If this were his father's day to die, Charboneau would do it his way.

The chief ignored the insult and continued. "Two quick shots to the back of the head, execution style." He walked slowly before each one. Cocking his hand like a gun, he imitated the action, as if they needed help to imagine it. "My men will not sweat over digging a shallow mass grave in this heat. No one will discover your bodies out here. In days, exposed to the elements and the animals of the Amazon jungle, there will be nothing left to find."

He stopped directly in front of Charboneau, grinning. His father glared back, losing none of his attitude, but that didn't stop Zharan.

"Shortly, you will mean nothing more than a full

belly for some jaguar or puma after they rip the meat off your bones and devour your entrails, their muzzles red with your blood. Nothing will go to waste, I understand."

Hands in front with wrists cuffed together, Christian stood next to Raven, his gut twisted with guilt. An overwhelming rush of powerlessness swept through him, compounding his agony. One of Fuentes's men had searched him and confiscated not only his Glock 19, but also his Marine Corps Ka-Bar knife and his backup gun, a .357 short-barreled revolver he had in an ankle holster strapped to his leg. The man also took away his international cell phone.

Bad enough to be stripped of his weapons, but now Raven would be searched and Fuentes took over, knowing what it would do to Christian. The bastard took his time. From the corner of his eye, Fuentes toyed with his reaction.

His father watched from a distance. In a subtle move, he shook his head to get him to cool down, but that only fanned the flames of Christian's anger. He wouldn't stand for this, not with Raven.

"Get your hands off her."

"Christian, please. Don't." Raven tried to intervene, more for his sake than her own. "I can handle it."

"Yes. Listen to your woman, Christian." Fuentes grinned and flashed a wink at him. "Besides, maybe she wants to handle what I've got. Or perhaps one man isn't enough for her."

The men around Fuentes laughed, a low guttural sound that quickly died when their eyes trailed down her body like unwanted fingers. Hiding her terror, Raven glared at the detective, but defiance didn't stop him.

She gritted her teeth when the cop plunged a filthy hand down her shirt, manhandling her left breast. With his other hand, he squeezed her ass, letting his fingers probe deep between her legs. Raven held herself rigid, but there was nothing she could do. The rest of the men closed in, some licking their lips with eyes following every move Fuentes made. Any minute, Christian would lose it. Raven saw it in his eyes. And if he did, Fuentes would not hesitate to kill him here and now.

Fire raged in Christian's eyes. His fear for her had taken over. Christian knew everything could change in a heartbeat. One spark. One nod from Zharan and these men could pounce on Raven and take what they wanted. And he could do nothing to stop them. His heart pumped rapid fire in his chest. He gasped for air as if he was drowning.

When he took a step toward the bastard, Zharan's men grabbed his arms and held him in place. He jerked and tried to break free, but more men grappled him into submission. Finally, a beefy guy emerged from the rabble and punched him hard in the stomach. Once. Twice. Three times. It got his attention.

Fuentes smiled at Christian, doubled over in pain. Then the man looked down at Raven and rubbed her body harder, undeterred. She fought the degradation and the pain, trying not to show how much it hurt.

"I'm gonna bring you down, Fuentes." The words were out of Christian's mouth before he realized he'd said them. The voice of the predator. "Some way . . . somehow. I'm gonna take you out."

"You threatening me, Delacorte?"

The dirty cop laughed again, but didn't stop abusing Raven. He held her against his chest, an arm around her throat. In crude fashion, Fuentes ground his pelvis into her backside, giving Christian a tormenting preview of what would happen. Christian charged the bastard, nearly toppling the men holding him back.

"You talk big when you've got me handcuffed with men holding me down. Come over here and bring it, you coward."

From across the clearing, Nicholas Charboneau had watched the whole exchange and finally had enough. When he burst out laughing, all heads turned.

"No, that's not a threat, you ignorant jerk." Directing his comment at Fuentes, his father grinned and shook his head. "I'd say that sounded like a promise worth keeping." Then he shrugged and cocked his head. "Ricardo? Who's in charge here? You're gonna kill us anyway. Do you have to subject us to this damned Brazilian soap opera? Really, man. I know it's hard, but show some class."

Christian did a double take, unsure whose side his father was on. But when Zharan waved Fuentes off, Christian knew his father had done the right thing.

"Get off her, Arturo," the chief ordered, waving a hand for another man to resume the search for weapons and identification. "Be patient. If things go as planned, you and your men will get your chance with her. And you can make him watch." Zharan pointed at Christian. "In the meantime, follow orders and finish up. We pull out in five minutes."

His father had only bought a cease-fire. Once they got back to the clearing, all bets would be off. If Christian orchestrated a plan, he'd have little time to do it. His mind raced with ideas until a strange sensation churned heat across his skin, a slow and steady buildup.

The talisman Bianca Salvador had made for him began to burn. And he felt the weight of the trinket against his chest. He'd forgotten it was there. *What the hell was happening?* In his confusion, he shifted his gaze toward Raven. Her eyes fixed on him with a questioning look, but how could he explain what he didn't understand himself?

Bound and defenseless, Christian should have felt the building anxiety of his childhood terror—being powerless. Instead, he discovered a newfound clarity to his thinking and strength he found only when he hunted, the predator alive within him.

He'd get one moment to act and he'd take it, regardless of the risk to him. Raven's life would depend on it.

Although if anyone asked about it point-blank, Christian would deny any belief in Bianca's talisman, yet he'd still hedged his bet and worn the damned thing hidden under his shirt. How could a charm calling upon a protective spirit make things any worse?

Today, he'd confront superior numbers with greater firepower than the gangs on the south side of Chicago. And believing in himself made more sense than giving up. So when it came time to putting faith in something tangible, Christian thought of the special ops shock troopers' motto.

Always outnumbered, seldom outgunned, but never outclassed.

Today he'd be outgunned with hands cuffed, not exactly an even playing field. But if these men wanted to hurt Raven Mackenzie, he'd show them what Chicago tough was all about. To get to her, they'd have to come through him. Easier said than done.

CHAPTER 24

A cold razor edge of tension sliced through the muggy air of the jungle. Pinpricks of goose bumps rippled across Raven's skin, feeling like needles beneath the surface.

The return trip to the clearing was happening way too fast. And the reality of knowing when and how she and Christian would die had dominated her mind and robbed her ability to appreciate what little time they might have left.

Christian walked behind her. Raven took solace in listening to every footstep he made and hearing each breath he took. She knew he'd picked that spot to watch over her. Even now, she felt his love.

Araujo and Charboneau were ahead of her. Fuentes led the way and had a small cadre of men dedicated to keeping his prisoners moving and in line. His men were well-armed and trudged through the jungle in silence with stern faces, a few stealing glances of her when they thought she wasn't looking. On occasion, the more aggressive ones didn't bother to hide their hunger. They raked their eyes over her, taking what she would never give, as if they had a right.

Soon, they would. She'd be nothing more than an afternoon's entertainment, a token reward for their lack of shame. Raven knew precisely what Fuentes and Zharan had in store for her. And damned if she'd be led to slaughter with her chin down. She deliberately let them believe they had won. Her body language gave them no cause for alarm.

But Raven kept her head in the game and eyes alert. And above all, she trusted and believed in Christian. They weren't going down without a fight.

It all happened so fast, Christian never saw what instigated Raven's accident. She stumbled and fell to the ground in front of him. He'd been too preoccupied, streaming various escape scenarios through his mind like fast forwarding a movie.

He rushed to her side. When he helped Raven to her feet, she came up with a limp and lunged for a fallen tree along the trail, a place to sit.

"Ow . . . sorry. Can't believe this," she cursed under her breath.

Christian knelt in front of her and started to remove her boot to assess the injury. His handcuffs made it awkward.

Fuentes walked up and stood over his left shoulder. "Don't take it off," the man said. "If it's sprained, the boot will keep the swelling down. Either way, we're not stopping."

Christian looked up, keeping his face unreadable and his tone civil. "At least let her sit for a minute. And she could use some water. We all could." He pleaded his case, hoping Raven had staged her fall and would milk the stall tactic for all its worth.

"Ouch. Watch it . . . please." She laid a hand on her shin.

Rattling off some Portuguese, Fuentes grunted his irritation and snapped his fingers. Two men gripped their weapons and stood at attention, ordered to pull guard duty while the rest took a breather. Another young man came up with a canteen.

Raven took it and thanked him with a nod and a faint smile. Christian couldn't imagine what was going through her mind. Shortly, that kid with the canteen would be standing in line to rape her with wild eyes and his brain turned to mush. The blinding urges of his libido would give in to the chaos of mob mentality and the animal cries of his fellow officers. But to look at him now, the kid smiled and blushed like a shy teenager. *Unbelievable.*

Christian wiped the image from his head. He tried to stay focused, holding back his anger. As Raven drank small sips of water from the canteen, he felt her ankle and played with her bootlaces.

"Are you okay?" he muttered under his breath.

"Yeah. Could use an AR-15 or a Browning M2 right about now, but hey, a girl can dream, can't she?" She shrugged, keeping her voice down. "Thought we should talk."

"Smart girl." He winked. "We need to pick our spot and come up with a diversion. Any ideas?" He gazed into Raven's beautiful eyes, as if he were speaking to her, but also directed his comments to the other captives. "We won't get a second chance at this."

Araujo and his father closed ranks, moving slowly so they wouldn't generate suspicion.

"Are you in on this?" he asked the native man. When he nodded, Christian went on. "What's Fuentes doing?" He didn't dare turn around. Christian relied on Raven to be his eyes and ears. "And where's Zharan?"

"Fuentes has a cell phone in his hand," Raven said. "He just pulled it from his vest." She narrowed her eyes and grimaced with a show of pain, as if Christian had just hurt her. "Zharan hasn't come up the trail yet. Can't see him. What's with that phone? Fuentes looks pissed."

"Is he making a call?"

"No. Looks like he's scrolling. Doesn't look like your phone, Christian."

Araujo jumped in. "No. It's mine."

"Yeah, and he's fascinated with your hardware, my friend," Nicholas chimed in, keeping his voice low. His lips were concealed behind another water bottle and his cuffed hands. "You got a calling plan we should all know about? Care to share who's in your circle?"

"You are a strange one, Nicholas Charboneau." Araujo shook his head. "I don't understand your questions, but I only use that phone to contact one person."

"Your broker? The Psychic Hotline?" Charboneau raised an eyebrow.

Araujo narrowed his eyes in question, but his expression softened into a fleeting smile.

At that moment, Chief Zharan came over the rise and Fuentes went to meet him. The two men pulled off the trail, away from the rest. An intense conversation followed, the strain very apparent. Araujo took the opportunity to fill them in on his mystery caller, the man who'd made contact to cut himself in for the ransom. When he was done, Christian glanced over his shoulder to Zharan and Fuentes, then back at his father.

"You thinking what I'm thinking?" He smiled.

"Don't think you're in need of that much psychiatric help, but I'd bet serious cash Fuentes recognized the phone number on Araujo's phone."

"And?" he prompted.

His father thought about it, then continued, "Ricardo isn't known for working and playing well with others. No doubt a big disappointment to his mother, but I think he's been flying solo on a very lucrative side business that Fuentes is only just figuring out."

Christian nodded. "I think we've just found a chink in their armor. Maybe we can capitalize on it, parlay it into a diversion when the time comes."

They fixed their eyes on him, making their silent pledge to back him up. When the time came, he knew they'd have his backside. They were still outnumbered and would probably not make it. But in his book, going down fighting edged out two to the back of the head any day.

"Damn it. What the hell . . . ?" Christian tugged at his shirt. The talisman had begun to burn again. He pulled it out and rubbed the skin of his chest, unsure what to make of it. Mario Araujo reached for the dangling charm.

"Ayza the Protector. Who made this for you?" the man asked.

"Bianca Salvador. She insisted I wear it." He tucked it back into his shirt. "But the damned thing burns like hell. I must be allergic to something she used."

"Or maybe Ayza is only trying to get the attention of a nonbeliever." Araujo smiled and cocked his head. "Perhaps our predicament is not as hopeless as it appears."

"Not you too." He grimaced, his chest still feeling the effects.

But the native man only shrugged.

Christian shook his head, then took a discreet look over his shoulder. Zharan yanked Araujo's cell phone from the hands of his number two man and didn't look like he planned to return it. The chief turned his back and ended their conversation, but nothing looked resolved for Fuentes.

"Looks like our break is done. Follow my lead and be ready to move," Christian whispered.

Fuentes stalked up the trail. When he passed his prisoners, he yelled to his men.

"Fall in. Move. We're heading out." And to Christian, he threatened with a finger thrust inches from his face. "If she slows us down, I will personally drag her by the hair off this ridge. Do you understand me?"

Christian returned his glare, his only reply.

The men scrambled. And he and Raven were hauled to their feet. Fuentes didn't say another word. He looked like a man with something far more urgent on his mind.

Up ahead, a third helicopter occupied the marshy clearing—the end of the line. With rotor blade motionless, the aircraft faced them and sat apart from the other two, its engine long since cooled. One guard in uniform leaned against the craft, then stood at attention as they approached.

It's now or never, hotshot. What's the plan?

Christian let his eyes strafe the treeline, his senses on hyper alert. All the way back, he'd pictured how this might play out. In his hip pocket, he had the new intel of a rift between Zharan and Fuentes. A theory, nothing more. And he needed a diversion. Once he got it, he'd have to move, no hesitation.

He'd given thought to overpowering one of the guards in the jungle and making a run for it through the brush. But it would've only been a matter of time before they got a bullet to the back or been run down by the much younger men in Fuentes's horde.

And even though the clearing had little cover, it had the helicopters, their best means of escape. If they launched a quick assault and took one or two weapons, they might stand a chance to use the choppers for cover in the interim and as a means of escape later. He knew enough about flying one to get them off the ground.

Outnumbered as they were, they'd have to hit hard and fast, taking out command personnel like Zharan and Fuentes first. Next, they'd have to target key weapons experts and neutralize any with long range capability or grenade launchers. A nearly impossible feat since they didn't know these men or have a clear inventory of their firearms.

Scenarios played through his head, but the reality of these men returning fire interfered with the outcome. Christian needed something to tip the scales in his favor. That's what was on his mind when the lone guard patrolling the aircraft turned to face them. And the sneer of Captain Luis Duarte stopped him dead in his tracks. Hell, the man stared right at him.

"Ah, shit!" Christian muttered. "This day just keeps getting better."

All hope drained with the same sickening effects of rapid blood loss. *What the hell would they do now?*

CHAPTER 25

"Good afternoon, Chief Zharan." Duarte moved away from the aircraft. Dressed in fatigues, he looked like one of the men. Surprisingly, he was alone. "I've been listening to the chatter on your radio frequency. You've had an excellent day, it would appear. But all good things come to an end, I'm afraid."

For a second, the chief flinched his surprise at seeing Duarte, but he recovered quickly. "What are you talking about?" Zharan stepped forward and faced the captain. "You're a wanted man, Duarte. What are you doing here?" The man spoke with all the casualness of meeting an acquaintance at a cocktail party.

"Ah, the best defense is a good offense, is that it?" The captain's smile broadened to a grin. "Funny. I feel the same way."

Fuentes got the reference and understood the implications. He searched the thick vegetation of the jungle, craning his neck to get a better view. His face tightened. His nerves wired. He gripped his weapon and pulled it from his holster, leaving it by his side.

Christian exchanged a quick glance at Raven, his father, and Araujo. They stood ready.

Duarte continued, "Detective Eduardo Silva sends his regrets, but he was unable to make it. If he survives, he might be willing to share what he knows for immunity. Who's to say?"

"Even a man as loyal as Detective Silva would say anything under torture. You have nothing admissible in a court of law." The chief opened his mouth to go on, but Duarte raised a finger.

"Perhaps, but before you insult my intelligence again, I would like to share the reason I'm standing here in this clearing with you and not taking cover in the trees like the rest of my team."

Zharan's men suddenly realized their vulnerability, standing in the open. They fidgeted and started to talk. The chief raised a hand, but that didn't stop the commotion. He was losing control.

"Say it, Luis. No more melodrama," Zharan demanded.

"I have snipers positioned in the trees. Once you left the jungle, they closed the gap and now have you completely surrounded. They've been given their orders whether I'm alive or not, but I had to look you in the eye to deliver the news. An indulgence I couldn't resist."

Zharan shrugged and held out both hands in question. "What's this all about, Captain Duarte? Revenge?" The man had the audacity to laugh. The sound of it was as abrasive as nails on a chalkboard. "Charges can be dropped. I can restore your good name with the stroke of my pen. And if you killed that Asian woman, you won't hear any complaints from me. The bitch had it coming—if not for this, then something else. What do you want? Name your price."

At the mention of Jasmine, his father stepped forward with venom in his eyes, but Christian and Raven held him back.

"Now's not the time. Be patient. We still need a diversion." Christian kept his voice low. He dared to hope he'd been wrong about Duarte, but the jury was still out. This could be nothing more than a falling out among thieves.

Instead of responding to the chief's question, Captain Duarte did a strange thing. Christian watched as the man stepped toward the helicopter closest to him and opened the cargo bay door. He stood back from the aircraft and beckoned with a wave of his fingers.

All eyes were on the shadowy cargo hold of the chopper. The fuselage rocked with a faint motion. Jasmine Lee slid from a seat in the dark and leapt to the ground with all the grace of a cunning feline on the prowl.

"Am I the Asian bitch you referred to, Ricardo?" She narrowed her eyes. If looks could indeed kill, Chief Zharan would be slit cock to gullet with a very dull knife. "As you can see, Captain Duarte hasn't hurt me. In fact, he's been quite cordial. He made me see that we needed to talk. So I believe there's been a misunderstanding. And I, for one, would like to clear it up with the proper authorities as soon as possible."

"This is bullshit!" Zharan spat. The man was more than angry. His charges against the captain would never hold up now. Like two gunslingers, Zharan and Duarte glared at each other, waiting for one to blink.

But Jasmine tempered the tension with something else on her mind. Slowly, she walked across the clearing toward Nicholas as if no one else were there. Her stern expression and steely eyes melted as she approached him with each step, replaced by the face of a woman in love. Raven watched the two of them change before her eyes, influenced by a reserved dignity all their own. The amazing transformation in both of them surprised her. Ignoring all the danger, they held each other's gaze. Nothing seemed more important than feeling that first touch of a hand or catching the soft tremble of a lip fighting to hold back the emotion.

Raven glanced over to Christian. He hadn't missed the exchange between his father and Jasmine. He still stood spellbound by it, and that made her smile. Even with a war on the verge of happening, the man Raven loved took the time to witness the quiet reuniting of two lovers.

God, how I love this man!

But no one else noticed Jasmine and Nicholas. With tensions high, Duarte sat on the proverbial powder keg, still trying to diffuse it. He made his point again.

"As for what I want? I'd like for your men to lay down their weapons." He raised his voice so the men behind Zharan would hear. "As far as I'm concerned, they were only following orders."

This caused a stir within the rank and file. Those able to speak English translated for those who couldn't. Duarte's offer swept through the men like a grass fire in high winds.

"Don't make matters worse, Ricardo. Charboneau and his people are foreigners. Killing them would only stir up the American consulate, something our government would frown upon. And who would believe Mario Araujo, a man who had made his living off kidnappings at gunpoint? Advise your men to put down their weapons. We can settle this back in Cuiabá."

Christian saw the tension mounting in Fuentes and pulled Raven closer. Duarte tried to downplay what lay in store for Zharan, but too much had happened. The captain had no idea of the friction building between Zharan and his top dog. Perhaps Fuentes had much more to lose with everything unraveling. The detective looked like a man faced with a harsh reality and all his options gone.

Once again, Duarte yelled at the top of his lungs, *"Put down your weapons and back away with your hands up!"* He repeated his demands in Portuguese.

But Zharan interrupted and countered with his own power play. *"Anyone putting down their weapons will be shot. Do you hear me?"* he screamed, red faced. "Fuentes? Captain Duarte is an armed fugitive. Take him into custody. If he resists, kill him."

Most of the men backed off, but a handful near Fuentes reached for their weapons. In the second it took to raise them, a high-pitched whine shrieked through the air. Faint at first, then loud and distinct. It deadened with a sharp final crack. A man standing too close to Fuentes jerked to the right and pitched backward, but not before the back of his head exploded. A sniper with suppressed fire made the sound of silent death hard to forget. Fuentes had moved enough to change his fate.

"Hit the deck!" Christian cried out, and hunched over, covering Raven with his body.

But Jasmine had another agenda. And it had nothing to do with avoiding a fight.

Even as men scrambled for cover, she ignored the risk to protect Nicholas. With a fist, she coldcocked the guy next to Nicky and grabbed the man's Taurus 1911 pistol. She had intended to disarm him and give the weapon to Nicholas, but two more men lunged for them.

She shot one point-blank in the face. His blood spattered her cheek, making her flinch. When she turned, the other man had grappled Nicholas to the ground. They wrestled for a gun, but Nicky was bound in handcuffs. In seconds, it would be over if the bastard got off a shot. Jasmine wouldn't wait for the outcome. She could have shot him in the head, but a muscle spasm might force a nervous reflex in the man's trigger finger. She jammed the Taurus into the waistband of her pants and pulled a knife from a sheath on her belt.

Jasmine knocked off the man's helmet and grabbed his hair. She yanked him back with one hand and gripped the knife hard in the other. In the same motion, she dug the blade deep under the man's ear and twisted it, severing the artery. His warm blood spurt up the knife and sprayed, but at least he released his grip on the gun enough for Nicky to grab it. The dying man clutched his neck and rolled to the ground, his face distorted with fear and pain. In a matter of minutes he would bleed out, but she wouldn't be around to witness it.

Nicky tried to scramble to his feet, ready to do his part, but Jasmine wasn't done doing her duty. She had to get him to safety. Without hesitation, she grabbed his arm and hauled him behind one of the choppers, the nearest cover. Her sudden move caught him by surprise. Still off balance, he half-crawled to keep up and not be such a burden. Jasmine didn't have time to slow down. Moving targets were harder to hit.

Nicholas was covered in blood, but she knew it wasn't his. When he was out of the line of fire, she breathed a sigh of relief and prepared to jump back into the fray to help Duarte end this, but something made her stop. For one brief instant, Jasmine stood over Nicky awash in euphoria. She had saved him, had done her job. She smiled, and in response, his expression softened into a crooked grin.

But a shot rang out and took it all away.

She felt a strong punch to her arm and chest. And the left side of her body flushed with heat. A bloom of red erupted on her chest. In shock, she looked down, the pain not yet registered. Her eyes rolled into her head and she collapsed onto Nicky. The blackness swallowed her.

"*Nooo!*" he cried.

Confined by handcuffs, Nicholas broke her fall as best he could. Once he had her, he gripped her hard to his chest as if he could make it all better by willing it done. He sat rocking her in his arms, his mouth gaped open with an unspoken *Why?* on his lips.

Nicholas peered around the helicopter that Jasmine had used to protect him. She had shoved him to safety, leaving her in the open, a clear target. Across the clearing, Zharan stood with his gun still aimed.

Nicholas blinked. He wanted to find a gun and shoot the smug bastard, but he only thought of one thing. *Stop the bleeding!* With his heart hammering in his chest, he laid her to the ground, cradling her head. Jasmine had a faint pulse and was barely breathing. He tore open her blouse and the body armor under it. In a fluke mishap, the bullet went through her arm and into her chest, bypassing her body armor via the armhole. As much as he hated seeing an exit wound, he knew enough to know it went clean through, preferable to a round that expended all its energy inside her.

But no telling how close the bullet had come to her lungs or what arteries were hit. The handcuffs made his work almost impossible. He pressed both wounds, his hands spread as far as they would reach. Shooting and chaos swelled around him, but all he thought about was Jasmine.

Her beautiful face blurred through his tears.

Damn it! She's not dead yet! Anger took control.

"Don't leave me. Not now," he cried. "You hear me, Jasmine? Please . . . don't leave me."

Nicholas blocked out everything. Now, nothing else mattered.

But Christian couldn't say the same.

Beside his father, a sniper round exploded and ripped through the chest of another of Zharan's men. Christian heard it from where he stood. It tore through flesh with a wet beefy sound. The hot smell of blood assaulted his nose, sickening and sweet. By the time the dead man hit the turf, a pool of crimson leaked out from under him, soaking the ground. Ignoring the horror, Christian lunged for the man's handgun.

"Christian!" Raven screamed. "Look out!"

Fuentes kicked the weapon aside and stood over

him with a gun pointed to his forehead, a self-satisfied smirk on his face. Christian stared down the barrel. He would die on his knees after all. But in that instant, a cold wave surged through his body, initiating from deep in his chest. Suddenly, he felt the weight of the talisman, fortifying him with its strength.

It all rushed by in a blur, happening way too fast, until time abruptly stopped. The change punched him like a blow to the head, then muted to a calming hush.

Christian felt every sensation as if he were the only one moving, like an out of body experience. In his head, he heard his own breaths and the rhythm of his heart, muffled and steady. And he saw Raven crying off to his right, her voice garbled. Two men had grabbed her arms and were pulling her away. Raven didn't fight back. She only watched the drama being played out between him and Fuentes.

Near one of the helicopters, Charboneau was covered in blood and held Jasmine in his arms, but when his father cried out, no sound came from his mouth. Even Fuentes tensed his muscles and moved in slow motion.

Christian saw everything with such clarity, as if he wasn't a part of it.

But just as quickly the sluggish sensation came to a sudden stop. When it did, Christian stared into the barrel of a gun pointed between his eyes. And the sound of the detective's voice came through loud and clear.

"See you in hell, Delacorte."

That's when Fuentes pulled the trigger.

CHAPTER 26

Click. At the sound, Christian flinched. His breath caught in his throat, even with his heart thrashing in his chest.

Fuentes's eyes flared, his face distorted with rage. Without hesitation, he slapped the bottom of the magazine, racked the slide of his weapon, and pulled the trigger. A glint of flying brass from the ejected live round caught the dying rays of the sun. All of it happened so fast, Christian had no time to react.

Click. The gun misfired again.

He wasn't about to give the bastard a third try. Christian shoved the man's arm aside with his cuffed hands and broke free from the line of fire. He leapt to his feet and moved in tight to Fuentes. Putting muscle behind it, he jabbed the man's throat with a brutal forward thrust of his elbow, cutting off the cop's air. Stunned, Fuentes dropped his chin with eyes watering and mouth gaped open. Spittle drooled from his lips. He grasped his neck.

Christian wrenched the gun free from his other hand. It dropped to the ground. All he could do was kick it out of reach. He shifted his weight and drove an elbow back into the detective's stomach. When Fuentes doubled over, Christian turned to ram a knee high and sharp into his face. The man's head snapped back. He staggered backward like a drunk on a bender. Blood oozed from his nose and down his chin.

"That's for me." Christian panted, his chest heaving with the adrenaline rush. "But this? This is for Raven."

Fuentes shook his head and tried holding up a hand, but no words came from his mouth. Christian wasn't about to accept his surrender so easily. A flood of memories bubbled to the surface, fueling his fire. He lunged for Fuentes with a shoulder, picking the man off the ground with force. He slammed his back into one of the helicopters, then hit him with a flurry of punches to his body and face. Even with his hands restrained, he made every blow count.

Fuentes cried out. "*Arrghh . . .* p-please."

But Christian ignored his plea for leniency. He pictured Raven's face as the man degraded her in front of his men. Out of love, she came to Brazil to help, but Fuentes and his arrogant boss would have turned her good deed into tragedy by raping and killing her, leaving her body for the animals. And the images of the dead men back at the cave faded in and out of the shadows in his mind.

He pounded and kicked the man's ribs until he heard a crack and felt one bone give. With the force of each blow, Fuentes's body lurched off the ground. His head lolled from side to side like a macabre rag doll. Fuentes could no longer defend himself. His arms hung limp at his sides. Only his legs kept him propped against the chopper.

Christian shoved him to the ground onto his knees, then came up behind him. He wrapped his cuffed hands around the man's neck and yanked back. A fatal stranglehold or a crushed larynx, Christian didn't much care. With his head turning a deathlike purple, Fuentes grappled against his hands, grunting and writhing, the weight of his own body working against him. Christian pulled harder. As the man weakened, it got easier.

"Christian . . . please." He heard a familiar voice, but couldn't stop.

Even the tears he imagined in his father's eyes, when he looked him in the face for the first time, ramped up his anger. His father had narrowly escaped a living hell in that damned cave, only to be thrown into another nightmare, being forced to witness Jasmine dying.

Christian's rage took hold and wouldn't let go. Not until he finally heard her voice.

"Please . . . he's had enough. You're going to kill him!" Raven cried. "Please stop . . . for me. You're not like him. You're not a killer."

When Christian looked up, he stared at her as if she were a stranger. She'd seen that look before and it always scared her. He loosened his grip and shoved Fuentes face first into the dirt. Raven reached for his arm and pulled him toward her, to reclaim him. He staggered, his chest sucking air. His fists were raw and covered in blood. When his rage finally subsided, he stared at Fuentes, unconscious on the ground. A bloody heap.

Christian turned and shook his head, unable to look her in the eye or say a word. His shame took over. He'd given in to the dark beast he'd fought his entire life.

Raven knew she had to distract him from his agony or the monster would find a foothold in his guilt. "Duarte's rounding up the rest of Zharan's men. It's over." Tears brimmed in her eyes. She couldn't believe it herself. They'd made it.

The skirmish had been brief but had taken its toll with the number of dead and dying. Most of Zharan's tactical team had their hands up and knelt in the marshy sod, their faces young and scared. Duarte's men were searching them for weapons, then binding their hands with plastic restraints and shoving them to the ground. Those trained as medics were taking care of the wounded. The more serious were being loaded onto stretchers for the ride back.

Zharan was handcuffed and under guard. By the looks of him, Duarte must have rearranged the chief's face with his fists after the man shot Jasmine. His hair was gnarled into a tangled mess and his polished smile was tarnished with blood and a chipped tooth. And that perfect nose now had character. A noticeable improvement all the way around.

"It's over, but not for Jasmine, Christian." Raven fixed her eyes on Nicholas Charboneau, the man's hands and arms slick with Jasmine's blood.

It didn't look good.

Christian rushed by her and knelt near Jasmine. The sucking sound coming from the exit wound on her chest made his skin crawl. Unconscious, she struggled to breathe. Not a good sign. One of Duarte's men had an opened medical kit on the ground by her.

The man had to act quickly. He fumbled through the packages of dressing and found what he needed.

But soon, he cried out in broken English, "This . . . no good. Look for another." The young officer held out an occlusive dressing, an air- and watertight trauma dressing used to treat sucking chest wounds.

Christian saw what he meant. The package had been torn open, exposed to the air. It made the blasted thing useless. The waxy coating of the dressing had dried out.

"Get these off me. Hurry." Christian held out his hands. The young officer found his key and unlocked his cuffs, then did the same for Raven and Nicholas. With hands free, Christian rummaged through the med supplies for another one, but came up empty. "Damn it!"

He remembered Zharan had ordered both helicopters be equipped with med supplies. Christian sprang to his feet and raced across the clearing. One of the field medics had the other kit, using it to treat a head wound. Christian knelt by the man and dug through the other medical supplies. All the while, the moist hissing of Jasmine's wound played on his nerves, a sound not easily forgotten.

"Damn it," he cursed under his breath. The dressing he needed was missing from the second kit or had been used already. Now, he'd have to get creative. He grabbed what he needed and rushed back.

"I got nothing, but maybe you can use these . . . to improvise."

The young man was still working on Jasmine to stop the bleeding and get two large-bore IVs into her. But when he looked up and saw what Christian held in his hands, he shook his head and shrugged.

"How?" Pity edged his eyes. He'd probably received limited training, but had no idea how to make due with what he had.

Christian looked down at the rubber gloves, empty IV bag wrapper, scissors, and tape in his hands. For a second, he shut his eyes. She needed a hospital and a chest tube, not his clumsy attempt at playing doctor.

"What's happening? Why can't he help her?" His father tugged at his arm, smearing Jasmine's blood on his sleeve. When he figured out Christian was her last chance, his father asked, "Do you know what to do?"

"Yeah, but I've got no time to explain." Christian nodded, acting more confident than he felt. "You gotta trust me."

A cavity surrounded the lungs. Pierced by a bullet, the pocket would let air in and prevent the lungs from inflating right. To complicate matters, air wouldn't leave the lungs like it normally did, so each breath Jasmine took filled the cavity and the surrounding lung tissue with more and more air. If they left the wound untreated and waited for the trip back to a hospital, Jasmine would die from a growing pressure in her chest cavity, one that would push against her heart and twist the major veins and arteries closed. She'd strangle with the serious complications of a collapsed lung. Christian had seen it happen.

He needed to move. *Now!*

He tugged on a pair of rubber gloves and leaned closer, listening to the left side of her chest. Her breathing only came from the one side. A lung had collapsed. Unconscious as she was, she had taken a turn for the worse. Her skin looked moist and clammy. And her heart rate was shallow and rapid.

He had no time to lose. Christian clipped off a section from an empty IV bag wrapper with a pair of scissors. He cleared the wound and swabbed the surrounding area with antiseptic.

"Cut me some tape." He nudged his chin at Raven, fixing his eyes on her.

She didn't hesitate. Raven yanked on a rubber glove and did as he asked, tearing off pieces of tape, ready to assist him.

Christian placed a piece of the bag wrapper over the wound and taped three sides down, leaving one section open to act as a flutter valve for Jasmine's exhale. He had to use his gut instincts on how much to tape down. He hoped he guessed right.

"Gotta treat the entrance wound too." He applied a similar patch of the wrapper to the left side of her chest, under her arm. He taped it completely closed this time.

With the distance to the hospital, he knew she'd have a better chance if he got her lung inflated. He leaned closer and listened again. With her shallow breathing, she may not be able to fill her lung naturally. Christian couldn't wait for something that might not happen. He tilted her head back and pinched off her nose, applying a measured mouth-to-mouth, matching her breathing as she inhaled. After a few tries, it worked.

"Got it." He grinned and gave a reassuring glance at his father and Raven. Any small victory felt like a major milestone.

The lung inflated enough to move her, but he wasn't done yet. He had to treat her arm wound. Christian secured a mound of gauze to her arm to stop the bleeding there. But she could still have internal bleeding into her chest cavity. He may only have bought her a few precious minutes.

"Now we gotta get her to a trauma center. Fast." He looked up into the worried eyes of his father, knowing Charboneau would take charge now.

"Please . . . help us." Nicholas pleaded his case to the men witnessing the drama being played out. "We need a hospital."

Captain Duarte stepped in and ordered his men to load the nearest chopper with the wounded. "Take those most seriously injured. And these hostages are to accompany them. Move. Move!"

The men around them scrambled to help.

"I will call ahead to make sure the hospital knows what to expect," another man offered.

Christian nodded. He stared down at his gloved hands, caked with Jasmine's blood. Doubt crept into his mind. He had no idea if he'd done the right thing. Now it would be a race against time to get her the help she needed. He yanked off his gloves and threw them to the ground.

"Come on." He helped his father to his feet. "We gotta go."

With great care, Duarte's men loaded Jasmine onto a stretcher with her IVs, carrying her toward the cargo hold of a helicopter. Others crawled in behind them. Another man lay on a stretcher next to Jasmine. A tight squeeze.

After the door slammed shut, the thick smell of blood and fear hung heavy in the air. Miserable groans and strained breathing filled the cramped space. One man whispered a prayer. Christian shut his eyes, wanting to block out the waking nightmare and the ghosts it conjured for him. Once the crew jumped into the cockpit and revved the engine, the sound masked the pitiable suffering and desperation. A small mercy.

Every second felt like an eternity.

After they lifted off the ground, Christian felt Raven's hand on his. He had almost lost her. Turning, he kissed her cheek and held her in his arms, not wanting to let go. Like a shot of adrenaline, she infused his soul with her strength . . . and her love. He fought a lump wedged in his throat. So many thoughts . . . so many regrets raced through his head. Christian had no idea how to make it up to her.

"When I think what could have happened . . ." he whispered in her ear.

She pulled from him enough to touch a gentle finger to his lips. "Don't say it. We're still here." She swallowed, her eyes glistening. "We can talk later. Your father needs you now."

Raven was right. Cradling her face in his hands, Christian kissed her again, then shifted his gaze to his father. The man looked lost.

"Jasmine's tough," Christian said. "She's gonna make it."

He stared into the inconsolable eyes of Nicholas Charboneau, unsure he'd even heard him. His father nodded, more out of reflex, but he didn't look up. Instead, he stroked the pale fingers of Jasmine's hand as if she were made of delicate crystal and would shatter.

"This can't be happening. Not to her." His father's voice barely carried over the chopper noise, his words not meant for anyone else to hear.

When Christian reached for his neck to give his father a reassuring squeeze, Nicholas lowered his chin and let out a gasping sob, fighting hard to hold back. Christian didn't know his father well enough to understand the depth of his sadness. A part of him deeply regretted that. Maybe Charboneau cried for all he'd suffered, but more than likely, he dreaded what still lay ahead.

Christian hesitated, then wrapped his arms around his father, the most natural thing in the world for some. When he did, Nicholas finally let go. He buried his face in Christian's shoulder, his body shaking.

"Jasmine loves you, Nicholas. She has for a long time." He spoke only loud enough for his father to hear over the rotor. "And if you don't put your money on her pulling through this, she's gonna come back and kick your ass."

His father's body shook even more. How much of it was laughing or crying, he didn't know or care. He held his father, making up for lost time between a father and a son.

And it felt good.

With Nicholas in his arms, he looked down at Jasmine, her face a ghastly gray. He thought of the old saying—*Those who live by the sword, die by it.* Jasmine had certainly lived by it, but if she died, Christian had a feeling she'd haunt his dreams out of spite. And he knew she'd enjoy every minute of his hellish torment.

To her credit, Jasmine had done it. She'd rescued his father and saved his life.

Would they be too late to return the favor?

Chapter 27

Jasmine had been in surgery for several hours. And there had been no word when it would end. Not knowing was killing him. Nicholas realized he'd never known what the phrase "hell on earth" meant until now. The clock on the ICU waiting room wall ticked with an abrasive noise, a mundane and monotone mockery of the passage of sweet time.

If anything good came of this, it would center on Christian.

Nicholas watched him return from the bank of phones down the hall. His son's face looked grim, worry forged in the dark shadows under his eyes. When Christian wasn't looking, he fixed his eyes on his son, taking in every detail of the man he'd become.

His son.

He marveled at the words and let them resonate in

his head. Ever since he'd met Christian, he hadn't had the nerve to say them aloud. Perhaps in time. Thanks to his son, Jasmine, and many others, he might have that time. Time he didn't deserve.

He had a son, a courageous and trustworthy man. The irony of that fact wasn't wasted on him. He knew he had one woman to thank for such a gift, a woman he'd misjudged.

"How is your mother?" Nicholas asked.

Christian seemed surprised by the question.

"She's . . . better." He nodded. Resting his elbows on his knees, he leaned forward in his seat, one down from him. His son glanced at the clock on the wall . . . again. "Ever since I left, Fiona's been going through hell."

An awkward silence built between them. An announcement over the PA system filtered down to the waiting room, muffled yet persistent. Life went on, even though his world had stopped as cold and final as death.

"Then you'll have to make it up to her," Nicholas offered. He ventured a hand to his son's shoulder. He took it as a good sign Christian didn't flinch. "A man like you can be counted on to do the right thing." After a beat, he added, "Lord knows you didn't get that quality from my side of the family. You have Fiona to thank for that."

Christian dropped his head and stifled a soft chuckle.

"Yeah? Kind of worried about the flip side to the coin. What did I inherit from you?" He crooked his lip into a grin and let the question hang in the air. Neither of them wanted to hear the answer, but Nicholas ventured one anyway.

"I'd pray you inherited nothing from me, but the powers that be stopped listening to me long ago." He squeezed his son's shoulder again and let go. "For what it's worth, I'm proud of you, Christian. Proud of the man you are, despite all the odds stacked against you. Fiona did the right thing to keep us apart. You be sure and tell her I said so."

"Maybe you should tell her yourself."

Nicholas furrowed his brow at the thought of seeing Fiona in that place, dressed in prison garb and plagued by the haunted eyes of the institutionalized.

"I never intended for her to pay for her sin. I only wanted to protect her." Nicholas hadn't realized he'd spoken aloud.

"What are you talking about? Protect her from what?" Christian asked.

Nicholas had played a part in Fiona's incarceration as surely as if he'd turned state's evidence against her. He had nothing to do with the murder of her husband, Charles Dunhill. That had been her choice. She'd shown such strength to do what must be done back then. But when he'd learned about what she did, he had no idea of the real reason behind the killing and jumped to the wrong conclusion.

He didn't find out the truth until it was too late. Fiona had only been trying to save her child . . . their child. Christian.

Anger and a taste for revenge had colored his motives, but for the most part, he had arranged for the killing of the hit man that she'd used to assassinate her husband in order to protect her. The man was a loose thread and she hadn't the strength to cut it off. In the end, he had shed light on the old Dunhill murder-for-hire case.

Fiona's guilt proved to be too much for her. He

should have known better. The very vulnerability he had tried to protect her against had also been her downfall. A self-inflicted wound. He couldn't shield her from her own conscience and the pervasive guilt that had been eating away at her all those years.

Guilt made a person weak. He found it a mercy not to be troubled by such things.

Nicholas didn't try to reply to his son's questions. Instead, he shifted his gaze down the hall. Showered and changed, Raven Mackenzie headed their way, carrying two small bags.

"She's lovely, you know." He jutted his chin in her direction. Christian turned to see what he meant. "Women like her don't come along every day. I hope you don't let her go."

Christian kept staring down the hall, smiling at the woman he loved. "Don't intend to. And you could take a little of that advice yourself."

He turned and smiled at his father. It felt surprisingly comfortable to sit with him like this.

"Any word? Is she out of surgery?" Raven asked, hope in her beautiful eyes.

Christian stood and shook his head. "None yet. What's in the bags?"

"I brought a change of clothes for you." She handed him a carryon. "And I thought Nicholas could use some things also. I went to the hotel, looking to pack a bag, and found one already done. Did you do it, Christian?"

"No." He looked down at his father. "Jasmine did."

At the mention of her name, the harsh reality of the situation hit home. Christian set his bag down and glanced at the clock once again.

"I'll stay until you get back," he offered, leaning up against a wall with arms crossed.

"Thank you for your kindness, Raven." His father's smile came and went. "I think I'll do us all a favor and freshen up. Excuse me." He stood and went to the nearest washroom, but turned at the last minute. "Please come get me if anything . . ." He couldn't finish.

"Yeah, we will." Christian nodded. After his father left, he said, "Waiting is pure torture, but I know it's been harder on him."

"Then he's lucky to have you here. So am I." She walked toward him with arms open wide.

"Risky business getting this close to me. I don't smell much better than . . . my father."

"I'll take my chances. Some things don't require second thought."

She nuzzled into his embrace, her familiar warmth washing through him like a cleansing summer rain. It felt good to hold her. He burrowed his head into her neck and breathed in the scent of her skin.

"I love you so much, Christian. And what you did for your father . . . and for Jasmine? It makes me love you all the more. I was selfish and wrong when I asked you not to go. I just want you to know that."

Christian heard her soft sob and knew she was crying. He pulled her closer, murmuring in her ear.

"I'm not sure I could make that decision a second time. It scares me what I almost lost . . . what we almost lost. I don't ever want to be in that situation again. I love you more than my own life, Raven Mackenzie. And there will be no more secrets between us. I swear it."

He held her, knowing he'd crossed a threshold with

the woman in his arms. A threshold he'd been looking for his whole life. Finally, he'd come home.

When the doctor came down the hall toward them, Nicholas stood, unable to hide the dread and expectation on his face. Christian couldn't read the surgeon's expression, grim and edged by exhaustion. But the man raised his hands as he approached, allaying their worst fears.

"She made it through surgery." He forced a cautious smile. "But the next forty-eight hours will be critical. She's in recovery now. We'll be moving her to ICU soon. You can see her then, one visitor at a time."

Charboneau looked as if he'd collapse back into his chair. He let out the breath he'd been holding and almost doubled over in relief. Raven didn't say anything, but smiled at Christian, wrapping her arms around his waist.

The doctor gave them more on how the surgery went. Although Nicholas looked as if he listened to every word, Christian knew his mind was a blur with relief. He felt the same. As strong as Jasmine was, he knew she'd make it through the critical time with flying colors. The woman was too stubborn to die with a whimper.

When the doctor left, Christian spoke to his father. "Sounds like she's gonna make it. I'm glad."

"She's tough," Raven agreed, smiling at Charboneau.

His father let out a sigh, but avoided his gaze, coughing and clearing his throat. No doubt, something in the air made eyes watery and red.

"Yes, she is." He nodded. When he looked up,

his attention shifted down the hall. His shoulders slumped and his face registered his sudden wariness.

"What the hell does he want?" Nicholas, slouched in his chair, crossed his arms over his chest. "Do we have to deal with this now?"

True to form, Captain Luis Duarte headed straight for them, his gaze locked on Charboneau. The man had cleaned up, dressed in uniform—all business and looking like pure trouble.

"I heard Ms. Lee has come through surgery. Good to hear." No smile. "But you and I have business, Mr. Charboneau. You want to discuss the matter in private?"

"No need. Say what you're going to say, Captain." His father narrowed his eyes. "I have nothing to hide."

The captain found amusement in his father's declaration of innocence. Christian wanted to believe his father had nothing to do with events at Genotech Labs and the nightly deliveries of the drug-addicted to the research facility's gate by a secret faction of the Cuiabá police, but he wasn't delusional. He shifted his attention to Charboneau, eager to hear what he'd say.

"I have had Chief Zharan under my own surveillance for quite a while. I've tracked his activities and his conversations. Anything you care to offer before I file my report?" The cop added, "My government might be more lenient if you cooperated."

Duarte had disclosed enough for a guilty man to leap to his own defense, trying to cover his tracks. Cops used this tactic all the time, hoping their suspect would admit to something. But unfortunately for the good captain, Christian knew he'd met his match with a man like Charboneau who'd dodged charges his whole life. Such a simple ruse wouldn't catch a man like his father.

"How thoughtful of you to consider my well-being, Captain. And, of course, I will cooperate with your government in any way I can. This man should be brought to justice."

Charboneau sat up and leaned forward in his chair, challenging the policeman to spell it out. Daring him to do it.

"I'll be eager to learn what transpired while I was out of the country. Your chief of police has used his position to undermine the noteworthy work of the genetics research being conducted at a facility I support financially. I'm sure he's set back our work, and I'll be contacting my lawyer to see what can be done about it."

Cagey to the bitter end. If Duarte had a trump card to play, now was the time to spring it. And Nicholas knew it.

"Chief Zharan is cooperating too. And Fuentes. With what I have, we shall soon know everything that happened. I will need a statement from you."

"Yes, about the kidnapping. I understand."

"The kidnapping and other things."

"Ah, then I will need time to contact my lawyer. A man would be ill-advised not to seek counsel on such matters."

His father raised his chin, baiting the captain. Duarte looked as if he'd won. With Nicholas asking for a lawyer, it raised the red guilt flag to a cop.

But his father quickly shifted gears, deflating Duarte's small victory. "After all, I would hate to cast a dark light on the impressive research of Genotech

Labs. I would want my attorney to protect the lab's reputation, of course. I'm sure you understand."

He stared the police captain straight in the eyes without flinching. He'd asked for a lawyer and made it seem like his concern was for the reputation of the research facility, not his own backside. Christian never wanted to play a game of chess or poker with the man.

"I would imagine Dr. Phillips was coerced to participate in Zharan's scheme, but certainly, if there is more to it, I'd want to know the extent of his involvement. As a financial contributor, I'd have every right to know such things . . . for the sake of the facility and its research, you understand," his father added.

Checkmate. Duarte gritted his teeth, his dark eyes set on Charboneau.

"I can expect your cooperation then." The man held back his disdain, but Christian felt the heat. "I will be in touch. Don't leave town."

Duarte turned toward Christian. "I'd like to speak to you in private, Mr. Delacorte. My request is not open to debate."

Christian followed the cop down the hall, glancing back over his shoulder at Raven. She did not look pleased. When they found an empty hospital room, Duarte closed the door behind him and started in.

"I don't know what your involvement is with Nicholas Charboneau, but you don't seem like the sort of man who would work for such a . . ." He didn't finish, but the man glared at him, expecting his response.

"I told you. I don't work for him. I did this as a favor for Jasmine. What are you trying to say?"

"Men like Charboneau come to my country and take what they want. They give nothing in return.

This I am used to, but I suspect he's involved in something subtle and far more sinister."

"You have proof?" Christian leapt to a conclusion about the evidence, but by the look on Duarte's face, he'd hit the bull's-eye dead center.

"Not yet, but I plan to do everything in my power to determine his guilt."

"Or his innocence. Did you leave that part out?" He wasn't sure why he was defending his father, a man he didn't really know.

Duarte fixed his eyes on him, then turned to walk away, gathering his thoughts with a heavy sigh and hands on his hips. Keeping his back to Christian, he began again.

"Chief Zharan has openly talked about Charboneau's involvement, but as you can imagine, his testimony would carry little weight against a man like him. And Dr. Phillips is far too scared to point a finger at either man. It seems the passports for his entire family were withheld to force him to stay and cooperate. Zharan is in possession of these passports, so I still have no connection to Nicholas Charboneau," he admitted. "And Zharan is blaming Fuentes for his overzealous approach in carrying out his orders regarding the homeless men they delivered to the lab for testing. Dr. Phillips may have conducted the tests and experiments, but he claims not to know how they disposed of these men. Fuentes was ordered to dispose of them afterward. We will get to the bottom of this, but I suspect there's a mass grave out there that we may never find. Someone should pay for such an atrocity."

He was right. Someone should be held accountable for what happened to those men.

"Aren't you afraid I'll pass this on to Charboneau?" Christian asked. "Why are you telling me this?"

A long awkward silence passed between them. Finally, Captain Duarte turned around to face him.

"Because you risked your life to protect the others. And I pride myself on being a good judge of character. I believe the actions of a man say much about his true nature." Duarte smiled for the first time, the effort taxing.

"You did the same. Thank you, Captain."

"I think by now you can call me Luis, yes?"

Christian shrugged and nodded. "It took guts to go against your chief of police."

"The man thought of himself as superior, and he used his position of power to corrupt those around him. I came from one of the *favela* you see on the edge of town. My parents were dirt poor. Zharan and men like him consider me nothing more than filth on their shoes. I may not have much even now, but at least I can look at myself in the mirror. Who's to say what wealth truly is?"

"You are a philosopher, Luis." Christian smiled, seeing the man for perhaps the first time. "I suppose the research at Genotech will come to a halt until things are sorted out."

"Yes, but there are many credible facilities throughout the world. If I have my say, I will shut the place down. That message you can take back to Mr. Charboneau. No matter how he wants to color his benevolence, his money will no longer be required."

"I appreciate your candor, but why didn't you come forward and tell me what was going on? Raven and I nearly got killed out there."

"I know, and I am very sorry for my part in that,

but you have to understand. I did not know your connection to Charboneau. You could have been working for his syndicate and lying to me. My case against Zharan was in its infancy. I could not afford to make a mistake." He shook his head. "I deeply regret what might have happened. I escalated my actions to help. I hope you understand. So much was at stake, the lives of many."

"So what happens now?" Christian crossed his arms.

Duarte's contrite expression grew stern. "Chief Zharan and Fuentes will have many charges against them, not the least of which will be aggravated kidnapping and extortion on the man I suspect was his partner. I hope you appreciate the irony. Mario Araujo will testify. He should receive a light sentence for his cooperation. By the end of all this, Zharan's list of offenses should surpass his arrogance."

Duarte scaled back his stern attitude. "I cannot say how the case against Charboneau will end. That remains to be seen. I ask only your discretion, and one other thing."

"Yeah? What's that?"

"Don't disappoint me, Mr. Delacorte." He grinned, almost a smirk.

"Don't plan to, Captain Duarte." Christian shook his hand and watched him leave the room, but felt rooted where he stood, unable to rejoin his father.

He wasn't sure he could ignore his doubts about his father. Nothing might ever be proven, yet a wall had been erected in his mind by a presumption of guilt rather than innocence. Christian couldn't shake the feeling, and knew that any future with his newfound father would be tainted by it.

The harsh reality stacked up to an impenetrable wall and the truth glared at him in the face. His mother, Fiona, had been right to keep the man's name a secret from him all these years. Nicholas Charboneau made his wealth off criminal activities. End of story. His fantasy of having a relationship with the man after all these years had been just that—a fantasy.

How would he face the man now? And worse, did he care what his father thought?

CHAPTER 28

The next few days were filled by hours at the hospital, with time spent in between at police headquarters. In the end, Duarte reluctantly gave Nicholas the clearance to leave the country—the sooner the better. The cop was not a happy man, but he had an impressive case built against Chief Zharan and Fuentes. Both men turned finger pointing into a lost art. Once they got going, neither would shut up.

Even though Christian had doubts about his father's involvement, he'd probably never know the truth now. He found it hard to act as if nothing had changed between them but he'd come to terms with his own feelings. In the end, he had to settle for doing the right thing and saving the man's life, returning the favor Jasmine had done for him.

He was okay with that.

On the day they were scheduled to leave Brazil, Christian found his father exactly where he thought

he'd be, at the bedside of Jasmine Lee. It didn't look
like he'd gotten much sleep. Charboneau hadn't noticed him and Raven standing in the doorway to the
private hospital room.

Recovering from an almost lethal bullet wound,
Jasmine looked pale but beautiful, her fresh-faced
childlike innocence had been restored as she slept.
Nicholas sat near the bed, his chair pushed close. He
held her hand and stroked her hair, his eyes fixed on
her as if he might awaken her by sheer force of will.

Maybe he could.

Christian had no desire to intrude. He only wanted
one last look as reassurance Jasmine would be okay.
Because of her strength and unflinching love for his
father, she had done what she came to Brazil to do—
save his life. Thanks to her, Christian knew he would
have some semblance of a future with his father, such
as he was. The last piece to the puzzle of his life was
named Nicholas Charboneau. In the grand scheme
of things, the man was no prize in the humanitarian department, but Christian felt a certain serenity
just having met him. He had to be satisfied with that.
Maybe one day he would be.

He watched his father. So much remained unsaid
between them, all the questions without answers.
Given all that had happened, he would not find a
resolution today. And he hated awkward good-byes,
especially those tinged with the implied obligation
between an estranged father and son.

His trip to Brazil had taught him what mattered
most was not where he'd come from, but where he
was going. His past didn't define him anymore.
He could paint a life worth living, one paintbrush
stroke at a time, on the blank canvas of his future.

And Raven had more to do with that than Nicholas Charboneau. He knew that now. With reluctance, Christian backed out of the room and turned to go, slipping his hand in Raven's. He stopped when he heard his father's voice.

"Were you going to leave without saying good-bye?"

So much for the old man not noticing.

"I figured the next step was yours." Christian stuck his head back in the room with Raven at his side. He kept his voice low with Jasmine sleeping. "You know where to reach me in Chicago. I think you've known that for a while."

"Yes, I suppose so." Nicholas stood and joined him at the doorway. "But I'm not exactly father of the year material, if you know what I mean."

"Really? I find that hard to believe, but I'll take your word for it." He grinned and leaned a shoulder against the door frame.

"How is she?" Raven asked.

"She gets better with each passing day. Doctors are expecting her to make a full recovery."

"That's good." Raven nodded and smiled.

After a long moment of silence, Charboneau cleared his throat.

"One thing you will learn about me—that is, if you care to—I'm not the type of man who ignores an elephant standing in the middle of a hospital doorway. Aren't you even a little curious about my involvement with Genotech Labs? You've never really asked me about it." He directed his question to Christian. "And I know it's put a strain on any chance we might have."

The man had balls. A brass pair.

"I think I have a pretty good idea about your interest in the lab. Just because the police don't have grounds to arrest you doesn't mean your slate is clean."

Nicholas narrowed his eyes. "Whatever happened to the presumption of innocence?" he asked. "Would it surprise you to find that a man my age and in my line of work might have regrets? I've assessed my life and found I'm not perfect. There . . . I've said it. Alert the media."

Christian shook his head, unable to hold back a lazy grin. *Yep, a brass pair of whoppers.* "You're a crime boss, for crying out loud. That's not exactly a minor character flaw."

"I wasn't the one who ramped up the experiments and instigated that bogus and disreputable medical clinic. The chief of police knew it would be easy to place the blame on someone like me, for exactly the reasons you brought up." His father splayed a hand over his chest. "Why is it so difficult for you to believe I would want to turn over a new leaf?"

Christian stared at his father. The man didn't flinch and he didn't turn away or divert his eyes. If body language could be trusted, he wasn't lying. Yet why would a man like Charboneau care what he thought? And why was he fighting so hard to convince him of his innocence?

"So let me get this straight. You came to Brazil to put your capital dollars in a genetics facility geared to fight drug addiction . . . even though you and your crime syndicate make money off the other end of that coin. Is that it?"

Nicholas shrugged again. "Do you think my business associates would support such a benevolent act? Why do you think I came to a country half a world away . . . and invested my personal funds? There are some things a man would be wise not to share. I just figured if I did this, it might balance the scales a little."

What he said was beginning to make sense in a strange sort of way. And Charboneau certainly was pulling out all the stops to convince him.

"It's a pity Dr. Phillips isn't talking," Nicholas said. "Otherwise he might back me up." He rubbed a hand against the back of his neck, his fatigue showing.

Christian smiled and cocked his head. "Yeah, too bad the doctor's so scared. But I suppose a man's got to put his family first."

"Yes, I would feel the same, if I were in his shoes. I think I'm beginning to understand the importance of family."

Before Christian could reply, Captain Duarte walked up behind them.

"Sorry to disturb you, but I wanted to find out how Ms. Lee is doing today." He smiled with his uniform cap in hand. The humble act looked as if it pained him, a smile as much of a hardship for the captain to summon as speaking before a crowded auditorium. Duarte was living proof that a person shouldn't judge a book by the austerity of its cover.

"She's better." Nicholas nodded and shook the man's hand. "No offense, Captain, but we'll be happy to take leave of your company . . . and your beautiful country. I just want to get her home."

Home. The word sounded good to Christian.

"No offense taken, Mr. Charboneau. I for one will be happy to see you go. And I hope you don't take this personally, but I would rather we not cross paths again. Do I make myself clear?"

"Very. We are in complete agreement. And believe me, I don't say that often with an officer of the law." His father smiled.

Turning to Christian, Duarte said, "I came to see you and your lovely lady to the airport. Your jet is fueled and ready for departure."

Christian put his arm around Raven and shook his head, fighting a smile.

"How did you know we'd be leaving, Captain?" Raven asked.

Christian rolled his eyes. He'd stopped questioning the captain's superhuman powers. "Let's just say the guy's a real know-it-all. And I mean that, literally." He turned his attention toward the cop. "We'd appreciate the lift. Thanks."

"It would be my pleasure." Duarte nodded and moved down the hall, sensing Christian had unfinished business.

He turned toward his father, dreading this moment. *See you around* wouldn't cut it. Yet he didn't know what to say. Nicholas saw his uncertainty and made it easy.

"The next time we meet, it'll be hard to top this, you know." His father grinned.

"Yeah, well. If it's all the same to you, I could do with a little less excitement."

Nicholas's face grew solemn. "Doctor said that what you did for Jasmine back there, you saved her life. I have no idea how to thank you."

"Just tell her we're even. She'll know what I'm talking about." He reached out his hand to his father. "Don't be a stranger."

Nicholas looked at his outstretched hand, then opened his arms and pulled Christian into his embrace. "If you need anything, don't hesitate to call. I mean it," he whispered in his ear. "If you'll give me a chance, maybe we can take this father-son thing a day at a time, see what happens. Can you handle that?"

"A day at a time sounds like a plan." He wondered if his father noticed that he didn't answer the question.

Christian pulled from Charboneau's arms and stared into his eyes long enough to know his father accepted what he said, for now. He watched him rejoin Jasmine at her bedside and found himself wishing things had been different, but trust had to be earned. And they had a long way to go before that happened, if it ever did.

As he turned, Raven slipped her hand into his, an endearing gesture he'd grown to love. She fixed her eyes on him, giving him the quiet reassurance he knew he could count on for a lifetime. They walked to where Captain Duarte stood, then headed for the bank of elevators a few steps away.

"As you said before, Christian, I do know things." Duarte shrugged with a self-satisfied smirk on his face. "Things that might surprise you."

He shifted his gaze to the captain but didn't respond. He didn't have to.

"Such as?" Raven took the bait, then hit the button calling for an elevator.

"Nicholas Charboneau is Christian's father, isn't he?" Duarte asked, looking as if he really didn't expect an answer.

A little shocked by the man's abrupt declaration, Christian cocked his head and stared at him. He would have guessed the family resemblance didn't get by the detective's keen observation, but he would have been wrong. It would appear Duarte was a mind reader as well.

"I saw it in his eyes. Your father's," the cop added without hesitation. "Even for a man as complicated as Nicholas Charboneau, the undeniable connection was plain to see."

Christian let Raven and Duarte into the elevator before him, then punched the button for the ground floor. The cop had looked behind the curtain of Oz and saw something even he had missed.

"Nothing gets by you, Luis." He shook his head, giving the man his due.

"Yes. Just remember that." The man tapped the bridge of his nose, and a corner of his lips twitched.

When they got to the first floor, Duarte spoke again.

"We will pick up your luggage at the hotel. Then we have a quick stop to make before you leave. It won't take long."

"Lead the way." Christian extended his arm toward the revolving front door of the hospital. "I'm placing my trust in you."

Duarte grinned, for real this time. With chest out, the police captain sauntered across the hospital reception area in his neatly pressed uniform and shiny black shoes, his footsteps resonating across the marble floor.

"It's about damned time, Delacorte."

Jasmine cleared her throat, a painful look on her face. Opening her eyes looked like an effort. Nicholas grabbed a cup of half-melted shaved ice and held up a spoon with an ice chip in it. Without words, she opened her mouth and accepted it. After she cooled her parched throat, she spoke in a soft raspy voice.

"You think Christian bought what you said about regrets and your act of benevolence?" Jasmine forced a weak smile, putting up a good front. The fire was gone, but she looked more beautiful than he'd ever seen her.

"I can be very convincing, you know." He winked and leaned closer, filling his eyes and his senses with everything about her.

"With all that talk about reform, I was worried you might actually be telling the truth."

Nicholas traced a finger down the side of her cheek, letting a sad expression linger on his face. "The best lie comes with an element of the truth, my dear Jasmine. I do have regrets in my life. Some are worth rectifying . . . and some I consider . . . terminal character defects."

She raised a pale hand toward him, the one without the IV.

"I love you, Nicky. Just the way you are."

"Yes, I know."

After a long silence, Jasmine raised an eyebrow. Her lips pursed into a weak pout. "Admit it. You love me too."

"I will do no such thing." Nicholas leaned closer and gazed into her eyes. "I prefer to show you instead."

He bent down and touched his lips to hers, a loving gentle kiss. In all their years together, Jasmine had never known such tenderness. She wanted the moment to last forever, but she would take what he was willing to give.

With a man like her Nicky, a woman could live a lifetime in a day.

* * *

Duarte's unmarked police car was parked at the curb in the front parking lot of the hospital. While the captain got into the driver's seat, Raven gestured her preference to sit in the back, no doubt wanting some distance from the male bonding ritual he and Duarte had started. Christian opened the door, but before she got in, she looked at him with a question on her mind.

"A reformed drug kingpin with a conscience? Out of curiosity, did you buy any of that?"

Christian's expression melted into a grin. "Not a word." He shook his head. "Let's just say Father's Day got a hell of a lot more . . . complicated."

He kissed her on the cheek and closed the car door behind her.

It didn't take long to pick up their luggage from the penthouse suite at the Hotel Palma Dourada. They didn't have to check out. Nicholas needed the suite while Jasmine was in the hospital and would pick up the tab when he left.

All the while, Captain Duarte chatted about the weather and the charm of his city—a proud ambassador for his country and his people. This Duarte was a completely different man than the one Christian had met, the guy with all the suspicion and menace for unwanted foreigners to his country. Their brief, casual exchange left Christian wishing he had more time to get to know the man. But one thing Duarte did not talk about was where they'd be going next.

When he turned down a familiar street, Christian fought the growing grin on his face.

"So how are Bianca and Hector?" He turned

toward Duarte as the captain parked in front of the Guia Do Espírito. "They going to be all right?"

"You know what they say, Christian." Duarte got out of the car before he finished. "'That which does not kill us, makes us stronger.' They will be fine, I think. I promise to look in on them from time to time."

"I'm sure she would appreciate that, Luis." He smirked. "Having a good woman in your life may not be a bad thing."

Before Duarte could react beyond his shocked expression, Christian reached for the front door, but didn't have to opened it. It swept from his reach with the tinkle of a bell overhead and Bianca Salvador greeted them on the street with outstretched arms. He couldn't help but notice the special smile Bianca gave to the dashing man in uniform.

"Oh, you've come." The woman's eyes glistened, but the beaming smile on her face challenged the idea her tears were spawned from sadness. "Please . . . please come in," she greeted them, then yelled into the back of the store. "Hector. They're here."

Hector came from the back storage room with a grin on his face. His bruises had yellowed, but the cuts were still visible. Bianca had endured much the same abuse. It pained him to see it. If they were hurting, they never showed it.

Bianca had a plate of cookies from the café down the street. She served coffee and they chatted as if they were family, catching up on old times. It reminded Christian of the Delacortes, the family he had lost all those years ago. He stood on the periphery and watched the others, recalling the faces and voices that lurked in his memory, entwined in the nightmare of his past. One day he hoped he could sort them out and discard the pain, keeping what remained.

When the time felt right, he spoke up, addressing Hector.

"I was going to contact you once I got back to the U.S., but you stuck your neck out when you thought Jasmine was in trouble and you ended up on Chief Zharan's radar. For that, I'm sorry, but very grateful. And we had an agreement. Do you remember?"

Hector looked sheepishly at his aunt. His cheeks blushed.

"Yes, but you don't have to worry about that anymore. We are friends, yes?" Hector raised his eyebrows, a glimmer of hope on his face. "Friends don't exchange money to do what is right." He stuck out his chest and stood tall, exchanging a look with Bianca. She nodded, tussling with a smile.

"But friends help each other," Christian insisted, catching the attention of a curious Raven. "I want to set up a trust fund for you and Bianca, to help while you're away at school."

"Oh, no. That is too generous." Hector shook his head and waved his hands in objection. "Away at school? I don't go to university."

"Yet. At least, it will be up to you whether you take me up on my offer. The trust fund will be set up. I want to pay for your education, like I promised. I insist. Personally, I think it's a wise investment. You can attend a college in Brazil or come to the U.S. I'll sponsor you, once I learn what I need to do. It will be your choice. What do you say?"

Bianca clasped a hand over her mouth, her eyes welling with tears. Hector looked like a stunned rabbit. His eyes darted between Christian and his aunt. His mouth gaped open. He had no idea what to say.

"Then it's settled." Christian handed them both a business card. "I'll be in touch."

Bianca burst forth with a stream of Portuguese, hugging and kissing Christian on the cheek. She did the same with Raven. But when it came time to show her appreciation to Captain Duarte, he noticed she lingered a bit longer. Christian shook his head. If he were a betting man, he'd put money that Duarte felt the same way toward her.

"And I've got one more thing to say."

Everyone turned toward him.

Christian reached under the collar of his shirt and pulled out the Ayza talisman Bianca had made for him. He slipped the chain over his head and walked toward Captain Duarte.

"I don't know if Bianca made this talisman for me, but I want you to have it. I've got a feeling you're gonna need it."

Christian heard a soft chuckle in the room behind him. Duarte looked surprised but hid it well, as usual.

"A man with your brand of honor is rare, Luis. It was a privilege meeting you."

He slipped the chain over Duarte's head. The captain accepted his gift with a nod and a nervous clearing of his throat. For a nonbeliever, the man held the talisman in his hand with surprising reverence. Christian knew he had done the right thing.

When Duarte saw he was the center of attention, he shrugged. "We probably should get both of you to the airport."

They headed for the door, but Raven stopped them.

"I have to ask about that talisman," she said, looking at Bianca. "Fuentes had his gun pointed at Christian." She shuddered. "Yet when he pulled the trigger, the gun misfired. Do you think . . . ?"

She looked at Christian, then at Duarte. When he shrugged and saw Duarte do the same, avoiding his eyes, Raven turned to Bianca for an answer.

"You can choose to believe or not," she said. "There are things we will never understand, but I believe Ayza intervened when Christian was in trouble. And I am glad he did."

Their faces turned toward him, expecting a rebuttal.

"Don't look at me. I'm the last one who's gonna argue with that logic." He joined them in a laugh, shaking his head.

As Christian said his good-byes, he hoped it would not be for the last time. And he sincerely wanted Hector to attend college. Time would tell if the kid would take him up on his offer. Perhaps for Hector and Bianca, it was enough that he had asked.

The Dunhill jet engine droned in the background, the aircraft hurling above a sea of billowing white against an azure sky. They were finally heading home.

With the armrest raised, they sat as close as they could to one another. Raven had her head on his shoulder, her arms around his waist. The scent of her shampoo made him imagine a hot bath with her naked body next to his, bubbles up to their necks. Not a bad way to celebrate their first night back.

But Christian had one more thing that wouldn't

wait until they returned. He nudged her chin with his finger, letting him look into the eyes that could hold him spellbound for eternity. He had something to ask the woman he loved.

"This may not be the time or place, but I didn't want to wait. Life's too short."

He undid his seat belt and reached into a pocket. By the time he got down on one knee, Raven's eyes were brimming with tears. Her sweet fingers cupped her lips. Christian opened the small red velvet ring case, revealing the most beautiful diamond ring she had ever seen.

A *black diamond*.

"It's one of the most breathtaking diamonds in the world, mined in Brazil. Its beauty caught my eye the minute I saw it. But when I found out how precious and rare it was, it reminded me of our love. I want to spend the rest of my life with you, Raven Mackenzie. Will you marry me?"

Tears streamed down Raven's cheeks, and at first she couldn't speak. Thoughts of how she had almost lost him raced through her mind, but faded to a delicate and harmless mist when she imagined the life they would have together.

She pulled him to her, kissed his face and neck and whispered over and over, "Yes, yes, yes. Oh, sweet Ayza, yes."

At that moment, strange images drifted through her mind as she kissed and held the man she loved. Maybe Bianca's spirits graced her with their powers after all.

Raven remembered the family portraits hanging on the wall of her home.

The underlying strength shown in the portrait of

her dead father and the unforgettable smile of the mother she had never really known. Soon her wedding portrait would join the collection of her life. She and Christian would begin their future together as man and wife, creating memories of their own. She had always believed in the enduring strength of their love, even when Christian had his doubts whether he deserved her at all.

Raven smiled at the thought. She would have the future she'd always dreamt about and a lifetime to share it with him. Between everything that had happened to them and the miracle of their love, why would Bianca's conjuring be such a stretch?